The Race

Clive Cussler is the author or co-author of forty-six books, including the famous Dirk Pitt® adventures; the NUMA® Files adventures; the *Oregon* Files, such as *The Jungle*; the Isaac Bell adventures; and the Fargo adventures, most recently *The Kingdom*. His non-fiction works include *The Sea Hunters* and *The Sea Hunters II*; these describe the true adventures of the real NUMA, which, led by Cussler, searches for lost ships of historic significance. With his crew of volunteers, Cussler has discovered more than sixty ships, including the long-lost Confederate submarine *Hunley*. He lives in Arizona.

Justin Scott is the author of twenty-six novels, including *The Shipkiller* and *Normandie Triangle*; the Ben Abbot detective series; and five modern sea thrillers under his pen name Paul Garrison. He lives in Connecticut.

Find out more about the world of Clive Cussler by visiting: www.clivecussler.co.uk

The Race

CLIVE CUSSLER
and JUSTIN SCOTT

MICHAEL JOSEPH
an imprint of
PENGUIN BOOKS

MICHAEL JOSEPH

Published by the Penguin Group
Penguin Books Ltd, 80 Strand, London WC2R ORL, England
Penguin Group (USA) Inc., 375 Hudson Street, New York, New York 10014, USA
Penguin Group (Canada), 90 Eglinton Avenue East, Suite 700, Toronto, Ontario, Canada M4P 2Y3
(a division of Pearson Penguin Canada Inc.)
Penguin Ireland, 25 St Stephen's Green, Dublin 2, Ireland (a division of Penguin Books Ltd)
Penguin Group (Australia), 250 Camberwell Road,
Camberwell, Victoria 3124, Australia (a division of Pearson Australia Group Pty Ltd)
Penguin Books India Pvt Ltd, 11 Community Centre,
Panchsheel Park, New Delhi – 110 017, India
Penguin Group (NZ), 67 Apollo Drive, Rosedale, Auckland 0632, New Zealand
(a division of Pearson New Zealand Ltd)
Penguin Books (South Africa) (Pty) Ltd, 24 Sturdee Avenue,
Rosebank, Johannesburg 2196, South Africa

Penguin Books Ltd, Registered Offices: 80 Strand, London WC2R ORL, England

www.penguin.com

First published in the United States of America by G. P. Putnam's Sons 2011
First published in Great Britain by Michael Joseph 2011

1

Printed in Great Britain by Clays Ltd, St Ives plc

A CIP catalogue record for this book is available from the British Library

HARDBACK ISBN: 978–0–718–15724–1

TRADE PAPERBACK ISBN: 978–0–718–15725–8

www.greenpenguin.co.uk

Penguin Books is committed to a sustainable
future for our business, our readers and our
planet. This book is made from paper certified
by the Forest Stewardship Council.

A Drunk Danced Alone in the Gutter

Chicago
1899

A TALL DRUNK DANCED ALONE IN THE GUTTER, singing a Stephen Foster song loved by the Anti-Saloon League. The melody was mournful, reminiscent of Scottish pipes, the tempo a slow waltz. His voice, a warm baritone, rang with heartfelt regret for promises broken.

"Oh! comrades, fill no glass for me
"To drown my soul in liquid flame . . ."

He had a golden head of hair, and a fine, strong profile. His extreme youth—he could not have been more than twenty—made his condition even sadder. His clothes looked slept in, matted with straw, and short in the arms and legs, like handouts from a church basement or lifted from a clothesline. His linen collar was askew, his shirt was missing a cuff, and he had no hat despite the cold. Of gentleman's treasures to sell for drink, made-to-order calfskin boots were all he had left.

He bumped into a lamppost and lost the thread of the lyric. Still humming the poignant tune, still trying to waltz, he dodged a potter's field morgue wagon pulling up at the curb. The driver tied his horses and bounded through the swinging doors of the nearest of the many saloons spilling yellow light on the cobble-stones.

The drunken youth reeled against the somber black wagon and held on tight.

He studied the saloon. Was it one where he would be welcomed? Or had he already been thrown out? He patted empty pockets. He shrugged sadly. His eyes roved the storefronts: five-cent lodging houses, brothels, pawnbrokers. He considered his boots. Then he lifted his gaze to the newspaper dealer's depot on the corner, where press wagons were delivering Chicago's early editions.

Could he beg a few pennies' work unloading the bundled news-papers? He squared his shoulders and commenced a slow waltz toward the depot.

"*When I was young I felt the tide*
"*Of aspiration undefiled.*
"*But manhood's years have wronged the pride*
"*My parents centered in their child.*"

The newsboys lining up to buy their papers were street-toughened twelve-year-olds. They made fun of the drunk as he approached until one of them locked gazes with his strangely soft violet-blue eyes. "Leave him alone!" he told his friends, and the tall young man whispered, "Thanks, shonny. Whuss yer name?"

"Wally Laughlin."

"You've a kind soul, Wally Laughlin. Don't end up like me."

"I TOLD YOU TO GET RID OF THE DRUNK," said Harry Frost, a giant of a man with a heavy jaw and merciless eyes. He straddled a crate of Vulcan dynamite inside the morgue wagon. Two ex-prizefighters from his West Side gang crouched at his feet. They were watching the newspaper depot through peepholes drilled in the side, waiting for the owner to return from his supper.

"I chased him off. He came back."

"Run him in that alley. I don't want to see him again, except carried on a shutter."

"He's just a drunk, Mr. Frost."

"Yeah? What if that newspaper dealer hired detectives to protect his depot?"

"Are you crazy? That's no detective."

Harry Frost's fist shot fifteen inches with the concentrated power of a forge hammer. The man he hit fell over, clutching his side in pain and disbelief. One second he'd been crouched beside the boss, the next he was on the floor, trying to breathe as splintered bone pierced his lung. "You busted my ribs," he gasped.

Frost's face was red. His own breath raced with anger. "I am not crazy."

"You don't know your own strength, Mr. Frost," protested the other boxer. "You could have killed him."

"If I meant to kill him, I would have hit him harder. *Get rid of that drunk!*"

The boxer scrambled out of the back of the wagon, closed the door behind him, and shoved through the sleepy newsboys lined up to buy their papers.

"Hey, you!" he yelled after the drunk, who didn't hear him but did him the favor of stepping into the alley under his own steam, saving him the trouble of dragging him, kicking and screaming. He plunged in after him, tugging a lead sap from his coat. It was a narrow alley, with blank walls on either side, barely wide enough for a wheelbarrow. The drunk was stumbling toward a doorway at the far end, lit by a hanging lantern.

"Hey, you!"

The drunk turned around. His golden hair shone in kerosene light. A tentative smile crossed his handsome face.

"Have we met, sir?" he asked, as if suddenly hopeful of arranging a loan.

"We're gonna meet."

The boxer swung his sap underhanded. It was a brutal weapon, a leather bag filled with buckshot. The buckshot made it pliable so that it would mold to its target, pulverize flesh and bone, and pound the young man's fine, strong profile flat as beefsteak. To the boxer's surprise, the drunk moved quickly. He stepped inside the arc of the sap and knocked the boxer off his feet with a right cross as expert as it was powerful.

The door sprang open.

"Nice going, kid."

Two middle-aged Van Dorn private detectives—ice-eyed Mack Fulton and Walter Kisley in a checkerboard drummer's suit—grabbed the fallen man's arms and dragged him inside. "Is Harry Frost hiding in that morgue wagon?"

But the boxer could not answer.

"Down for the count," said Fulton, slapping him hard and getting no response. "Young Isaac, you don't know your own strength."

"So much for our fledgling investigator's first lesson in interrogating criminals," said Kisley.

"And what is that first lesson?" Fulton echoed. They were nicknamed Weber and Fields at the Van Dorn Detective Agency, for the vaudeville comics.

"Permit your suspect to remain conscious," answered Kisley.

"So," they chorused, "he may *answer* your questions."

Apprentice detective Isaac Bell hung his head.

"I'm sorry, Mr. Kisley. Mr. Fulton. I didn't mean to hit him so hard."

"Live and learn, kid. That's why Mr. Van Dorn teamed a college man like you with such wise old ignoramuses as we."

"By our grizzled example, the boss hopes, even a rich kid from the right side of the tracks might flourish into brilliant detectivehood."

"Meantime, what do you say we go knock on that morgue wagon and see if Harry Frost is home?"

The partners drew heavy revolvers as they headed up the alley.

"Stay back, Isaac. You do not want to brace Harry Frost without a gun in your hand."

"Which, being an apprentice, you are not allowed to carry."

"I bought a derringer," Bell said.

"Enterprising of you. Don't let the boss get wind of it."

"Stay back anyway, a derringer won't stop Harry Frost."

They rounded the corner into the street. A knife glittered in the lamplight, slicing through the reins that tied the morgue wagon's horses, and a heavyset figure lashed their rumps with the driver's whip. The animals bolted, stampeding past the wagons lined up at the depot. The newsboys scattered from flying hooves and spinning wheels. Just as the runaway reached the depot, it exploded with a thunderous roar and a brilliant flash. The shock wave slammed into the detectives and threw them through the swinging doors and front windows of the nearest saloon.

Isaac Bell picked himself up and stormed back into the street. Flames were leaping from the newspaper depot. The wagons had been tumbled on their sides, their horses staggering on shattered legs. The street was filled with broken glass and burning paper. Bell looked for the newsboys. Three were huddled in a doorway, their faces white with shock. Three more were sprawled lifeless on the sidewalk. The first he knelt by was Wally Laughlin.

COME, JOSEPHINE IN MY FLYING MACHINE.

BY ALFRED BRYAN & FRED FISCHER

Oh! Say! Let us fly, dear
Where, kid? To the sky, dear
Oh you flying machine
Jump in, Miss Josephine
Ship ahoy! Oh joy, what a feeling
Where, boy? In the ceiling
Ho, High, Hoopla we fly
To the sky so high

Come Josephine, in my flying machine,
Going up, she goes! up she goes!
Balance yourself like a bird on a beam
In the air she goes! There she goes!
Up, up, a little bit higher
Oh! My! The moon is on fire
Come, Josephine in my flying machine,
Going up, all on, Goodbye!

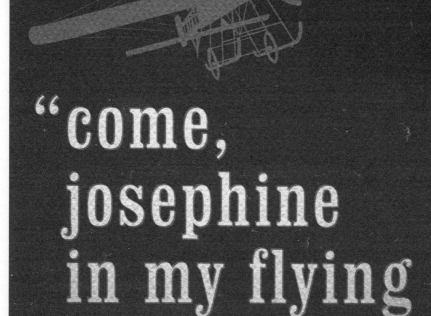

"come, josephine in my flying machine"

The Big-Game Rifle

1

The Adirondack Mountains, Upper New York State
1909

MRS. JOSEPHINE JOSEPHS FROST—a petite, rosy-cheeked young woman with a tomboy's pert manner, a farm girl's strong hands, and lively hazel eyes—flew her Celere Twin Pusher biplane eight hundred feet above the dark forested hills of her husband's Adirondack estate. Driving in the open air, in a low wicker chair in front, she was bundled against the cold headwind in padded coat and jodhpurs, a leather helmet and wool scarf, gloves, goggles, and boots. Her motor drummed a steady tune behind her, syncopated by the ragtime clatter of the drive chains spinning her propellers.

Her flying machine was a light framework of wood and bamboo braced with wire and covered with fabric. The entire contraption weighed less than a thousand pounds and was stronger than it looked. But it was not as strong as the violent updrafts that cliffs and ravines bounced into the atmosphere. Rushing columns of air would roll her over if she let them. Holes in the sky would swallow her whole.

A gust of wind snuck up behind and snatched the air that held her wings.

The biplane dropped like an anvil.

Josephine's exuberant grin leaped ear to ear.

She dipped her elevator. The machine pitched downward, which made it go faster, and Josephine felt the air lift her back onto an even keel.

"Good girl, Elsie!"

Flying machines stayed up by pushing air down. She had figured that out the first time she left the ground. Air was strong. Speed made it stronger. And the better the machine, the more it *wanted* to fly. This "Elsie" was her third, but definitely not her last.

People called her brave for flying, but she didn't think of herself that way. She just felt completely at home in the air, more at home than on the ground where things didn't always work out the way she hoped. Up here, she always knew what to do. Even better, she knew what would happen when she did it.

Her eyes were everywhere: glinting ahead at the blue mountains on the horizon, glancing up repeatedly at the aneroid barometer that she had hung from the upper wing to tell her her altitude, down at the motor's oil pressure gauge between her legs, and searching the ground for breaks in the forest big enough to alight on if her motor suddenly quit. She had sewn a ladies' pendant watch to her sleeve to time how much gasoline she had left. The map case, and compass ordinarily strapped to her knee, were back at the house. Born in these mountains, she steered by lakes, railroad tracks, and the North River.

She saw its dark gorge ahead, so deep and sheer that it looked like an angry giant had split the mountain with an ax. The river gleamed at the bottom. A break in the trees beside the gorge revealed a golden meadow, the first sizable opening she had seen since she had taken to the air.

She spied a tiny splash of red, like a flicker's red crest.

It was a hunting hat worn by Marco Celere, the Italian inventor who built her flying machines. Marco was perched on the cliff, rifle slung over his back, scanning for bear through field glasses. Across the meadow, at the edge of the trees, she saw the hulking silhouette of her husband.

Harry Frost raised his rifle and aimed it at Marco.

Josephine heard the shot, louder than the motor and drive chains clattering behind her.

HARRY FROST HAD A WEIRD FEELING he had missed the Italian.

He was a seasoned big-game hunter. Since retiring rich, he had shot elk and bighorn sheep in Montana, lion in South Africa, and elephants in Rhodesia, and he could have sworn the bullet had gone high. But there was his wife's swarthy boyfriend squirming on the edge of the cliff, hit but not dead.

Frost levered a fresh .45-70 shell into his Marlin 1895 and found him in the scope. He hated the sight of Marco Celere—oily black hair brilliantined slick to his skull, high forehead like a vaudeville Julius Caesar, thick eyebrows, deep-set dark eyes, waxed mustache curled at the tips like pigs' tails—and he was taking great pleasure in smoothly squeezing the trigger when suddenly a strange noise clattered in his head. It sounded like the threshing machine at the farm at the Matawan Asylum for the Criminally Insane, where his enemies had locked him up for shooting his chauffeur at the country club.

The bughouse had been worse than the most monstrous orphanage in his memory. Powerful politicians and high-priced lawyers claimed credit for springing him. But it was only right to let him out. The chauffeur had been romancing his first wife.

Unbelievably, it was happening again with his new bride. He could see it written on their faces every time Josephine hit him up for more dough to pay for Marco's inventions. Now she was begging him to buy the Italian's latest flying machine back from his creditors so she could win the Atlantic–Pacific Cross-Country Air Race and claim the fifty-thousand-dollar Whiteway Cup.

Wouldn't that be swell? Winning the biggest air race in the world would make his aviatrix wife and her inventor boyfriend famous. Preston Whiteway—the snoot-in-the-air, born-with-a-silver-spoon-in-his-mouth San Francisco newspaper publisher who was sponsoring the race—would make them stars, and sell fifty million newspapers in the process. The chump husband would be famous, too—a famously cuckolded, fat old rich husband—the laughingstock of all who despised him.

Rich he was, one of the richest men in America, every damned dollar earned himself. But Harry Frost wasn't old yet. A little over forty wasn't that old. And anyone who said he was more fat than muscle hadn't seen him kill a horse with a single punch—a trick he had performed famously in his youth and lately had made a birthday ritual.

Unlike the treachery with the chauffeur, this time they wouldn't catch him. No more flying off the handle. He had planned this one down to the last detail. Savoring revenge, going about it like a business, he had resurrected his formidable talents for management and deception to lure the unsuspecting Celere on a bear hunt. Bears couldn't talk. There'd be no witnesses deep in the North Country woods.

Convinced he had shot higher than he meant to, Frost aimed low and fired again.

JOSEPHINE SAW CELERE whiplashed from the cliff by the force of the bullet.

"Marco!"

THE CLATTER IN HARRY FROST'S SKULL GREW LOUD. Still peering down the barrel of his rifle at the wonderful empty space where Marco Celere had been, he suddenly realized that the noise was not a memory of the Matawan farm but real as the 405-grain lead bullet that had just blown the bride thief into the gorge. He looked up. Josephine was flying over him in her damned biplane. She had seen him shoot her aeroplane inventor.

Frost had three cartridges left in his magazine.

He raised the rifle.

But he didn't want to kill *her*. She'd stay with him now that Marco was out of the way. But she saw him kill Marco. They would lock him back in the bughouse. Second time around he'd never get out. That wouldn't be fair. He wasn't the betrayer. *She* was.

Frost whipped the rifle skyward and fired twice.

He misjudged her speed. At least one shot passed behind her. With only a single bullet left, he gathered his wits, settled his nerves, and led the biplane like a pheasant.

Bull's-eye!

He had scored a hit, for sure. Her flying machine lurched into a wide, clumsy turn. He waited for it to fall. But it kept turning, wobbling back in the direction of the camp. It was too high to hit with a pistol, but Frost jerked one from his belt anyway. Bracing the barrel on his powerful forearm, he fired until it was empty. Eyes bugging with rage, he flicked a snub-nosed derringer out of his sleeve. He emptied its two shots futilely in her direction and pawed at his hunting knife, to cut her heart out when she smashed into the trees.

The clatter grew fainter and fainter and fainter, and Harry Frost could do nothing but watch helplessly as his treacherous wife disappeared beyond the tree line and escaped his righteous wrath.

At least he had blown her lover into the gorge.

He lumbered across the meadow, hoping for a glimpse of Celere's body smashed on the river rocks. But halfway to the rim of the cliff, he stopped dead, poleaxed by a horrible realization. He had to run before they locked him back in the bughouse.

JOSEPHINE FOUGHT WITH ALL HER SKILL to guide her machine safely to the ground.

Harry had hit it twice. One bullet had nicked the two-gallon gasoline tank behind her. The second was worse. It had jammed the link between her control lever and the wire that twisted the shape of her wings. Unable to warp them to bank the machine into a turn, she was dependent entirely on its rudder. But trying to turn without banking was like flying a glider before the Wright brothers invented wing warping—god-awful awkward and likely to slide her sideways into a deadly flat spin.

Lips tight, she worked the rudder like a surgeon's scalpel, taking measured slices of the wind. Her mother, a frantic woman unable to cope with the simplest task, used to accuse her of having "ice water in her veins." But wasn't ice water handy on a crippled flying machine, Mother? Slowly, she brought the biplane back on course.

When the wind gusted from behind, she smelled gasoline. She looked for the source and saw it dripping from the fuel tank. Harry's bullet had punctured it.

Which would happen first? she wondered coolly. Would the gasoline all leak out and stop her motor before she could alight on Harry's lawn? Or would sparks from the engine and chains ignite the gasoline? Fire was deadly on a flying machine. The varnish of nitrate fabric dope that stiffened and sealed the cotton canvas covering her wings was as flammable as flash powder.

The only field nearer was the meadow. But if she alighted there, Harry would kill her. She had no choice. She had to land the machine at the camp, if she had enough gasoline to reach it.

"Come on, Elsie. Take us home."

The forest inched slowly beneath her. Updrafts buffeted her wings and rolled the airship. Unable to warp them to counteract, she tried to keep the machine on an even keel using her elevators and rudder.

At last she saw the lake beside Harry's camp.

Just as she got close enough to see the main house and the dairy barns, her motor sputtered on the last fumes of gasoline. The propellers stopped turning. The pusher biplane went silent but for the wind whispering through the wire stays.

She had to volplane—to glide—all the way to the lawn.

But the propellers, which had been pushing her, were dragging in the air. They held her back, reducing her speed. In moments she would be gliding too slowly to stay aloft.

She reached behind her and jerked the cable that opened the engine's compression valve so the pistons would move freely and allow the propellers to spin. The difference was immediate. The aeroplane felt lighter, more like a glider.

Now she could see the dairy pasture. Speckled with cows and crisscrossed with fences, it offered no room to come down safely. There was the house, an elaborate log mansion, and behind it the sloping lawn of mowed grass from which she had earlier taken to the air. But first she had to clear the house, and she was dropping fast. She threaded a path between the tall chimneys, skimmed the roof, and then coaxed the rudder to turn into the wind, taking great care not to slide into a spin.

Eight feet above the grass, she saw that she was moving too fast. Air squeezed between the wings and the ground had the effect of holding her up. The biplane was refusing to stop flying. Ahead loomed a wall of trees.

The gasoline that had soaked into the varnished canvas ignited in a sheet of orange flame.

Trailing fire, unable to slant her wings sharply to slow enough to touch her wheels to the grass, Josephine reached back and jerked the compression cable. Closing the valve locked the eight-foot propellers. They grabbed the air like two fists, and her wheels and skids banged hard on the grass.

The burning biplane slid for fifty yards. As it slowed, the fire spread, scattering flame. When she felt it singe the back of her helmet, Josephine jumped. She hit the ground and threw herself flat to let the machine roll past, then she sprang to her feet and ran for her life as flames engulfed it.

Harry's butler came running. He was trailed by the gardener, the cook, and Harry's bodyguards.

"Mrs. Frost! Are you all right?"

Josephine's eyes locked on the pillar of flame and smoke. Marco's beautiful machine was burning like a funeral pyre. Poor Marco. The steadiness that had gotten her through the ordeal was dissolving, and she felt her lips quiver. The fire looked like it was underwater. She realized that she was shaking and crying, and that tears were filling her eyes. She couldn't tell if she was crying for Marco or herself.

"Mrs. Frost!" the butler repeated. "Are you all right?"

It was the closest by far she had ever come to getting killed in an aeroplane.

She tried to pull her handkerchief from her sleeve. She couldn't get it out. She had to take her glove off. When she did, she saw her skin was dead white, as if her blood had gone into hiding. Everything was different. She now knew what it felt like to be afraid.

"Mrs. Frost?"

They were all staring at her. Like she had cheated death or was standing among them like a ghost.

"I'm O.K."

"May I do anything to help, Mrs. Frost?"

Her brain was whirling. She had to do something. She pressed her handkerchief to her face. A thousand men and women had learned to fly since Wilbur Wright won the Michelin Cup in France, and until this moment Josephine Josephs Frost had never doubted that she could drive an aeroplane just as fast and as far as any of them. Now every time she climbed onto a flying machine she would have to be brave. Well, it still beat being stuck on the ground.

She mopped her cheeks and blew her nose.

"Yes," she said. "Drive into town, please, and tell Constable Hodge that Mr. Frost just shot Mr. Celere."

The butler gasped, *"What?"*

She glanced at him sharply. How surprised could he be that her violent husband had killed someone? Again.

"Are you quite sure of that, Mrs. Frost?"

"Am I quite sure?" she echoed. "Yes, I saw it happen with my own eyes."

The butler's dubious expression was a chilling reminder that it was Harry who paid his salary, Harry who paid for everything, and Mrs. Frost was now a woman alone with no one to count on but herself.

The bodyguards didn't look surprised. Their long faces said, There goes our meal ticket. The butler, too, was already getting over it, asking as routinely as if she had just ordered a glass of iced tea, "Will there be anything else, Mrs. Frost?"

"Please do what I asked," she said in a voice with a slight tremor as she stared at the fire. "Tell the constable my husband killed Mr. Celere."

"Yes, madam," he replied in a blank tone.

Josephine turned her back on the fire. Her hazel eyes were wont to shift toward green or gray. She did not have to look in a mirror to know that right now they reflected a colorless fear. She was alone and she was vulnerable. With Marco Celere dead and her husband an insane killer, she had no one to turn to. Then the thought of Preston Whiteway flowed into her mind.

Yes, that's who would protect her.

"One more thing," she said to the butler as he started to walk away. "Send a telegram to Mr. Preston Whiteway at the *San Francisco Inquirer*. Say that I will visit him next week."

2

"Hoopla!"

ISAAC BELL, CHIEF INVESTIGATOR of the Van Dorn Detective Agency, thundered up San Francisco's Market Street in a fire-engine red gasoline-powered Locomobile racer with its exhaust cutout wide open for maximum power. Bell was a tall man of thirty with a thick mustache that glowed as golden as his precisely groomed blond hair. He wore an immaculate white suit and a low-crowned white hat with a wide brim. His frame was whipcord lean.

As he drove, his boots, well-kept and freshly polished, rarely touched the brake, an infamously ineffective Locomobile accessory. His long hands and fingers moved nimbly between throttle and shifter. His eyes, ordinarily a compelling violet shade of blue, were dark with concentration. A no-nonsense expression and a determined set of his jaw were tempered by a grin of pure pleasure as he raced the auto at breakneck speed, overtaking trolleys, trucks, horse carts, motorcycles, and slow automobiles.

In the red-leather passenger seat to Bell's left sat the boss, Joseph Van Dorn.

The burly, red-whiskered founder of the nationwide detective agency was a brave man feared across the continent as the scourge of criminals. But he turned pale as Bell aimed the big machine at the dwindling space between a coal wagon and a Buick motor-truck stacked to the rails with tins of kerosene and naphtha.

"We're actually on time," Van Dorn remarked. "Even a little early."

Isaac Bell did not appear to hear him.

With relief, Van Dorn saw their destination looming over its shorter neighbors: Preston Whiteway's twelve-story *San Francisco Inquirer* building, headquarters of the flamboyant publisher's news-paper empire.

"Will you look at that!" Van Dorn shouted over the roar of the motor.

An enormous yellow advertising banner draped the top floor proclaiming in yard-high letters that Whiteway's newspapers were sponsoring the

WHITEWAY ATLANTIC-TO-PACIFIC CROSS-COUNTRY AIR RACE
The Whiteway Cup and $50,000
To be awarded to the
First Flier
To Cross America in Fifty Days

"It's a magnificent challenge," Bell shouted back without taking his eyes from the crowded street.

Isaac Bell was fascinated by flying machines. He had been fol-lowing their rapid development avidly, with the object of buying a top flier himself. There had been scores of improved aerial in-ventions in the past two years, each producing faster and stronger aeroplanes: the Wright Flyer III, the June Bug, the bamboo-framed Silver Dart, the enormous French Voisins and Antoinettes pow-

ered by V-8 racing-boat engines, Santos Dumont's petite Demoi-
selle, the cross–English Channel Blériot, the rugged Curtiss Pusher,
the Wright Signal Corps machine, the Farman III, and the Celere
wire-braced monoplane.

If anyone could actually navigate a flying machine all the way
across the United States of America—a very big *if*—the Whiteway Cup would be won in equal parts by the nerve and skill of the
airmen and by how ingeniously the inventors increased the power
of their engines and improved systems of shaping their wings to
make the airships turn more agilely and climb faster. The winner
would have to average eighty miles a day, nearly two hours in the
air, every day. Each day lost to wind, storm, fog, accidents, and
repairs would increase dramatically those hours aloft.

"Whiteway's newspapers claim that the cup is made of solid
gold," Van Dorn laughed. "Say," he joked, "maybe *that's* what he
wants to see us about—afraid some crook will steal it."

"Last year his papers claimed that Japan would sink the Great
White Fleet," Bell said drily. "Somehow they made it home safe to
Hampton Roads. There's Whiteway now!"

The fair-haired publisher was steering a yellow Rolls-Royce
roadster toward the only parking space left in front of his building.

"Looks like Whiteway has it," said Van Dorn.

Bell pressed hard on his accelerator. The big red Locomobile
surged ahead of the yellow Rolls-Royce. Bell stomped the anemic
brakes, shifted down, and swerved on smoking tires into the parking space.

"Hey!" Whiteway shook a fist. "That's my space." He was a big
man, a former college football star running to fat. An arrogant
cock to his head boasted that he was still handsome, deserved
whatever he wanted, and was strong enough to insist on it.

Isaac Bell bounded from his auto to extend a powerful hand with a friendly smile.

"Oh, it's you, Bell. That's my space!"

"Hello, Preston, it's been a while. When I told Marion we'd be calling on you, she asked me to send her regards."

Whiteway's scowl faded at the mention of Isaac Bell's fiancée, Marion Morgan, a beautiful woman in the moving-picture line. Marion had worked with Whiteway, directing his Picture World scheme, which was enjoying great success exhibiting films of news events in vaudeville theaters and nickelodeons.

"Tell Marion that I'm counting on her to shoot great movies of my air race."

"I'm sure she can't wait. This is Joseph Van Dorn."

The newspaper magnate and the founder of the nation's premier detective agency sized each other up while shaking hands. Van Dorn pointed skyward. "We were just admiring your banner. Ought to be quite an affair."

"That's why I called for you. Come up to my office."

A detail of uniformed doormen were saluting as if an admiral had arrived in a dreadnought. Whiteway snapped his fingers. Two men ran to park the yellow Rolls-Royce.

Whiteway received more salutes in the lobby.

A gilded elevator cage carried them to the top floor, where a mob of editors and secretaries were gathered in the foyer with pencils and notepads at the ready. Whiteway barked orders, scattering some on urgent missions. Others raced after him, scribbling rapidly, as the publisher dictated the end of the afternoon edition's editorial that he had started before lunch.

"'The *Inquirer* decries the deplorable state of American aviation. Europeans have staked a claim in the sky while we molder on the earth, left behind in the dust of innovation. But the *Inquirer* never merely decries, the *Inquirer* acts! We invite every red-blooded American aviator and aviatrix to carry our banner skyward in the Great Whiteway Atlantic-to-Pacific Cross-Country Air Race to fly across America in fifty days!' Print it!

"And now . . ." He whipped a newspaper clipping from his coat and read aloud, "'The brave pilot dipped his planes to salute the spectators before his horizontal rudder and spinning airscrew lofted the aeronaut's heavier-than-air flying machine to the heavens.' Who wrote this?"

"I did, sir."

"You're fired!"

Thugs from the circulation department escorted the unfortunate to the stairs. Whiteway crumpled the clipping in his plump fist and glowered at his terrified employees.

"The *Inquirer* speaks to the average man, not the technical man. Write these words down: In the pages of the *Inquirer*, 'flying machines' and 'aeroplanes' are 'driven' or 'navigated' or 'flown' by 'drivers,' 'birdmen,' 'aviators,' and 'aviatrixes.' Not 'pilots,' who dock the *Lusitania*, nor 'aeronauts,' who sound like Greeks. You and I may know that 'planes' are components of wings and that 'horizontal rudders' are elevators. The average man wants his wings to be wings, his rudders to turn, and his elevators to ascend. He wants his airscrews to be 'propellers.' He is well aware that if flying machines are *not* heavier than air, they are balloons. And soon he will want that back East and European affectation 'aeroplane' to be an 'airplane.' Get to work!"

Isaac Bell reckoned that Whiteway's private office made Joseph Van Dorn's mighty "throne room" in Washington, D.C., look modest.

The publisher sat behind his desk and announced, "Gentlemen, you are the first to know that I have decided to sponsor my own personal entry in the Great Whiteway Atlantic-to-Pacific Cross-Country Air Race for the Whiteway Cup and the fifty-thousand-dollar prize."

He paused dramatically.

"Her name—yes, you heard me right, gentlemen—*her* name is Josephine Josephs."

Isaac Bell and Joseph Van Dorn exchanged a glance that Whiteway misinterpreted as astonished rather than confirmation of a foregone conclusion.

"I know what you're thinking, gentlemen: I'm either a brave man backing a girl or I'm a fool. *Neither!* I say. There is no reason why a girl can't win the cross-country aerial race. It takes more nerve than brawn to drive a flying machine, and this little girl has nerve enough for a regiment."

Isaac Bell asked, "Are you referring to Josephine Josephs *Frost?*"

"We will not be using her husband's name," Whiteway replied curtly. "The reason for this will shock you to the core."

"Josephine Josephs Frost?" asked Van Dorn. "The young bride whose husband took potshots at her flying machine last fall in upper New York State?"

"Where did you hear that?" Whiteway bristled. "I kept it out of the papers."

"In our business," Van Dorn replied mildly, "we tend to hear before you do."

Bell asked, "Why did you keep it out of the papers?"

"Because my publicists are booming Josephine to build interest in the race. They are promoting her with a new song that I commissioned entitled 'Come, Josephine in My Flying Machine.'

They'll plaster her picture on sheet music, Edison cylinders, piano rolls, magazines, and posters to keep people excited about the outcome."

"I'd have thought they'd be excited anyway."

"If you don't lead the public, they get bored," Whiteway replied scornfully. "In fact, the best thing that could happen to keep people excited about the race will be if half the male contestants smash to the ground before Chicago."

Bell and Van Dorn exchanged another look, and Van Dorn said, disapprovingly, "We presume that you utter that statement in confidence."

"A natural winnowing of the field will turn it into a contest that pits only the best airmen against plucky tomboy Josephine," Whiteway explained without apology. "Newspaper readers root for the underdog. Come with me! You'll see what I'm talking about."

Trailed by an ever-expanding entourage of editors, writers, lawyers, and managers, Preston Whiteway led the detectives down two floors to the art department, a lofty room lit by north windows and crammed with artists hunched over drawing boards, illustrating the day's events.

Bell counted twenty men crowding in after the publisher, some with pencils and pens in hand, all with panic in their eyes. The artists ducked their heads and drew faster. Whiteway snapped his fingers. Two ran to him, bearing mock-ups of sheet music covers.

"What have you got?"

They held up a sketch of a girl on a flying machine soaring over a field of cows. "'The Flying Farm Girl.'"

"No!"

Abashed, they held up a second drawing. This depicted a girl

in overalls with her hair stuffed under what looked to Bell like a
taxi driver's cap. "'The Aerial Tomboy.'"

"No! God in Heaven, no. What do you men do down here for
your salaries?"

"But Mr. Whiteway, you said readers like farm girls and
tomboys."

"I said, 'She's a girl!' Newspaper readers like girls. Draw her
prettier! Josephine is beautiful."

Isaac Bell took pity on the artists, who looked ready to jump
out the window, and interjected, "Why don't you make her look
like a fellow's sweetheart?"

"I've got it!" yelled Whiteway. He spread his arms and stared
bug-eyed at the ceiling, as if he could see through it all the way to
the sun.

"'*America's Sweetheart of the Air.*'"

The artists' eyes widened. They looked carefully at the writers
and editors and managers, who looked carefully at Whiteway.

"What do you think of that?" Whiteway demanded.

Isaac Bell observed quietly to Van Dorn, "I've seen men more
at ease in gun battles."

Van Dorn said, "Rest assured the agency will bill Whiteway for
your idea."

A brave old senior editor not far from retirement spoke up at
last: "Very good, sir. Very, very good."

Whiteway beamed.

" 'America's Sweetheart of the Air'!" cried the managing editor,
and the others took up the chant.

"Draw that! Put her on a flying machine. Make her pretty—no,
make her beautiful."

Invisible smiles passed between the detectives. Sounded to

Isaac Bell and Joseph Van Dorn like Preston Whiteway had fallen for his personal entry.

Back in Whiteway's private office, the publisher turned grave. "I imagine you can guess what I want from you."

"We can," Joseph Van Dorn answered. "But perhaps it would be better to hear it in your own words."

"Before we start," Bell interrupted, turning to the only member of the entourage who had followed them back into Whiteway's office and taken a faraway chair in the corner, "may I ask who you are, sir?"

He was dressed in a brown suit and vest, celluloid stand-up collar, and bow tie. His hair was brilliantined to his skull like a shiny helmet. He blinked at Bell's question. Whiteway answered for him.

"Weiner from Accounting. I had him deputized by the American Aeronautical Society, which will officially sanction the race, to preside as Chief Rule Keeper. You'll be seeing a lot him. Weiner will keep a record of every contestant's time and settle disputes. His word is final. Even *I* can't overrule him."

"And he enjoys your confidence in this meeting?"

"I pay his salary and own the property he rents to house his family."

"Then we will speak openly," said Van Dorn. "Welcome, Mr. Weiner. We are about to hear why Mr. Whiteway wants to engage my detective agency."

"Protection," said Whiteway. "I want Josephine protected from her husband. Before Harry Frost shot at her, he murdered Marco Celere, the inventor who built her aeroplanes, in an insane fit of jealous rage. The vicious lunatic is on the run, and I fear that he is stalking her—the only witness to his crime."

"There are rumors of murder," said Isaac Bell. "But, in fact, no one has seen Marco Celere dead, and the district attorney has filed no charges as there is no body."

"Find it!" Whiteway shot back. "Charges are pending. Josephine witnessed Frost shooting Celere. Why do you think Frost ran? Van Dorn, I want your agency to investigate the disappearance of Marco Celere and build a murder case that will require that hicktown prosecutor to get Harry Frost locked up forever. Or hanged. Do what you must, and damn the expense! Anything to protect the girl from that raving lunatic."

"Would that Frost were only a raving lunatic," said Joseph Van Dorn.

"What do you mean?"

"Harry Frost is the most dangerous criminal not currently behind bars that I know of."

"No," Whiteway protested. "Harry Frost was a first-class businessman before he lost his mind."

ISAAC BELL DIRECTED A COLD GLARE at the newspaper publisher. "Perhaps you are not aware how Mr. Frost got started in business."

"I am aware of his success. Frost was the top newsstand distributor in the nation when I took command of my father's papers. When he retired—at the age of thirty-five, I might add—he controlled every newsstand in every railroad station in the country. However cruel he's been to poor Josephine, Frost commanded great success in forging his continental chain. Frankly, as one businessman to another, I would admire him, if he weren't trying to kill his wife."

"I'd sooner admire a rabid wolf," Isaac Bell countered grimly.

"Harry Frost is a brutal mastermind. He 'forged his continental chain,' as you put it, by slaughtering every rival in his path."

"I still say he was a fine businessman before he became a lunatic," Whiteway objected. "Instead of living on the interest of his wealth when he retired, he invested it in steel, railroads, and Postum Cereals. He possesses a fortune that would do J. P. Morgan proud."

Joseph Van Dorn's cheeks flamed with such fury that they were suddenly redder than his whiskers. He retorted sharply, the normally faint Irish lilt in his voice thickening into a brogue as heavy as a Dublin ferry captain's.

"J. P. Morgan has been accused of many things, sir, but even if they were all true, he would not be proud of such a fortune. Harry Frost possesses the managemental skills of General Grant, the strength of a grizzly, and the scruples of Satan."

Isaac Bell put it plainly: "We know how Frost operates. The Van Dorn Detective Agency tangled with him ten years ago."

Whiteway snickered. "Isaac, ten years ago you were in prep school."

"Not so," Van Dorn interrupted. "Isaac had just signed on as an apprentice and the god-awful truth is Harry Frost got the best of both of us. When the dust had settled, he controlled every railroad newsstand within five hundred miles of Chicago, and those of our clients who were not bankrupted were dead. Having established that blood-soaked foundation right under our noses, he expanded east and west. He's as slippery as they come. We could never build a case that would stand up in court."

Whiteway saw an opportunity to negotiate a low fee for the Van Dorn services.

"Have I put too much faith in the famous Van Dorn motto, 'We Never Give Up. Never'? Ought I shop around for better detectives?"

Isaac Bell and Joseph Van Dorn stood up and put on their hats.

"Good day, sir," said Van Dorn. "As your cross-country race will span the continent, I recommend you 'shop around' for an investigative outfit with a national reach equal to mine."

"Hold on! Hold on! Don't go off half-cocked. I was merely—"

"We admitted the drubbing Frost dealt us in order to warn you not to underestimate him. Harry Frost is mad as a hatter and violent as a longhorn, but, unlike most madmen, he is coldly efficient."

Bell said, "Faced with the choice between the asylum or the hangman, Frost has nothing to lose, which makes him even more lethal. Don't think for a moment he'll be content harming Josephine. Now that you've made her your champion in the race, he will attack your entire enterprise."

"One man? What can one man do? Particularly a man on the run."

"Frost organized gangs of outlaws in every city in the country to build his empire—thieves, arsonists, strikebreaker thugs, and murderers."

"I have no objection to strikebreakers," Whiteway said staunchly. "Someone's got to keep labor in line."

"You'll object to them beating up your fliers' mechanicians," Isaac Bell shot back coldly. "The infields of racetracks and fairgrounds where your racers will land their machines at night are a favored habitat of gamblers. The gamblers will make book on your race. Gambling draws criminals. Frost knows where to find them, and they'll be glad to see him."

"Which is why," said Van Dorn, "you must prepare to battle Frost at every stop on the route."

"This sounds expensive," Whiteway said. "Appallingly expensive."

Bell and Van Dorn still had their hats on. Bell reached for the door.

"Wait— How many men will it take to cover the entire route?"

Isaac Bell said, "I traced it on my way west this past week. It's fully four thousand miles."

"How could you trace my route?" Whiteway demanded. "I haven't published it yet."

The detectives exchanged another invisible smile. No Van Dorn worth his salt arrived at a meeting ignorant of a potential client's needs. That went double for the founder of the agency and his chief investigator.

Bell said, "There is a necessary logic to your route: Flying machines can't cross high mountains like the Appalachians and the Rockies, the competitors' support trains will have to follow the railroad lines, and your newspapers will want the greatest number of spectators to take notice. Consequently, I rode the Twentieth Century Limited from New York City to Chicago on the Water Level Route up the Hudson River and along the Erie Canal and Lake Erie. At Chicago I transferred to the Golden State Limited through Kansas City, south to Texas, and crossed the Rockies at the lowest point in the Continental Divide through the New Mexico and Arizona territories and across California to Los Angeles and up the Central Valley to San Francisco."

Bell had traveled on the excess-fare express trains under the guise of an insurance executive. Local Van Dorns, alerted by telegraph, had reported at the station stops about the fairgrounds and racetracks where the fliers were likely to land each night. Their dossiers on gamblers, criminals, informants, and law officers had made compelling reading, and by the time his train eased alongside the ferry on Oakland Mole, Isaac Bell's encyclopedic knowledge of American crime had been brought thoroughly up to date.

Weiner spoke suddenly from his chair in the corner.

"The rules stipulate that to conclude the final leg of the race the winner must first fly a circle completely around this building— the San Francisco Inquirer Building—before he alights on the Army Signal Corps's grounds at the Presidio."

"Protecting such an ambitious route will be an enormous job," Van Dorn said with a stern smile. "As I advised earlier, you need a detective agency with field offices that span the nation."

Isaac Bell removed his hat and spoke earnestly. "We believe that your cross-country race is important, Preston. The United States lags far behind France and Italy in feats of distance flying."

Whiteway agreed. "Excitable foreigners like the French and Italians have a flair for flying."

"Phlegmatic Germans and Britons are making a go of it, too," Bell observed drily.

"With war brewing in Europe," Van Dorn chimed in, "their armies offer enormous prizes for feats of aviation to be employed on the battlefield."

Whiteway intoned solemnly, "A terrible gulf yawns between warlike kings and autocrats and us overly peaceable Americans."

"All the more reason," said Isaac Bell, "for 'America's Sweetheart of the Air' to vault our nation to a new level above the heroic exploits of the Wright brothers and aerial daredevils circling crowds of spectators on sunny days. And as Josephine advances the United States, she will also advance the brand-new field of aviation."

Bell's words pleased Whiteway, and Van Dorn looked at his chief investigator admiringly for deftly flattering a potential client. But Isaac Bell meant what he said. To make aeroplanes a fast, reliable mode of modern transportation, their drivers had to tackle wind and weather across the vast and lonely American landscape.

"Harry Frost must not be allowed to derail this great race."

"The future of air flight is at stake. And, of course, the life of your young aviatrix."

"All right!" said Whiteway. "Blanket the nation from coast to coast. And to hell with what it costs."

Van Dorn offered his hand to shake on the deal. "We will get on it straightaway."

"There is one other thing," Whiteway said.

"Yes?"

"The squad of detectives who protect Josephine?"

"Handpicked, I assure you."

"They must all be married men."

"Of course," said Van Dorn. "That goes without saying."

BACK IN BELL'S AUTO, roaring down Market Street, a beaming Van Dorn chuckled, "Married detectives?"

"Sounds like Josephine traded a jealous husband for a jealous sponsor."

Isaac Bell left unspoken the thought that the supposedly naive farm girl had made a swift transition from a rich husband to pay for her airships to a rich newspaper publisher to pay for her air-ships. Clearly, a single-minded woman who got what she wanted. He looked forward to meeting her.

Van Dorn said, "I had a strong impression that Whiteway would prefer Frost *hanged* to being locked up."

"You will recall that Whiteway's mother—a forceful woman—writes articles on the immorality of divorce that Whiteway is obliged to publish in his Sunday supplements. If Preston desires Josephine's hand in marriage, he will definitely prefer *hanged* in order to receive his mother's blessing, and his inheritance."

"I would love to make Josephine a widow," growled Van Dorn. "It's the least that Harry Frost deserves. Only, first we've got to catch him."

Isaac Bell said, "May I recommend you put Archie Abbott in charge of protecting Josephine? There's no more happily married detective in America."

"He'd be a fool not to be," Van Dorn replied. "His wife is not only remarkably beautiful but very wealthy. I often wonder why he bothers to keep working for me."

"Archie's a first-class detective. Why would he stop doing what he excels at?"

"All right, I'll give your friend Archie the protective squad."

Bell said, "I presume you will assign detectives to Josephine, not PS boys."

Van Dorn Protective Services was a highly profitable offshoot of the business that supplied top-notch hotel house detectives, bodyguards, valuables escorts, and night watchmen. But few PS boys possessed the spirit, vigor, enterprise, skill, and shrewdness to rise to the rank of full-fledged detective.

"I will assign as many full detectives as I can," the boss replied.

"But I do not have an army of detectives for this job—not while I'm sending so many of my best men abroad to set up our overseas offices."

Bell said, "If you can spare only a limited corps to protect Josephine, may I recommend that you comb the agency for detectives who have worked as mechanicians?"

"Excellent! Disguised as mechanicians, a small squad can stick close by, working on her flying machine—"

"And set me loose on Frost."

Van Dorn heard the harsh note in Bell's voice. He shot an inquiring glance at him. Seen in profile, as he maneuvered the big auto through heavy traffic, his chief investigator's hawk nose and set jaw looked to be chiseled from steel.

"Can you keep a clear head?"

"Of course."

"He bested you last time, Isaac."

Bell returned a wintery smile. "He bested a lot of detectives older than I was back then. Including you, Joe."

"Promise to keep that in mind, and you can have the job."

Bell let go of the shifter and reached across the Locomobile's gasoline tank to envelop the boss's big hand in his. "You have my word."

3

"MAULED BY A BEAR," said North River town constable John Hodge, as Isaac Bell's eyes roamed inquiringly over his scarred face, withered arm, and wooden leg. "Used to be a guide, taking the sports hunting and fishing. When the bear got done, I was only fit for police work."

"How did the bear make out?" asked Bell.

The constable grinned.

"Winter nights, I sleep warm as toast under his skin. Civil of you to ask—most people won't even look me in the face. Welcome to the North Country, Mr. Bell. What can I do for you?"

"Why do you suppose they never recovered Marco Celere's body?"

"Same reason we never find any body that falls in that gorge. It's a long way down to the bottom, the river's swift and deep, and there's plenty of hungry animals, from wolverine to pike. They fall in the North, they're gone, mister."

"Were you surprised when you heard that Harry Frost shot Celere?"

"I was."

"Why? I understand Frost was known to be a violent man. Long before he was sent up for murdering his chauffeur."

"Early the same morning that Mrs. Frost's butler reported the shooting, Mr. Frost had already filed a complaint that his rifle had been stolen."

"Do you think he owned another?"

"He said that one was his favorite."

"Do you think he reported it falsely, to throw off suspicion?"

"Don't know."

"Was the rifle ever found?"

"Boys playing on the railroad tracks found it."

"When?"

"That same afternoon."

"Do you suppose Frost might have dropped it if he hopped a freight train to escape?"

"I never heard about rich sports riding the rails like hobos."

"Harry Frost wasn't always rich," said Bell. "He escaped from a Kansas City orphanage when he was eight years old and rode the rails to Philadelphia. He could hop a freight in his sleep."

"Plenty of trains come through" was all the constable would concede.

Bell changed the subject. "What sort of man was Marco Celere?"

"Don't know."

"Did you never see Celere? I understand he arrived last summer."

"Stuck to himself, up there at the Frost camp."

Bell looked out the window at North River's muddy Main Street. It was a warm spring day, but the blackflies were biting, so few people stirred out of doors. It was also what the stationmaster had called "Mud Week," when the long winter freeze finally melted, leaving the ground knee-deep in mud. The only facts that the closemouthed constable had volunteered concerned being mauled by the bear. Now Hodge waited in silence, and Bell suspected that if he did not ask another question, the taciturn backwoodsman would not speak another word.

"Other than Josephine Frost's report," Bell asked, "what proof of the shooting do you have?"

"Celere disappeared. So did Mr. Frost."

"But no direct evidence?"

Constable Hodge pulled open a drawer, reached inside, and spread five spent brass cartridge shells on the desk. "Found these at the edge of the meadow just where Mrs. Frost said she saw him shooting."

"May I?"

"Go right ahead."

Bell picked one up in his handkerchief and examined it. ".45-70."

"That's what his Marlin shoots."

"Why didn't you give these to the district attorney?"

"He didn't ask."

"Did it occur to you to mention them?" Bell asked patiently.

"Figured he had his case with Mrs. Frost being the witness."

"Is there anyone who could show me where the shooting occurred?"

To Bell's surprise, Hodge sprang from his chair. He circled his desk, wooden leg clumping the floor. "I'll take you. We better stop at the general store for a bunch of stogies. Shoo away the blackflies."

Puffing clouds of cigar smoke beneath their hat brims, the North River constable and the tall detective drove up the mountain in Hodge's Model A Ford. When they ran out of road, Hodge attached a circle of wood to his peg so he didn't sink into the mud, and they continued on foot. They climbed deer trails for an hour until the thick stands of fir trees and birch opened onto a wide meadow of matted winter-browned grass.

"By this here tree is where I found the shell casings. Clear shot across to the lip of the gorge where Mrs. Frost saw Celere fall off."

Bell nodded. The cliff was a hundred and fifty yards across the meadow from the trees. An easy shot with a Marlin, even without a telescopic sight.

"What do you suppose Celere was doing out on the rim?"

"Scouting. The butler told me they went out for bear."

"So to go ahead like that, Celere must have trusted Frost?"

"Folks said Mr. Frost was buying airplanes for his wife. I guess he'd trust a good customer."

"Did you find Celere's rifle?" Bell asked.

"Nope."

"What do you suppose happened to it?"

"Bottom of the river."

"And the same for his field glasses?"

"If he had 'em."

They walked out to the edge of the gorge. Isaac Bell walked along it, aware that he was not likely to see any signs of an event that occurred before winter snows had fallen and melted. At a point near a single tree that stood lonely sentinel with its roots clinging to the rim, he noticed a narrow shelf immediately below. It thrust out like a second cliff, six feet down and barely four feet wide. A falling body would have to clear it to plummet to the river. Gripping the roots where erosion had exposed them, he lowered himself to it and looked around. No rusty rifle. No field glasses. He peered over the side. It was a long way down to the glint of water at the bottom.

He hauled himself back up to the meadow. As he stood, resting his hand on the tree for balance, he felt a hole in the bark. He looked more closely. "Constable Hodge? May I borrow your hunting knife?"

Hodge unsheathed a strong blade that had been fashioned by honing a steel file. "Whatcha got there?"

"A bullet lodged in the tree, I suspect." Bell used Hodge's knife to gouge the bark around the hole. He carved an opening large enough to dislodge a soft lead wad with his fingers in an effort not to scratch it with the blade.

"Where the heck did that come from?"

"Maybe Harry Frost's rifle."

"Maybe, maybe not. You'll never know."

"Maybe I will," said Bell, recalling a court case argued a few years earlier by Oliver Wendell Holmes where a bullet was matched to the gun that fired it. "Do you happen to have that rifle the boys found on the tracks?"

"In my office. I'd have given it back to Mrs. Frost, but she left. Mr. Frost of course was long gone. Anyone left on the property out there is no one I would give a fine rifle to."

They returned to North River. Hodge helped Bell find a bale of cotton wool packing material at the railroad depot. They set it up at the empty end of the freight yard. Bell stuck his calling card in the center of the bale and paced off one hundred and fifty yards. Then he loaded two .45-70 shells into Frost's Marlin, found the calling card like a bull's-eye in the telescopic sight, and squeezed off a round.

The bullet missed the card, missed the cotton wool bale, and *twanged* off an iron signal post above it.

Constable Hodge looked pityingly at Isaac Bell. "I naturally assumed that a Van Dorn private detective would be conversant with firearms. Would you like me to shoot it for you?"

"The scope is off-kilter."

"That'll happen," Constable Hodge said, dubiously. "Sometimes."

"It could have been damaged when it was dropped on the tracks."

Bell sighted in on the mark the bullet had pocked in the iron post and calculated the distance down. He levered out the spent shell, which loaded a fresh cartridge into the chamber, and squeezed the trigger. His calling card flew from the bale.

"Now you're getting the hang of it," Hodge said. "Keep it up you could be a pretty good shot, young feller."

Bell dug the bullet out of the bale and wrapped it in a handkerchief along with the slug he had pulled from tree. He walked to the post office and mailed them to the Van Dorn laboratory in Chicago, requesting examination under a microscope to determine whether the bullet he had test-fired revealed rifling marks that resembled those on the bullet in the tree.

"Is anyone living out at Frost's camp?" he asked Hodge.

"No one you'd want to meet. About the only thing still going is the creamery. They send milk into town to sell. Cook, maids, butler, gardeners, and gatekeeper, they all left when Mrs. Frost did."

Bell rented a Ford auto at the livery stable, and followed directions for several miles to the Frost camp. The first he saw of it was the gatehouse, an elaborate structure built of boulders and a grillwork of massive logs under its steep roof that gave the lie to the term "camp," an Adirondack affectation similar to dubbing a

Newport mansion a "cottage." The gatekeeper's living quarters, a large, handsome bungalow, was attached to it. No one came when he called and pounded on the door.

He drove under the stone arch and onto a broad carriage drive. The drive was surfaced with crushed slate and graded in a manner far superior to the muddy, potholed public road from town. Piercing mile after mile of forest, the level roadbed gouged through hillsides and was carried across countless streams and brooks on hand-hewn stone culverts and bridges ornamented in the Arts and Crafts style.

Bell drove through five miles of Harry Frost's land before he finally saw the lake. Across the water stood a sprawling house of timbers, shingles, and stone. Large cottages and outbuildings surrounded the house, and in the distance were the barns and silos of the creamery. As the smooth slate drive skirted the lake and drew closer to the compound, he saw numerous outbuildings: blacksmith shop, smokehouse, laundry, and, at the far end of a broad lawn, an aeroplane hangar—a large, wide shed recognizable by the front elevators of a biplane poking out the gable end.

Isaac Bell stopped the Ford under the porte-cochere of the main house, accelerated the motor slightly, and opened the coil switch. The place seemed deserted. With the motor off, the only sounds he could hear were the faint ticking of hot metal and the soft sigh of a cool breeze blowing off the lake.

He knocked on the front door. No one answered. He tried the door. It was unlocked, a massive affair.

"Hello!" Bell called loudly. "Is anyone home?"

No one answered.

He stepped inside. The foyer opened into a great hall, an immense chamber brightly lighted by tall windows. Twenty-foot-tall stone fireplaces dominated each end. Rustic chairs and couches clustered on woven carpets. Gloomy European oil paintings were hung in gold frames that glittered. Timbers soared high overhead. The walls and ceiling were papered with birch bark.

The tall detective stalked from opulent room to opulent room.

Anger began to heat his breast. Scion of a Boston banking family, and bequeathed a personal fortune by his grandfather, Isaac Bell was accustomed to the accoutrements of great wealth and no stranger to privilege. But this so-called camp had been paid for with riches founded on the suffering of innocent men, women, and children. Harry Frost had committed so many crimes forging his empire that it would be difficult to single one out were it not for a Chicago depot bombing he had engineered to destroy a rival distributor. Frost's dynamite had killed three newsboys waiting for their papers. The oldest had been twelve.

Bell's boot heels echoed though an empty corridor and down a stairway.

At the foot of the stairs hulked a heavy oak door, studded with nailheads.

Bell jimmied the lock and discovered a vast wine cellar carved from the living stone. He strode among the racks, noting excellent vintages from the last twenty years, a large number of the fine '69 and '71 clarets and some astonishingly rare bottles of 1848 Lafite, laid down nearly twenty years before Baron Rothschild bought the Médoc estate. Frost had even purchased a long row of Château d'Yquem bottles of the 1811 Comet Vintage. Although, based on the low quality of the art hanging upstairs, Bell suspected a crooked wine merchant's variant on fake Academy paintings.

Upon leaving the wine cellar, he stopped suddenly, arrested by the sight of a wedding photograph on a center table. Harry Frost, dressed up in top hat and morning coat, glowered truculently at the camera. Expensive tailoring could not hide his bulk, and the top hat made him appear even wider. Bell studied the photograph closely. Frost, he realized, was not the fat man a first glance might suggest. There was something lithe and long-legged about his stance, a man poised to spring. Violent as a longhorn, Joe Van Dorn had characterized him. Quick as one, too, Bell suspected. And as strong.

Josephine stood like a child beside him, her youthful face expressing bravery, Bell thought, and something more—a sense of adventure as if she were embarking into the unknown and hoping for the best.

Arrayed stiffly behind the couple was a family of what looked like farm folk dressed for church. Bell recognized the stone fireplace behind them. They had been married here at the camp in this vast, echoing room. A strong resemblance in all the faces, but Frost's told Bell that no one but Josephine's own family had attended.

He went outside. He circled the house and inspected the outbuildings. A carriage house had been converted to a firing range, with an arsenal of pistols and rifles locked in a glass case. Similar cases held collections of swords, cutlasses, flick-knives, and daggers.

The garage contained expensive automobiles—a Packard limousine, a Palmer-Singer Skimabout, a Lancia Torpedo—and several motorcycles. The stable of vehicles fit the picture forming in Bell's mind of Frost as a restless recluse. He lived like a king but also like an outlaw. The camp was as much a hideout as it was an estate, and Frost, like all successful criminals, was prepared for a quick getaway. It seemed as if Harry Frost knew that, despite his wealth and power, it was only a matter of time before he would commit an atrocity that would make him a fugitive.

Bell looked into the blacksmith shop. The forge was cold. In the smithy's scrap heap he saw horseshoes that had been twisted out of shape. Harry Frost's Chicago calling card, Bell recalled, bent with Frost's bare hands to demonstrate his almost inhuman strength, then thrown by his thugs through the bedroom windows of his rivals. It was an article of faith among the drunks in the West Side saloons that Frost had killed a Clydesdale with his fist.

Hanging above the twisted shoes, grimy with smoke, was a framed award that Frost had received for contributing money to a civic group. Bell turned on his heel and walked into the sun, whispering the newsboys' names: Wally Laughlin, Bobby Kerouac, Joey Lansdowne. It had been an elaborate funeral, their fellows maintaining the newsboy tradition of hiring hearses and mourners and paying clerks to write obituaries and letters of condolence. Wally Laughlin, Bobby Kerouac, Joey Lansdowne, barely out of childhood, priests promising their mothers they'd find a better place in Heaven.

Bell entered the boathouse at the edge of the lake. Inside, he found flatboats and canoes and a sailboat with its mast shipped. From the boathouse he walked through tall grass to the aeroplane hangar. It contained enough parts to assemble several flying machines. But the machine he had seen through the open end was missing its engine and propellers.

He heard voices in the direction of the smokehouse.

Bell walked quietly toward them, keeping the squat windowless stone structure between him and whoever was talking on the other side. He stopped beside it. A voice was droning on and on. It sounded like a middle-aged or older man, talking some trapped listener's ear off. Bell's own ear was struck by the accent. The speaker spoke the flat *a*'s heard in the Adirondack region. But this was no local Upstate New Yorker, not with the unmistakable *d*'s for *th* sounds and snaky *s*'s of Chicago.

The subject of his monologue tagged him as a denizen of the notorious Levee District, where crime and vice were daily fare.

4

"YOU WANT TO MAKE A PILE MONEY, you get yourself a bordello—What's that? No, no, no. *Not here!* Who's your customers here? Cows? You go to Chicago! You go over dere by the West Side. You purchase a house for six thousand. You bring a carpenter by to build a buncha walls for a couple hundred bucks. You get ten girls. Twenty visits a night. Dollar a visit—you don't want no cheap fifty-cent house—and you let the girls keep half. You pay the house off in two months. From then on, you're making three thousand a month. *Profit!*"

"I gotta go do my chores," said a younger, slower voice.

Bell removed his broad-brimmed hat to venture a quick glance around the corner. The middle-aged talker was sitting on a barrel with his back to him. He had a bottle of beer in his hand and was wearing a city man's derby, shirtsleeves, and vest. The younger was a farm boy in a straw hat. He was clutching a bucket and a rake.

"And don't forget your profits selling booze to the visitors. And the girls. The girls always blow their easy money. They want morphine, cocaine, wine, you take your cut. Salesman comes by to sell 'em dresses, you take your cut."

"I gotta go, Mr. Spillane."

The farmhand shuffled out of sight in the direction of the creamery.

When Bell rounded the corner of the smokehouse, and the man on the barrel whirled to face him, he instantly recognized the grizzled fifty-year-old from the wanted posters.

"Sammy Spillane."

Spillane stared long and hard, trying to place him. It had been ten years. He pointed at Bell, shaking his finger, nodding his head. "I know you."

"What are you doing here, Sammy? Was Harry Frost running an old folks' home for retired bruisers?"

"You're a goddamned Van Dorn, that's who you are."

"How did you get out of Joliet?" Sammy's pale skin told him he'd been locked up until recently.

"Time off for good behavior. Time to paste your nose into that pretty face."

"You're getting a little long in the tooth to mix it up, aren't you, Sammy?"

"I am," Sammy conceded. "But me old gal Sadie blessed me with two fine sons. Come out here, boys!" he called loudly. "Say hello to a genuine Van Dorn detective, who forgot to bring his pals with 'im."

Two younger and bigger versions of Sammy Spillane stepped into the sunlight, yawning and rubbing sleep from their eyes. At the sight of Isaac Bell they darted back inside and returned with pick handles, slapping the heavy bulging ends menacingly in their palms. Bell did not doubt that they had learned their trade as strikebreakers intimidating union marchers. Their father, meanwhile, had drawn a Smith & Wesson revolver, which he pointed at Bell.

"What do you think of my boys, detective?" Spillane chortled. "Chips off the old block?"

"I'd have recognized them anywhere," said Isaac Bell, looking the big young men up and down. "The resemblance is strongest in the squinty pig eyes. Though I do see a bit of their mother in those sloping foreheads. Say, Sammy, did you ever get around to marrying Sadie?"

The insult provoked them to charge simultaneously.

They came at the tall detective from both sides. They raised the pick handles expertly, tucking their elbows close to their torsos so they didn't expose themselves and trusting in wrist action to swing the thick hickory shafts with sufficient power to smash bone.

Their attack momentarily blocked Sammy's field of fire.

Bell kept it blocked by slewing sideways. When Sammy Spillane could see him again, Isaac Bell's white hat was falling to the grass and the two-shot .44 derringer the detective had drawn from inside the crown was aimed squarely at his face. Sammy swung his revolver toward Bell. Bell fired first, and the Chicago gangster dropped his gun and fell off the barrel.

His sons halted their rush, surprised by the crack of gunfire and the sight of their father curled up on the ground, clutching his right arm and moaning in pain.

"Boys," Bell told them, "your old man has decided to sit this one out. Why don't you drop the lumber before you get hurt?"

They separated, flaring to either side. They stood twelve feet apart, each only six feet from Bell, an easy reach with the pick handles.

"You got one shot left, Mr. Detective," said the bigger of the two. "What are you going do with it?"

Bell scooped his hat off the ground, clapped it on his head, and aimed at a spot between them. "I was fixing to shoot your brother in the knee, figuring he could use that pick handle as a cane for the rest of his life. Now I'm reassessing the situation. Wondering if you're the one." The gun barrel yawned from one to the other, then settled between them, rock steady.

"You shoot him, you've gotta deal with me," the smaller warned.

"Same here," said the bigger, adding with a harsh laugh, "Mexican standoff. 'Cept you're short a Mexican— Daddy, you all right?"

"No, dammit," Sammy groaned. "I'm shot in the arm. Kill him before he blows your fool head off! Get him, both of you. Stick and slug! *Now!*"

Sammy Spillane's sons charged.

Bell dropped the big one with his last bullet and shifted abruptly to let his brother's pick handle whiz an inch from his face. Young Spillane's momentum threw him off balance, and Bell raked the back of his neck with the derringer as he tumbled past.

He sensed movement behind him.

Too late. Sammy Spillane had retrieved the pick handle dropped by the son Bell had shot. Still on the ground, he swung it hard with his unwounded arm.

The hardwood shaft slammed into the back of Bell's knee. It hardly hurt at all, but his leg buckled as if his tendons had turned to macaroni. He went down backwards, falling so hard that it knocked the wind out of his lungs.

For what felt like an eternity, Isaac Bell could neither see, breathe, nor move. A shadow enveloped him. He blinked his eyes, trying to see. When he could, he saw Spillane's smaller son was standing astride him, lifting his pick handle over his head with both hands. Bell could see the thick bulge of wood blot out a chunk of the sky. He saw the man's entire body tighten to put every ounce of his strength into the downward blow.

Bell knew that his only hope was to draw his automatic from

the shoulder holster under his coat, but he still couldn't move. The pick handle was about to descend on his skull.

Suddenly fueled by a rush of adrenaline, Bell found the strength to reach into his coat. Realizing he could move again, he immediately changed tactics, and instead of drawing his pistol, he kicked up between the man's legs. He connected solidly with the hard toe of his boot.

Young Spillane froze, rigid as a statue. He stood with his arms locked high in the air. The pick handle began slipping from his paralyzed fingers. Before it hit the ground, an inch from Bell's head, he tumbled backwards, screaming.

Isaac Bell stood up, brushed off his suit, and stepped on Sammy's hand when he reached for his fallen Smith & Wesson.

"Behave yourself. It's over."

He checked that the brother he had shot was not bleeding from an artery and would survive. The man he had kicked caught his breath in deep gasps. He glowered at his father and brother on the ground beside him and up at the tall detective standing over them. Sucking air into his lungs, he groaned, "You got lucky."

Isaac Bell opened his coat to reveal the Browning pistol in his shoulder holster. "No, sonny, *you* got lucky."

"You had another gun? Why didn't you use it?"

"Mr. Van Dorn's a skinflint."

"What? What are you talking about?"

"The agency has strict rules about wasting lead on stumblebum skunks. We also make a practice of leaving at least one skunk conscious to answer our questions. Where's Harry Frost?"

"Why the hell would I tell you?"

"Because if you tell me, I won't turn you in. But if you don't tell me, your daddy is going back to Joliet for assaulting me with a firearm, and you two are going down to Elmira for assaulting me with pick handles. And I'll bet those New York cons doing their bit don't like Chicago fellows."

"The boys don't know where Harry is," Sammy Spillane groaned.

"But you do."

"Harry went on the lam. Why would he tell me where he's running?"

"He would tell you," Bell answered with elaborate patience, "so that you would know where to go to help him, Sammy, with money, weapons, and your crook colleagues. Where is he?"

"Harry Frost don't need no money from me. And he don't need no 'crook colleagues,' neither."

"A man can't run without help."

"You don't get it, Mr. Detective. Harry has dough stashed in every bank in the country. You track him in New York, he'll get dough in Ohio. You follow him to Ohio, he'll be shaking hands with a bank manager in California."

Bell watched the wounded gangster through narrowed eyes. Spillane was describing a fugitive who thoroughly understood how big and fragmented America was, the kind of modern criminal that even a continental outfit like the Van Dorn Detective Agency found difficult to track across state lines and through myriad jurisdictions. He made a mental note to have the Van Dorn field offices circulate wanted posters to every bank manager in their territory. Admittedly a long shot, as banks numbered in the tens of thousands.

"I suppose he has pals everywhere, too?"

"Not 'pals' you'd call friends. But guys he helped so they'd help him back. How do you think I got here after Joliet? Harry looked out for people who could help when he needed it. Always. From the first newsie I beat—from the first time I worked in his sales department—Harry Frost was always there for me."

"If he knows you'll help him, he must have told you where he was headed. Where is he?"

"Daddy don't know, mister," chorused Sammy's sons.

"Mr. Frost was scared they'd throw him back in the bughouse."

"He wouldn't tell nobody."

Isaac Bell saw that this was going nowhere. "How did Frost make his getaway?"

"Hopped a freight."

The railroad tracks through the village of North River ran north and south. North to Canada. South to Saratoga and Albany, and from there Boston, Chicago, or New York Any direction he chose. "Northbound freight?" Bell asked. "Or southbound?"

"North."

South, thought Bell. And with Whiteway's publicists "booming" Josephine's participation in the race, locating the aviatrix would be as simple as buying a newspaper.

"I have one more question," said Isaac Bell. "If you lie again, I'll put all three of you back in prison. Where is Marco Celere?"

Sammy Spillane and his sons exchanged baffled glances.

"The Italian? What do you mean, *where*?"

"Where is he?"

"Dead."

"Are you sure?"

"What the hell do you think Harry's running from?"

BELL GOT BUSY ON THE QUESTIONS he had to answer to capture Harry Frost before he hurt Josephine. Waiting for the train to

Albany, he wired Grady Forrer, Van Dorn's research man in New York, for a report on what Harry Frost had been up to since he retired at the young age of thirty-five and asked him to scour the newspapers for a wedding announcement that might shed light on how Frost had met and married Josephine.

As his train was approaching, he fired off a telegram to Archie Abbott at Belmont Park, where the competitors were gathering in the mile-and-a-half racetrack's infield, instructing him to ask Josephine when and how she first met Marco Celere.

Archie's reply was waiting at the Albany station.

Josephine met Celere last year in San Francisco, when she and her husband went to California for an aviation meet. Marco Celere had recently immigrated there from Italy.

Who, exactly, was the flying-machine inventor?

Bell wired James Dashwood, a hardworking young Van Dorn detective in the San Francisco office, to investigate Marco Celere's activities there.

Were the aviatrix and her instructor lovers? Or was Frost jealous for no reason? It was a difficult question. Constable Hodge had reported that Frost and his wife did not socialize in North River. No one in the town knew them as a couple. And Marco Celere was an outsider who lived at the Frosts' secluded camp while working on his aeroplane. Bell would have to pose the delicate question to Josephine himself.

The Interboro Rapid Transit subway whisked Bell from Grand Central Terminal to the basement entrance of the Hotel Knickerbocker, where the Van Dorn Detective Agency maintained New York offices. He found Grady Forrer in the subterranean bar off the downstairs lobby. Research had failed to find any newspaper announcement about Frost's wedding, but Forrer had managed to turn up some gossip. Josephine was an Adirondack dairy farmer's daughter—a local North River girl who had grown up a few short miles from Frost's lavish camp—information that the close-mouthed Constable Hodge had not volunteered.

Bell went upstairs to the office and telephoned him long-distance.

"Joe Josephs's girl," John Hodge answered. "Heck of a tomboy, but pretty as a picture—and about as independent as I've ever seen. A good kid, though. Sweet-natured."

"Do you know how she and Frost met?"

"Not the sort of thing I'd busy my head about."

As for Harry Frost's activities since he retired, Research reported that he traveled around the world on big-game hunts. In which case, why had Frost missed such an easy shot at Celere? The hunter fired five shots. The last three at Josephine's flying machine, two of which hit, she had reported to Constable Hodge. If the scope was improperly sighted, and he missed the first shot, an experienced rifleman would have noticed and compensated, even if he had to rely on the rifle's iron sight. It seems highly unlikely he missed twice, Bell reasoned. The bullet in the tree could have been the first shot, the one that Josephine had seen wing Celere but not kill him. So the second killed him. Frost missed the third when he shot at her aeroplane—understandable, as big-game hunters had little experience shooting at flying machines. But he had corrected again, and the fourth and fifth nearly killed her.

TWO DAYS LATER, the Chicago laboratory reported that, under a microscope, the bullet Bell had test-fired had revealed rifling marks that *might* resemble those on the bullet in the tree, but the bullet in the tree was too battered for the laboratory to be positive. The Van Dorn gunsmith did agree with Bell's speculation that the bullet in the tree could have passed through the body of the man it killed. Or only creased him, he suggested. Or missed him completely. Which was a reason, other than the river, to explain the lack of a corpse.

5

"GOOD THING THE HORSES AREN'T RUNNING," Harry Frost muttered aloud. "They'd choke on the smoke."

Frost had never seen so many trains crowding the Belmont Park Terminal.

Back in the old days, when he was one of the regular sporting men arriving at the brand-new track in their private cars, it would get pretty crowded on race day, with thirty ten-car electrics delivering spectators from the city. But nothing like this. It looked to him like every birdman in the country was steaming in, with support trains of hangar cars and Pullmans and diners and dormitories for their mechanicians—every car painted with the hero's name like a rolling billboard. Locomotives belched about the rail yard, switch engines shuttled express and freight cars onto extra sidings. When the electric train he had ridden out from Long Island City let him off, it was on the last open platform.

He spotted Josephine's train first off.

All six cars, even her hangar car, were painted yellow—the color that that San Francisco snake Whiteway painted everything he owned. All six cars shouted "Josephine" from their sides in a bold red headline font, outlined and drop-shadowed like the cover of the sheet music for that damned song.

The song Preston Whiteway had commissioned had marched across the country like an invading army. No matter where Harry Frost fled, it was impossible to escape the tune, banged out by saloon piano players, rattling from gramophones, hummed by men and women in the street, storming through his skull like a steam calliope.

Up, up . . . higher . . . The moon is on fire . . . Josephine . . . Goodbye!

Good-bye, it would be. Red-faced with rage, Harry Frost strode out of the terminal. Not only had Josephine betrayed their marriage, not only had Celere betrayed the trust that had suckered him into investing thousands in his inventions, now they had made him a fugitive.

He had consulted lawyers secretly. Every single one warned that if it ever went to trial, a conviction for a second murder charge would be a catastrophe. His wealth would not help a second time around. His political connections, the best money could buy, would disappear when the newspapers whipped his "day in court" into a Roman circus. When he cornered a New York Court of Appeals judge in his mistress's Park Avenue apartment, the man had told Frost flat out that his only hope of escaping the hangman would be to rot the rest of his life in the insane asylum.

But capturing him would not be easy, they would discover. He had lived like a hermit since he was released from Matawan. Even before, his face had never been well known to the public. That "Newsstand King" stuff was confined to the business. Average citizens, like those leading the rush out of the terminal toward the Belmont grandstand, had never seen his picture.

Besides, he smiled, stroking the full beard and mustache he had grown, now he himself saw a stranger in the mirror. The beard had made him look twenty years older by growing in surprisingly gray compared to his heavy crown of black hair, which had barely begun to be salt-and-peppered. Eyeglasses with the lenses tinted in the European way made him look a little like a German professor. Although wearing his flat sportsman's cap, he might even pass himself off as an Irish writer.

His only fear was that his bulk would give him away. The middle-aged professor in the beard and tinted glasses filled as much space as the Newsstand King. More, even, because his dark sack suit was a veritable tent of loosely cut wool, deliberately chosen to conceal his weapons and "bulletproof" vest. He had no intention of being stopped from killing Josephine, much less locked up for murdering a woman who deserved it. His firearms included a highly accurate Browning pistol for covering his escape, a pocket pistol and derringer for emergencies, and a powerful Webley-Fosbery automatic revolver. He had sawed four inches off the barrel to hide it in his pocket and loaded it with the "man-stopper" hollow-point expanding bullets.

A Chicago priest had manufactured the bulletproof vest of multiple layers of silk specially woven in Austria. Frost had invested secretly in the enterprise and owned shares in the company formed to market the inch-thick garment. The Army had rejected it for being too heavy and too hot. Frost's weighed thirty-six pounds, a negligible burden for a man of his size and strength. But it was undeniably hot. On the short walk from the train he was wiping his brow with a handkerchief. But it was worth the discomfort, as it would stop modern high-velocity, smokeless-powder slugs fired from revolvers and pistols.

He had been disappointed when he shot at Marco Celere long-range. He had missed seeing the betrayer's fear as he died. Didn't even get to see the body. He'd do it up close, this time, and squeeze the life out of Josephine with his bare hands.

He stayed within the crowd lining up to buy tickets, then shuffled among them toward the grandstand. He knew she was here because the incessantly buzzing, droning motors overhead told him they were practicing today. The wind was light, so a dozen machines were up in the sky. Josephine would be either flying or in the infield adjusting and tuning the machine that Preston Whiteway had bought for her.

He had to hand it to the race organizers, they knew their business. With weeks to go before the starting day, they had convinced fifty thousand people to ride out to Nassau County and pay twenty-five cents each to watch the birdmen practice. The aviators weren't racing around pylons or trying to set altitude records—none of the usual exhibitions of soaring, diving, and altitude climbing expected at flying fairs—just buzzing about in the air when they felt like it. But the stands were noisy with men and women cheering their heads off, and Frost could tell by the awe on their faces and their ceaseless "ooohhhs" and "aaahhhs" why they paid their quarters. The sight of enormous machines held up by invisible forces took the breath away. They weren't as fast as locomotives and racing cars, but it didn't matter. Big as they were, they hung in the blue like they belonged there.

Suddenly he saw her!

Josephine came streaking down from the sky like a yellow sword. There was no mistaking her machine. It was painted that same damned Whiteway Yellow that the born-with-a-silver-spoon-in-his-mouth sissy boy had trademarked.

Harry Frost had accompanied his wife to many an air meet to

buy her aeroplanes, and he watched this one with a knowledgeable eye. He was impressed. The Italian's final invention was a hell of a machine, as different from the last aeroplane Frost had bought for Josephine as a hawk was from a pigeon. The previous, the one from which Josephine had seen him shoot the bastard, had been a sturdy biplane. This was a mono, with a single wing, and even after it stopped rolling across the infield it still looked fast and nimble just sitting there.

His jaw tightened as he focused his horse-racing field glasses. There she was, jumping off, with the big grin she got on her face when she really liked an aeroplane. She didn't look like she was mourning her boyfriend, and she didn't look like she was missing her husband, either. He felt the blood flush hot under his beard. He mopped his brow. Time to do the deed.

He started down from the grandstand. The guard at the gate stopped him. He showed the infield entry badge he had bought the night before from a drunken track official in a Hempstead saloon, and the guard let him pass. He walked across the horse track and stopped dead, rocked by the sight of his own face on a poster nailed to the inside rail.

WANTED
Murder Suspect
HARRY FROST
REWARD
*** $5,000 ***
(Armed and Dangerous—*Do Not Approach!!!*)
Wire or Telephone
VAN DORN DETECTIVE AGENCY
"We Never Give Up. Never."

Frost's brain started racing. Why were Van Dorns hunting him with wanted posters? What did Van Dorns care about him killing Marco Celere? What the hell was going on?

His printed face glared back at him.

It was the standard Van Dorn poster. Frost remembered it well from his Chicago days, when the private detectives were careening around the city trying to stop him by arresting the people who worked for him. When that failed, they had tried to get people to inform on him. A few dead informants put a stop to that, he recalled, grunting a laugh.

We Never Give Up?

Never?

Oh yeah? You gave up on me, pal.

He laughed again because the drawing they had mocked up of his face looked pretty much like he used to *before* he grew his beard. Frost was only vaguely aware that laughing to himself out loud drew the attention of others heading to the infield. None, however, connected his bearded face to the beardless poster.

Suddenly the laughter turned sour on his tongue.

Another wanted poster blared from the rail—same as the first—"WANTED / Murder Suspect / HARRY FROST / REWARD / *** $5,000 *** / (Armed and Dangerous—*Do Not Approach!!!*) / Wire or Telephone / VAN DORN DETECTIVE AGENCY / 'We Never Give Up. Never'"—except this one had a picture that showed what they guessed he would look like if he had grown a beard.

A cold shiver traveled up his spine. The artist had come damned close. It wasn't quite like looking in the mirror, and it didn't show his glasses, but the face looked familiar. He stopped to study the poster, angrily shrugging off people who bumped into him, ignor-

ing their complaints, which died on their lips when they took in the
size of him. Finally, he stood taller, and strolled slowly on, deciding
that it was unlikely that people would link even the bearded face
on the poster to his. Not in these crowds. Besides, anyone who
knew his name would not dare turn him in.

To hell with the Van Dorns. He beat them ten years ago, and
he would beat them again.

He walked among the flying machines, inhaling the familiar
smells of gasoline and oil, rubber and canvas, and doping varnish,
and worked his way circuitously toward her yellow machine. When
he got within fifty feet, he plunged his hands into his pockets,
caressing the sawed-off Webley with his right while his left gripped
the haft of a spring-loaded dagger, which offered the option of
dispatching a protector quietly.

Josephine had her back to him. She was standing on a soapbox,
with her head buried in the motor. Frost closed in on her. His
heart was pounding with anticipation. His face felt hot, his hands
were sweating. He gripped his weapons harder.

Abruptly, he stopped.

He didn't like the look of Josephine's mechanicians. He hid
beside a Wright Model A biplane and observed them through the
front rudders. It did not take long to confirm his suspicions.

They wore the right clothes, the typical vests, bow ties, shirtsleeves, and flat caps. And they were a younger bunch, as he expected of men who tinkered with flying machines. But they were
watching the crowds more than they were watching Josephine's
machine. Van Dorns! The mechanicians were detectives.

His brain raced again. Not only were Van Dorns hunting him
with wanted posters, they were guarding Josephine. Why?

Whiteway! It had to be Whiteway. Buying the Italian's flying

machine out of hock would have cost a pretty penny. So would
that yellow support train. But it would pay in spades by using
Josephine to boom the race and sell newspapers. Preston Whiteway
had hired the detectives to protect his investment in Josephine.

Or was it more than protecting his investment?

Frost's skull suddenly felt like it would explode.

Was Whiteway sweet on her?

Machines were roaring on the ground and buzzing in the air.
Everywhere he looked, everything was moving—loud machines,
drivers, Van Dorns. He had to get a grip on himself. Deal with
Whiteway later. First, Josephine.

But the Van Dorns guarding Josephine would carry those
wanted posters in their memories. Her guards would stop anyone
who looked even slightly like either picture.

He noticed that their eyes kept shifting toward a tall redheaded
man standing nearby in a sack suit and bowler. A suspect? Did they
think that Harry Frost had dyed his hair red, lost seventy pounds,
and gained two inches? The fellow looked like a Fifth Avenue
swell. But he had thin white lines of a boxer's scarring on his brow.
And his eyes were busy, looking everywhere even as he pretended
not to.

Not a suspect, Frost surmised. Another goddamned Van
Dorn—the chief of their squad, from the way the others were
looking to him. Suddenly Frost realized who the swell was—
Archibald Angel Abbott IV. No wonder they hadn't bothered dis-
guising him as a mechanician.

Archibald Angel Abbott IV was too well known to work co-
vertly. He had always been a big deal in the blue-blooded society
set—New York's most eligible bachelor. Then the newspapers had
made him famous when he married the daughter of the railroad

tycoon Osgood Hennessy. She stood to inherit it all. Frost wondered why the hell Abbott hadn't traded his guns in for golf clubs.

That question pierced Harry Frost's seething skull like a lightning bolt.

Archibald Abbott had the right idea, continuing to work for the Van Dorn Detective Agency for a measly few bucks after he married rich. Retiring was a mug's game. Harry Frost had learned that too late. He had lost his edge. From the time he was eight years old, Harry Frost had dreamed of not having to work to survive. He had achieved his dream. And what did it get him? Being made a monkey of. That was how he had been taken by Josephine and Marco—bunco artists he would have smoked in a flash in the old days.

Frost fingered his weapons. Josephine still had her head in the motor. He could seize her by the throat, let her see that it was him, then cut her heart out. But the awful truth was that he could not get near her. There were too many Van Dorns masquerading as mechanicians. He couldn't kill them all. They would gun him down first. He was not afraid to die. But he was damned if he would die in vain.

He needed help.

He hurried back to the train terminal and boarded an electric to Flatbush, where he entered a Brooklyn savings bank. Fleeing poverty, riding the rails as a child, begging for pennies for food, he had vowed never to be caught short anywhere ever again. As he flourished—as he plowed the profits of the distribution empire into stocks that returned fortunes—he had banked money in states across the continent.

He withdrew three thousand dollars from an account that held twenty. The bank manager counted it out personally in his private office. After Frost picked it up, the banker casually laid on his desk a wanted poster similar to those Frost had seen at the racetrack.

This poster was tailored to bankers. It warned them to be on the lookout for Harry Frost, or someone who looked like Harry Frost, drawing from his account. Frost acknowledged the banker's loyalty with a brusque nod. They both knew that it was the least the banker could do. If Frost hadn't covered his losses on an ill-advised scheme involving other men's money, the banker would be serving time in Sing Sing.

A trolley took him to the waterfront.

He walked to a Pennsylvania Railroad stockyard pier. Tugboats were shoving car floats alongside. Trainloads of cows, sheep, and pigs were herded from the freight cars into cattle pens. Frost headed for the pier building and pushed through a door that said "No Admittance." Thugs masquerading as railroad police tried to stop him. Frost knocked both men down with his open hand and pushed through another door at the back of the building into a stable. A dozen beef cattle, each with a distinctive Mexican brand burned on its flank, were tethered to posts set in the floor.

There were two men with the cows. One was seated at a table on which were scattered cow horns. The other was removing a horn from one of the tethered animals by turning it in his hands, unscrewing it from a threaded rod that had been drilled in the base of the horn. Rod Sweets, the man at the table, didn't recognize Harry Frost in his beard. He pulled a pocket pistol.

"Don't," said Frost. "It's me."

Sweets stared. "Well, I'll be damned."

"You will be if you don't put that gun away."

Sweets shoved it hastily back his vest. "Don't tell me you've developed a taste for dope."

The cow horns—sawn from the steers in Mexico, hollowed out, and fitted with threads—had been stuffed with Hong Kong opium before being screwed back on. Sweets smuggled hundreds of pounds of raw opium yearly into New York in this manner and presided over a vast refining and distribution network that supplied morphine to thousands of druggists and physicians. Protecting such an enterprise took an army.

"No dope," said Frost. "I want to hire a crew."

Rod Sweets's men would not care that he hated Josephine for buncoing him nor that he hated Preston Whiteway for seducing her. Money was all they cared for. And money, he had plenty of.

Frost made arrangements with Sweets quickly. Then he hurried to the Red Hook saloon where could be found the brothers George and Peter Jonas, who specialized in tampering with the brakes and gasoline tanks of newspaper-delivery trucks. Again, money was all that was needed, and the saboteurs were falling all over themselves trying to persuade him that it was even easier to smash a flying machine than a motortruck.

"It's all in the wires that hold 'em together," said George, and Peter finished his brother's thought: "A wire lets go, the wing falls off, down she goes."

Harry Frost had spent many a long hour watching his wife at air meets. "The birdmen know that. They check their wires every time they go up."

The brothers exchanged a quick glance. They didn't know much about flying machines, but they knew the logic of machines in general, which was all they really had to know to break one.

"Sure, they check 'em," said George. "They look for nicks, for kinks, for weak spots."

Peter said, "So, like you says, Mr. Frost, we're not going to sneak up on 'em with a hacksaw."

"But," said George, "they don't always check the fittings that anchor the wire to the wing." He glanced at his brother, who said, "We pull a steel anchor bolt."

"We replace it with a cast-aluminum anchor bolt that looks just the same but ain't so strong."

"They don't see it."

"They go up."

"They jerk hard in the air."

"The anchor lets go."

"The wing falls off."

"They're flying a cinder block."

FROST TOOK A TROLLEY BACK TO FLATBUSH.

He felt an unexpected sense of well-being.

Back in harness. He'd been idle too long. For the first time since the nightmare of Josephine's betrayal, he felt restored, alive again, even as he hid in the dark. The important thing, as always, was to move quickly, move before anyone knew what he was doing, and never do what they expected.

He rode an electric Long Island Rail Road train to Jamaica in the borough of Queens. At an auto rental, he hired the most expensive car they had—a Pierce. He drove it through truck and dairy farms across the Nassau county line to Garden City, and swept under the porte-cochere of the Garden City Hotel. It was a grand place. Before Josephine, before the chauffeur and the asylum, he had rubbed shoulders with Schuylers, Astors, and Vanderbilts here.

The staff did not recognize him behind his gray beard. He paid for a large suite on the top floor, where he ordered dinner served in his room. He drank a bottle of wine with it and turned in for a fitful sleep haunted by strange dreams.

He sat bolt upright at dawn, thunderstruck by the clatter of threshing machines. His heart pounded, as he listened for the squealing of the wheels when the guards rolled the morning break- fast slop down the corridor and the clanging of the ladle striking the cauldron. The same morning racket he still remembered from the orphanage. Only, gradually, did he begin to notice things. The bed was soft and the room was quiet. He glanced at the open windows, where white curtains fluttered in a warm breeze. There were no bars. He wasn't in the bughouse. They hadn't dragged him back to the orphanage. A smile crept across Harry Frost's face. Not threshing machines. *Flying* machines. Morning practice at Belmont Park.

He had breakfast in bed, three short miles from the racetrack where Josephine and her new admirers were tuning their airships for the race.

"WHERE'S JOSEPHINE?" Isaac Bell inquired of the Van Dorn detectives guarding the gate to the Belmont Park Race Track infield.

"In the air, Mr. Bell."

"Where's Archie Abbott?"

"Over by the yellow tent."

Bell had driven out to Belmont in a borrowed Pierce-Arrow to interview Josephine about her husband's habits and the associates he might recruit. As the only person who had spent time with him in his reclusive years, she might even have an idea of where he would hide.

Bell saw right off that Whiteway had chosen a perfect place to start the air race. The Belmont infield was enormous. Encompassed by the longest racetrack in the country, a mile and a half, it was the size of a small farm. Nearly fifty acres of flat grass inside the track were overlooked by a grandstand that could seat thousands of paying spectators. It offered numerous two-hundred-yard stretches of grass on which the machines could gather speed to take to the sky and return to the ground, as well as room for tents, temporary wooden aeroplane hangars, trucks, and autos. The rail yard for the support trains was just on the other side of the stands.

Bell breathed deeply of the air—an exhilarating mix of burnt oil, rubber, and gasoline—and felt instantly at home. It smelled like a race-car meet made all the richer by the scent of the fabric dope that the aviators varnished their machines with to seal the fabric covering the frames. The ground was alive with machines and men rushing about, like at an auto meet. But here at Belmont, all eyes were aimed at the sharp blue sky.

Machines swept into the air, swooped and darted about— boundless as birds but a hundred times bigger. A vast variety of shapes and sizes sailed through the sky. Bell saw airships triple the length of racing cars lumber overhead on wings that spread forty feet, and smaller ones flitted by, some flimsy, some supple as dragonflies.

The noise was as thrilling, each type of motor blasting its own unique sound: the *Smack! Smack!* of a radial three-cylinder Anzani, the harsh rumble of Curtiss and Wright four-cylinders, the smooth burble of the admirable Antoinette V-8s that Bell knew from speedboats, and the exuberant *Blat! Blat! Blat!* of the French-built rotary Gnome Omegas whose seven cylinders whirled improbably around a central crankshaft, spewing castor oil smoke that smelled like smoldering candle wax.

He located Archie by making a beeline for an enormous tent of the same bright yellow as the banner he had seen on top of Whiteway's Inquirer building, and they shook hands warmly. Archie Abbott was nearly as tall as Isaac Bell, redheaded, with compelling gray eyes and a sparkling smile. He was clean-shaven. Faint white lines of scar tissue on this aristocratic brow indicated experience in the prize ring. They had been best friends since college, when Archie boxed for Princeton and Bell had floored him for Yale.

Bell saw that Archie had used his time here well. He was friendly with all the participants and officials. His detectives—

those disguised as mechanicians, newspaper reporters, hot dog salesmen, and Cracker Jack vendors, and those patrolling in sack suits and derbies—appeared familiar with their territory and alert. But Archie could not tell Bell any more than he already knew about Josephine's relationship with Marco Celere, which was little more than speculation.

"Were they lovers?"

Archie shrugged. "I can't answer that. She does get a little misty-eyed when his name comes up. But what she's really nuts about is that flying machine."

"Could it be that she's misty-eyed for his mechanical expertise?"

"Except that Josephine is a whiz of a mechanician herself. She can take that machine apart and put it back together on her own, if she has to. She told me that the places she'll be flying won't have a mechanician."

"I'm looking forward to meeting her. Where is she?"

Archie pointed at the sky. "Up there."

The two friends scanned the blue, where a dozen flying machines were maneuvering. "I'd have thought that Whiteway would have painted her machine yellow."

"He did. Yellow as this tent."

"I don't see her."

"She doesn't circle around with the others. She flies off by herself."

"How long has she been gone?"

Archie pulled out his watch. "One hour and ten minutes, this time," he reported, clearly not happy to admit that the young woman whose safety and very life were his responsibility was nowhere in sight.

Bell said, "How in heck can we watch over her if we can't see her?"

"If I had my way," said Archie, "I'd ride in the machine with her. But it's against the rules. If they carry a passenger, they're disqualified. They have to fly alone. That Weiner accounting fellow explained that it wouldn't be fair to the others if the passenger helped drive."

"We've got to find a better way to keep an eye on her," said Bell. "Once the race starts, it will be a simple matter for Frost to lie in wait along the route."

"I plan to post men on the roof of the support train with field glasses and rifles."

Bell shook his head. "Have you seen all the support trains in the yard? You could get stuck behind a traffic jam of locomotives blocking the tracks."

"I've been considering a team of autoists to run ahead."

"That will help. Two autos, if I can find the men to drive them. Mr. Van Dorn's already complaining that I'm gutting the agency. Who is on this machine approaching? The green pusher?"

"Billy Thomas, the auto racer. The Vanderbilt syndicate hired him."

"That's a Curtiss he's driving."

"The syndicate bought three of them, so he can choose the fastest. Six thousand apiece. They really want to win. Here comes a Frenchman. Renee Chevalier."

"Chevalier navigated that machine across the English Channel."

Bell's eye had already been drawn to the graceful Blériot monoplane. The single-wing craft looked light as a dragonfly. An open girder of strut work connected the cloth-covered wings to the tailpiece of rudder and elevators. Chevalier sat behind the wing, partially enclosed in a boxlike compartment that shielded him nearly to his chest. He was switching his Gnome rotary engine on and off to slow it as he landed.

"I'm buying one of those when this job is over."

"I envy you," said Archie. "I'd love to take a crack at flying."

"Do it. We'll learn together."

"I can't. It's different when you're married."

"What are you talking about? Lillian wouldn't mind. She drives race cars. In fact she'll want one, too."

"Things are changing," Archie said gravely.

"What do you mean?"

Archie glanced around and lowered his voice. "We haven't wanted to tell anyone until we're sure everything's O.K. But I'm not about to start a dangerous new hobby now that it looks like we're going to have children."

Isaac Bell grabbed Archie underneath the arms and lifted him joyfully off the ground. "Wonderful! Congratulations."

"Thank you," said Archie. "You can put me down now." People were staring. It was not often they saw a tall man raise another high in the air and shake him like a terrier.

Isaac Bell was beside himself with happiness. "Wait 'til Marion hears! She'll be so happy for you. What are you going to name it?"

"We'll wait 'til we see what sort of 'it' it is."

"You can get a flying machine soon as it's in school. By then flying will be even less dangerous than it is now."

Another machine was approaching the grass.

"Who's driving that blue Farman?"

The Farman, another French-built airship, was a single-propeller pusher biplane. It looked extremely stable, descending as steadily as if it were gliding down a track.

"Sir Eddison-Sydney-Martin."

"He could be a winner. He's won all of England's cross-country races, flying the best machines."

"Poor as a church mouse," Archie noted, "but married well."

The socially prominent Archibald Angel Abbott IV, whose ancestors included the earliest rulers of New Amsterdam, could gossip as knowledgeably about Germans, Frenchmen, and Britons as about New York blue bloods, thanks to a long honeymoon in Europe—sanctioned by Joe Van Dorn in exchange for scouting overseas branches for the agency.

"The baronet's wife's father is a wealthy Connecticut physician. She buys the machines and looks after him. He's extremely shy. Look there, speaking of having a wealthy benefactor, here comes Uncle Sam's—U.S. Army Lieutenant Chet Bass."

"That's the Signal Corps Wright he's driving."

"I knew Chet at school. When he starts in on the future of aerial bombs and torpedoes, you'll have to shoot him to shut him up. Though he has a point. With the constant war talk in Europe, Army officers haunt the aviation meets."

"Is that red one another Wright?" Bell asked, puzzled by an odd mix of similarities and differences. "No, it can't be," he said as it drew nearer. "The propeller's in front. It's a tractor biplane."

"That's the 'workingman's' entry, Joe Mudd driving. It started out as a Wright, 'til it collided with an oak tree. Some labor unionists trying to improve their reputation bought the wreck and cobbled it together out of spare parts. They call it the 'American Liberator.'"

"Which unions?"

"Bricklayers, Masons and Plasterers teamed up with the Brotherhood of Locomotive Firemen. It's a good little machine, considering that they're operating on a shoestring. Whiteway's trying to bar them."

"On what grounds?" Bell asked.

"'If workingmen find themselves with excess funds,'" Archie mimicked Whiteway's pompous delivery, "'they should contribute them to the Anti-Saloon League.'"

"Temperance? I've seen Preston Whiteway drunk as a lord."

"On champagne, not beer. Drink is a privilege, to his way of thinking, which should be reserved for those who can afford it. Needless to say, when he had Josephine's flying machine painted 'Whiteway Yellow,' Joe Mudd and the boys varnished theirs 'Revolution Red.'"

Bell searched the sky for her. "Where is our girl?"

"She'll be back," Archie assured him, peering anxiously. "She'll run out of gas soon. She'll have to come back."

A scream at a high pitch suddenly pierced the air like a pneumatic siren.

Bell looked for the source. It sounded loud enough to rouse a sleeping firehouse. Oddly, none of the mechancians and birdmen in the infield paid it any mind. The noise ceased as suddenly as it had begun.

"What was that?"

"Platov's thermo engine," said Archie. "A crazy Russian. He's invented a new kind of aeroplane motor."

Still watching the sky for Josephine, Bell let Archie lead him to a three hundred length of rail at the beginning of which perched a strange mechanism. Mechanicians were assembling a large white biplane beside it.

"There's Platov."

Women in long white summer dresses and elaborate Merry Widow hats were gazing spellbound upon the handsome Russian inventor, whose thick, curly dark hair, springy as a heap of steel shavings, spilled from a straw boater with a bright red hatband, and tumbled down his cheeks in equally curly mutton-chop whiskers.

"Seems to have a way with the ladies," said Bell.

Archie explained that they were competitors' wives, girlfriends, and mothers traveling aboard the support trains.

Platov was gesturing energetically with an engineering slide rule, and Bell noted the gleam in his dark eyes of the "mad scientist." Though in Platov's case, the Russian appeared less dangerous than eccentric, particularly as he was busy romancing his admirers.

"He's prospecting for investors," Archie said, "hoping some fliers will try it in the race. So far, no one's ready to give up propellers. But his luck might have changed. That fat fellow in white is a Mississippi cotton farmer with more money than brains. He's paying to test the motor on a real flying machine. Mr. Platov? Come tell my friend Mr. Bell how your contraption works."

The inventor touched his lips to several of the ladies' gloves, tipped his boater, and bustled over. He shook Bell's hand, bowed, and clicked his heels. "Dmitri Platov. De idea is dat superior motor-powering fly machine Platov is demonstrating."

Bell listened closely. The "thermo engine" used a small automobile motor to power a compressor. The compressor forced liquid kerosene through a nozzle. An electric spark ignited the volatile spray, creating thrust.

"Is making jet! Jet is pushing."

Bell noticed that the voluble Russian appeared to be well liked. His fractured English provoked snickers among the grease-stained mechanicians who gathered to watch, but Bell overheard them discussing the new engine with respect. Just like mechanicians at an automobile race, they were tinkerers, always on the lookout for ways to make machines faster and stronger.

If it worked, they were saying, the thermo engine had a good chance of winning because it tackled head-on the three biggest problems holding back flying machines: excess weight, insufficient power, and the vibration that threatened to shake their flimsy frames to pieces. So far, it was tethered to a rail, down which it had "flown" repeatedly at a high rate of speed. The real test would come when the artificers finished assembling the cotton farmer's airship.

"De idea is dat no pistons is shaking, no propeller is breaking."

Again Bell overheard agreement among the gathering of flying-machine workmen. Platov's engine could be, in theory at least, as smooth as a turbine, unlike most gasoline engines, which rattled an airman's molars loose. Another mechanician ran up. "Mr. Platov! Mr. Platov! Could you please come quickly to our hangar car?"

Platov grabbed a leather tool bag and hurried after him.

"What was that about?" asked Bell.

"He's a tip-top machinist," said Archie. "Supports himself working freelance, fashioning parts. The hangar cars have lathes, drill presses, hones, and gear shapers. If all of a sudden they need a part, Platov can make it faster than the factory can ship it."

"Here comes our girl!" said Isaac Bell.

"At last," said Archie, clearly relieved despite his earlier assurances.

Bell watched the yellow speck that his sharp eyes had spotted on the horizon. It grew larger rapidly. Sooner than Bell expected, it was close enough to present the shape of a sleek monoplane. He could hear the motor make an authoritative smooth burble.

Archie said, "That's the Celere that Preston Whiteway bought back from Marco's creditors."

Isaac Bell eyed it appreciatively. "Marco's last effort makes most of these others look like box kites."

"It's a speedster, all right," Archie agreed. "But the talk around the infield is it's not as strongly constructed as the biplanes. And there are rumors that that's how Marco went broke."

"What rumors?"

"Back in Italy, they say, Marco sold a machine to the Italian Army, borrowed against future royalties, and immigrated to America and built a couple of standard biplanes he sold to Josephine's husband. Then he borrowed more money to build that one she's flying on now. Unfortunately, they say, back in Italy a wing fell off the one he sold to the Italian Army, and a general broke both legs in the smash. The Army canceled the contract, and Marco was however you say *persona non grata* in Italian. True story or not, the mechanicians agree that monoplanes aren't as strong as biplanes."

"But all that biplane strength comes at the expense of speed."

"Maybe so, but the birdmen and mechanicians I talked to all say that just getting to San Francisco is going to be the hard part. Machines that strive only for speed can't stay the whole race."

Bell nodded. "The sixty-horsepower, four-cylinder Model 35 Thomas Flyer that won the New York–to–Paris automobile race probably wasn't the fastest, but it was the strongest. Let's hope that Preston didn't buy our client a death trap."

"Considering the flocks of telegrams Whiteway sends her every day, you can bet he had that machine examined from stem to stern before he bought it. Whiteway wouldn't take chances with her life. The man's in love."

"What does Josephine think of Preston?" Bell asked.

It was not an idle question. If anyone knew her state of mind regarding Whiteway, it would be Archie. Before he became the most happily married detective in America, Archibald Angel Abbott IV had enjoyed many years as New York City's most avidly pursued eligible bachelor.

"In my opinion," Archie smiled knowingly, "Josephine admires the aeroplane that Preston bought her very much."

"No one has ever accused Preston Whiteway of exercising intelligence in his personal affairs."

"Didn't he once carry a torch for Marion?"

"Blithely unaware that he was risking life and limb," Bell said grimly. "My point exactly."

He started toward the open section of infield where the machines were alighting. Joe Mudd's sturdy red tractor biplane had taken to the sky while Bell was listening to Platov and was approaching to land ahead of the yellow monoplane. While Josephine circled around to let it go first, the red biplane floated to the grass and rolled along for a hundred yards to a stop.

Josephine's machine came down to earth at a steeper angle and a much higher rate of speed. It was traveling so swiftly that it seemed that she had somehow lost control of it and was falling out of the sky.

7

CONVERSATIONS CEASED.

Men put down tools and stared.

The yellow aeroplane was mere yards from smashing into the grass when Josephine hauled back on a lever that raised small flaps on the back of her wings and the elevator on her tailpiece. The airship leveled out, slowed, bounced on the grass, and rolled to a gentle stop.

There was a long moment of stunned silence. Then, from one end of the infield to the other, mechanicians and airmen whistled, clapped, and cheered her stunt, for it was clear that she had come down exactly as she had intended, relying on her skill to thumb her nose at gravity.

And when a slight figure dressed head to toe in white climbed out of her compartment behind the wing, a roar of approval thundered from spectators in the grandstand. She waved to the crowd and flashed a gleaming smile.

"Well done!" said Isaac Bell. "Preston Whiteway may be an idiot in his personal affairs, but he can spot a winner."

He strode to the yellow machine, pulling ahead of the long-legged Archie. A burly detective dressed as a mechanician blocked his way. "Where you going, mister?"

"I am Van Dorn Chief Investigator Isaac Bell."

The man stepped back, though he still eyed him carefully. "Sorry, I didn't know you, Mr. Bell. Tom LaGuardia, Saint Louis office. I just got shifted here. I saw you talking to Mr. Abbott. I should have assumed you were on the level."

"You did the right thing. Never assume when your client's life is at risk. If you stop the wrong person, you can always apologize. If you don't stop the right person, you can't apologize to a dead client."

Archie caught up. "Good job, Tom. I'll vouch for him."

Bell was already heading for Josephine. She had climbed onto a crosspiece that connected the landing wheels to lean into her motor and was adjusting the carburetor with a screwdriver.

Bell said, "Those hinged appendages on the back of your wings appear to give you extraordinary control."

She looked down at him with lively eyes. Hazel, Bell noticed, a warm green color in the sunlight, edging toward a cooler gray. "They're called *alettoni*. That's Italian. It means 'little wings.'"

"Did they slow your airship's descent by enlarging the wing's surface?"

Returning her attention to the carburetor, she answered, "They deflect more air."

"Do *alettoni* work better than warping?"

"I'm not sure yet," she said. "They don't always do what I want them to. Sometimes they act as a brake and slow me down instead of keeping me level."

"Can they be adjusted?"

"The man who invented them is dead. So now we have to fig-ure it out without his help." She made a final adjustment, sheathed her screwdriver in a back pocket, jumped to the ground, and offered her gloved hand. "I'm Josephine, by the way. Who are you?"

"Sorry, I should have introduced myself. I'm Isaac Bell. I'm Van Dorn's chief investigator."

"My brave protectors," she said with a frank and open smile.

She was tiny, Bell thought. Barely an inch over five feet tall, with a pretty upturned nose. Her direct gaze was older than her years, though she had a young woman's voice, thin and girlish. "I'm pleased to meet you, Mr. Bell. I hope 'chief investigator' doesn't mean Archie's been fired?"

"Not at all. Archie is in charge of your personal safety. My job is to intercept your husband before he gets close enough to harm you."

Her eyes darkened, and she looked fearful. "You'll never catch him, you know."

"Why not?"

"He's too sly. He thinks like a wild animal."

Bell smiled to put her at ease, for he saw that she was really afraid of Frost. "We'll do what we have to to deal with him. I wonder whether you might give me any clues to his behavior. Anything that would help me run him to ground."

"I can only tell you things about him that *won't* help. I'm afraid I don't know anything that will."

"Then tell me what *won't* help."

"Harry is completely unpredictable. I never knew what to expect. He'll change his mind in a flash." As she spoke her eyes glinted toward the field where Joe Mudd's red tractor biplane was taking to the air again, and Bell realized that she was assessing the competition as coolly as he would an outlaw in a knife fight.

"Can you tell me about friends he would call on?"

"I never saw him with a friend. I don't know if he ever had any. He kept to himself. Completely to himself."

"I encountered some Chicago men at your camp yesterday. I had the impression they were living there."

"They're just bodyguards. Harry kept them around for protection, but he never had anything to do with them."

"Protection from what?"

She made a face. "His 'enemies.'"

"Who were they?"

"I asked him. Once. He started screaming and hollering. I thought he would kill me. I never asked again. They're in his head, I think. I mean, he was in the nuthouse once."

Bell gently changed the subject. "Did he ever take friends when he went big-game hunting? Did he shoot with a party?"

"He hired guides and bearers. But otherwise he was alone."

"Did you go with him?"

"I was busy flying."

"Did that disappoint him?"

"No. He knew I was flying before we married." Her eyes tracked a Blériot swooping past at sixty miles an hour.

"Before? May I ask how you got started in flying?"

A high-spirited grin lighted her open face. "I ran away from home—stuffed my hair under a cap and pretended to be a boy." It wouldn't be hard, thought Bell. She didn't look like she weighed over a hundred pounds.

"I found a job in a bicycle factory in Schenectady. The owner was building flying machines on the weekend, and I helped him with the motors. I knew all about them from fixing my dad's farm machinery. One Monday, instead of going to work, I snuck out to the field and flew the machine."

"Without lessons?"

"Who was there to teach me? There weren't any schools back then. Most of us learned on our own."

"How old were you?"

"Seventeen."

"And you just climbed on the machine and flew it?"

"Why not? I could see how it worked. I mean, all it is, really, is the aeroplane goes up by pushing the air down."

"So with no formal training," Bell smiled, "you proved both Bernoulli's theorem and the existence of the Venturi effect."

"What?"

"I only mean that you taught yourself how to shape the wings to create the vacuum over the wing which makes it rise."

"No," she laughed. "No, Mr. Bell. Venturi and all that is too complicated. My friend Marco Celere was always rattling on about Bernoulli. But the fact of the matter is, the flying machine goes up by pushing the air down. Warping the wings is just a way to deflect the air away from where you want to go—up, down, around. Air is wonderful, Mr. Bell. Air is strong, much stronger than you think. A good flying machine like this one—" She laid an affectionate hand on its fabric flank. "Marco's best—makes the air hold you up."

Bell absorbed this with a certain amount of amazement. He liked young people and routinely took apprentice detectives under his wing, but he could not recall speaking with any twenty-year-old who sounded more clear and more certain than did this dairy farmer's daughter from the wilds of the North Country.

"I've never heard it put so simply."

But she had shed no light so far on her husband's habits. When he queried her further, he developed the impression that she had known little about Harry Frost before she married him, and all she had learned since was to fear him. He noticed that her eyes kept darting to the other airships rolling about the infield and climbing into the sky. Whatever confusion or youthful ignorance had led Josephine into marriage with a man like Harry Frost, the vulnerable, naive girl on the ground became a confident woman in the air.

"Having taught yourself, did you then learn a lot more from your friend Marco?"

Josephine sighed. "I could not understand his Italian, and he spoke very little English and was always working on the machines." She brightened. "But he did teach me one thing. It took me quite a while to understand what he was trying to say in English. But I finally pried it out of him. He said, 'A good flying machine has to fly—it *wants* to fly.' Isn't that wonderful?"

"Is it true?" asked Isaac Bell.

"Absolutely." She laid a firm hand on the machine again. "So if you will excuse me, Mr. Bell, if you have no more questions, I hope that this one wants to fly. But it is going to take a while to find out for sure."

"Do you miss Marco Celere?"

Her eyes did not fill, as Archie had reported, but Josephine did admit that she missed the inventor very much. "He was kind and gentle. Not at all like my husband. I miss him very much."

"Then it must be a comfort to be flying his latest machine."

"Thanks to Mr. Whiteway's kindness and generosity. He bought it from Marco's creditors, you know." She glanced sidelong at Bell. "It puts me deep in his debt."

"I imagine you'll more than pay it back by making a strong pull for the Whiteway Cup."

"I have to make more than a strong pull. I have to *win* the Whiteway Cup. I have no money of my own. I was completely dependent on Harry, and now I'm dependent on Mr. Whiteway."

"I'm sure he will be grateful if you win the race."

"Not *if*, Mr. Bell." Her gaze fixed on the sky where a parchment-colored Blériot was rising, and when she looked back at Bell her eyes had turned opaque. "I will win, Mr. Bell. But not to make him grateful. I will win because I will do my best, and because Marco built the best flying machine in the race."

Later, when Isaac spoke with Archie, he told his friend, "If I were a betting man, I'd lay money on her."

"You *are* a betting man!" Archie reminded him.

"So I am."

"Belmont Park is swarming with unemployed gamblers who would be delighted to relieve you of your money. The New York reformers just passed a law banning horse-race betting. The Atlantic–Pacific race is the bookies' godsend."

"What odds are they offering on Josephine?"

"Twenty-to-one."

"*Twenty?* You're joking. There's a fortune to be won."

"The bookies reckon she's up against the top birdmen in America. And they're betting we'll get our pants beat off by the Europeans, who hold all the records in cross-country flying."

Isaac Bell went looking for a bookmaker who could handle a thousand-dollar bet on Josephine. Only one accepted bets that large, he was told, and was directed to Johnny Musto, a short, wide middle-aged fellow in a checkerboard suit who reeked of an expensive cologne Bell had last smelled in the Plaza Hotel barbershop.

The old betting ring under the stands had been replaced, since the Legislature banned horse gambling, with an exhibit hall, showing motors and accessories for aircraft, race cars, and motorboats. Musto was lurking just outside it in the forest of steel pillars that supported the grandstand. He had as thick a Brooklyn accent as Bell had ever heard outside a vaudeville theater.

"Youse sure youse wanna do dis?" asked the bookie, who knew a private detective when he saw one.

"I am absolutely positive," said Isaac Bell. "In fact, now that you ask, let's make it two thousand."

"It's your funeral, mister. But would it be O.K. if I ask youse a little somethin' first?"

"What?"

"Is de fix in?"

"Fix? It's not a horse race."

"I know it ain't no horse race. But it's still a race. Is de fix in?"

"Absolutely not. There's no fix," said Isaac Bell. "The race is sanctioned by the American Aeronautical Society. It's honest as the day is long."

"Yeah, yeah, yeah, only dis girl is Harry Frost's wife."

"She has nothing to do with Harry Frost anymore."

"Oh yeah?"

Bell caught a mocking note in the man's voice. A suggestion that Musto was in on a joke that Bell hadn't heard yet. "What do you mean by that, Johnny?"

"She ain't with Harry no more? Den why's he hangin' 'round?"

"*What?*" Bell gripped Musto's arm so hard, the bookie winced.

"I saw dis fellow yesterday looked just like him."

Bell loosened his grip but fixed him just as sternly with his eye.

"How well do you know Frost?" All the evidence he'd gathered thus far pointed to a man who'd not been seen in public in years.

Johnny Musto puffed up proudly. "The biggest sportin' men come to Johnny Musto. I took Mr. Frost's bets when he used to visit Belmont Park."

"How long ago was that?"

"I dunno. Four years, I guess."

"You mean the year the track first opened?"

"Yeah, I guess so. Seems longer."

"What did he look like, Johnny?"

"Big fella, shoulders like a bull. Grew himself a beard. Like's drawn on dat poster dere." He nodded at a Van Dorn wanted poster glued to a pillar that depicted Frost with a beard.

"He looks like that picture?"

" 'Ceptin' his grew in all gray. Makes him look a lot older than he used to."

"A lot older? Then what makes you so sure it's him?"

"He was mutterin' to himself just like he used to. Shovin' past folks like they weren't dere. Turnin' red in de face for no reason. Red as a beefsteak. Just like he used to before they locked him in de bughouse."

"If you were so sure it was Frost, Johnny, why didn't you turn him in for the reward? Five thousand dollars is a lot of money even for a bookmaker who handles the biggest sportsmen."

The Belmont Park bookie looked at the tall detective with an expression of disbelief. "You ever go to da circus, mister?"

"Circus? What are you talking about?"

"I'm askin', do ya go to da circus?"

Bell decided to humor him. "Often. In fact, when I was a youngster, I ran away from home to join a circus."

"Did ya ever stick your head in de lion's mouth?"

"Come on, Johnny. You've been around. You know that Van Dorns protect people who help them."

"From Harry Frost? Don't make me laugh."

8

WHEN NIGHT FELL ON BELMONT PARK, the aviators and mechanicians pulled canvas shrouds over their airships to protect their fabric wings from dampness. They anchored the machines to tent pegs driven deep in the ground in case a wind sprang up. Then they trooped off to the rail yard to sleep on their support trains. Somewhere in the distance a bell clock chimed eleven.

Then all was quiet in the infield.

Two shadows materialized from beneath the grandstand.

The Jonas brothers had driven out from Brooklyn in an ice truck, arriving in daylight to get the lay of the land. Now, with the moon and stars hidden by clouds, they walked boldly in the dark, crossing the racetrack and scrambling over the inside rail into the infield. They headed for Joe Mudd's aeroplane, choosing it because it was off to one side and easy to find. But as they approached they heard snoring. They slowed and crept closer. Two mechanicians, built like hod carriers, were sleeping under the wings. The Jonases slithered off to the far side of the infield, steering clear of Josephine Joseph's Celere monoplane, which they had seen earlier, before night fell, was surrounded by humorless Van Dorn detectives armed with shotguns. Far across the field, they chose a different victim, not knowing it was the French-built

Farman biplane owned by the Channel-crossing English baronet Sir Eddison-Sydney-Martin.

They confirmed that no one was sleeping nearby, removed the canvas shroud from one double wing, which was faintly silhouetted against the dark sky, and studied its construction. They did not know a lot about flying machines, but they recognized a truss when they saw one. The only difference between this double wing and a railroad bridge was that instead of the truss being constructed of steel uprights and diagonals, the two planes of the wing were supported by wood uprights counterbraced by diagonal wire stays.

Having figured out what made the Farman's wing strong, the Jonas brothers set about weakening it. They felt in the dark for the turnbuckle used to tighten the strong multistranded stay that angled from the top plane to the bottom plane.

"Roebling wire," George whispered. "Good thing Frost said no hacksaw. It would take all night to cut this."

Shielding a flashlight in their hands, they inspected the turnbuckle. A strand of safety wire had been wrapped around it to prevent it from loosening from vibration. They carefully unwound the safety wire, unscrewed the turnbuckle to slacken the Roebling wire stay until they could remove the end from its connection to the wing, and replaced the steel anchor in that connection with a fragile one made of aluminum.

They tightened the turnbuckle until the stay hummed again, carefully rewound the safety wire exactly as they'd found it, and draped the shroud back over the wing. They took care to note which aeroplane they had sabotaged—Harry Frost had made it clear he had to know—checked the color of the wing fabric with their flashlight, left the infield and the track, found their truck, and drove to a nearby farm, where they parked and fell asleep. An hour after dawn they met Harry Frost in Hempstead where he had told them to and reported which machine they had sabotaged.

"Describe it!"

"Biplane. One propeller."

"Front or back?"

"Back."

"What color?"

"Blue."

Frost paid them one hundred dollars each—more than a month's salary for a skilled mechanician even if he had a generous boss.

"Not bad for one night," Georgie Jonas said to Peter Jonas on the long drive home to Brooklyn. But first they had to fill the ice truck as payment to their brother-in-law, who owned it. They weighed out a load at a waterfront "bridge" controlled by the American Ice Company trust. Four dollars a ton.

George asked, "How about the fifty-cent rebate?"

"Independent dealers don't get rebates."

Peter said, "There's supposed to be two thousand pounds in a ton. How come the ton you charged us for only weighs eighteen hundred pounds?"

"It's ice. It melted."

"But you're supposed to slip in a couple of hundred extra pounds to cover melting."

"Not for independents," said the trust man. "Move your truck, you're blocking the bridge."

"This isn't fair."

"What are you going to do about it?"

They rode the trolley home to their favorite saloon, laughing how they should persuade Harry Frost to reform the ice business. What a racket. Add it all up, the trust controlled ice harvesting, shipping it, storing it, distributing it, and selling it. Had to be ten million bucks a year. The Jonas boys laughed louder. Harry Frost would reform it, all right. Harry Frost would take it over.

It was a beautiful morning. With several beers and a couple of hard-boiled eggs under their belts, they decided to ride the electric train back to Belmont Park to watch the blue biplane fall out of the sky.

ISAAC BELL EYED A MOB OF REPORTERS. They were descending on the English contender Sir Eddison-Sydney-Martin as he waited for his mechanicians to pour oil and gasoline into his Farman. The fact that the journalists moved about the infield as a group made him extra alert. It would be so easy for a killer to hide among them.

Archie was nearby, keeping a close eye on Josephine, who for once had not vanished into the blue sky but was waiting her turn in the exhibition speed race. The infield was unusually crowded with visitors—it seemed everyone and his brother had procured a pass somewhere, so Archie had doubled the guard. At the moment, ten Van Dorns, four disguised as mechanicians, were within easy reach of Josephine.

Bell satisfied himself that he recognized all of the reporters. So far, only newspapers owned by Whiteway were covering the race, which made it a little easier to keep track. When and if the public got sufficiently fired up over the race, Whiteway had told him, other papers would have to write about it. Bell figured they would cross that bridge when they came to it. In the meantime, Whiteway was taking full advantage of his monopoly, and his reporters were telling the story exactly as he wanted it told. American fliers were the underdogs, and the lowest underdog of all was "America's Sweetheart of the Air."

A drinking man from the flagship *Inquirer* led the way, shouting at Eddison-Sydney-Martin, "If England's champion could say anything he wanted to American readers, what would that be?"

"May the best man, or woman, win."

Bell noticed that Eddison-Sydney-Martin's hands were shaking. Apparently Archie had been correct about the baronet being painfully shy. Bell could see that addressing a group of people held greater terrors than flying three thousand feet in the air. His wife, Abby, a beautiful brunette, was at his elbow to lend support, but Bell was struck by the man's courage. Despite his shaking hands, and a deer-blinded-by-a-searchlight rounding of his eyes, he stood his ground.

The Whiteway reporter pretended incredulity. "You can't mean that, Sir Eddison-Sydney-Martin. The London papers are proclaiming to the whole world that you are racing for England and the honor of Great Britain."

"We Britons have in common with Americans an enthusiastic press," the baronet replied. "In actual fact, you could say that I am virtually half American by the great good fortune of marrying my lovely Abby, who is a Connecticut Yankee. Nor do I believe, frankly, that the Whiteway Cup Air Race is anything like a boxing match, where only one man remains standing at the end. Every aviator here will win by his or her very presence. The knowledge we gain will lead to better flying machines and better drivers."

A reporter who shouted out the name of a Whiteway business journal published in New York asked, "Do you see a commercial future in flying machines?"

"Will passengers pay to fly? Lord knows when we'll see an 'aero bus' with such lifting capability. But just moments ago I saw a commercial venture that might hold lessons for the future. As I passed above Garden City, three miles to the north, and was vol-planing down to Belmont Park, I noticed motoring beneath me a trades van headed here in the employ of the publishing house Doubleday, Page and Company. How, you might well ask, could I see that it was a Doubleday, Page and Company motor van from high above? Well, the answer is that in addition to the signs painted on the sides of the van, an alert advertising manager in their Garden City headquarters looked up at a sky filled with flying machines from Belmont Park and painted 'Doubleday, Page and Company' on top to catch the attention of aviators."

The reporters scribbled.

The baronet added, "Obviously, it caught mine as I sailed above it. So perhaps the commercial future in flying machines lies in supine billboards."

Isaac Bell joined in the laughter.

Eddison-Sydney-Martin's long face brightened with sudden relief, like a man released early from prison. "Hallo, Josephine!" he called.

Josephine was hurrying toward her yellow airship, head down as if hoping to slip by unobserved, but she paused to return his wave, and then call warmly to the baronet's wife, "Hello, Abby."

"Here, you journalist chaps," said the English airman, "wouldn't you have a jollier time interviewing an attractive woman?"

As the reporters caught sight of Josephine, he vaulted onto his Farman and shouted urgently, "Spin it, Ruggs."

Lionel Ruggs, his chief mechanician, spun the propeller. The Gnome rotary engine caught on the first pull, and the baronet rose from the grass, trailing blue smoke.

Isaac Bell moved swiftly to intercept the reporters stampeding toward Josephine, all too aware that anyone who wanted to do her harm could jam a press card in his hatband and unobtrusively join the mob.

Archie had already anticipated the possibility. Before the reporters reached her, she was surrounded by detectives, who gave each and every journalist the gimlet eye.

"Smooth," Bell complimented Archie.

"That's what Mr. Van Dorn pays me so much money for," Archie grinned.

"He told me he wonders why you work at all, now that you're rich."

"I wonder, too," said Archie. "Particularly when I'm demoted to 'classy' bodyguard."

"I asked specifically for you. You're not demoted."

"Don't get me wrong, Josephine's a crackerjack, and I'm glad to look after her. But the fact is, it's a job for the PS boys."

"No!"

Bell whirled about to look his old friend full in the face. "Don't make that mistake, Archie. Harry Frost intends to kill her, and there isn't a Protective Services man on the entire Van Dorn roster who can stop him."

Archie was nearly as tall as Bell and as rangily built. Bell may have floored him in their long-ago college boxing match, but he was the only one who ever did. Archie's easygoing style, handsome looks, and patrician manner concealed a toughness that Bell had rarely encountered among men of his class. "You give Frost too much credit," he said.

"I've seen him operate. You haven't."

"You saw him operate ten years ago, when you were a kid. You're not a kid anymore. And Frost is ten years older."

"Do you want me to replace you?" Bell asked coldly.

"Try firing me, I'll appeal straight to Mr. Van Dorn."

They stared hard at each other. Men standing nearby backed away assuming punches would fly. But their friendship ran too deeply for fisticuffs. Bell laughed. "If he catches wind of us bull moose locking horns, he'll fire both of us."

Archie said, "I swear to you, Isaac, no one will hurt Josephine while I'm on watch. If anyone dares try, I will defend her to my dying breath."

Isaac Bell felt reassured, not so much because of Archie's words but because during their entire exchange he never took his eyes off her.

A HEAVILY LADEN, immaculately lacquered Doubleday, Page delivery van rolled into Belmont Park. The driver and his helper wore uniform caps with polished visors that were the same dark green color as the van. They pulled up at the grandstand service entrance and unloaded bales of *World's Work* and *Country Life in America* magazines. Then, instead of leaving the grounds, they steered onto the stone-dust road that connected the train yard to the infield and followed a flatbed Model T truck that was carrying a Wright motor from a hangar car to the flying machine it was meant to power.

The gate that barred the way across the racetrack into the infield was manned by Van Dorn detectives. They waved the Model T through but stopped the Doubleday, Page van and regarded the duo, attired like trustworthy deliverymen, with puzzled expressions.

"Where do you think you're going?"

The driver grinned. "I bet you wouldn't believe me if I said we was delivering reading matter to the birdmen."

"You're right about that. What's up?"

"We got a motor in the back for the Liberator. The mechanicians just got done with it and asked us to lend a hand."

"Where's their truck?"

"They had to pull the bands."

"Joe Mudd's my brother-in-law," interjected the helper. "Knew we was delivering magazines. Long as the boss don't find out, we're O.K."

"All right, come on through. You know where to find him?"

"We'll find him."

The green-lacquered van wove through the busy infield. The driver steered around flying machines, mechanicians, autos, trucks, wheelbarrows, and bicycles. Crammed in the back of the van, so tightly they had to stand, were a dozen of Rod Sweets's fighters. Dressed in suits and derbies, they were a clear cut above the usual pug uglies in order to ensure the smooth flow of opium and morphine to doctors and pharmacists. They stood in tense silence, hoping their outfits would help them disappear into the crush of paying spectators when the clouting was over. No one wanted to tangle with Van Dorns, but the money Harry Frost had paid in advance was too rich to refuse. They would take their lumps. Some of them would get collared. But those who escaped back to Brooklyn intact wouldn't have to work for months.

Harry Frost stood with them, watching Sir Eddison-Sydney-Martin's blue Farman biplane through a peephole drilled in the side. He felt strangely calm. His plan would work.

Sir Eddison-Sydney-Martin was tearing up the sky, fighting to set a speed record for biplanes on an oval course marked by pylons fifteen hundred yards apart. The course was three miles. To beat the record, he had to circle twenty laps in less than an hour, and he was cutting the corners tightly by banking with great skill. But unbeknownst to the Englishman, every high-speed turn he hurled the sturdy Farman into could be his last. When the Jonas boys' aluminum anchor failed under the terrific forces, the sabotaged wire tension stay would rip from the wing it counterbraced, and the wing would break. At that fatal moment, every eye in the grandstand and every eye in the infield would fly to the falling machine.

Frost had seen them fall. From five hundred feet, it took a remarkably long time to hit the ground. In that time, no one, not even the Van Dorns, would see his fighters emerge from the van. Once out, it would be too late to stop them. They would slash a swath like a football wedge, and he would charge through the cleared space straight at Josephine.

ISAAC BELL WAS ADMIRING how sharply Eddison-Sydney-Martin cut the corners when, thirty minutes into the speed record attempt, a wing came off. It seemed like an illusion. The engine kept roaring, and the biplane kept racing. The broken wing separated into two parts, the top and bottom planes, which remained loosely attached to each other by wire braces. The rest of the airship hurtled past them on a steep downward trajectory.

Thousands in the grandstand gasped. As one, they surged to their feet, blood draining from their faces, eyes locked on the sky. The mechanicians in the infield looked up in anguish. A woman screamed—Eddison-Sydney-Martin's wife, Bell saw. The stricken aeroplane was falling nose down, when it began to spin. Terrible forces tore its canvas, and it shed ragged strips of fabric that trailed after it like long hair.

Bell could see Sir Eddison-Sydney-Martin grappling with the controls. But it was hopeless. The biplane was beyond control. It hit the ground with a loud bang. Bell felt it shake the earth a quarter mile away. A collective moan rippled across the infield and was echoed by the crowd in the grandstand.

Bell heard another scream.

The tall detective's heart sank even as he exploded into action. The English airman's wife was running toward the wreckage, but it wasn't Abby who had screamed. She held both hands pressed to her mouth. The scream, a hopeless shriek of terror, had come from behind him.

Josephine.

BOOK TWO

"balance yourself like a bird on a beam"

Balance Yourself Like a Bird on a Beam

10

ISAAC BELL YANKED HIS BROWNING PISTOL from his shoulder holster and ran full tilt up the middle of a double row of flying machines.

The sight of a tall man in a white suit running toward them with a gun in his hand scattered the mechanicians who were staring at the wreckage behind him. At the end of the path they cleared for him Bell saw Josephine with her back to him. In front of her, the red-haired Archie Abbott was shielding her with his own body. In front of Archie, six Van Dorn detectives fought shoulder to shoulder to block a flying wedge of thugs charging with fists, clubs, and lengths of sharpened bicycle chain.

Behind the attackers stood a dark green Doubleday, Page delivery van with its back doors open wide. Harry Frost leaped through the doors with a gun in one hand and a knife in the other.

A Van Dorn drew his gun. A bicycle chain snaked it out of his bloodied hand. A club to his skull sent him pinwheeling. A second detective was knocked to the trampled grass. The remaining four fought to hold the line, but they were overwhelmed by the flying wedge and flung aside, opening a clear path to Archie and Josephine. Harry Frost charged up it with the speed and power of a maddened rhino.

Isaac Bell triggered his Browning. It was a highly accurate weapon, but he was running at full speed so he aimed for the larger target of Frost's body instead of his head. Bell's bullet went home. He saw it pluck Frost's coat, but it did not slow the big man's charge. Nor did it prevent Frost from leveling his gun at Archie.

Bell was almost to them, close enough to recognize Frost's gun as a Webley-Fosbery. Knowing Frost's predilection for brutality, Bell feared that the weapon was loaded with the .455 "Manstopper" hollow-points.

Archie stood his ground and aimed his pistol at Frost. It was a small-scale 6.35mm Mauser pocket pistol, an experimental model that the factory owners had presented to him when his honeymoon took him through Germany. Bell had argued that it was too light to count on. But Archie had smiled, "It's a keepsake of our honeymoon, and it doesn't wrinkle my suit."

Coolly, he let Frost close the range before he squeezed off three bullets.

Bell saw the bullets pierce Frost's lapels. But Frost kept coming. Speed, weight, and momentum were stronger forces than three 6.35mm slugs. Archie's well-aimed bullets would ultimately kill Harry Frost, but not before the charging man wreaked bloody destruction. Bell aimed for Frost's head. Archie blocked his line of fire.

Cool as ice, the redheaded detective tipped up the barrel to place the coup de grâce between Frost's eyes. Before he could fire, another of the attackers' sharpened chains whistled through the air like a bullwhip and slashed the Mauser out of his hand.

Isaac Bell jinked to the left and fired over Archie's shoulder. He was sure he had hit Frost again. But the angry red-faced giant triggered his own weapon point-blank at Archie Abbott. The Webley boomed like a cannon.

Archie staggered as the hollow-point bored a tunnel through

his chest. His legs crumpled under him. Frost jammed his revolver in his pocket and switched the knife to his right hand, burning eyes locking on Josephine as he brushed past Archie.

Archie hurled a mighty left hook as he fell.

Bell knew that with his body shattered, the punch was born of all that Archie had left—his courage and his skill. It caught Frost square on the side of his jaw with such force that bone cracked. Frost's eyes widened with shock. His fist convulsed open. The knife dropped.

Bell was almost on him. He couldn't shoot. Josephine was in his way.

Frost whirled and ran.

Bell started to chase after him. But as he leaped across his fallen friend's body he saw bright red blood frothing from Archie's coat. Without hesitating, he dropped to the ground beside him.

"Doctors!" he shouted. "Get doctors!"

Bell opened Archie's coat and shirt and pulled a razor-sharp throwing knife from his own boot to cut away Archie's undershirt. Air was bubbling from the wound. Bell looked around. People were gaping. But one set of eyes was cool and ready to help.

"Josephine!"

He handed her the knife.

"Quick. Cut me a patch of wing fabric. Like this."

He indicated the size with his hands.

"Doctors!" Bell shouted to those watching. "Get moving, you men! Find doctors!"

Josephine was back in seconds with a neatly cut square of yellow fabric.

Isaac Bell pressed it over the wound and held three sides of the square down tight to Archie's skin. As Archie's chest rose and fell,

Bell let air escape from the wound but allowed no more air to be sucked in.

"Josephine!"

"I'm here."

"I need cloth to tie this down."

Without hesitation, she removed her heavy flying tunic and then her blouse, which she sliced into long strips.

"Help me slip it under him."

Bell rolled Archie onto the side of the wound while Josephine worked the cloth under him. Bell tied the ends.

"Grab those shrouds to keep him warm. *Doctors!*"

A doctor ran up at last. He banged his bag down, knelt beside Archie, and felt for a pulse. "Good job," he said of the patch. "Are you a physician?"

"I've seen it done," Bell answered tersely. On his own chest, he could have added, when he was twenty-two years old, by Joseph Van Dorn, calmly trying to save his apprentice's life while tears were soaking his whiskers.

"What put the hole in him?" asked the doctor.

"Hollow-point .455."

The doctor looked at Bell. "Is he a friend?"

"He is my best friend."

The doctor shook his head. "I'm sorry, son. There's a reason they call it a manstopper."

"We need an ambulance."

"One's coming right now. The English birdman didn't need it."

WITHIN MINUTES ARCHIE was loaded into the ambulance and on his way to the hospital with two doctors riding with him. By then the

Van Dorns had regrouped, and formed a powerful cordon around Josephine.

Harry Frost had escaped in the confusion.

Bell quickly organized a manhunt, which included alerting every hospital in the area.

"He's carrying at least three slugs in him," he said, "maybe four. And Archie broke his jaw."

"We caught two of their crew, Isaac. Brooklyn toughs. I recognize one. He works for Rod Sweets, the opium king. What do we do with them?"

"See what you can get out of them before you hand them to the cops." Bell had no doubt that Archie had romanced the local police when he first arrived at the racetrack. It was standard practice to cozy up and find who should be paid off to be friends in an emergency.

"They're singing already. Frost paid them a hundred bucks a head. Gave them the dough up front so they could bank it with their girlfriends in case they got caught."

"O.K. I doubt they'll know anything useful about Frost. But see what you can learn. Then turn them in. Tell the cops Van Dorn will press charges. Give them a reason to hold them."

Bell spoke briefly with Josephine to make sure she felt safe and to assure her that he had ordered up additional guards until they caught Frost. "Are you all right?"

"I'm going up," she said.

"Now?"

"Flying clears my mind."

"Don't you have to replace the fabric you cut out of your airship?"

"I didn't cut it from an essential surface."

———

BELL HURRIED TO WHERE Eddison-Sydney-Martin's biplane had struck the ground. It was a very odd coincidence that the English-man's accident had distracted everyone in Belmont Park, including his detectives, at the moment Harry Frost's thugs attacked. In fact, it could not be a coincidence. Frost must have somehow engi-neered it.

Bell saw from a distance that the Farman had crashed nose first. Its fuselage was sticking straight up in the air like a monument, a tombstone, to poor Eddison-Sydney-Martin, who, if Bell's suspi-cions were correct, was the victim of a murder, not an accident. The baronet's wife was standing beside the wrecked biplane. A tall man in a flying helmet had his arm around her as if to comfort her. He was smoking a cigarette. He leaned down and whispered in her ear. She laughed.

Bell circled so he could see their faces. The man was Eddison-Sydney-Martin himself. He was dead white in the face, with a trickle of blood seeping from a bandage over his eye, and he was leaning heavily on Abby. But, miraculously, the Englishman was standing on his own two feet.

Bell looked again at the =wrecked Farman, and asked, "Who was driving your machine?"

Sir Eddison-Sydney-Martin laughed. "I'm afraid I attended the entire adventure in person."

"Something of a miracle."

"The framework tends to absorb the impact—all that wood and bamboo collapses in a cushiony manner, if you know what I mean. So long as one doesn't tumble out and snap one's neck, or one's motor doesn't jump its moorings and crush one, one has a fair shot at surviving a smash. Not that a chap is not immensely grateful for whatever part luck plays, what?"

"I'm sorry to see you're out of the race."

"I'm not out of the race. But I do need another machine straightaway."

Bell glanced at his wife, wondering whether, as she wrote checks, she would risk sending her husband up in the air again. Abby said, "Some clever folk in New Haven are experimenting with a sort of 'headless' Curtiss that has a lot of go."

"They've a license from Breguet, who make an excellent machine," her husband added.

"What went wrong?" Bell asked. "Why did she go down?"

"I heard a loud bang. Then a wire stay shrieked past my head. It would appear that a counterbracer parted. Unsupported, the wing collapsed."

"Why did the counterbracing stay break?"

"That is something of a mystery. I mean, one never encounters shoddy construction on a Farman machine." He shrugged. "My chaps are looking into it. But it's all in the game, isn't it? Accidents do happen."

"Sometimes," said Bell, even more convinced that the Englishman's accident was no accident. He stepped closer to the wreck, where Lionel Ruggs, the Farman's chief mechanician, was removing parts to be salvaged. "Did you find the wire that broke?" he asked.

"Bloody little that didn't break," Ruggs retorted. "She hit so hard, she's mostly splinters."

"I mean, the wire that broke that caused the accident. The baronet said he heard one let loose."

"I've laid them all over there." He pointed at a row of wires.

"So far, I find none broken. It's Roebling wire. Same as was spun into the cables that hold up the Brooklyn Bridge. Virtually indestructible."

Bell went to look for himself. A helper, a boy no more than fourteen, came and went with more wire. He was puzzling over one end of a strand when Bell asked, "What do you have there, sonny?"

"Nothing."

Bell took a shiny silver dollar from his pocket. "But you're staring like something struck you—here."

The boy grabbed the coin. "Thank you, sir."

"Why don't you show this to your boss?"

The boy dragged the wire to the chief mechanician. "Look at this, Mr. Ruggs."

"Lay it out with the rest, laddie."

"But, sir. Look at this, sir."

Lionel Ruggs put on reading spectacles and held it to the light. "Bloody hell . . . Bloody, bloody hell!"

Just then, Dmitri Platov came running up. He shook his head at the remains of the Farman. Then he looked at Eddison-Sydney-Martin, who was lighting a fresh smoke. "Is surviving? Is lucky."

Bell asked, "What do you make of this, Mr. Platov?"

Platov took the fitting in his fingers and studied it, puzzlement growing on his face. "Is strange. Is very strange."

Bell asked, "Why is it strange?"

"Is aluminum."

Chief Mechanician Ruggs exploded, "What the bloody hell was it doing on our machine?"

"What do you mean?" asked Isaac Bell.

Platov said, "Is something should not be. Is—how you say— link-ed weak."

"This anchor at the end of the wire is made of cast aluminum," Ruggs seethed. "It should be steel. There's tons of tension on those wires, tons more when the machine moves sharply. The anchor bolt should be as least as strong as the wire. Otherwise, like Mr. Platov says, it's a weak link."

"Where did it come from?" asked Bell.

"I've seen it used. But not on our machines, thank you very much."

Bell turned to the Russian. "Have you seen aluminum used this way?"

"Aluminum lightweight. Aluminum on struts, aluminum on crossing members, aluminum on framing. But counterbracing anchor? Only fools." He handed it back to Lionel Ruggs, his ordinarily cheery face stern. "Is person doing should being shot."

"I'll pull the trigger myself if I find the bloody bastard," said the mechanician.

11

ISAAC BELL RAN TO THE RAIL YARD, where Archie had set up a field office in a corner of Josephine's hangar car. He scanned the reports that were coming in by telegraph, telephone, and Van Dorn messenger. Harry Frost was still on the run despite his wounds.

Or to put it more accurately, Bell had to admit, Harry Frost had vanished.

All hospitals had been alerted to look out for the wounded man. None had responded. Frost could be dying in a ditch or dead already. He could be hiding in the farmland around the racetrack. Or he could have made his way to Brooklyn, where gangsters would take him in, for a price, and provide midwives and crooked pharmacists to treat his wounds. He could have run east into rural Nassau and Suffolk counties. Or north to the vast, thinly populated Long Island hunt country, where the owners of great American fortunes rode to the hounds.

Bell telephoned the New York office. He ordered more agents sent out from Manhattan, and others to double the watch on the railroad and subway stations and the ferries. And he dispatched apprentices to hospitals with stern instructions not to engage but to call for help. When he had done all he could to encourage the manhunt, Bell left a dozen detectives with orders to stick close to

Josephine and raced his borrowed Pierce to the Nassau Hospital in Mineola, where they had taken Archie.

Archie's beautiful wife, Lillian, a young blond-haired woman of nineteen, was standing outside the operating room in a long duster, having driven from New York. Her astonishingly pale blue eyes were dry and alert, but her face was a mask of dread.

Bell took her in his arms. He had introduced her to Archie, sensing that the high-spirited only child of a widowed "shirt-sleeve" railroad tycoon would bring particular joy to his friend's life. He had been more than right. They adored each other. He had persuaded her crusty father to see Archie for the man he was and not a fortune hunter. *You changed my life,* Archie had thanked him simply at the wedding where Bell was best man. Ironically, years earlier, he had already changed Archie's life when he proposed that Archie become a Van Dorn detective. If only he hadn't.

Bell watched over the top of her head as a surgeon came out of the operating room, his expression grave. When he saw Bell holding Lillian, relief flickered in his eyes as if the fact that a friend was comforting her would make it easier to tell her that her husband had died.

"The doctor is here," Bell whispered.

She turned to the doctor. "Tell me."

The doctor hesitated. To Isaac Bell, Lillian Osgood Abbott was the little sister he had never had. He could forget that she was so exquisitely beautiful that most men found it very difficult to speak to her on first meeting. In this awful instance, Bell guessed that the doctor could not bear to utter any word that would cause tears to track her cheeks or her brave mouth to crumble.

"Tell me," she repeated, and took the doctor's hand. Her firm touch gave the man courage.

"I'm sorry, Mrs. Abbott. The bullet did much damage, barely missed the heart and shattered two ribs."

Bell felt a cavern open in his own heart. "Is he dead?"

"No! . . . Not yet."

"Is it hopeless?" Lillian asked.

"I wish I could . . ."

Bell held tighter as she sagged in his arms.

He said, "Is there nothing that can be done?"

"I . . . nothing I can do."

"Is there *anyone* who can save him?" Isaac Bell demanded.

The doctor gave a deep sigh and stared sightlessly back at him. "There is only one man who could even attempt to operate. The surgeon S. D. Nuland-Novicki. In the Boer War, he developed new procedures for treating gunshot wounds. Unfortunately, Dr. Nuland-Novicki—"

"Get him!" cried Lillian.

"He is away. He's lecturing in Chicago."

Isaac Bell and Lillian Osgood Abbott locked eyes in sudden hope.

The doctor said, "But even if Nuland-Novicki could board the Twentieth Century Limited in time, your husband will never last the eighteen hours it will take to get here. Nineteen, with the extra time from here to Long Island. We can't move him to New York."

"How long does he have?"

"Twelve or fourteen hours at most."

"Take us to a telephone," Bell demanded.

The doctor led them at a dead run through echoing halls to the hospital's central telephone station. "Thank God, Father's at home," said Lillian. "New York," she told the operator. "Murray Hill four-four-four."

The connection was made to Osgood Hennessy's limestone mansion on Park Avenue. The butler summoned Hennessy to the telephone.

"Father. Listen to me. Archie's been shot . . . Yes, he is desperately wounded. There is a surgeon in Chicago. I need him here in twelve hours."

The doctor shook his head, and said to Bell, "The Twentieth Century and the Broadway Limited take eighteen hours. What train could possibly make it from Chicago to New York faster than those crack fliers?"

Isaac Bell allowed himself a hopeful smile. "A special steaming on tracks cleared by a railroad baron who loves his daughter."

"COMMISSIONER BAKER'S ENEMIES call him a lightweight," growled Osgood Hennessy, referring to New York City's recently appointed police commissioner. "I call him a damned good fellow."

Six Traffic Squad touring cars and a motorcycle that the department was testing with a view to forming a motorcycle squad were racing their engines outside Grand Central Terminal, prepared to escort Hennessy's limousine at the highest possible speed over the Manhattan Bridge, across Brooklyn, and into Nassau County. The streets were dark, dawn a faint hint of pink in the eastern sky.

"Here they are!" cried Lillian.

Isaac Bell exploded from the railroad terminal, running hard, with his hand locked on the arm of a youthful, fit-looking Nuland-Novicki, who was scampering alongside like an eager schnauzer.

Engines roared, sirens howled, and in seconds the limousine

was tearing down Park Avenue. Lillian handed Nuland-Novicki the latest wire from the hospital. He read it, nodding his head. "The patient is a strong man," he said reassuringly. "That always helps."

AT BELMONT PARK that same pink hint of dawn reflected on the shiny steel rail down which Dmitri Platov's revolutionary thermo engine was scheduled to speed on its final test run. The freshening sky gave urgency to the task of a man crouched under it. If he stayed much longer, early risers would see him loosening bolts with a monkey wrench. Already, he smelled breakfast. The breeze traveling across the infield carried whiffs of bacon frying on the support trains in the yards on the other side of the grandstand.

Mechanicians would appear any minute. But sabotage was slow work. He had to wait before he turned each nut to sluice the threads with penetrating oil to prevent the loud screech of rusty metal. Then he had to mop the drips that would be noticed by sharp eyes performing the last earthbound tests before experimenting on Steve Stevens's biplane, which was waiting near the rail under canvas.

He would have finished by now, except that the detectives guarding Josephine Josephs's flying machine made a habit of sweeping the infield. Silent, unpredictable, they would appear out of nowhere shining flashlights, then vanish just as suddenly, leaving him to wonder when they were coming next and from which direction. Twice he had crouched, nervously rubbing his arm, while he waited for them to move on.

His final step, when he had loosened the fishtail that held two abutting ends of rail, was to work matchsticks into the space he had opened. If anyone tested the joint, it would not feel loose. But when assaulted by the enormous forces unleashed by the thermo engine, the rails would part and the joint burst open. Its effect would be like a railroad switch opened to shunt a train from one track to another. The difference was, this was a single rail, and the "train," Platov's miracle engine, would have no track to shunt onto but would fly through the air like a self-propelled cannonball. And God help anyone who got in its way.

12

"HARRY FROST IS NOT DEAD," said Isaac Bell.

"By all accounts," said Joseph Van Dorn, "Harry Frost was shot twice by you and three times by poor Archie. He's got more lead in him than a tinsmith."

"Not enough to kill him."

"We've not seen hide nor hair of him. No hospital has heard of him. No doctor has reported treating a broken jaw accompanied by unexplained gunshot wounds."

"Outlaw doctors charge extra not to report gunshot wounds."

"Nor have we received proof of any sightings by the public."

"We received numerous tips," said Bell.

"None panned out."

"That doesn't mean he's dead."

"At least he's out of commission."

"I wouldn't bet on that," said Isaac Bell.

Joseph Van Dorn smacked a strong hand on his desk. "Now, listen to me, Isaac. We've been down this road repeatedly. I would love that Harry Frost were not dead. It would be good for business. Preston Whiteway would continue paying a fortune for cross-country protection of our Sweetheart of the Air. Happily, he's willing to pay us to find Frost's corpse. But I cannot in good conscience continue to bill him for a dozen agents around the clock."

"There is no corpse," Bell replied.

The boss asked, "What evidence do you have that he is not dead?"

Bell jumped up and paced long-leggedly around the Hotel Knickerbocker suite that Van Dorn commandeered for his private office on the occasions he was in New York. "Sir," he addressed him formally, "you have been a detective longer than I."

"A lot longer."

"As such, you know that a so-called hunch by an experienced investigator is bedded in reality. A hunch does not come from nothing."

"Next you'll be defending sixth senses," Van Dorn retorted.

"I don't have to defend sixth senses," Bell shot back, "because you know better than I, from your long experience, that sixth senses are the same as hunches. Both are inspired by observations of things and events that we're not yet aware we have seen."

"Do you have any idea what you observed that provokes your hunch?"

"Sarcasm is the boss's privilege, sir," Bell answered. "Perhaps I observed how agilely Frost carried himself when he ran, sir. Or that shock registered on his face only when Archie broke his jaw, sir. Not when we shot him, sir."

"Will you please stop calling me sir?"

"Yes, sir," Bell grinned.

"You're darned chipper today."

"I am so relieved that Archie has a fighting chance. Dr. Nuland-Novicki said the most important thing was getting through the first twenty-four hours, and he has."

"When can I visit him?" asked Van Dorn.

"Not yet. Lillian's the only one they'll allow in his room. Even

Archie's mother is cooling her heels in the hallway. The other reason I'm chipper is, Marion arrives any day from San Francisco. She's hired on with Whiteway to take moving pictures of the race."

Van Dorn fell silent for a moment, reflecting on their exchange. When he spoke again, it was soberly. "What you say is true about hunches—or, if not entirely true, is certainly agreed upon by experienced fieldmen."

"The unrecognized observation is a compelling phenomenon."

"But," said Van Dorn, raising a meaty finger for emphasis, "experienced fieldmen also agree that hunches and sixth senses have enriched bookmakers since the first horse race in human history. This morning I learned that you've *doubled* your bets, summoning to Belmont Park some of my best men who are already thinly dispersed about the continent."

"'Texas' Walt Hatfield," Bell answered boldly and without apology. "Eddie Edwards from Kansas City. Arthur Curtis from Denver. James Dashwood from San Francisco."

"I wouldn't put Dashwood in that company."

"I've worked with the kid in California," said Bell. "What Dash lacks in experience he makes up in doggedness. He is also the finest pistol shot in the agency. He would have drilled Harry Frost a third eye in his forehead."

"Be that as it may, it costs money to move men around. Not to mention the danger of derailing cases they're working on."

"I conversed with their field office managers before I summoned them."

"You should have conversed with me. I can tell you right now that I am sending Texas Walt straight back to Texas to finish his San Antone train robbery case and Arthur Curtis to Europe to open the Berlin office. Archie Abbott turned up some good locals. Arthur's the man to run them, as he speaks German."

"I need the best, too, Joe. I'm juggling four jobs: protecting Josephine, protecting the cross-country air race, hunting Frost, and investigating what exactly happened to Marco Celere."

"There, too, evidence points squarely at dead."

"There, too, we're short a corpse."

"I exchanged wires with Preston Whiteway last night. He'll settle for either body: Celere's so we can convict Frost or Frost's so we can bury him."

"Frost dead, is my vote, too," said Bell. "Josephine would be safe, and I could hunt for Celere at my leisure."

"Why bother if Frost is dead?"

"I don't like murders without bodies. Something is off-kilter."

"Another hunch?"

"Do you like murders without bodies, Joe?"

"No. You're right. Something's off."

There was a quiet, tentative knock at the door. Van Dorn barked, "Enter!"

An apprentice scuttled in with a telegram for Isaac Bell.

Bell read it, his expression darkening, and he told the apprentice, who was balanced on his toes poised to flee, "Wire them that I want a darned good explanation for why it took so long to get those wanted posters into that bank."

The apprentice ran out. Van Dorn asked, "What's up?"

"Frost is not dead."

"Another hunch?"

"Harry Frost just withdrew ten thousand dollars from the First National Bank of Cincinnati. Shortly after he left, our office there finally managed to drop off the special banks-only wanted post-ers, warning that Frost might come in looking for money. By the time the bank manager called us, he was gone."

"A long shot that paid off, those posters," said Van Dorn. "Well done."

"It would have been a lot better done if someone did their job properly in Cincinnati."

"I've been considering cleaning house in Cincinnati. This tears it. Did they say anything about Frost's wounds?"

"No." Bell stood up. "Joe, I have to ask you to personally over-see the Josephine squad until I get back."

"Where are you going?"

"Massachusetts, east of Albany."

"What are you looking for?"

"Young Dashwood unearthed an interesting fact. I had asked him to look into Marco Celere's background. Turns out Frost wasn't the only one who wanted to kill him."

Van Dorn shot his chief investigator an inquiring glance. "I'm intrigued when more than one person wants to kill a man. Who is it?"

"A deranged Italian woman—Danielle Di Vecchio—stabbed Celere, screaming, *'Ladro! Ladro!' Ladro* means 'thief' in Italian."

"Any idea what set her off?"

"None at all. They locked her up in a private insane asylum. I'm going up to see what I can learn from her."

"Word to the wise, Isaac: these private asylum fellows can be difficult. They hold such sway over patients, they become little Napoleons— Ironic, since many of their patients think *they're* Napoleon."

"I'll ask Grady to research a chink in his armor."

"Just make sure you're back before the race starts. You younger fellows are better suited to chasing flying machines around the countryside and sleeping out of doors. Don't worry about Josephine. I'll look after her personally."

BELL CAUGHT the Empire State Express to Albany, rented a powerful Ford Model K, and sped east on twenty miles of dirt roads into a thinly populated section of northwestern Massachusetts. It was hilly country, with scattered farms separated by dense stands of forest. Twice he stopped to ask directions. The second time, he got them from a mournful-looking young truck driver who was changing a flat tire by the side of the dusty road. A wagon in tow contained a disassembled flying machine with its wings folded.

"Ryder Private Asylum for the Insane?" the driver echoed Bell's question.

"Do you know where it is?"

"I should think I do. Just over that hill. You'll see it from the top."

The driver's costume—flat cap, vest, bow tie, and banded shirtsleeves—told Bell that he was likely the aeroplane's mechanician. "Where are you taking the flying machine?"

"Nowhere," he answered with a woebegone finality that brooked no further questions.

Bell drove the Model K to the crest of the hill and saw below a dark red brick building hulking in the shadows of a narrow valley. Fortresslike crenellations and towers at either end did nothing to lighten the aura of despair. The windows were small and, Bell saw as he drew near, barred like a penitentiary's. A high wall of the same bleak-colored brick surrounded the grounds. He had to stop the auto at an iron gate, where he pressed a bell button that eventually drew the attention of a surly guard with a billy club dangling from his belt.

"I am Isaac Bell. I have an appointment with Dr. Ryder."

"You can't bring that in here," he said, pointing at the car.

Bell parked the Ford on the side of the driveway. The guard let him through the gate. "I ain't responsible for what happens to that auto out there," he smirked. "All the loonies ain't inside."

Bell stepped closer and gave him a cold smile. "Consider that auto your primary responsibility until I return."

"What did you say?"

"If anything happens to that auto, I will take it out of your hide. Do you believe me? Good. Now, take me to Dr. Ryder."

The owner of the asylum was a trim, precise, exquisitely dressed man in his forties. He looked, Bell thought, like a fussy sort, overly pleased with a situation that gave him total control over the lives of hundreds of patients. He was glad he had heeded Joe Van Dorn's warning about little Napoleons.

"I don't know that it will be convenient for you to visit Miss Di Vecchio this afternoon," said Dr. Ryder.

"You and I spoke by long-distance telephone this morning," Bell reminded him. "You agreed to a meeting with Miss Di Vecchio."

"The lunatic patient's state of mind does not always concur with an outsider's convenience. An untimely encounter could be distressing for both of you."

"I'm willing to risk it," said Bell.

"Ah, but what of the patient?"

Isaac Bell looked Dr. Ryder in the eye. "Does the name An-drew Rubenoff ring a bell?"

"Sounds like a Jew."

"In fact, he is a Jew," Bell answered with a dangerous flash in his eye. He would never abide bigotry, which was going to make taking Ryder down a peg even more satisfying. "And a fine Jew he is. Heck of a piano player, too."

"I am afraid I have not met the, ah, gentleman."

"Mr. Rubenoff is a banker. He's an old friend of my father's. Practically an uncle to me."

"I have no banker named Rubenoff. And now if you'll excuse—"

"I am not surprised that you don't know Mr. Rubenoff. His clients tend toward up-and-coming lines like automobile manu-facture and moving pictures. But, out of sentiment, he allows his holding companies to retain their grip on some smaller, more con-ventional banks, and even buy another now and then. In fact, 'Uncle Andrew' asked me would I pay a visit on his behalf to one nearby while I was in your neighborhood. I believe it's called the First Farmers Bank of Pittsfield."

Dr. Ryder turned white.

Bell said, "The Van Dorn Detective Agency's Research boys root up the darnedest information. First Farmers of Pittsfield holds your mortgage, Dr. Ryder, the terms of which allow the bank to call in your loan if the value of the collateral plummets—as it has for most private asylums, including the Ryder Private Asylum for the Insane, as the new state-run institutions siphon off patients. I will meet with Miss Di Vecchio in a clean, pleasant, well-lighted room. Your personal quarters, which I understand are on the top floor of the turret, will be ideal."

———

DANIELLE DI VECCHIO took Bell's breath away. She entered Ryder's cozy apartment tentatively, a little fearful—understandably, Bell thought—but also curious, a tall, well-built, very beautiful woman in a shabby white dress. She had long black hair and enormous dark eyes.

Bell removed his hat and gestured for the matron to leave them and close the door. He offered his hand. "Miss Di Vecchio. Thank you for coming to see me. I am Isaac Bell."

He spoke softly and gently, mindful that she had been incarcerated under court order for slashing a man with a knife. Her eyes, which were darting around the room, drinking in furniture, carpets, paintings, and books, settled on him.

"Who are you?" Her accent was Italian, her English pronunciation clear.

"I am a private detective. I am investigating the shooting of Marco Celere."

"*Ladro!*"

"Yes. Why do you call him a thief?"

"He stole," she answered simply. Her eyes roamed to the window, and the way her face lit up told Isaac Bell that she had not been out of doors for a long time and probably not seen green trees and grass and blue sky even from a distance.

"Why don't we sit in this window seat?" Bell asked, moving slowly toward it. She followed him carefully, warily as a cat yet aching to be caressed by the breeze that stirred the curtains. Bell positioned himself so he could stop her if she tried to jump out the window.

"Can you tell me what Marco Celere stole?"

"Is he dead from this shooting?"

"Probably," answered Bell.

"Good," she said, then crossed herself.

"Why did you make the sign of the cross?"

"I'm glad he's dead. But I'm glad it wasn't me who took life. That is God's work."

Doubting that God had deputized Harry Frost, Isaac Bell took a chance on Di Vecchio's mental state. "But you tried to kill him, didn't you?"

"And failed," she answered. She looked Bell in the face. "I have had months to think about it. I believe that a part of my soul held back. I don't remember everything that happened that day, but I do recall that when the knife missed his neck it carved a long cut in his arm. Here . . ." She ran her fingers in an electric glide down the inside of Bell's forearm.

"I was glad. But I can't remember whether I was glad because I drew blood or glad because I didn't kill."

"What did Marco steal?"

"My father's work."

"What work was that?"

"My father was *aeroplano cervellone*—how do you say?—brain. Genius!"

"Your father invented flying machines?"

"Yes! *Bella monoplano.* He named it *Aquila. Aquila* means 'eagle' in American. When he brought his *Aquila* to America, he was so proud to immigrate to your country that he named her *American Eagle.*"

She began talking a mile a minute. Marco Celere had worked

for her father in Italy as a mechanician, helping him build the aeroplanes he invented. "Back in Italy. Before he made his name short."

"Marco changed his name? What was it?"

"Prestogiacomo."

"Prestogiacomo," Bell imitated the sound that rolled off her tongue. He asked her to spell it and wrote it in his notebook.

"When Marco came here, he said it was too long for Americans. But that was a lie. Everyone knew Prestogiacomo was *ladro*. Here, his new name, Celere, only means 'quick.' No one knew the kind of man he really was."

"What did he steal from your father?"

What Marco Celere had stolen, Di Vecchio claimed, were new methods of wing strengthening and roll control.

"Can you explain what you mean by roll control?" Bell asked, still testing her lucidity.

She gestured, using her long graceful arms like wings. "When the *aeroplano* tilts this way, the *conduttore—pilota*—changes the shape of wing to make it tilt that way so to be straight."

Recalling his first conversation with Josephine, Bell asked, "Did your father happen to invent *alettoni*?"

"*Yes! Si! Si!* That's what I am telling you. *Alettoni.*"

"Little wings."

"My father," she said, tapping her chest proudly, "my wonderful *babbo*. Instead of warping the whole wing, he moved only small parts of it. Much better."

Bell passed his notepad to her and handed over his Waterman fountain pen. "Can you show me?"

She sketched a monoplane, and depicted the movable hinged

parts at the back of the outer edges of the wings. It looked very much like the yellow machine that Josephine was flying.

"*Alettoni*—hinged little wings—is what Marco stole from your father?"

"Not only. He stole strength, too."

"I don't understand."

"My father learned how wings act to make them strong."

In a fresh torrent of English peppered with Italian and illustrated with another sketch, Danielle explained that monoplanes had a habit of crashing when their wings suddenly collapsed in flight, unlike biplanes, whose double wings were structurally more sound. Bell nodded his understanding. He had heard this repeatedly in the Belmont Park infield. Monoplanes were slightly faster than biplanes because they presented less wind resistance and weighed less. Biplanes were stronger—one of the reasons they were all surprised when Eddison-Sydney-Martin's Farman had broken up. According to Danielle Di Vecchio, Marco Celere had proposed that the monoplane's weakness came not from the "flying wire" stays underneath the wings but the "landing wires" above them.

"Marco tested his *monoplano* with sandbags to make like the strain of flying—what is your word?"

"Simulate?"

"*Sì*. Simulate the strain of flying. My father said a static test was too simplistic. Marco was pretending the wings do not move. He pretended that forces on them do not change. But wings do move in flight! Don't you see, Mr. Bell? Forces of wind gusts and strains of the machine's maneuvers—*carico dinamico*—attack its wings from many directions and not only push but *twist* the wings. Marco's silly tests took no account of these," she said scornfully. "He made his wings too stiff. He is *meccanico*, not *artista!*"

She handed Bell the drawings.

Bell saw a strong similarity to the machine that Josephine had persuaded Preston Whiteway to buy back from Marco Celere's creditors. "Is Marco's monoplane dangerous?" he asked.

"The one he made in San Francisco? It would be dangerous if he had not stolen my father's design."

Bell said, "I heard a rumor that a monoplane Marco sold to the Italian Army broke a wing."

"*Si!*" she said angrily. "That's the one that made all the trouble. His too-stiff *monoplano*—the one he tested with sandbags back in Italy—smashed."

"But why couldn't your father sell his *Eagle monoplano* to the Italian Army if it was better than Marco's?"

"Marco ruined the market. He poisoned the generals' minds against all *monoplano*. My father's *monoplano* factory went bankrupt."

"Interesting," said Bell, watching her reaction. "Both your father and Marco had to leave Italy."

"Marco fled!" she answered defiantly. "He took my father's drawing to San Francisco, where he sold machines to that rich woman Josephine. My father *emigrated* to New York. He had high hopes of selling his *Aquila monoplano* in New York. Wall Street bankers would invest in a new factory. Before he could interest them, creditors seized everything in Italy. He was ruined. So ruined that he killed himself. With gas, in a cheap San Francisco hotel room."

"San Francisco? You said he came to New York."

"Marco lured him there, promising money for his inventions. But all he wanted was my father to fix his machines. He died all alone. Not even a priest. That is why I tried to kill Marco Celere."

She crossed her shapely arms and looked Bell in the eye. "I am angry. Not insane."

"I can see that," said Isaac Bell.

"But I am locked with insane."

"Are you treated well?"

She shrugged. Her long graceful fingers picked at her dress, which a hundred launderings had turned gray. "When I am angry, they lock me alone."

"I will take Dr. Ryder aside and have a word with him." Firmly aside, by the scruff of his neck, with his face jammed against a wall.

"I have no money for lawyers. No money for 'medical experts' to tell the court I am not lunatic."

"May I ask why your father could not find other buyers for his *Eagle* flying machine?"

"My father's *monoplano* is so much better, so fresh and new, that some of it is still—how do you say?—*innato*. Tempestuous."

"Temperamental?"

"Yes. She is not yet tamed."

"Is your father's flying machine dangerous?"

"Shall we say 'interesting'?" Danielle Di Vecchio replied with an elegant smile. And at that moment, thought the tall detective, they could be thousands of miles from Massachusetts, flirting in a Roman salon.

"Where is it?" he asked.

The Italian woman's dark-eyed gaze drifted past Bell, out the window, and locked on the hilltop. Her face lighted in a broad smile. "There," she said.

Bell looked out the window. What on earth was she imagining?

The truck with the flat tire had towed its wagon to the crest of the hill. "A boy," she explained. "A nice boy. He loves me."

"But what is he doing with your father's machine?"

"My father took it with him from Italy. His creditors can't touch it here. It is his legacy. My inheritance. That boy helped my father in America. He is *eccellente meccanico*!"

"Not *artista*?" Bell asked, testing her reaction with a smile. He could not be sure, but she seemed as sane as he was.

"Artists are rare, Mr. Bell. I'm sure you know that. He wrote that he was coming. I thought he was dreaming." She jumped up and waved out the window, but it was unlikely that he could see her. Bell passed her the hem of the white curtain. "Wave this. Maybe he'll see it." She did. But he did not respond, his gaze likely on the myriad barred windows.

She slumped down on the window seat. "He's still dreaming. Does he imagine I can just walk out of here?"

"What is his name?" Bell asked.

"Andy. Andy Moser. My father liked him very much."

Isaac Bell was struck by a wonderful possibility. He asked, "How fast is your father's monoplane?"

"Very fast. Father believed that only speed would overcome winds. The more speedy the *aeroplano*, the safer in bad weather, Father said."

"Faster than sixty miles per hour?"

"Father hoped for seventy."

"Miss Di Vecchio, I have a proposition for you."

13

"MR. MOSER, YOUR SITUATION is about to improve vastly," Isaac Bell said to the sad-faced mechanician who was grilling a frankfurter on a fire he had built a safe distance from the crated *American Eagle* monoplane.

"How do you know my name?"

"Read this!"

Bell thrust a fine parchment-paper envelope he had lifted from Dr. Ryder's writing desk into Moser's grease-stained hand.

"Open it."

Andy Moser slid a finger under the seal, unfolded a sheet of writing paper covered in an elegant Florentine cursive script, and read slowly, moving his lips.

Isaac Bell had seized an opportunity to help the beautiful Italian woman while helping himself solve the vexing problem he had warned Archie about. The field of competitors vying for the Whiteway Cup was growing so large that too many support trains would be jockeying for the same railroad tracks. Keeping up with Josephine's flying machine to guard her life would be a nightmare even with the help of the auto patrols that Archie had envisioned.

But what, Bell had asked himself, if he took "the high ground"?

With his own airship, he could ride herd on the race. He could watch Josephine in the air while he stationed men ahead at the racetracks and fairgrounds that would provide infields to alight on.

Danielle Di Vecchio needed money to plead her case to get out of Ryder's asylum.

Isaac Bell needed a speedy airship. He bought hers.

"Danielle says I'm supposed to go with you, Mr. Bell."

"And bring my flying machine," said Bell, grinning at the wagon. Disassembled and folded up for travel, it looked like a dragonfly in a cage.

"And teach you how to *drive* it?"

"As soon as I set you up in a first-class hangar car."

"But I don't know how to fly it. I'm only a mechanician."

"Don't worry about that. Just get her running, and show me the controls. How long will it take to put it back together?"

"A day, with a good helper. Have you ever driven a flying machine?"

"I drive a one-hundred-mile-an-hour Locomobile. I have driven a V-Twin Indian racer motorcycle, a 4-6-2 Pacific locomotive, and a fifty-knot steel-hulled turbine yacht built by Sir Charles Algernon Parsons himself. I imagine I'll pick it up."

"Locomotives and steel yachts don't leave the ground, Mr. Bell."

"That's why I'm so fired up! Finish your lunch and wave goodbye to Danielle. She's watching from the fourteenth window from the left, second from the bottom. She can't wave through the bars, but she can see you."

Moser gazed sadly down the hill. "I hate leaving her behind, but she says you're going to help get her out."

"Don't you worry, we'll get her out. And in the meantime,

Dr. Ryder has promised that her treatment will improve, dramatically. Will your truck make it to Albany?"

"Yes, sir."

"I'll go ahead and charter a train. It will be waiting in the Albany yards, steam up for Belmont Park. Mechanicians will be standing by to help you reassemble the *American Eagle* the second you arrive."

"Belmont Park? Are you intending to enter the *American Eagle* in the cross-country race?"

"No," Bell laughed. "But it's going to help me keep an eye on Josephine Josephs."

Andy Moser looked incredulous. Of all he had read and heard since Isaac raced up in his Model K Ford, this took the cake. "You *know* the Sweetheart of the Air?"

"I am a private detective. Josephine's husband is trying to kill her. The *American Eagle* is going to help me save her life."

After Bell chartered his support train in Albany, he wired San Francisco to alert Dashwood to the fact that Marco Celere's original name was Marco Prestogiacomo. He might well have still been Prestogiacomo when he landed in San Francisco, and Bell hoped that this new information would speed up Dashwood's unusually slow progress.

"I'M NOT GOING TO WASTE flying time watching Dmitri Platov demonstrate his thermo engine," Josephine told Isaac Bell a day later. "I doubt it will work. And even if it does, that horrible Steve Stevens is too fat to drive a flying machine, even one of Marco's."

"One of Marco's? What do you mean?"

"It's a biplane he invented for heavy lifting, to carry a bunch of passengers."

Bell said, "I wasn't aware that Marco had another machine in the race."

"Steve Stevens bought it from his creditors. Lucky him. It's the only machine in the world that will lift him. He paid twenty cents on the dollar. Poor Marco got nothing."

Bell escorted her to her monoplane. Van Dorn mechanicians spun her propeller, and when the blue smoke of her motor turned white, she tore down the field and took to the sky for yet another of her long-distance practice runs.

Bell watched her dwindle to a yellow dot, secure in the thought that soon he would be flying beside her. The *Eagle* had arrived late last night on a four-car special train that Bell had chartered for the duration. Andy Moser and a Van Dorn crew were already trundling the pieces from the rail yard to the infield.

Then, thought Bell, all he had to do was learn to drive the thing before the race started. Or at least well enough to keep learning on the job, as he tracked Josephine across the country. By the time the race ended in San Francisco, he'd have gotten pretty good at it, and the first thing he would do was take Marion Morgan for a ride. The *Eagle*'s motor had plenty of extra power, Andy had told him, to carry a passenger. Marion could even bring a moving-picture camera. And wouldn't that adventure be a wedding gift?

He watched Josephine disappear in the east. "All right, boys," he told the Van Dorns, "stay here and wait for Josephine to come back. Stick close to her. If you need me, I'll be over at the thermo engine."

"Do you think Frost will attack here like he did before? He knows we're primed."

"He's surprised us before. Stick close. I'll come back before she lands."

Bell walked across the infield to the three-hundred-foot-long steel rail on which Platov had promised his engine would race in a final experiment before they installed it in Steve Stevens's biplane.

The enormously fat Stevens, bulging in a white planter's suit and glowering impatiently, sat at a breakfast table that his elderly servants had set with linen and silver. Platov and Stevens's chief mechanician were tinkering with the still-silent jet motor, the mechanician setting valves and switches while Platov consulted his slide rule. Stevens was venting his restlessness by upbraiding his servants. His coffee was cold, he was complaining. His sweet rolls were stale, and there weren't enough of them. The docile old men attending the cotton planter looked terrified.

Stevens's arrogant gaze fell on Bell's white suit.

"Surely Southern blood courses in your veins, suh," he drawled in dulcet Southern tones. "Ah have never laid eyes on a Yankee who could do justice to the pure white duds of the Old South."

"My father spent time in the Old South."

"And taught you to dress like a gentleman. Do Ah presume correctly that he was buyin' cotton for New England mills?"

"He was a Union Army intelligence officer, carrying out President Lincoln's order to free the slaves."

"Ready, sirs," Dmitri Platov called out.

The Russian inventor's springy mutton-chop whiskers were quivering with excitement and his dark eyes were flashing.

"Thermo engine ready."

Stevens glared at his chief mechanician. "Is it, Judd?"

Judd muttered, "Ready as it ever will be, Mr. Stevens."

"About time. Ah've had just about enough sittin' and waitin' . . . *Now*, where you goin'?"

Judd had picked up a baseball bat and started walking along the rail. "I gotta whack the stop switch as she's nearing the end to shut the motor off."

"Is that how you're goin' to stop the motor on my flyin' machine? Are you-all fixin' to stand in front of me with a *baseball bat*?"

"No worry!" cried Platov. "Automatic switch in machine. This only test. See?" He pointed at the thermo engine, resting on the rail. "Big switch. Just touch with bat as engine go by."

"All right, get on with it, for God's sake. The rest of the race'll be across the Mississippi before Ah take to the sky."

Judd ran two hundred feet down the rail and positioned himself. Bell thought he looked as unhappy as a long-ball hitter ordered to bunt.

"Is action!" cried Platov.

The thermo engine ignited with a low whine that soared to an earsplitting shriek. Bell covered his ears to protect his acute hearing and watched the motor begin to shake with awesome power. No wonder the mechanicians all respected Platov. That steel box he had invented was smaller than a steamer trunk, but it seemed to contain the amazing energy of a modern locomotive.

Platov jerked the release lever, and the latches holding it back opened.

The thermo engine shot down the rail.

Bell could scarcely believe his eyes. In one instant, it was throbbing next to him. In the next, it reached the man with the bat. It really worked, and the speed was phenomenal. Then all hell broke loose. Just as Judd was about to bunt the bat against the stop switch, the thermo engine jumped the rail.

It smashed through the chief mechanician as if he were a paper target, knocked what little remained of his body to the ground, and flew a hundred yards, crashing through Sir Eddison-Sydney-Martin's brand-new New Haven Curtiss parked on the grass and tearing the tail off a Blériot, before it came to rest inside a truck owned by the Vanderbilt syndicate, where it burst into flames.

Isaac Bell ran to the fallen Judd and saw immediately that there was nothing to be done for the man. Then while others ran to the destroyed New Haven and the burning truck, Bell inspected the rail where the engine had escaped.

Dmitri Platov was wringing his hands. "Was so good, 'til then. So good. Oh, that poor man. Look at that poor man."

Steve Stevens waddled up. "If this don't beat all! My head mechanician's been killed, and Ah got no jet engine for my machine. How in hell am Ah supposed to run a race?"

Platov wept. He tore at his thick black hair and beat his hands on his chest. "What terrible thing I have done. Did he have wife?"

"Who the hell would marry Judd?"

"Is terrible, is terrible."

Isaac Bell stood up from where he was crouching beneath the rail, brushed Stevens out of his way, and placed a firm hand on Platov's shoulder. "I wouldn't blame myself, if I were you, Mr. Platov."

"Is me. Is captain of ship. Is my machine. Is my error. I have killed a man."

"But you didn't intend to. Nor did your amazing machine. It had some help."

"What the devil are you talkin' about?" said Stevens.

"The rail broke. That's what made the machine jump it."

"That's Platov's rail," shouted Stevens. "That's his responsibility. He's the one who put it there. He's the one responsible for it breakin'. Ah'm callin' my lawyers. We're goin' to sue."

"Look at this joint," said Bell. He led Platov to the point where two lengths of rail had parted. Platov crouched beside him, lips pursed tighter and tighter. "Is bolts loosen-ed," he said angrily.

"Loose?" howled Stevens. "'Cause you-all didn't make it tight . . . What are you doin', sir?" he said, recoiling, as Bell shoved his fingers under his nose.

"Smell that and shut up."

"I smell oil. So what?"

"Penetrating oil, to make it easier to unscrew the bolts."

"No squeak," Platov said miserably. "No noise."

"The rail was sabotaged," said Isaac Bell. "The fishtail bolts were loosened just enough to let the rail slip under pressure."

"No!" said Platov. "I check rail every test. I check this morning."

"Ah," said Bell, "that's what those are." He knelt down and picked up some oil-soaked matchsticks. "That's how he did it," he mused. "Jammed these into the crack to damp the motion when you tested it. But they would have fallen out when the rail started vibrating as the thermo engine approached. Diabolical."

"Rail move," said Platov. "Thermo engine fly away . . . But why!"

"Do you have enemies, Mr. Platov?"

"Platov likes. Platov like-ed."

"Perhaps back in Russia?" asked Bell, aware that Russian immigrants of every political stripe from radical to reactionary had fled their restive land.

"No. I leave friends, family. I send money home."

"Then who'd do such a thing?" demanded Steve Stevens.

Isaac Bell said, "Could it be that someone didn't want you to win the race with Mr. Platov's amazing motor?"

"Ah'll show 'em! Platov, make me a new motor!"

"Not possible. Take time. I am being sorry. You need to find ordinary gasoline motor. In fact, you need two motors, mounted on lower wings."

"Two! What for?"

Platov spread his arms wide as if measuring Stevens's girth. "For lifting heaviness. Powering equal to thermo engine. Two motors, mounted on lower wing."

"Well, how the hell am Ah goin' to find two motors, and who the hell is goin' to install 'em, with Judd dead?"

"Judd's assistants."

"Farm boys, tractor hands. Fine doin' what Judd told them to do, but they're not real mechanicians." Stevens jammed plump fists on his broad hips and glared around the infield. "If this don't beat all. Here, Ah got my machine. Ah got money to buy new motors, but no hands to install 'em. Say, how 'bout you, Platov? Want a job?"

"No thank you. I am having new thermo engine to manufacture."

"But Ah seen you runnin' around takin' jobs for money. Ah'll pay top dollar."

"My thermo engine come first."

"Tell you what. When you're not workin' on my flyin' machine, you can work on your thermo engine."

"Could your train tow my shop car?"

"Sure thing. Glad to have your tools along."

"And can I still being freelance machinist to make money for new thermo engine?"

"Just as long as my machine comes first." Stevens beckoned his servants. "Tom! You, there, Tom. Fetch Mr. Platov some breakfast. Can't expect a top hand to work hard on an empty stomach."

Platov looked at Isaac Bell as if to ask what he should do.

Bell said, "It looks like you're back in the race."

He saw Josephine returning and hurried toward the open stretch where she would come down. His brow was furrowed. He was thinking hard about coincidences. The Englishman's accident occurring simultaneously with Frost's attack was no coincidence. It had been deliberate sabotage to create a distraction to support the attack.

But what was the distraction, this time? There had been no attack. Josephine was high in the sky, and Bell had seen nothing amiss on the ground. When last heard of, Harry Frost was in Cincinnati. It was possible he could have returned to New York. But it seemed unlikely that he would attack again at Belmont Park in broad daylight, particularly since Bell had assigned Van Dorns, backed up by local police, to check the loads inside every closed van and wagon that entered the infield. It was logical to assume that Frost reckoned he would do better to lie in wait and spring from ambush.

Bell found Josephine's Van Dorn mechanicians watching her yellow monoplane spiral-dipping down toward the infield in a series of steep dives and sharp turns. "Have you boys seen anything out of order?"

"Not a thing, Mr. Bell. Except that thermo engine running wild."

Was this sabotage a genuine coincidence? Had Platov's engine been destroyed by a saboteur not employed by Frost? Not by the saboteur who caused the Farman to lose a wing but by another,

operating on his own? For what purpose? To eliminate a potentially strong competitor, seemed the only answer.

"Did you say something, Mr. Bell?"

Isaac Bell repeated through gritted teeth what he had just
growled under his breath. "I hate coincidences."

"Yes, sir! First thing they taught me when I joined the Van
Dorns."

"YOUR FLYING MACHINE IS BEAUTIFUL!" Josephine exclaimed de-
lightedly. "And look at you, Mr. Bell! You look happy as a jaybird
in a cherry tree."

Bell was grinning. Andy Moser and the mechanicians Bell
had hired to help him were tightening the flying and landing
wires that braced the wing. They still had work to do on the tail
and the control links, and the motor was scattered in small pieces
in their spick-and-span hangar car, but with the wing spreading
across the fuselage, it was beginning to look like something that
would fly.

"I must say, I've never in my life bought anything I've liked
as much."

Josephine kept striding around it, eyeing it professionally.

Bell watched for her reaction as he said, "Andy Moser tells me
that Di Vecchio licensed the controlling system from Breguet."

"So I see."

"That wheel turns it like an automobile. Turn left to make the
rudder turn you left. Tilt the wheel post left, and it warps the wings
by moving the *alettoni* to bank left into the turn. Push the wheel
post, and she'll go down. Pull it, and the elevators make her go up."

"You can drive it with only one hand, when you get good at it," said Josephine.

Leaving a hand free for a pistol, which meant that Bell could counterpunch if someone attacked Josephine in her flying machine. He said, "It works just like yours."

"It's the up-to-date thing."

"It ought to make it easier to learn to fly," said Bell.

"You bought yourself a beauty, Mr. Bell. But I'll warn you, she's going to be a handful. The trouble with going fast is you land fast. And that Gnome motor makes it even worse, since you won't have a real throttle like my Antoinette's."

While the similarities were striking, Bell had to admit that, when it came to their French-made power plants, the Celere and Di Vecchio monoplanes were radically different. Josephine's Celere was powered by a conventional water-cooled V-8 Antoinette, a strong, lightweight motor, whereas Di Vecchio had installed the new and revolutionary air-cooled rotary Gnome Omega in his. With its cylinders spinning around a central crankshaft, the Gnome offered smooth running and superior cooling at the expense of fuel consumption, ticklish maintenance, and a primitive carburetor that made it almost impossible to run the motor at any speed but wide open.

"Can you give me some tips on slowing down to land like I've seen you do?"

Josephine leveled a stern finger at the control wheel. "Before you get fancy, practice blipping your magneto on and off with that *coupe* button."

Bell shook his head. Switching the ignition on and off, interrupting electricity to the spark plug, was a means, of sorts, to slow the motor. "Andy Moser says to go easy on the *coupe* button or I'll burn up the valves."

"Better the valves than you, Mr. Bell," Josephine grinned. "I need my protector alive. And don't worry about stalling the motor, it's got plenty of inertia to keep it spinning." Her face fell. "I'm sorry, that was really stupid of me about needing you alive. How is Archie?"

"He's hanging on. They let me see him this morning. His eyes were open, and I believe he recognized me . . . Josephine, I have to ask you something."

"What?"

"Look at the wing stays."

"What about them?"

"Do you notice how they converge at these triangular king posts, top and bottom?"

"Of course."

"Do you notice how the triangles form in essence single light-weight steel struts? The point thrusting above the wing is actually the top of the broad base that extends below the wing."

"Of course. It's very strong, that way."

"And do you see how ingeniously it's braced by the chassis?" She crouched down beside him, and they studied the strong X-braced support that connected the body of the aeroplane to its skids and wheels.

"It's the same system as on your Celere, isn't it?" Bell asked.

"It looks similar," she admitted.

"I haven't seen anything like it on any other monoplane. I have to ask you, is it possible that Marco Celere, shall we say, 'borrowed' his wing-strengthening innovation from Di Vecchio?"

"Absolutely not!" Josephine said vehemently.

Bell observed that the ordinarily exuberant aviatrix seemed troubled by his blunt accusation. She jumped to her feet. Her grin had gone out like a light, and a flush was gathering on her cheeks. Did she suspect, even fear, that it was true?

"Or, perhaps, could Marco have unconsciously copied it?" he asked gently.

"No."

"Did Marco ever tell you he worked for Di Vecchio?"

"No."

Then, oddly, she was smiling again. Smugly, Bell thought. And he wondered why. The tension had left her slim frame, and she stood in her usual pert manner, as if about to spring into motion.

"Did Marco never mention that he worked for Di Vecchio?"

"Di Vecchio worked for *Marco*," she retorted, which explained her peaceful smile. "Until Marco had to fire him."

"I heard it was the other way around."

"You heard wrong."

"Perhaps I misunderstood. Did Marco tell you that Di Vecchio's daughter stabbed him last year?"

"That crazy woman almost killed him. She left a terrible scar on his arm."

"Did Marco tell you why?"

"Of course. She was jealous. She wanted to marry him. But Marco wasn't interested. In fact, he told me that her father was pushing her into it, hoping that Marco would rehire him."

"Did Marco tell you that she accused him of being a thief?"

Josephine said, "That poor lunatic. All that talk about 'stealing her heart'? She's insane. That's why they locked her up. It was all in her head."

"I see," said Bell.

"Marco had no feelings for her. He never did. Never. I can guarantee you that, Mr. Bell."

Isaac Bell thought quickly. He did not believe her, but in order to protect her life he needed Josephine to trust him.

"Josephine," he smiled warmly, "you are a very polite young lady, but we're going to be working very closely. Don't you think it's time you call me Isaac?"

"Sure thing, Isaac. If you like." She studied the detective's face as if seeing him for the first time. "Do you have a girl, Isaac?"

"Yes. I am engaged to be married."

She gave him a flirtatious grin. "Who's the lucky lady?"

"Miss Marion Morgan of San Francisco."

"Oh! Mr. Whiteway mentioned her. Isn't she the lady who will be taking moving pictures?"

"Yes, she'll be here soon."

"So will Mr. Whiteway."

Josephine glanced at the ladies' watch she wore sewn to her flying jacket sleeve.

"Which reminds me, I've got to get back to the train. He's sent a dress designer and a seamstress with another flying costume I'm supposed to wear for the newspaper reporters." She raised her pretty eyes longingly to the sky. It was the soft blue color of the warm and windless early afternoons before strong sea breezes swept across Belmont Park and made it dangerous to fly.

"You look like you'd rather go flying," said Bell.

"I sure as heck would. I don't need a special costume. Did you see that white getup he made me wear the other day? Didn't stay white long when we pulled the head off the Antoinette. This is all

I need," she said, indicating her worn flared leather gloves, wool jacket belted at her tiny waist, jodhpurs tucked into high laced boots. "Now Mr. Whiteway wants me to pose in a purple silk flying costume. And at night I'm supposed to wear long white dresses and black silk gloves."

"I saw your outfit last night. Very becoming."

"Thank you," she said with another flirtatious grin. "But just between us chickens, Isaac, I couldn't wait to get back into my overalls and help the boys fixing my machine. I'm not complaining. I know that Mr. Whiteway is anxious for me to draw any publicity I can to help the race."

Bell walked her to the train yard. "Hasn't he asked you to call him Preston instead of Mr. Whiteway?"

"All the time. But I don't want him to get the wrong idea, using first names."

After Bell got her safely aboard the bright yellow *Josephine Special* and in the care of the dress designer and the Van Dorn who guarded her train, he hurried to the headquarters car, which had a telegraph key linked to the detective agency's private system.

"Anything yet from San Francisco?" he asked the duty officer.

"Sorry, Mr. Bell. Not yet."

"Wire James Dashwood again."

The young man reached for the key. "Ready, sir."

"NEED CELERE AND PRESTOGIACOMO INFORMATION SOONEST."

Bell paused. The widely divergent opinions of Marco Celere held by Danielle Di Vecchio and Josephine Josephs Frost would raise interesting questions about any murder victim, but they were particularly interesting when the victim had disappeared.

"Is that it, sir? Shall I send it?"

"Continue: *'PARTIAL STORY BETTER THAN NONE.'*

"And then add: 'ON THE JUMP.'

"In fact, add 'ON THE JUMP' twice."

"There it is, sir. Shall I send it?"

Bell considered. If only it were possible to telephone long-distance all the way to San Francisco, he could query the usually reliable Dashwood as to what was taking him so long and impress upon him the urgency he felt.

"Add another 'ON THE JUMP'!"

14

"I HEAR THE WRIGHT BROTHERS started a flying school, Mr. Bell," Andy Moser called from the front of the *Eagle* when Isaac Bell ordered him to spin the propeller to start the sleek machine.

"I don't have time to go to Ohio. The race starts next week. Besides, how many teachers have driven flying machines for more than a year? Most aviators pick it up on their own, just like Josephine. Spin her over."

It was a perfect day for flying, a sunny late-spring morning at Belmont Park with a light west wind. Andy and the mechanicians who Bell had hired to assist him had rolled the *Eagle* to a distant stretch of grass far from the main activity of the infield. They had chocked the wheels, and when they heard Bell order Andy to start the motor, they grabbed the chocks' ropes and prepared to steady the machine as wing runners.

Bell was seated behind the wing, with his head, shoulders, and chest exposed. The motor was ahead of him—the safest place for it, Eddison-Sydney-Martin insisted, where it wouldn't crush the driver in a smash. Ahead of the motor gleamed a nine-foot, two-bladed propeller of polished walnut—the most expensive place for it, Joe Mudd had noted. "If you come down hard on the nose, it'll cost you a hundred bucks for a new one."

Bell tilted the wheel post and watched the effect on the wings.

Out at the tips, eighteen feet to his right and left, the *alettoni* hinged up and down. He looked back along the slim fuselage, whose booms and struts were covered in tightly drawn silk fabric to reduce drag, and turned the wheel. The rudder moved left and right. He pulled the wheel toward him. The elevators hinged to the horizontal tail keel tilted. In theory, when he did that in the air, the machine would go up.

"Spin her over!"

"A hundred fliers have died in accidents," Andy reminded him for the third time that morning.

"More mountain climbers die falling off cliffs. Spin her over!"

Moser crossed his arms over his chest. He was one of the stubbornest men Bell had met. His father was a policeman, and Moser had the policeman's wall-like resistance to anything he didn't like. This resistance was stiffened by an unshakable belief in machinery. He knew machinery, loved it, and swore by it.

"I know the machine is ready to fly because I put it together with my own hands. I know we walked around it and tested every moving part and every brace. And I know the motor is ready to fly because I pulled the cylinder heads off to tune the timing and the pressure. The only thing I do not know is ready to fly is the driver, Mr. Bell."

Isaac Bell fixed his overanxious mechanician with a no-nonsense eye.

"If you're going to help me protect Josephine, you better get used to the idea that Van Dorn operators go about their business promptly. I have observed how aviators take to the air since I first arrived at Belmont Park. When I purchased my *American Eagle*, I questioned both Josephine Josephs and Sir Eddison-Sydney-Martin on their techniques. I have also grilled Joe Mudd, whose navigation of his Liberator indicates an especially steady hand in the flying line. All agree that these Breguet controls make it a lot easier to learn. Last, but not least," Bell smiled, "I have read every issue of both *Aeronautics* and *Flight* since those magazines were first published—*I know what I'm doing.*"

Bell's smile vanished like a shotgunned searchlight. His eyes turned dark as December. *"Spin! Her! Over!"*

"Yes, sir!"

Bell opened the gasoline valve and moved the air valve to the idle setting. On the Gnome rotary engine, he had learned, the driver was the carburetor.

Andy Moser turned the propeller repeatedly, drawing fuel into the motor. Bell moved the magneto switch.

"Contact!"

Andy clutched the propeller with both hands, threw his long, lean back into a powerful tug, and jumped back before it cut him in half. The motor caught, chugged, and spewed pale blue smoke. Bell let it warm. When it sounded ready, he opened the air valve fully. The smoke thinned. The gleaming nickel-steel cylinders and the shiny propeller begin to blur as they spun toward top speed with a powerful-sounding *Blat! Blat! Blat!* He had never felt a motor spin so smoothly. At twelve hundred rpms, it ran slick as a turbine.

He glanced down at Andy.

"Ready!"

Andy nodded agreement and signaled the mechanicians to pull the chocks and run alongside to steady the wings in case of a crosswind. The *Eagle* began to roll, bouncing on pneumatic tires that were connected to the chassis's skids with springy bands of rubber, and swiftly picked up speed. The wing runners dropped behind. Bell felt a smooth, muscular impulse as the tail lifted from the ground.

He had a hundred yards of open space ahead of him before the grass ended at the rail that separated the infield from the racetrack. He could blip the magneto button to slow the motor so he could practice rolling on the ground. Or he could pull back on the wheel and try the air.

Isaac Bell pulled back on the wheel and tried the air.

In a heartbeat, the *Eagle* stopped bouncing. The grass was five feet under him. Unlike trains and autos that shook as they went faster, when the machine left the ground Bell felt like it was floating on glassy water. But he was not floating. He was hurtling straight at the white wooden rail that separated the field from the racetrack.

He was barely off the ground. His wheels would not clear it. He tugged a little harder on the wheel to go higher. Too hard. He felt the machine tip upward sharply. In the next instant, he felt a sudden void open up under him, and the *Eagle* started to fall.

He had been in comparable fixes in autos and motorcycles, and even on boats and horseback.

The solution was always the same.

Stop thinking.

He allowed his hands to ease the wheel forward a hair. He felt a shove from below. The propeller bit the air. Suddenly the railing was safely below his wheels, and the sky looked immense.

A pylon was suddenly standing in front of him, one of the hundred-foot-tall racecourse markers around which they timed the speed trials. Just as Andy and Josephine had warned him, the gyroscopic force exerted by the spinning weight of the rotary engine had dragged him to the right. Bell turned the wheel to the left. The *Eagle* rolled sideways and drifted left. He straightened up, banked too far right, compensated again, compensated repeatedly, and gradually worked her onto an even keel.

It was like sailing, he realized in a flash of insight that made everything clearer. Even though he had to counteract the engine pull, the *Eagle* would point where he wanted it to as long as he knew where the wind was coming from. The wind—the air—was his to use, keeping in mind that, with his propeller pulling him through the air, most of the wind he encountered he was producing himself.

He drew back on the wheel to climb. The same principle seemed to hold. He climbed in stages, stepping into the sky as if going up stairs, leveling off when it felt too slow, angling up when he picked up speed. Speed made air stronger, Josephine had told him.

Belmont Park grew small beneath him, as if he were gazing through the wrong end of a telescope. Farms and villages spread below. To his left he saw the deep dark blue of the Atlantic Ocean. Smoke ahead and scores and scores of converging rail and trolley tracks pointed toward New York City.

A rational thought rambled through his mind, surprising him. He let go of the wheel with one hand to pull his watch chain. He tugged his gold watch from its pocket and deftly thumbed it open. It had occurred to him that this was so much fun that he had better check the time. Andy Moser had poured enough gas and castor oil into the tanks to run the motor for an hour. All by himself, in the middle of the sky, Isaac Bell laughed out loud. He had a strong feeling that he had changed his life forever and might never return to earth.

"A BANDAGE," said Sir Eddison-Sydney-Martin, applying one to Isaac Bell's forehead, "tends to unsettle my wife less than an open wound. I imagine you'll find the same holds true with your fiancée."

"It's just a scratch," said Bell. "My poor flying machine suffered a lot worse."

"Only your wheels and skids," said the baronet. "Your chassis seems intact, although I must say your mechanician appears put out."

Bell glanced at Andy Moser, who was stalking circles around the machine and shouting at his helper. Eddison-Sydney-Martin stepped back to survey his handiwork.

"All done, and the bleeding has stopped. In fact, by the look of you, I expect you're more in need of courage for reporting to your fiancée than when you took to the air. Be brave, old chap. I'm told Miss Morgan is a remarkable woman."

Bell drove to the Garden City Hotel to meet Marion, who was arriving from San Francisco that afternoon. The instant he walked into the hotel he knew that Marion was there ahead of him. Gentlemen seated in the lobby were staring over the tops of unread newspapers, bellboys eager to be summoned were lined up like tin soldiers, and the Palm Court maître d' was personally pouring Marion's tea.

Bell paused a moment to gaze upon the tall, willowy blond beauty of thirty who had taken his heart. She was still in her traveling clothes, an ankle-length pleated mauve skirt with a matching vest and high-collared blouse cinched at her narrow waist and a stylish hat with a high crown and down-swept brim. Her coral-sea green eyes outshone the emerald engagement ring on her finger.

Bell swept her into his arms and kissed her. "I have never seen you looking lovelier."

"Fisticuffs?" she inquired of the bandage.

"My first flying lesson. I discovered an aeronautical phenomenon called ground effect, which made bringing the *Eagle* back down to earth something of a challenge. Andy and his helper will be up half the night fixing the wheels."

"Was your instructor put out?"

Bell squared his broad shoulders. "Actually," he admitted, "I taught myself."

Marion raised one exquisite eyebrow and regarded him with the collected gaze of a woman who had graduated with the first class at Stanford Law School and worked in banking before flourishing in the new trade of moving pictures. She said, "I understand that Orville and Wilbur Wright learned the same way. Of course, they were busy inventing the aeroplane."

"I had the advantage of advice from seasoned aviators . . . You are regarding me with a strange look."

"Your eyes are as bright as I've ever seen them, and you're grinning ear to ear. You look like you're still flying."

Isaac Bell laughed. "I suppose I am. I suppose I always will be. Though what you're seeing at the moment is also the effect of being so very happy to see you."

"I am overjoyed to see you, too, my dear, and glad of a 'love effect.' It's been too long." She stood up from her chair.

"What are you doing?"

"I am standing up to kiss you again."

Bell kissed her back until she said, "The house detective will be coming over to ask what we're doing in public."

"No worry there," said Bell. "The Garden City Hotel just signed a contract with Van Dorn Protective Services. Our man took over house detective duties this very morning."

"So," she said, sitting back down, "tell me about the bump on your noggin. And this 'ground effect.'"

"Ground effect prevents you from alighting when a cushion of air develops between your wings and the ground. Air turns out to be strong—stronger than you'd imagine. Essentially, the machine does not want to stop flying, and you have to somehow persuade it—like when a horse takes the bit in its teeth."

"A flying horse," Marion remarked.

"Apparently the effect is strongest on a monoplane because—"

"You must tell me," Marion interrupted, "what did you *see* when you were up there?"

"Speed looks different in the air. The land didn't appear to blur as it does beside a train or my Locomobile. It seemed to flow under me, more slowly the higher I went."

"How high did you go?"

"High enough to see the Hudson River. When I saw it, I knew I had to fly to it."

Marion's beautiful eyes widened. "You flew all the way to the Hudson River?"

Bell laughed. "It seemed safer than flying over the ocean—I could see that, too."

Marion marveled, "At the same time you saw the Hudson River, you saw the Atlantic Ocean? Then surely you saw the skyscrapers of New York."

"Like spikes in the smoke."

"You must take me up to shoot moving pictures."

"You will love it," Bell answered. "I saw a giant sturgeon swimming on the bottom of the river."

"When are we going?" she asked as excitement rose in her voice.

"Well, umm, flying is perfectly safe, of course. But not yet safe with me."

Isaac Bell was reminded that his beloved could be as single-minded as Josephine when she asked with a challenging smile, "I wonder if Preston Whiteway would hire an aviator to take me up?"

"Let me practice first. By the end of the race I'll have the hang of it."

"Wonderful! We'll do it over San Francisco. I can't wait! But you will be careful while you learn?"

"Promise," said Bell.

"I refuse to worry about gun battles and knife fights. But flying? You're out of your element."

"Not for long. Next time I see the wind has shifted, I'll land accordingly."

"How could you tell the direction of the wind when you yourself were in it? Did you see a flag blowing?"

"I watched the cows."

"Cows?"

"There are dairy farms around the park, and Josephine taught me that cows always graze facing upwind. They point true as a weather vane and are easier to see from above."

"What else has America's Sweetheart of the Air taught you?"

"Keep an eye peeled for emergency landing spaces. But steer clear of bright green fields. They're too wet to land on." Bell left out Josephine's warning to avoid extreme movements that would cause his wings to collapse. Neither would he repeat Eddison-Sydney-Martin's dry "I'd avoid blundering into flat spins if I were you, old chap," or Joe Mudd's blunt "Don't get fancy before you know your business."

Marion said, "By all accounts, including Preston's fulsome praise of her, Josephine sounds like an interesting character."

"Josephine's a character, all right, and I could use your help reading her. In the meantime, I would not mind another kiss. Shall I instruct the house detective to erect a barricade of Chinese screens and potted palms?"

"I have a better idea. By now, the maids have unpacked my bags. Let me get out of my traveling things and into a bath. And perhaps you'll come up and join me for supper, or something."

"Shall I order champagne?"

"I already have."

"SERIOUSLY, DARLING, why did you decide not to take flying lessons?" Marion asked later upstairs. Bathed, perfumed, and arrayed in a long emerald green peignoir, she patted the chaise longue. Bell brought their glasses and sat beside her.

"No time. The race starts next week, and I've got my hands full, with Harry Frost trying to murder Josephine and a saboteur wrecking flying machines."

"I thought Archie shot Frost."

"Three times, with that little German pistol he insisted on carrying." Bell shook his head in dismay. "I thought I shot Frost, too. He's wounded but definitely not out of action. A Cincinnati banker reported that Frost's jaw was swollen and that he was slurring his speech, but otherwise he was healthy, which hardly sounds like a man carrying a bunch of lead in him."

"Maybe you missed?"

"Not with my Browning. It doesn't miss. And I *know* I saw Archie pepper him point-blank. He couldn't have missed. But Frost is a big man. If the slugs missed his vitals, who knows? Still, it's something of a mystery."

It was Isaac Bell's habit to discuss his cases with Marion. She was an educated woman, with a quick and insightful mind, and always brought a new perspective to a problem. He said, "Speaking of mysterious misses, Frost himself apparently missed one of his shots at Marco Celere. An easy shot no hunter would fluff. I discovered that the rifle he probably used had a damaged telescopic sight. Yet another reason why I want to see Celere's remains."

"Could Harry Frost have worn some sort of *armor* when he attacked?"

"Armor won't deflect bullets. That's why gunpowder put the knights out of business."

"Chain mail?"

"That's an interesting thought because with modern alloy steel perhaps you could manufacture chain mail strong enough to stop a bullet. Lord knows what it would weigh. Some years ago the Army was testing so-called bulletproof vests. But they were too hot and heavy to be practical . . . Interesting thought, my dear. I'll have Grady Forrer sic his Research boys on it first thing in the morning."

Marion stretched luxuriously. "Are there any other mysteries I can solve for you?"

"Several."

"Starting with?"

"Where is Marco Celere's body?"

"Any others?"

"Why does the Italian lady I bought my aeroplane from insist that Marco Celere stole her father's secrets while Josephine insists that Miss Di Vecchio's father worked for Celere and therefore had no secrets to steal?"

"What is Miss Di Vecchio like?"

"Startlingly attractive."

"Really?"

"In fact, so attractive that it is hard to believe that Marco Celere, or any man, would turn his back on her."

"How did you escape?"

Bell touched his glass to hers. "I'm immune."

"Blind to beauty?" she teased.

"I am in love with Marion Morgan, and she has spoken for my heart."

Marion returned his smile. "Maybe Marco had his eye on Josephine."

"Josephine is cute as a button but hardly in Miss Di Vecchio's class. She's a pretty little thing, pert and flirtatious, but more farm girl than femme fatale."

"But ambitious? At least about flying," Bell said, "and very skilled navigating flying machines. There are men who are drawn to accomplished women."

"Well, love is strange, isn't it?"

"If Marco and Josephine were lovers at all. Archie thinks she was in love with Marco's flying machines. And as you know Archie has a pretty good eye for that sort of thing."

Marion asked, "What does *your* eye tell you?"

"Frankly, I don't know. Except she vehemently defends Marco on the question of who stole whose invention."

"Could it be that Josephine is defending her flying machine more than she's defending her lover?"

"That is very possible," said Bell. "While Marco, I suspect, was in love with a girl who could afford to *buy* his flying machines."

"Then everyone got what they wanted."

"Except Harry Frost." Bell's eyes grew bleak, then hot with anger. "Poor Archie. Frost did such a terrible thing. How a man would load such monstrous ammunition into a weapon is beyond me."

Marion took his hand. "I spoke with Lillian on the telephone. I'll see her at the hospital tomorrow."

"How did she sound?"

"Tired and hopeful. Poor thing. It's a nightmare—both of our nightmares—only I'm older and have loved you longer, and I don't worry in that same way. Lillian admitted to me that since Archie returned to work after their honeymoon, she was afraid every day until he came home safe. Darling, are you taking such chances learning to fly because you're worried about Archie? Or trying to make up for what happened to him?"

"I've always been keen to fly."

"But are you keen to fly for the wrong reasons? Isaac, you know I never trouble you with worrying about your safety. But this seems unusually risky. What can you possibly do up in the air if Frost shoots at her?"

"Shoot back, and finish Harry Frost once and for all."

"Who will fly the aeroplane while you're busy shooting?"

"I can drive it with one hand . . . Well, actually, to be perfectly honest," he admitted with a rueful smile, "I *will* be able to drive with one hand soon. Today, I was hanging on tight with both."

Marion extended her arms. "Can you demonstrate that?"

15

"WOULD YOU GIVE ME SOME ADVICE on that straightening-up-fast stunt just before you touch the ground?" Isaac Bell asked Josephine. The race was starting in three days, and he had scheduled a certification test to get an official pilot's license from the Aero Club.

"*Don't!*" Josephine grinned, "is the best advice I can give you. Practice blipping your magneto instead, and don't try stunts your machine isn't up to."

"My *alettoni* are the same as yours."

"No, they're not," she retorted, her grin fading.

"The wing bracing is the same."

"Similar."

"Just as strong."

"I wouldn't count on that," she said seriously.

The subject always turned her prickly, but Bell noticed that she no longer repeated her earlier assertion that Danielle's father had worked for Marco Celere. It was almost as if she suspected that the opposite was true.

Gently he said, "Maybe you mean *I'm* not up to it."

She smiled, as if grateful Bell had let her off the hook. "You will be. I've been watching you. You have the touch—that's the important thing."

"Glad to hear it," said Bell. "I can't fall too far behind you if I'm going to protect you."

In fact, Bell had devised a defense in which he was only one element. Van Dorn riflemen would spell one another on the roof of the support car, easily climbing to their gun perch through a hatch in the roof. Two roadsters in a boxcar with a ramp would be ready to light out after her if for any reason Josephine strayed from the railroad tracks. And every day detectives would take their places in advance at the next scheduled stop.

A commotion broke out at the hangar door.

Bell glided in front of Josephine as he drew the Browning from his coat.

"Josephine! Josephine! Where is that woman?"

"Oh my God," said Josephine. "It's Preston Whiteway."

"Josephine! Josephine!" Whiteway barreled in. "There you are! I bring good news! Great news!"

Bell holstered his weapon. The best news he could think of was that Van Dorns had arrested Harry Frost.

"My lawyers," shouted Whiteway, "have persuaded the court to annul your marriage to Harry Frost on the grounds that the madman tried to kill you!"

"Annulled?"

"You are free . . . Free!"

Isaac Bell observed the meeting between Josephine and Whiteway long enough to form an opinion of its nature, then slipped out the door.

"Cut!" he heard Marion Morgan order sharply. Her camera operator—hunched over a large machine on a strong tripod—stopped cranking as if a hawk had swooped down and seized his arm. It was well known among Miss Morgan's operators that Mr. Bell did *not* want his picture taken.

"My darling, how wonderful to see you." He thought she

looked lovely in her working outfit, a shirtwaist and long skirt, with her hair gathered high to be out of her way when she looked through the camera lens.

She explained that she and her crew had been trailing Preston Whiteway all morning to shoot scenes for the title card that would read

The Race Sponsor's Arrival!!!!

Bell took her into his arms. "What a treat. Can we have lunch?"

"No, I've got to shoot all of this." She lowered her voice. "How did Josephine take the news?"

"I got the impression she was trying to dampen Whiteway's excitement over the prospect of her being 'Free! Free!'"

"I imagine that Preston's working around to asking her to marry him."

"The signs are all there," Bell agreed. "He's beaming like bonfire. He's wearing a fine new suit of clothes. And he shines like he's been barbered within an inch of his life."

MARION HAD HER CREW IN PLACE, cranking their camera, when Preston Whiteway lured the New York press to Josephine's big yellow tent in the infield with the promise of an important change in the race. Bell kept a close eye on the gathering, accompanied by Harry Warren, Van Dorn's New York gang expert, who Bell had asked to take over the Belmont Park squad for the wounded Archie.

Bell saw that Whiteway had gotten his fondest wish: other newspapers could no longer ignore the Whiteway Cup. The aerial race was the biggest story in the country. But his rivals did not love him for it, and the questioning, two days before the race was to start, was openly hostile. Forty newspapermen were shouting questions, egged on by Van Dorn detective Scudder Smith, who had once been an actual newspaper reporter, or so he said.

"If that detective has imbibed as excessively as it appears," Isaac Bell told Harry Warren, "suspend him for a week, and dock his pay for a month."

"Scudder's O.K.," Harry assured him. "That's just part of his disguise."

"Disguised as what?"

"A drunken newspaper reporter."

"He's fooling me."

"Can you deny, Mr. Whiteway," a reporter from the *Telegram* howled aggrievedly, "that the extremely short hop from Belmont Park to Empire City Race Track in Yonkers is a ploy to charge more paying spectators from New York City?"

"Is it not true that you could fly from Belmont Park to Yonkers in a glider?" shouted the man from the *Tribune.*

"Ten miles, Mr. Whiteway?" asked the *Times.* "Could not the aviators simply walk?"

"Or ride bicycles?" chimed in Detective Smith.

Bell had to admire how cleverly Whiteway let his rivals' reporters have their fun before he fired back with both barrels. In fact, he suspected Whiteway had probably planned the change all along to draw the other papers into his trap.

"It is my pleasure to fulfill your expectation of some new sensation by announcing a last-minute change in the course. The first leg to Empire City Race Track in Yonkers will entail the competitors flying a full eighteen miles west from Belmont Park to the Statue of Liberty. Upon arriving at America's symbol of freedom, the aviators competing for the gold Whiteway Cup will circle the statue, for hundreds of thousands to see from riverbanks and spectator vessels, and then steer their machines another twenty-two miles north to Yonkers, for a grand total the first day of forty miles. These brave fliers will use the opportunity to 'work the kinks out' while crossing two bodies of water—the treacherous East River and the broad Upper Bay—then fly up the middle of the wide Hudson River to alight safely, God willing, in the infield of the Empire City Race Track, where an excellent aviation field is offered by the racing course . . . Thank you, gentlemen. I am sure that your editors anxiously await your stories to put extras on the street ahead of the competition."

He might have added that the Whiteway papers' "EXTRA"s were already in the hands of every newsboy in the city. But he didn't have to. The reporters were stampeding to the racetrack telephones, cursing that they had been hoodwinked and that the editors would take it out of their hides.

"I HATE THAT DAMNED STATUE," Harry Frost told Gene Weeks.

Weeks, a grizzled Staten Island waterman, was leaning on the tiller of his oyster scow, which was tied to a muddy bank of the Kill Van Kull. The boat, twenty-three feet long and nearly ten wide, looked like many of its type, but its peeling paint and faded decks concealed the existence of an oversize gasoline engine that made it go much faster than oyster scows engaged in legitimate trade.

"Why's that, mister?"

"Damned statue attracts foreigners. We got too many immigrants, we don't need no more mongrel blood."

Gene Weeks, whose family had emigrated from England before Frost's had stepped off the *Mayflower*, let the lunatic rant. Frost was flashing money for a ride on Weeks's boat. A lot of money. In his younger days, Weeks would have taken it away from him and tossed him overboard. Or tried, he admitted on second thought. The lunatic was a big fellow, and the bulges in his coat were probably not a flask and lunch. So if he wanted the lunatic's dough, he would have to earn it.

"Where'd you say you want me to take you, mister?"

Frost unfolded a newspaper, an EXTRA edition, and spread it on the salt-crusted bench beside Weeks's tiller. Mumbling cusswords at the harbor breeze that plucked at it, he showed Weeks a map of the first leg of the Whiteway Cup Cross-Country Air Race. "See how they're going to circle that damned statue and head up the river?"

"Yup."

The big fellow had penciled an X on the map.

"I want to be *here*, with the sun behind me."

16

"HAVE THE ODDS CHANGED FOR JOSEPHINE?" Isaac Bell asked the bookie Johnny Musto two nights before the race.

"Still holding at twenty-to-one, sir. A thousand dollars on the Sweetheart of the Air will pay youse twenty thousand."

"I've already bet *two* thousand."

"Indeed you have, sir. Admiring your brave sporting instincts, I'm speculating upon the potential value of increasing your initial investment. If the little gal wins, youse can buy yerself a roadster, and a country estate to drive it to."

Enveloped in clouds of violet cologne, and attended by marble-eyed thugs pocketing the cash and watching for the cops, Johnny Musto was strolling the infield, muttering, "Place yer bets, gentlemen, place yer bets! Odds? Name 'em, they're yers. One hundred dollars will earn youse fifty if Sir Eddison-Sydney-Thingamajig's brand-new Curtiss Pusher clocks the best time to San Francisco. Same holds for Frenchie Chevalier driving his Blériot. One-to-two, gents, one-to-two on Chevalier. But if Billy Thomas flies faster for the Vanderbilt syndicate, one hundred will receive one hundred back."

"How about Joe Mudd? What are the odds on Mudd?" asked a sporting man with a large cigar.

Johnny Musto smiled happily. Clearly, Bell thought, a man blessed by fortune.

"The workingman's flying machine offers a rare opportunity to win big—three-to-one. Three hundred dollars for a hundred ventured on Joe Mudd. But if you're looking for a sure thing, bet one hundred dollars on Sir Eddison–So-and-So–Thingamajig and win fifty bucks to take your goil to Atlantic City . . . Hold on! What's that?" A man dressed in mechanician's vest and flat cap was whispering in his ear. "Gents! The odds on Sir Eddison–So-and-So–Thingamajig are changing. One hundred will win you forty."

"Why?" howled a bettor, disappointed to see his potential winnings diminish.

"His chances of beating everybody just got better. His mechanicians chopped the canard off the front of his machine. They found out they don't need a front elevator, already got one in the back. Sir-Eddison–So-and-So–Thingamajig's Curtiss Pusher is racing headless. Nobody can beat him now."

THAT SAME NIGHT, the saboteur who had set the thermo engine on its murderously destructive final flight, killing Judd and laying waste to several aeroplanes, stood nervously rubbing his arm as he watched Sir Eddison-Sydney-Martin's mechanicians make final adjustments on the Englishman's newly headless Curtiss. Removing the front elevator had made the pusher look very trim.

The saboteur had studied it earlier while they were flying it in the last of the evening light, and he had agreed with all in the infield who knew their business that the Curtiss was flying considerably better than before, and somewhat faster. The bookmakers, who were already enamored of the Curtiss Motor Company's new ninety-horsepower, six-cylinder engine—a reliable "power unit," by all accounts—led the stampede to declare that the headless

Curtiss Pusher was the aeroplane to beat, particularly in the hands of a champion cross-country aviator like the English baronet.

At last the mechanicians covered the machine in canvas shrouds, turned off the generator powering their work lights, and trooped home to their bunks in the train yard. Keeping a sharp eye peeled for roving Van Dorn detectives, the saboteur took a carpenter's brace and bit from his tool bag and went to work.

"YOUR CERTIFYING EXAMINATION was scheduled to start five minutes ago, Mr. Bell."

The representative of the Aero Club, waiting beside Bell's machine, gestured impatiently with his clipboard.

Bell vaulted into the *American Eagle*'s driving seat, tossed his hat to a wing runner, and pulled on his goggles and helmet. "All set!"

He had just finished hammering out last-minute tactics with Harry Warren. Andy and the boys had the monoplane waiting on a grass strip, with the motor warmed and chocks holding the wheels.

"In order to qualify for your pilot's license, Mr. Bell, you are required to ascend to one hundred feet and fly around the pylon-marked course. Then you will ascend to five hundred feet and remain there ten minutes. Then you will demonstrate three methods of descent: a safe volplane in a series of circles, a gradual ocean-wave downward coast, and a sharper spiral dip. Is that clear?"

Bell grinned. "Is it O.K. if I keep moving while remaining at five hundred feet for ten minutes?"

"Of course. You have to keep moving. Otherwise, the machine will fall. Off you go! I haven't all day."

But no sooner had Bell's motor blatted to noisy life than the rotund Grady Forrer, Van Dorn's head of Research, galloped through the castor oil smoke, shouting for Isaac to wait.

Bell held down his blip switch. The Gnome sputtered to a grudging stop. Andy Moser brought the soapbox used to climb up to the monoplane. Grady heaved himself on it, saying, "Found out how Frost survived getting shot by you and Archie."

"Well done! How?"

"Remember I told you that ten years ago a Chicago priest manufactured a so-called bulletproof vest of multiple layers of a particularly tight silk cloth specially woven in Austria?"

"But the Army rejected it. It weighed forty pounds and was hot as Hades."

"Guess who invested in their manufacture anyway?"

"Chicago," said Bell. "Of course. Exactly the sort of thing Harry Frost would have gotten a line on and seen its potential. To be bulletproof is a criminal's dream."

"And a fellow his size could carry that weight."

"So the only wound Harry Frost suffered was the jaw Archie broke as he went down."

"Next time," said Grady Forrer, "bring a cannon."

Bell ordered Grady to pass the word to every man on the case. Sidearms—knives, revolvers, and automatics—would not pierce it. Bring rifles. And shoot for the head, just to be on the safe side.

"All right, sir," he called to the Aero Club certifier. "I'm ready for my test."

Andy reached to spin the propeller. Bell touched his blip switch. About to shout, "Contact!" he said instead, "Wait!"

"Now what?" exclaimed the Aero Club official.

From the corner of his eye, Bell saw running toward him a

hideously scarred young Van Dorn agent from the New York office. Bell signaled Andy, who was reaching to spin the propeller. Andy replaced the wooden soapbox. Eddie Tobin jumped on it and leaned in close so only Bell could hear.

"Looks like they spotted Harry Frost at Saint George."

St. George, on Staten Island, was a resort town where the Kill Van Kull met the Upper Bay. It was home to grand hotels with beautiful views of New York's harbor. The busy waterfront served ferries, tugs, coal barges, steam yachts, fishing boats, and oyster scows.

"How sure are you it was Frost?"

"You know some of my folks are in the oyster business."

"I do," said Bell without further comment.

For certain Staten Island families, the oyster business extended into realms of activity that the New York Police Department's Harbor Patrol dubbed piracy. Little Eddie was straight as they came, and Bell would trust the kid with his life. But blood was thick, which made Eddie Tobin an unusually well-informed private detective when it came to the dark side of maritime traffic in the Port of New York.

"A feller who looked a lot like Harry Frost—big, red-faced, gray beard—was flashing money to hire a boat."

"What kind of boat?"

"He said it had to be steady—wide like an oyster scow. And fast. Faster than the Harbor Patrol."

"Did he find one?"

"A couple of really fast ones kinda disappeared since then. Both run by fellers who'll do it for the dough. Frost—if it was Frost— was flashing plenty."

Isaac Bell slapped his shoulder. "Good work, Eddie."

The apprentice detective's face, branded by a brutal gang beating that had nearly killed him, shifted into a lopsided smile. His eyes had survived, though one was partly shaded by a drooping lid, and they glowed with pride at the chief investigator's compliment.

"Can I ask you what do you think it means, Mr. Bell?"

"If it was Frost—and not some crook trying to smuggle something off a ship or bust his pal out of jail and spirit him off to a friendlier jurisdiction—it means Harry Frost wants a stable gun platform and a fast getaway."

Bell extracted his long legs from the *Eagle*'s driving nacelle and leaped out, landing on the grass like an acrobat. "Andy! On the jump!"

"Hold on!" the Aero Club certifier cried. "Where are you going, Mr. Bell? We haven't even started the test."

"Sorry," said Bell. "We'll have to complete this another time."

"But you must hold your certificate to enter the race. It's in the rules."

"I'm not in the race. Andy! Paint her yellow."

"Yellow?"

"Whiteway Yellow. The same yellow as Josephine's. Tell her boys I said to give you as much dope as you need and to lend a hand with the brushes. I want my machine yellow by morning."

"How are people going to tell you apart? Your machines look near the same already. It's going to be very confusing."

"That's the idea." said Isaac Bell. "I'm not making this easy for Harry Frost."

"Yeah, but what if he shoots at you thinking you're her?"

"If he shoots, he'll reveal his position. Then he's all mine."

"What if he hits you?"

Isaac Bell didn't answer. He was already beckoning his detectives and addressing them urgently. "Young Eddie's turned up a heck of a clue. Station riflemen on boats on the East River and the Upper Bay and up the Hudson all the way to Yonkers. We've got Harry Frost where we want him."

BOOK THREE

"up, up, a little bit higher"

Smash at the Statue of Liberty

ISAAC BELL DROVE HIS *American Eagle* monoplane a thousand feet above Belmont Park to watch for trouble when the race began. The winds were tricky this afternoon—the firing of the start cannon was twice delayed by strong gusts—and novice though he was, the tall detective took to heart the expert birdmen's love of high flying. Josephine Josephs, Joe Mudd, Lt. Chet Bass, race-car driver Billy Thomas, cotton farmer Steve Stevens, and "Frenchie" Renee Chevalier all favored altitude for reasons put succinctly by Baronet Eddison-Sydney-Martin: "Falling from high, you can try to stop in time. Falling from low, you encounter the ground too soon."

The altitude gave Bell a spectacular view of the Belmont Park Race Track. The bright green infield was speckled with aeroplanes of every color. Gangs of mechanicians, distinguished by their vests and white shirtsleeves, milled about them, adjusting wire stays, tuning motors, topping off gasoline tanks and radiators. Fifty thousand spectators waving white handkerchiefs packed the grandstand.

Good thing he had planned for traffic jams. Clouds of coal smoke were billowing over the rail yard. Support trains were backed up already, trying to depart Belmont Park for the Empire City Race Track in Yonkers. The tracks heading out were one long line of crawling trains, locomotive to caboose, slow and ponderous as a procession of circus elephants. Locomotives jockeyed for position at the switches, engineers yanked shrieking whistles, brakemen scurried, dispatchers shouted, and conductors tore their hair in a noisy, smoky ballet that would be danced every morning the aviators took off for the next field. Bell's *American Eagle* hangar-car special was already in Yonkers, sent ahead at midnight with two Thomas Flyer touring autos.

The roofs of each and every boxcar and Pullman were painted with the racers' colors and names. A racer could tell at a glance whether a locomotive and cars below him was his support train, a competitor's, or merely an ordinary freight going about its business.

Josephine's jaunty yellow string was pulled by a fast, high-wheeled Atlantic 4-4-2. Preston Whiteway's palatial private car was coupled to the back, separated from her private sleeping car by the hangar car, diner, dormitory Pullmans for mechanicians, newspapermen, and detectives, and the roadster car with Whiteway's Rolls-Royce. It was well in the lead. Bell had seen to that, ordering it to depart before dawn, leaving behind an electric GMC moving van with a second set of tools. If all went as planned, the *Josephine Special* would be waiting in Yonkers when she alighted. Hopefully in the lead, thought Bell, having rashly pressed another thousand dollars into Johnny Musto's scented palm.

Ahead of the crawling trains he could see the smoke of New York City staining the blue sky ten miles to the west. The Wall Street skyscrapers, poking through the smoke, marked where Lower Manhattan thrust into the harbor, dividing the waters from which Harry Frost would attack.

Bell had deployed New York Van Dorns, led by Harry Warren

and guided by Staten Island waterman Eddie Tobin, on the East River, the Upper Bay, and the Hudson River in three fast boats, one for each body of water. They would be assisted, thanks to lavishly dispensed tips, by the New York Police Department's Harbor Patrol.

He was acutely aware that it was almost impossible to communicate with his widely scattered outfit. Were he ramrodding such an operation on the ground, he could issue orders and receive reports by telephone, telegraph, and motorcar. A Marconi radio, such as the U.S. Navy employed to communicate with battleships, would come in handy coordinating his far-flung, thinly spread forces. But a wireless telegraph weighed considerably more than the *American Eagle* and required an even heavier source of electricity, so he had to rely on the alertness and enterprising nature of the detectives on the ground and water.

The start cannon fired.

Isaac Bell did not hear it over the roar of the Gnome, but he saw a big white puff of gunpowder smoke.

They had drawn straws for start position. First to tear across the grass was cotton planter Steve Stevens, his enormous white biplane powered by twin pump-fed V-8 Antoinettes that were similar to the motor in Josephine's machine only bigger. Dmitri Platov had installed them, joking with the other mechanicians that the Antoinettes' high ratio of power to weight almost made up for the Southern cotton planter's tonnage. It took over two hundred yards to get off the ground. Wobbling into a turn, it circled the start pylon, where its departure time was recorded by Weiner of Accounting. But when it headed west, it appeared to Bell to move at a surprising clip.

Army Lieutenant Chet Bass rose next in his orange Signal Corps Wright 1909 Military Flyer. Joe Mudd followed in his "Revolution Red" biplane. Moments after Mudd circled the start pylon, Sir Eddison-Sydney-Martin passed him in his blue headless pusher. Machine after machine took to the air, had its time noted when it circled the start pylon, and headed for the Statue of Liberty.

Josephine had drawn the short straw. She rose last, leaping her Celere off the field in less than eighty yards, diving dangerously close to the ground to gain speed in the pylon turn, and whipped west as if fired from a slingshot. Bell flew above and slightly behind her, blessing Andy Moser for tuning the Gnome engine so finely that it could hold the pace of Josephine's powerful Antoinette.

The immensity of his task struck hard, as the land swiftly changed from the open farm fields of Nassau to the rooftops of densely developed Brooklyn. He could see everything for miles ahead but nothing in detail. If Harry Frost opened fire, shielded by chimneys, pigeon coops, and clotheslines of flapping laundry, the first clue in the air would be lead ripping into Josephine's machine.

Or his, Bell comforted himself grimly, since the two yellow craft looked so similar. Also of some relief, the aviatrix's course was constantly altered by air currents and wind gusts. If Frost ended up a quarter mile to either side of it, the same objects screening him would block a clear shot. Which made it all the more likely that the savvy hunter would attack from the water.

Bell saw it gleaming up ahead ten minutes after Josephine took to the air.

New York Harbor was a huge swath of rivers and bays cluttered with tugs, fleets of ferries carrying people to watch the race, barges, steamers, black freighters billowing smoke, four-masted ships, fishing boats, oyster boats, rowboats, speedboats, and lighters. To his right, Bell saw the Brooklyn Bridge draped across the East River, connecting Brooklyn to Manhattan Island. A white battleship surrounded by little tugboats was steaming toward the Navy Yard. Others, painted the new camouflage gray color, were moored pier side, being fitted with modern cage masts.

Dead ahead, Bell saw Brooklyn ending at Buttermilk Channel. Across that narrow strait lay Governors Island. A speedboat patrolled the middle of the strait, its deck marked with a white canvas *V* for Van Dorn. Beyond Governors Island, open water stretched nearly a mile to the Statue of Liberty.

The colossal copper green statue stood three hundred feet tall on a granite-clad pedestal set atop an ancient stone star-shaped fort on tiny Bedloe's Island. The Van Dorn Agency had another *V*-marked launch cruising near Bedloe's, weaving among the ferryboats, barges furnished with bleachers, and private yachts packed with spectators waving hats and handkerchiefs.

Bell saw that Steve Stevens's white biplane had already circled the waypoint and was disappearing far to the north up the Hudson River. He was closely followed by Billy Thomas in the race-car driver's green Curtiss Pusher. Four contestants trailed them. Joe Mudd's red biplane was just completing its turn around the tall statue, and two fliers were close behind him. Missing from the field was Eddison-Sydney-Martin's blue headless pusher, and Bell knew that Josephine had to be worried that the Englishman was so far ahead of Stevens that he was already sipping tea in Yonkers.

Bell took his left hand off the control wheel, gripped the field glasses suspended from his neck, and scanned the waters for small boats of the type Frost had supposedly hired. He noticed to the north a group of tugs, and two enormous ferries churning big wakes as they converged urgently toward a patch of water be-

tween Governors Island and the pier-bristled tip of Lower Manhattan. Bell swept the glasses ahead of them and saw a bright blue
flying machine sinking in the water. Sir Eddison-Sydney-Martin's
headless Curtiss had fallen into the bay. The lower wing and the
fuselage were already submerged.

The *Eagle* lurched like an auto skidding toward a ditch. Bell let
go of his glasses to use both hands. When he had coaxed her back
on an even keel, he resumed flying with one hand, spun the focus
wheel to narrow in on the wreckage, and found the Englishman
with his field glasses. The baronet was kneeling on the pusher's
top wing. His goggles were askew, and he had lost his helmet, but
he had somehow managed to light a cigarette. He greeted the first
tug to arrive to fish him out of the water with a grateful wave of
his smoke.

Before Bell could resume scrutinizing small boats with his field
glasses, he ran into a patch of rough air that required both hands
to control the *American Eagle*. It got rougher, roller-coastering him
fiercely. He guessed that he had driven into the precise junction in
the sky where opposing winds, blowing down the rivers and up
New York Bay, butted heads violently. Whatever the cause, he felt
them battering his monoplane, testing Di Vecchio's wing design
for weaknesses.

Suddenly the machine heeled on its side, turned to the right,
and fell.

18

ISAAC BELL ACTED INSTINCTIVELY, quickly, and decisively, and tried to steer out of the turn with the rudder. As he turned the rudder, he pulled back on the wheel to raise the nose. Neither rudder nor elevator had any effect. The *American Eagle* turned tighter and heeled more sharply.

His instincts had betrayed him. His propeller pointed into empty sky, and the ships in the harbor were suddenly under his right shoulder. And then, before he could reckon what he was doing wrong, everything began to spin.

He glimpsed a blur of yellow in the corner of his eye. In a flash, it was huge. Josephine's machine. He whizzed past it like an express train, missing her by yards, imagining Joe Van Dorn's reaction when, in the course of protecting America's Sweetheart of the Air, his chief investigator smashed into her in full view of a million spectators.

Speed! Josephine's first answer whenever he posed a question about flying technique. *Speed is your friend. Speed makes air strong.*

Bell turned his rudder back to a neutral position, stopped pulling on the control post and shoved it forward. Then, as gently as if he were commanding a frightened horse, he tilted the post sideways, raising the *alettone* on his left wing, lowering the one on the right. The *American Eagle* straightened out of its heel, stopped falling sideways, dipped its nose, and accelerated.

He was out of it in seconds. The gusts were still knocking him about, but the *Eagle* felt more like an aeroplane now than a falling rock. Speed, he thought ruefully, as the machine settled down. Easy to know in theory when flying on an even keel, hard to remember in the heat of the moment.

The confluence of river and sea winds that had nearly undone him proved to be as determined as it was deadly. It spawned a second maelstrom, more vicious than the first, that slammed into Josephine.

Bell had been lucky, he realized. It had hit him with a glancing blow. The full force of a band of crazily twirling wind gusts struck Josephine's Celere so hard that it knocked her out of the sky. Her machine flipped on its side. And, in an instant, the monoplane was falling in an uncontrollable flat spin.

As it plummeted under his machine, Bell saw a piece break off her left wing.

The broken piece trailed her, snared by control wires. He recognized an *alettone*, one of her hinged control flaps. Then the wires parted, and the flap blew away like a leaf in the wind. If Bell himself had not just battled the same gusts, he would have reckoned that Harry Frost had blasted the appendage with a heavy rifle slug. But this assault on Josephine was no criminal attack. This was Mother Nature at her worst. While not as malicious, the effect would be as deadly.

Josephine did not hesitate. *Speed!*

Bell saw her throw herself forward, thrusting all the weight of her slight frame to push her control wheel. She was trying to drop the nose, pushing the aeroplane to fall forward instead of sideways. At the same time, she was tilting her remaining *alettone* to turn against the spin.

Bell tensed every muscle, as if he could somehow help her machine survive by force of will. But it seemed certain that despite her cool courage, lightning reflexes, and vast experience, the power of the wind and the crippling loss of a control flap would smash her into the harbor.

He saw a blur of light ripple across the waters around the Statue of Liberty. Spectators on scores of boats were looking up at her falling craft, thousands of faces agape with horror.

Bell hit his blip switch, cutting off his motor, and put the monoplane into a steep volplane, dropping after Josephine's machine at a sharp angle, trying to stay with her, in a desperate impulse to help that was as impetuous as it was futile. The wind humming in the wire stays rose in pitch, shrieking, as the *Eagle* increased speed.

One hundred feet above the water, Josephine's aeroplane banked sharply into a turn that put her on a collision course with the colonnaded pedestal of the Statue of Liberty. Leveling off, her craft headed directly into the wind, which was blowing every flag in a stiff line from the south. It descended and wobbled left of the statue. She was attempting to alight, Bell realized with unexpected hope. She appeared to be aiming for a tiny patch of lawn beneath the stone walls of the star fort and the water.

The narrow space looked no bigger than a country vegetable garden, not more than sixty yards long and barely two wingspans wide. But as Bell leveled out of his glide and restarted the Gnome, he saw that that was all the room the aviatrix needed. Her

wheels touched at the start of the green grass, and the monoplane bounced, skidded, and stopped a foot from the water's edge
at the tip of the island.

Josephine scrambled out of the nacelle. She stood, arms
akimbo, inspecting the wing where the *alettone* had broken. Then,
mirroring the colossal green statue, she raised her right arm like
Lady Liberty lifting her torch of freedom and waved to the crowds
on the spectator boats. The pasty ripple of horror-stricken faces
exploded into the joyous flutter of thousands of handkerchiefs saluting her pluck and good fortune.

As soon as Isaac Bell saw a *V*-marked Van Dorn Agency steam
launch speed to Bedloe's Island, he whipped his flying machine
past the Statue of Liberty's stern Gallic nose and raced up the
Hudson River at sixty miles an hour. Nature had lent a hand with
her lethal wind gusts, and it was not a gift he would waste. Josephine was safely on the ground, soon to be protected by armed
detectives, and if Harry Frost was lurking on the route ahead,
Bell's decoy was now the only yellow flying machine the killer
would see to shoot at.

The tall detective did not have long to wait.

Four minutes later—four miles up the smoke-shrouded river,
with Midtown Manhattan on his right and the Weehawken piers
thrusting into the water on his left—a high-power rifle slug whistled past his head.

19

ANOTHER SLUG CRACKLED BY. A third slammed through the *Eagle*'s fuselage immediately behind Isaac Bell and shook the back of his seat. A fourth screeched off the tip of the triangular steel king post above the wing. Heavy bullets—Marlin .45-70s, Bell guessed—Frost's favorite. A fifth shot banged his rudder so hard, it rattled the control post. The gunfire was coming from behind him now. He had overflown Frost's position and was moving out of range.

Bell spun the *American Eagle* on a dime and roared back, searching the busy river for the boat from which the gunman had fired. He had been flying up the middle of the mile-wide Hudson when the shooting started, equidistant between the pier-lined shores of Manhattan Island and New Jersey. The resultant half-mile range was too far from land for Frost to have done such accurate shooting. He was directly under Bell, somewhere in the gloom of smoke and haze, screened by the moving traffic of tugs, barges, car floats, lighters, ferries, launches, and sailing vessels.

Bell spotted a short, wide, flat gray hull scooting between a triple-track car float carrying half a freight train, and a three-masted schooner under clouds of sail. He descended to investigate. It was an oyster scow moving at an unusual rate of speed, trailing a long white wake and blue exhaust from a straining gas-oline engine. The helmsman was hunched over his tiller in the stern. Its mast had been unstepped and shipped flat on the deck. A passenger was sprawled on his back beside the mast. He was a big man, Harry Frost's size, who appeared to have fallen. But as Bell's aeroplane caught up with the scow, he saw the sun glint on a long rifle.

Bell grabbed the control wheel in his left hand, drew his pis-tol with his right, and shoved the control post forward. If Harry Frost wondered why his wife's yellow monoplane had circled back, he was about to get the surprise of his life when he learned that he had mistaken a similar profile in an identical color for Jose-phine's Celere.

The *Eagle* dove at the oyster scow. Bell braced the automatic on the hull of the aeroplane, found the supine figure in his sights, and pulled the trigger three times. He saw one of his shots send wood chips flying from the deck and another tear a long furrow in the mast. The aeroplane lurched on an air current, and his third shot went wild.

The *Eagle* flew over the boat so close that Bell could hear the full-throated answering roar of Frost's rifle, three shots fired so fast that the closely spaced holes they stitched in the wing a yard from Bell's shoulder tore the fabric like a cannonball. So much for the surprise effect of two yellow aeroplanes.

"And you can shoot," Bell muttered. "I'll give you that."

He had flown over and past the oyster scow in a flash. When he got the *Eagle* turned around again and headed back, he saw the scow fleeing at high speed toward Weehawken. Seen from above, a great sprawl of railroad track fanned from a dozen piers into rail yards and a vast thirty-acre stockyard packed with milling cows, where, in the thousands, they were herded off trains coming in from the west, bound for cattle boats that would ferry them across the river to Manhattan slaughterhouses.

Bell swooped after him, coming up from behind, firing his pistol again and again. But at such a low altitude, the flying machine bounced and slid in the smoky surface wind, making it impossible to steady his aim, while Harry Frost, firing from the more stable platform of the oyster scow, was able to send another astonishingly accurate hail of lead straight at him. Bell saw another hole appear in his wing. A slug fanned his cheek.

Then a lucky shot hit a wing stay.

The wire broke with a loud bang, as tons of tension were suddenly released. Bell held his breath, expecting the entire wing to collapse from lack of support. Tight turns would increase the tension. But he had to turn, and turn quickly, to make another pass at the fleeing scow before it reached the piers. If Harry Frost managed to get ashore, he stood a good chance of getting away. Bell flew after the scow, firing his nearly useless pistol and vowing that, if he got out of this fix alive, he would order the mechanicians to fit the *American Eagle* with a swivel mount for an autoload rifle.

Frost's helmsmen steered for a pier where a gaff-rigged schooner was moored on one side and a four-hundred-foot steel-hull nitrate clipper was unloading guano on the other. The sailing ships screened the pier with forests of masts and thickets of crosstrees. It was impossible for Bell to shoot at Frost, much less attempt to land on the pier.

The oyster scow stopped alongside a ladder. Frost climbed fast as a grizzly. When he attained the pier's deck, he stood still for a long moment, watching Bell circle overhead. Then he waved a triumphant good-bye and bolted toward the shore. Two big men in slouch hats—railroad company detectives—blocked his path. Frost flattened both yard bulls without breaking stride.

Bell's eyes roved urgently over the industrial ground. There was no grass field in sight, of course. The rail yard was crisscrossed with freight trains, and the stockyards were thick with steers. He chose the only option. Battling a crosswind and hoping for eighty yards of open space, he tried to bring his aeroplane down on the pier that paralleled the one on which Frost had disembarked. A switch engine obligingly pulled a string of boxcars off it toward the yards. But stevedores scuttled about with wheelbarrows, and a team of horses ventured onto the pier, hauling a freight wagon.

The noisy racket of Bell's Gnome engine, blatting loudly as he blipped it on and off to slow down, spooked the horses. They stopped dead in their tracks. When they saw the bright yellow monoplane dropping out of the sky, they reared and backed up. The stevedores dove for cover, clearing a path except for the wheelbarrows they abandoned.

The pier was eighty feet wide. The *American Eagle*'s wings spread forty feet. Bell brought her in right down the middle on a smooth wooden deck between two railroad tracks. His rubber-sprung wheels took the first impact, which forced them up to let the skids act as brakes. But the timbers were smoother than turf, and the *Eagle* glided like a skier on snow, losing almost no speed until it hit a wheelbarrow. The barrow tangled in the skids and caused the *Eagle* to tip forward onto her propeller. The nine-foot polished walnut airscrew snapped like a matchstick.

Bell jumped from the aeroplane and hit the ground running, extracting the empty magazine from his pistol and shoving in a fresh one. The ships moored along the pier that Frost had mounted from the scow blocked his view of the fleeing man. Bell was almost to the shore before he glimpsed Harry Frost, already on solid ground, running full tilt toward the stockyards.

Another railroad cop made the mistake of attempting to stop him. Frost knocked him down and jerked a revolver from the yard bull's waistband. A fourth rail cop shouted at him and pulled a gun. Frost stopped, took careful aim, and shot him down. Now he stood his ground, turning on his heel, slowly, deliberately, daring any man to try to stop him.

Bell was a hundred yards behind, an impossibly long pistol shot, even with his modified No. 2 Browning. Pumping his long legs, he put on a burst of speed. At a distance of seventy-five yards, he aimed for Frost's head, assuming that the marauder was wearing his bulletproof vest. It was still extreme range. He braced his pistol on a rock-steady forearm, exhaled, and smoothly curled his trigger finger. He was rewarded with a howl of pain.

Frost's hand flew to his ear. The howl deepened to an angry animal roar, and he emptied the rail dick's revolver in Bell's direction. As the bullets whistled past, Bell fired again. Frost threw down his empty gun and ran toward the stockyards. Wild-eyed steers edged away. Frost vaulted a rail fence into their midst, and the animals stampeded from him, smashing into one another.

A steer jumped over the back of another and landed on the fence, knocking over a section. As fencing fell, animals crowded through the opening, leveling another section and then another, streaming in every direction, into the rail yard, onto a road to Weehawken, and toward the piers behind Bell. In seconds, hundreds of beef cattle were milling between him and Frost. Frost shoved through them, shouting and firing a gun he had pulled from his coat.

Bell was surrounded by horn-clashing, galloping animals. He

attempted to clear a space by firing in the air. But for every fear-maddened creature that shied from the gunfire, another charged straight at him. He slipped on the dung-slicked cobblestones. A heel went out from under him, and he almost lost his footing. If he went down, he would be trampled to a pulp. An enormous whiteface steer came at him—a Texas Longhorn–Hereford cross-breed he knew well from his years in the West. Ordinarily more docile than they looked, this one was knocking smaller cows out of its way like bowling pins.

Bell holstered his pistol to free his hands. Seeing nothing to lose and his life to gain if he could only get out of the herd, he jumped with lightning speed, grabbing the whiteface's horns with both hands and twisting himself over its head and onto its back. He clamped his knees with all his strength, grabbed the shaggy tuft between its horns with a steel fist, whipped off his flying helmet, and waved it like a bronco rider's.

The frightened bucking steer kicked its legs into a frantic gallop, shoved through the writhing mob, leaped a tumbled length of fence, and thundered back into the now empty stockyard. Bell tumbled off and staggered to his feet. Harry Frost was nowhere to be seen.

He scoured the acres of cobblestoned corrals for Frost's trampled body, peered into sheds and under the elevated office. He had no illusions about his own escape: he had been extremely lucky, and it was highly unlikely that Frost had been as fortunate. But he found no body, or even a dropped weapon or a torn coat or a mangled hat. It was as if the murderer had taken wing.

He kept hunting, as the stockmen began returning from the piers, the rail yards, and the city of Weehawken, driving captured steers that shambled into the yards too exhausted to pose any threat. Evening shadows cast by the stone cliffs of the Palisades were growing long when the Van Dorn detective stumbled upon a curved brick structure a few inches below the cobblestones. It was a circle of brick and mortar a full six feet in diameter, partly covered by a thick cast-iron disk. He knelt to inspect the disk. It had a date in raised numbers: 1877.

A stockman came along, cracking a whip. "What is this?" Bell demanded.

"Old manhole cover."

"I see that. What does it cover?"

"Old sewer, I guess. There's a few of 'em around. They used to drain the manure . . . Say, what the heck moved it? Must weigh a ton."

"A strong man," Bell mused. He peered into the darkness under it. He could see a brick-lined shaft. "Does it drain to the river?"

"Used to. Probably stops under one of them piers now. You see where they filled in the water and built the pier?"

Bell ran in search of a flashlight and hurried back with one he bought from a railroad cop. He lowered himself into the shaft, hunched under the low brick ceiling, and started walking. The tunnel ran straight and sloped slightly. It smelled of cow dung and decades of damp. And as the stockman predicted, after nearly a quarter mile he found a timber bisecting it vertically. Judging by the broken-brick rubble scattered around it, Bell reckoned it was a piling unknowingly driven down through the long-forgotten disused sewer by the builders of the pier.

The tall detective squeezed around it and walked toward the sound of rushing water. Now he could smell the river. The brick grew slippery, and the flashlight revealed streaks of moss, as if the

walls were wetted twice daily when the tide rose. He passed another vertical timber and came abruptly to the mouth of the
sewer. This would have been the end, underwater at high tide, originally extending into the river forty years ago before landfill extended the shore.

At his feet, a torrent of ebbing saltwater tide and freshwater
river current raced toward the sea. Overhead, he saw the shadows of a dense frame of piles and timbers—the underbelly of the
pier. He stepped onto a final crumbling lip of brick and looked
around.

"What took you so long?" said a voice.

Isaac Bell had a split second to train his light on a bearded face,
slick with blood, before Harry Frost hurled a pile-driver punch.

20

WITH FOUR YEARS of college boxing and ten years as a Van Dorn agent, including an investigation in the Arizona Territory disguised as an itinerant prizefighter, and another as a lumberjack, Isaac Bell reacted by rolling with the punch.

Memory speeded up, as if whirled in a turbine. He recalled events too fast to register as they had occurred. In memory, he could see Frost's fist swinging at him. He could see that he had been caught flat-footed. If he went down at Frost's feet, he was a dead man. His only chance to live was to make absolutely sure that Frost couldn't follow up with another blow.

Harry Frost had obliged Bell by knocking him backwards into the Hudson River.

The current was swift, tide and river speeding toward the sea.

Isaac Bell was barely conscious, with an aching jaw and a throbbing head.

He saw Frost scrambling along the narrow shelf of mud that the falling tide had exposed on the shore under the piers. Dodging the pilings that marched from the land into the river, Frost tried to keep up with the current. He scampered like a dog wanting to jump in the water after a ball but afraid of drowning.

The current slammed Bell against pilings in the water. Bell seized hold of one. Less than fifteen feet separated the detective and the murderer. *"Frost,"* he shouted, gripping the slimy wood, fighting the current. "Give it up!"

To Bell's surprise, Harry Frost laughed.

Bell had expected howling curses. Instead, the murderer was laughing. Nor was it insane laughter. He sounded almost cheerful when he said, "Go to hell."

"It's over," Bell shouted. "You can't get away from us."

Frost laughed again. "You won't get me before I get Josephine."

"Killing your poor wife won't do you any good, Harry. Give it up."

Frost stopped laughing. "Poor wife?" His bloodied face worked convulsively. *"Poor wife?"* He raised his voice in an angry cry: "You don't know what they were up to!"

"Who? What do you mean?"

Frost stared at him across the rushing tide. "You don't know nothing," he said bitterly. He shrugged his massive shoulders. An odd smile flickered across his mouth before his expression hardened like a death mask. "Say, look it this."

Harry Frost bent down and pawed in the mud. He straightened up, holding Bell's Browning.

"You dropped this when you ran away by jumpin' in the water. Here you go!" He flung the pistol in Bell's face.

Bell caught it on the fly. He juggled the muddy grip into his palm and flicked off the safety. "Elevate! Hands up!"

Harry Frost turned his back on the detective, clinging to the piling in the water, and stalked upstream against the flow of the tide.

"Hands up!"

"I'm not afraid of you," Frost called over his shoulder, taunting. "You are nothing. You couldn't even take one punch. You ran away."

"Stop right there."

"If you didn't have the belly to take another punch, you sure as hell don't have the nerve to shoot me in the back."

Bell aimed for Harry Frost's legs, intending to slow the man, climb out of the water, and get him. But he was numb with cold. His head was reeling from the punch. It took an act of will to steady the barrel, another to force his finger to curl smoothly around the trigger so he wouldn't miss.

The gun felt heavy.

"You don't have the guts to pull the trigger," Frost flung over his shoulder.

Strangely heavy. Was he losing consciousness? No. It was too heavy. Why did Frost throw it instead of simply shooting him? Why was he daring him to shoot? Bell let go the trigger, engaged the safety, turned the weapon around, and looked at the muzzle. It was cram-packed with mud.

Frost had jammed it into the river mud when he picked it up, deliberately tamping it into the barrel so it would blow up in Bell's hand. Characteristic Harry Frost. Like the bent horseshoes thrown through victims' windows to terrorize them, the chief investigator's maimed hand would warn every Van Dorn detective: Don't mess with Harry Frost.

Bell dunked the gun in the water and slammed it back and forth, sluicing out the mud. With any luck, it would fire a shot or two. But when he looked for his target, Harry Frost had melted into the shadows. Bell called, *"Frost!"* All he heard in response was laughter echoing under a distant pier.

"WHERE IS JOSEPHINE?" Isaac Bell shouted into the stockyard office telephone.

"Are you O.K., Isaac?" asked Joseph Van Dorn.

"Where is Josephine?"

"Camped out on Bedloe's Island, fixing her flying machine. Where are you?"

"Who's watching her?"

"Six of my best detectives and twenty-seven newspaper reporters. Not to mention Mr. Preston Whiteway, circling on a steam yacht, beaming searchlights for your fiancée to shoot moving pictures by. Are you O.K.?"

"Tip-top, soon as I get a propeller, a new wing stay, and a Remington autoload."

"I'll send word to Marion you're O.K. Where are you, Isaac?"

"Weehawken stockyards. Frost got away."

"Seems to be making a habit of that," the boss observed coolly. "Did you wing him at least?"

"I took off one of his ears."

"That's a start."

"But it didn't stop him."

"Where's he headed?"

"I don't know," Bell admitted. His head ached, and his jaw felt like he'd been chewing thornbushes.

"Do you think he'll try again?"

"He assured me he will not stop trying until he kills her."

"You spoke?" The tone of Van Dorn's voice suggested that if Bell could somehow see through telephone wire, he would be facing sharply raised eyebrows.

"Briefly."

"What's his state of mind?"

Isaac Bell had thought of little else since he swam ashore.

"Harry Frost is not insane," he said. "In fact, in a strange way he's enjoying himself. As I warned Whiteway in San Francisco, Frost knows he's been dealt his last hand. He's not going to fold his cards until he sets the casino on fire."

Joseph Van Dorn said, "Nonetheless, the lengths he's going to to avenge his wife's supposed seduction would fit most folks' definition of insane."

"Let me ask you something, Joe. Why do you suppose Frost didn't kill Josephine when they were still together?"

"What do you mean?"

"Why did Frost shoot Marco instead?"

"Put an end to the affair, hoping she'd come back."

"Yes. Except for one thing. Having killed Marco—assuming he is dead—"

"He is," Van Dorn interrupted. "We've been down that road."

"Having killed, or tried to kill, Marco," Bell replied evenly, "why is Frost now trying to kill Josephine?"

"He either *is* insane or just plain old-fashioned crazed with jealousy. The man was known for his temper."

"Why didn't he kill Josephine first?"

"You're asking me to explain the order of a madman's killings?"

"Do you know what he said to me?"

"I wasn't there when he escaped, Isaac," Van Dorn said pointedly.

Isaac Bell was too involved in his line of inquiry to countenance Van Dorn's jibe. "Harry Frost said to me, 'You don't know what they were up to.'"

"Up to? Marco and Josephine were running off together, that's what they were up to—or so Frost suspected."

"No. He didn't sound like he meant only a love affair. He indicated they were scheming. It was as if he had discovered that they had perpetuated some sort of betrayal *worse* than seduction."

"What?"

"I don't know. But I'm beginning to suspect that we are fighting something more complicated than we took on."

"We took on protecting Josephine from getting killed," Van Dorn retorted firmly. "So far, that's been complicated enough for *two* detective agencies. If what you're suggesting now has any bottom to it, we should call in a third."

"Send me that Remington autoload."

VAN DORN DISPATCHED an apprentice across on the Weehawken Ferry with the rifle and dry clothes from Bell's room at the Yale Club. Andy Moser arrived in one of the roadsters an hour later, with tools, stay wires, and a shiny new nine-foot propeller strapped to the fenders.

"Good thing you're rich, Mr. Bell. This baby cost a hundred bucks."

"Let's get to work. I want this machine flying by dawn. I already removed this broken stay."

Andy Moser whistled. "Wow! I've never seen Roebling wire snap."

"It had help from Harry Frost."

"It's amazing the wing didn't fall off."

Bell said, "The machine is resilient. These other stays, here and here, took up the slack."

"I always say, Mr. Di Vecchio built 'em to last."

They replaced the propeller and the broken stay and patched the holes Frost had shot in the wing fabric. Then Bell sawed twelve inches off the wooden stock of the Remington autoloading rifle, and Andy jury-rigged a swivel mount, promising to construct a more permanent installation "with a stop so you don't shoot your own propeller" when he got back to his shop in the hangar car. Next time Harry Frost fired at him he would discover that the *Eagle* had grown teeth.

21

FOUR MILES DOWNRIVER, at the foot of the Statue of Liberty, Josephine was trying to fix her flying machine. Blinded by the searchlights glaring from Preston Whiteway's steam yacht, choking on its coal smoke, and harried by reporters shouting puddingheaded questions, she and her Van Dorn detective-mechanicians, who had finally come over on a boat, addressed the mangled wing. But the damage was beyond their skills and the few tools they had with them, and the young aviatrix had begun to lose hope when help suddenly appeared in the last person she would have expected.

Dmitri Platov hopped off a Harbor Patrol launch from Manhattan Island, shook hands with the policemen who had given him a ride, and saluted her with a jaunty wave of his slide rule. Everyone said that the handsome Russian was the best mechanician in the race, but he had never come near her machine or offered his services. She was pretty sure she knew why.

"What are you doing here?" she asked.

He tipped his straw boater. "Platov come helping."

"Isn't Steve Stevens afraid I'll beat him if you help me?"

"Steve Stevens eating victory meal in Yonkers," Platov answered, flashing white teeth in his whiskers. "Platov own man."

"I need a savior, Mr. Platov. The damage is much worse than I thought."

"We are fixing, no fearing," said Platov.

"I don't know. You see, this sleeve—here, bring those lights!"

The Van Dorns hopped to obey, angling electric lights they had hooked up to the Statue of Liberty's dynamo.

"You see? The sleeve that holds the pintle for the *alettone* is not strong enough. Nor is it solidly seated in the frame. It's even worse on the other wing. Dumb luck that that one didn't fall off, too."

Platov felt the sleeve with his fingers, like a vet examining a calf. He turned to the nearest mechanician. "Please, you are bringing second tool bag from boat?"

The Van Dorn hurried to the dock.

Platov addressed the other detective. "Please, you bringing more lights."

Josephine said, "I can't believe my eyes. It's an amateurish design. The man who built the machine didn't seem to understand the stress on this part."

Dmitri Platov looked Josephine full in the face and stepped very close to her.

She was taken aback. Having never stood within twenty yards of him until this moment, she had never noticed how thoroughly his dark springy hair and mutton chops covered his brow, cheeks, chin, and lips, nor how brightly his eyes burned within that curly nest. She felt herself drawn to his eyes. There was something strangely familiar about them.

"Poor design?" he asked in straightforward, unaccented English. "I take that as a personal insult."

Josephine stared back in utter amazement.

She covered her mouth with her greasy glove, staining her cheek. Marco Celere's voice—the voice he had used only when they were alone—the faintest Italian accent, speaking the British phrases he had learned as a teenager apprenticed to a Birmingham machinist.

"Marco," she whispered. "Oh, my Marco, you're alive."

Marco Celere gave her the tiniest wink. "Shall I send our audience packing?" he murmured.

She nodded, still pressing her glove to her mouth.

Marco raised his voice and addressed the Van Dorn mechanicians in his familiar Dmitri Platov Russian accent. "Gentles-mens, de idea is dat too many cooks making cold soup. Let Platov being alone genius fixing Josephine aviatrix machine."

Josephine saw the detective-mechanicians exchange glances.

"Josephine being helper," Platov added.

The detectives were staring uncomfortably, Josephine thought. Did they suspect? Thank God, Isaac wasn't here. Chief Investigator Bell would question the shock on her face. These younger, less experienced operators sensed something out of kilter. But were they clever enough to challenge the mechanician-machinist who everyone in the race knew as "the crazy Russian" Platov?

"It's O.K.," said Josephine. "I'll be his helper."

The head Van Dorn nodded his assent. After all, she was a better mechanician than any of them. They retreated to the ropes they had strung to hold the newspaper reporters at bay. "We'll be right over here if you need us, Josephine."

Marco said, "Are passing Platov monkeying wrench, Josephine."

She fumbled for the tool. She could barely believe her senses. And yet she felt as if she had awakened from a nightmare that had started the week she married Harry Frost when she saw him punch and kick a man nearly to death for smiling at her. Her husband had never hurt her, but she had known from that moment on that he would one day, suddenly, without warning. What a fearful price she had paid for her aeroplanes, waiting, on tenterhooks, even as Harry applauded her passion for flying and bought her machines—until last autumn, when he grew suspicious of Marco.

He had moved like lightning. First, he cut her out of his will. Then he roared in her face that he would kill her if she ever dared ask him for a divorce. Having trapped her thoroughly, he refused to pay off Marco's debts on the machine they needed to compete for the Whiteway Cup. When he invited Marco to go hunting, she feared the worst. It was a trick to take Marco out in the woods and kill him in a "hunting accident."

But Marco had a plan to save them both and enter the race—a brilliant plan to fake his own murder and frame Harry for the crime.

He had jimmied the telescopic sight on Harry's hunting rifle so it would shoot high. He positioned himself so he could jump to a narrow ledge right below the rim of the cliff when Harry fired. Josephine would fly over, witnessing the shooting, so that Harry Frost would run. Marco would pretend to be dead, his body swept away by the North River. Josephine's violent, murderous husband would be permanently locked back in the insane asylum, where he belonged. And Josephine would be free to charm the wealthy San Francisco newspaper publisher Preston Whiteway into sponsoring her in the Atlantic–Pacific air race in a new Celere Monoplano. Later, after Harry was safely locked up, Marco would wander out of the Adirondack woods pretending amnesia, remembering nothing except being wounded by Harry Frost.

But things had gone badly wrong. Harry had actually shot Marco—she had seen him blasted off the cliff with her own eyes—and Harry was never caught.

Fearing Marco was dead, Josephine had felt punished for what was, she had to admit in retrospect, an evil plan. She had begun to wish she had not let Marco talk her into it. Just as now part of her regretted following through with their plan to make Whiteway her champion in the race. It had simply never occurred to her that the rich, handsome publisher would fall in love with a tomboy farm girl.

Some women might rate the opportunity to become the legal wife of a newspaper magnate as better luck than she deserved, but Josephine did not want any part of it. She loved Marco and she had grieved for him. And now, suddenly, unexpectedly, he was back, alive and well, like an unexpected Christmas gift delivered late.

"Marco?" she whispered. "Marco? What happened?"

"What happened?" Marco murmured, softly as he continued to appraise the monoplane's battered wing. "Your husband missed, but by not as much as we had hoped. That bloody .45-70 nearly blew my head off."

"I knew we should have used blanks. Changing the sights was too risky."

"Harry Frost was too smart for blanks. I told you that already. He'd have felt a lesser recoil, heard a lesser report. It had to be a real bullet. But I underestimated how canny he is. He sensed something was wrong with the sights in one shot. So bloody sharp that he compensated for the gun firing high on the second shot. Next I knew, I was flying off the cliff."

"I saw."

"Was I convincing?" Marco asked with another, almost imperceptible wink.

"I thought you were dead— Oh, my darling." It was all she could do to keep from hugging and kissing him.

A smile twitched his whiskers. "So did I. I fell on the ledge, like I was supposed to, but I passed out. It was dark when I woke. I was freezing. My head was splitting. I couldn't move my arm. All I knew was, I was still alive, and by some miracle Harry hadn't found me for the coup de grâce."

"That was because he knew I saw him shoot you. He ran."

"Just as we planned."

"But you weren't supposed to die. Or even be hurt."

Marco shrugged. "A minor detail. Nonetheless, the plan worked. Sort of. Harry's on the run. Unfortunately, he's overplaying his part—he should have been caught and locked up by now, or shot dead. But you have a wonderful *aeroplano* in the race, just as we planned."

"What about you, Marco?"

Marco didn't seem to hear her. He said, "You will win the greatest race in the world."

"Win? I'm a day behind already, and it just started."

"You will win. I will see that you win. Don't you worry. No one will stay ahead of you."

He sounded so sure, she thought. How could he be so sure? "But what about you, Marco?"

Again, he didn't seem to hear her question, saying, "And you have a suitor."

"What do you mean?"

"Every one at Belmont Park said that Preston Whiteway has fallen in love with you."

"That's ridiculous. It's just a crush."

"He had your marriage annulled."

"I didn't ask him to. He just went ahead and did it."

"You were supposed to charm him into buying you an aeroplane. But when you ask, 'What about you, Marco?' you seem to have already answered your own question."

"What do you mean?"

"It doesn't sound like there is anyplace in your scheme for Marco."

"It's not my scheme. I just wanted your aeroplane. Like we planned."

"You got more than we originally planned."

Josephine felt hot tears spring to her eyes. "Marco, you can't believe that I would prefer Whiteway to you."

"How can I blame you? You thought I was dead. He is rich. I am a poor aeroplane inventor."

"He could never replace you," she protested. "And now that you're back, we can—"

"What?" Marco asked bleakly. "Be together? How long would Whiteway let you fly my *monoplano* if he saw you with me?"

"Is that why you pretended you were dead?"

"I pretended I was dead for several important reasons. One, I was badly injured. If I stayed in North River, Harry would have killed me in my hospital bed."

"But how—"

"I rode a freight train to Canada. A kind farm family took me in and nursed me all winter. When I learned that you were with Whiteway and in the race and that Harry was still free, I decided to tag along, in disguise, keeping an eye on things, before miraculously walking out of the woods as Marco, as we planned."

"When will you?"

"After you win."

"Why wait so long?"

"I just told you, Whiteway would be as jealous of me as Harry. Maybe not as violent, but angry enough to cut you off and take his aeroplane. He does own it, doesn't he? Or did he give you the title?"

"No. He owns it."

"Too bad you didn't ask for the title."

She hung her head. "I didn't know how I could. He's paying for everything. Even my clothes."

"The rich are often kind, never generous."

"I don't know how long I can bear looking at you and pretending you're not you."

"Concentrate on my hairy disguise."

"But your eyes, your lips . . ." She pictured him as he had looked, his sleek black hair, noble forehead, elegant mustache, deep-set dark eyes.

"Lips do not bear thinking about until you win the race," he said. "Drive my airplane. Win the race. And don't forget, when you win the race, Josephine, America's Sweetheart of the Air will be a made woman with heaps of money. And Marco, the inventor of the winning Celere Monoplano, will be a made man, with Italian Army contracts to build hundreds of aeroplanes."

"What has it been like for you to look at me all this time?"

"What is it like? Like it has always been from the first day I set eyes on you. Like an ocean of joy that fills my heart. Now, let's get your machine fixed."

ISAAC BELL TRIED TO SLEEP in a blanket roll under the monoplane, but his mind kept seizing on Harry Frost's strange statement. Suddenly he sat up, galvanized by an entirely different and even stranger thought. He had been struck by his aeroplane's resilience—and grateful for it saving his life—even before Andy Moser's admiring remark that Di Vecchio "built 'em to last."

Bell pulled on his boots and ran to the rail-yard dispatch shack, where they had a telegraph. The peculiar strength of the *American Eagle* stemmed from multiple braces and redundant control links. Not only had its inventor used all the best materials, he had anticipated structural failure and designed to prevent catastrophe.

Such an inventor who built to last did not seem to be the sort of man to kill himself over a bankruptcy. Such a man, Bell thought, would rise above failure, seeing a bankruptcy as nothing worse than a temporary setback.

"Van Dorn," he told the New York Central Railroad dispatcher. He had a letter of introduction signed by the president of the line. But the dispatcher was delighted to help anyone in the air race.

"Yes, sir. What can I do for you?"

"I want to send a telegraph."

The dispatcher's hand poised over the brass key. "To whom?"

"James Dashwood. Van Dorn Agency. San Francisco."

"Message?"

Bell listened to the dispatcher tap the letters of his message into the Morse alphabet.

INVESTIGATE DI VECCHIO SUICIDE.

SPEED CELERE INVESTIGATION.

ON THE JUMP!

22

"LOOK AT HER GO!"

Throttle full, Antoinette engine discharging a high-pitched snarl that sounded like ripping canvas, Josephine's yellow monoplane streaked past Weehawken, New Jersey, at first light.

"Spin her over!"

Isaac Bell was already at the *Eagle*'s controls, having learned by telephone that Dmitri Platov and the Van Dorn mechanicians had worked all night to replace Josephine's *alettone* and its wind-mangled mounts. The aviatrix had just taken off from Bedloe's Island. Bell had his *Eagle* positioned at the head of the pier he had landed on the day before to take off over the river. His Gnome rotary was already warm and ready to fly. It blatted to life on one pull of the propeller.

"Chocks!"

They yanked the chocks from the wheels, and the monoplane started rolling. Andy and his helper ran beside the wings, steadying them, as Bell raced across the smooth boards between the railroad tracks and soared after Josephine.

He stayed close behind her as they flew up the middle of the Hudson River, eyeing the ships and boats for signs of Harry Frost, rehearsing flying with one hand and swiveling the rifle with the other. After fifteen miles, the two yellow aeroplanes veered toward the New York side, where the city of Yonkers stained the sky with smoke.

Although Bell was following Josephine's aeroplane, he practiced navigating by a race map sketched with pertinent landmarks. With the stiff paper strapped to his leg, he traced the oval Empire City Race Track, which grew visible a couple of miles inland beside a huge pit of mud where steam shovels were digging a new reservoir for New York City.

Bell saw Thoroughbreds cantering around the track on their morning workouts, but the racetrack's infield was deserted of flying machines, and the only hangar train in the rail yard was the long yellow *Josephine Special*. He learned upon alighting behind Josephine that every other flying machine still in the race had already taken off for Albany.

While the mechanicians poured gasoline, oil, and water in Josephine's tanks, and gasoline and castor oil in Bell's, they reported that even though Steve Stevens's double Antoinette twin-propellered tractor biplane had turned in the best time from Belmont Park to Yonkers, the cotton planter was mad as hell at Dmitri Platov for helping Josephine fix her plane at the Statue of Liberty.

"De idea is dat," they mimicked Platov affectionately, "every peoples racing together."

"So Mr. Stevens yelled at poor Dmitri," the mimics went on, switching to a Southern drawl, "Y'all is a *socialist*."

Bell noticed that Josephine did not join in the laughter. Her face was tight with tension. He assumed that she was deeply upset to be so far behind this early in the race. Ordinarily polite and pleasant to everyone, she was railing at her mechanicians to

"Hurry it up!" as they made further repairs to her whirlwind-damaged wing.

"Don't worry," Bell said gently, "you'll catch up."

The tall detective motioned one of the Van Dorns on her support train to join him. "Any idea why that flap fell off the wing?"

"She got caught in a pocket tornado."

"I know that. But could the hinge have been weakened beforehand?"

"Sabotage? First thing I looked for, Mr. Bell. Fact is, that machine's never been out of our sight on the ground. Mr. Abbott made that darned clear. We watched like hawks for sabotage. We slept next to it at Belmont. With one man always awake."

Andy and his helper arrived in a Thomas Flyer via a ferry from the Palisades of New Jersey before Josephine's mechanicians were finished. They drove it up the ramp into the *American Eagle Special*, and Bell sent the train ahead.

It was noon before Josephine could take to the sky.

She circled the grandstand for Weiner of Accounting's deputy to record her departure time, climbed to a thousand feet, and headed north. Isaac Bell flew a little above and a quarter mile behind. His race map said it was a hundred and forty miles to Albany's Altamont Fair Grounds. The route was easy to follow, the New York Central Railroad tracks hugging the east bank of the river, until, above the city of Hudson, he saw a number of short lines merge in from the east. At that confusing junction, the race stewards had marked the correct tracks to follow with long white canvas arrows.

The two monoplanes proceeded north without incident, eventually overtaking Bell's white-roofed *Eagle Special* train, which was loafing along waiting for them to catch up. The fireman shoveled on a little more coal to keep pace with the flying machines.

Suddenly, ten miles short of Albany, Bell saw Josephine drop in a steep volplane.

Isaac Bell followed her down in a longer series of descending loops and was still high up when she alighted on a freshly mown hayfield outside the village of Castleton-on-Hudson. Through his field glasses, he could see why she had found a place to land. Steam was gushing from the Antoinette. Something had gone wrong with the motor's water cooling.

Bell swung back toward the New York Central tracks. He flew low over the *Eagle Special* and pointed where he'd come from, and then spotted the yellow-roofed *Josephine Special*, which was high-balling to catch up. He swooped in front of the locomotive and turned in the direction where Josephine was. The train stopped at the next siding, where the Van Dorn had already parked. Brake-men jumped down, waving a red flag in back and throwing a switch in front so the special could pull off the main line.

Bell alighted beside Josephine and told her that help was on the way. It came aboard two roadsters, Preston Whiteway's Rolls-Royce, with two detective-mechanicians, who got straight to work on her machine, and Bell's Model 35 Thomas Flyer, with Andy Moser, who replenished gas and castor oil and adjusted the Gnome. Josephine's problem turned out to be more complicated than a broken water hose. The entire water pump was shot. The Thomas Flyer raced back to the train to get the new part.

"Mr. Bell," said Andy, "it's going to take them two hours at least."

"Looks that way."

"Could I ask you a favor?"

"Of course," said Bell, hand deep in his pocket, thinking Andy needed a loan. "What do you need?"

"Take me up."

"Flying?" Bell said, puzzled, because Andy was terrified of heights and never wanted to fly. "Are you sure, Andy?"

"Don't you realize where we are?"

"Ten miles short of Albany."

"Twenty miles west of *Danielle*. I was wondering could we fly over that Ryder Asylum, and you waggle the wings and maybe Danielle will see us?"

"It's the least we can do. Spin her over and hop on. We'll buzz by real close."

Bell was not surprised that Andy had a map. The lovesick mechanician had even marked the asylum with a red heart. They found a rail line they could follow into the closest town and took off, Andy squeezed in behind him, reading the map. At sixty miles per hour and boosted by a west wind, Bell was in sight of the gloomy red brick building in less than twenty minutes. He circled it repeatedly. A face appeared at every barred window. One of them had to be Danielle's. A flying machine was a startling sight for the vast majority of people outside a big city who had never seen one. The halls were probably alive with inmates, nurses, and guards, gawking, exclaiming. The Gnome's distinctive exhaust sound would surely alert Danielle that it was her father's machine even if she could not see it.

Poor Andy's face expressed a jumble of joy and sadness, excitement and frustration.

"I'm sure she hears us!" Bell shouted.

Andy nodded, understanding Bell was only trying to help. Bell descended deeper into the valley and circled close over the turret where he had interviewed Danielle in Ryder's private rooms. He checked the railroad watch he had hung from the king post. Plenty of time and fuel, he thought. Why not kill two birds with one stone: give poor Andy a break, and ask Danielle about the death of her father.

The lawn was broad inside the wall. He put the *Eagle* down easily. Guards came running, urged on by Dr. Ryder, who glued a smile to his face at the unwelcome sight of Isaac Bell.

"Quite an entrance, Mr. Bell."

"We've come to visit Miss Di Vecchio."

"Of course, Mr. Bell. She'll need a moment to get ready."

"Bring her out here. I imagine she will enjoy a breath of fresh air."

"As you wish. I'll bring her shortly."

Andy was staring at the bleak structure, with its small barred windows. "That man doesn't like you," he observed.

"No, he doesn't."

"But he obeys you."

"He has no choice. He knows that I know his banker. And he knows that if he ever harms a hair on Danielle's head, I will paste him in the snoot."

The first thing Bell noticed about Danielle was that her white patient's dress was brand-new. The second was that she regarded Andy Moser more like a kid brother than a boyfriend. He backed away to let them have a moment together. Andy was tongue-tied. Bell called, "Andy, why don't you show Danielle what you've done to her father's machine?"

Andy fell to the task eagerly, and Danielle walked around it with him, oohing and ahhing, and stroking the canvas with her fingertips. "Many improvements," she announced at last. "Is she still temperamental, Mr. Bell?"

"Andy's turned her into a lamb," said Bell. "She's rescued me more than once."

"I never realized you already knew how to fly."

"He's still learning," Andy said grimly.

"Your father built a real sweetheart," said Bell. "She's amazingly strong. The other day, a stay was damaged, and the others held together for it."

"*Elastico!*" said Danielle.

"Was your father *elastico*?" Bell asked gently.

Her big eyes lighted in happy memory. "Like *biglia*. India-rubber ball. *Rimbalzare!* He bounced."

"Were you shocked how he died?"

"That he killed himself? No. If you stretch *banda* too much, too many times, it breaks. A man breaks when too much goes bad. But before, he was *rimbalzare*. Is Josephine piloting Celere's *monoplano* in the race?"

"Yes."

"How does she fare?"

"Behind by a full day."

"*Brava!*" Danielle smiled.

"I was surprised to learn that Marco had another machine in the race. A big biplane with two motors."

Danielle sneered, "Who do you think he stole that from?"

"Your father?"

"No. Marco copied the biplane from a brilliant student he befriended in Paris. At the École Supérieure des Techniques Aéronautiques et de Construction Automobile."

"What was his name?"

"Sikorsky."

"Russian?"

"And part Polish."

"You knew him?"

"My father lectured at the École. We knew everyone."

"Do you know Dmitri Platov?"

"No."

"Did your father?"

"I never heard the name."

Bell weighed another question. What more could he learn about her father's suicide from her that might be worth the pain it might cause? Or should he rely on James Dashwood to ferret it out in San Francisco? Andy surprised him, stepping closer and muttering through tight lips, "Enough. Give her a break."

"Danielle?" Bell asked.

"Yes, Mr. Bell?"

"Marco Celere convinced Josephine that he is the sole inventor of her aeroplane."

Her nostrils flared and her eyes flashed. "Thief!"

"I wonder whether you could give me some . . . ammunition to convince her otherwise?"

"What does she care?"

"I sense disquiet. Doubt."

"What does it matter to her?"

"At her core is something honest."

"She is very ambitious, you know."

"I wouldn't believe everything I read in the papers. Preston Whiteway's competitors have only just begun to support his race."

Danielle gestured angrily at the wall. "I see no papers here. They say newspapers will confuse us."

"Then how do you know Josephine is ambitious?"

"Marco told me."

"When?"

"He was boasting when I stabbed. He said she was ambitious, but he was even more ambitious."

"*More* ambitious? She wants to fly. What did he want? Money?"

"Power. Marco didn't care about money. He would be a prince, or a king." She tossed her head and laughed angrily, "King of the toads."

"What is there about Josephine's machine that is indisputably your father's invention and not Marco Celere's?"

"Why do you care?"

"I am driving a machine your father invented. I have a strong sense of your father's genius and his skills and maybe his dreams. I don't think they should be stolen from him, particularly as he is not here to defend himself. Can you give me something I can use to defend him?"

Danielle closed her eyes and knitted her brow. "I understand," she said. "Let me think . . . You see, your *monoplano*, she was made later. After Marco made his copy. Marco is like a sponge. He remembers everything he ever sees but never has his own idea. So Marco's *monoplano* has no improvements that my father made in yours."

"Like what? What did he improve? What did he change?"

"*Alettoni.*"

"But they look exactly the same. I compared them."

"Look again," she said. "Closer."

"At what?"

"*Cardine*. How do you say? Pivot. Hinge! Look how the *alettoni* hinge to your aeroplane. Then look at Josephine's."

Bell saw the startled expression on Andy Moser's face. "What is it, Andy?"

"The boys were saying her flaps were lightly seated. The pintles were too small. That's why the flap fell off."

Bell nodded, thinking hard. "Thank you, Danielle," he said. It had been a productive visit. "We have to go. Are they treating you well?"

"Better, *grazie*. And I have lawyer." She turned to Andy and gave the mechanician a dazzling smile. "Thank you for visiting me, Andy." She extended her hand. Andy grabbed it and shook it hard. Danielle rolled her eyes at Bell and said, "Andy, when a lady gives you her hand, it is sometimes better to kiss it than shake it."

Bell said, "Andy, get the machine ready to start. I'll be there in a minute." He waited until Andy was out of earshot. "There is one other thing I must ask you, Danielle."

"What is it?"

"Were you ever in love with Marco Celere?"

"Marco?" she laughed. "Mr. Bell, you can't be serious."

"I have never met the man."

"I would love a sea urchin before I would love Marco Celere. A poisonous sea urchin. You have no idea how treacherous he is. He breathes lies as another man breathes air. He schemes, he pretends, he steals. He is *truffatore*."

"What is *truffatore*?"

"*Imbroglione*."

"What is *imbroglione*?"

"*Impostore! Defraudatore!*"

"A con man," said Bell.

"What is con man?" she asked.

"A confidence trickster. A thief who pretends to be your friend."

"Yes! That is Marco Celere. A thief who pretends to be your friend."

Isaac Bell's quick mind raced into high gear. A murdered thief whose body was never found was one sort of mystery. A murdered confidence man whose body disappeared was quite another. Particularly when Harry Frost had cried in bewildered anguish, "You don't know what they were up to."

Nor did you, Harry Frost, thought Bell. Not until after you tried to kill Marco Celere. That's why you didn't kill Josephine first. You didn't intend to kill her at all. That twisted desire came later, only after you learned something about them that you thought was even worse than seduction.

Bell was elated. It had been a most productive visit indeed. Although he still did not know what Marco and Josephine had been up to, he was sure now that Harry Frost was not merely raving.

He said, "Josephine told me that you wept that Marco stole your heart."

He was not surprised when Danielle answered, "Marco must have told her that lie. I've never met the girl."

Danielle helped Bell and Andy roll the *Eagle* to the far end of the asylum lawn and turned it into the wind. She gripped the cane tail skid, as Andy spun the propeller, and held fast, retarding its forward motion while he struggled to hold it back and scramble aboard at the same time. She was strong, Bell noticed, and when it came to flying machines she knew her business.

Bell cleared the asylum wall and followed the rail line to its connector to the New York Central line and followed the tracks to the Castleton-on-Hudson railroad station. Passing high over the main street, he saw white horses pulling fire engines and a close formation of brass horns and tubas gleaming in the sunlight.

A fire department marching band was heading up the street, leading a horde of people, in the direction of the hayfield where Josephine's machine was being repaired. They passed a brick schoolhouse, and the doors flew open and hundreds of children streamed out to join the parade. The word had gotten around, Bell realized. The whole town was coming to welcome her, and there were more people in the parade than would fit on the field.

Bell raced the mile to the hayfield, put down on it, and ran to warn his detectives. "The whole town's coming to greet Josephine. They let the kids out of school. We'll be stuck here all night if we don't go now."

23

JOSEPHINE WAS FRANTIC, "Hurry it up!" she cried to the mechanicians.

"I'll drive you down the road," said Bell. "Give them a speech. Let them see you so they won't mob the field."

"No," she said. "They don't want to see me, they want to touch the machine. I saw it happen in California last year. They wrote their names on the wings and poked pencils in the fabric."

"Their parents are coming, too."

"The parents were worse. They were tearing off parts for souvenirs."

"I'll block," said Bell.

He sent the Rolls-Royce roadster and the Thomas to try to intercept the parade on the road, a temporary solution, at best, as the excited townspeople would simply stream around the autos. He ran his *Eagle* on the ground to the head of the field to further distract them.

Small boys, who had run ahead of the parade, jumped the ditch that separated the road from the hayfield. Bell saw there would be no stopping the children, who had no concept of the danger of whirling propellers before they got in her way.

Just when it seemed they would block her path, everyone looked up.

Bell heard the unmistakably authoritative roar of a six-cylinder Curtiss. Baronet Eddison-Sydney-Martin's bright blue headless pusher, which Bell had last seen floating in New York Harbor, sailed overhead, making a beeline for Albany.

"That man," said Andy, "has nine lives."

Josephine dropped the wrench and jumped aboard her Celere.

The boys stopped running and stood stock-still, staring at the sky. Two yellow monoplanes on the ground had seemed the epitome of excitement. But the sight of a flying machine actually in the air was more remarkable, and less likely than July Fourth at Christmas.

"Spin her over!" Josephine shouted.

Her Antoinette howled. The wing runners turned her around into the wind, and she raced across the cut hay and into the sky. Isaac Bell was right behind her, one step ahead of the welcoming committee.

BELL FOUND ALBANY'S ALTAMONT Fairground buzzing with rumors of sabotage. The mechanicians tending the machines in the racecourse infield were debating whether the wings of Sir Eddison-Sydney-Martin's headless Curtiss Pusher had been deliberately weakened. Bell went looking for the Englishman. He found him and his wife, Abby, at a party in a yellow tent that had been pitched beside Preston Whiteway's private railroad car.

The newspaper publisher intercepted Bell and whispered urgently, "I don't like these rumors. Strange as it may seem, they suggest the presence of a second lunatic, someone other than Harry Frost. I want you to investigate whether there is a murderer among us, or if Frost is lashing out at everyone."

"I've already started," said Bell.

"I want constant reports, Bell. Constant reports."

Bell glanced around for something to distract Whiteway. "Who is that handsome Frenchman talking to Josephine?"

"Frenchman? Which Frenchman?"

"The dashing one."

Whiteway plowed through his guests to plant himself proprietorially next to Josephine and glower at the Blériot driver, Renee Chevalier, who had gotten her to smile despite her poor showing.

Bell joined Eddison-Sydney-Martin, congratulated him on his survival, and asked how his headless pusher had come to fall in the harbor.

"One of my chaps claims he found a hole drilled clean through the strut that snapped, causing the wing to collapse."

"Sabotage?"

"Rubbish."

"Why do you say rubbish?"

"I say it was a knothole in a timber selected poorly by the builder, though they'll never admit to it."

"Could I see it?"

"I'm afraid it floated off while she was extricated from the water. We lost several pieces plucking her onto the barge."

Bell located the mechanician working on the blue pusher, an American from the Curtiss Company, who scoffed at the knot explanation.

"If it wasn't a knot," Bell asked, "could someone have accidentally drilled a hole and covered it over to hide the mistake?"

"No."

"Why not?"

"No flying-machine maker would take the chance. They'd own

up to their mistake and replace the part even if it came out of their own pocket. Look, Mr. Bell, say a house carpenter mistakenly bores a hole in a board. He can plug it up, caulk it, paint it over, and no one's the wiser. But a flying-machine strut is a whole 'nother story. We all know that if something breaks up there, down she goes."

"Down she went," said Bell.

"Could have been murder. The Englishman's darned lucky they fished him out of the drink in one piece."

"Why do you suppose he insists it was a knothole?"

"The baronet is a babe in the woods. He can't imagine anyone doing him harm to win the race, just like he can't imagine a bird-man wanting to win it to collect the fifty thousand bucks. He's always saying 'the winning is prize enough,' at least when he's not saying 'the race is the prize.' Drives the boys nuts. He's, like, above it all, if you know what I mean, having a title and a rich wife. But the thing is, it's not fair to Mr. Curtiss. Glenn Hammond Curtiss would never let a patch job leave the factory."

"Was the pusher left unattended the night before the race started?"

"Along with all the others at Belmont Park. Your 'aviatrix' was the only one who had guards, but that's 'cause of the husband, I hear."

"So if neither a knothole nor a mistakenly drilled hole would ever get out of the Curtiss factory, how do you think that hole got in that broken strut?"

"Sabotage," said the mechanician. "Like everyone says. Bore a hole where we wouldn't see it. Where fabric lapped over it or a fitting concealed it. It happened to his Farman, too, didn't it? And look what happened to the Platov engine. Those were sabotage, right?"

"They were sabotage," Bell agreed.

"Excepting I don't see what none of them smashes had to do with Josephine's crazy husband. Do you, Mr. Bell?"

Bell pressed two dollars into the mechanician's hand. "Here, buy the boys a drink."

"Not 'til we reach San Francisco. We're sleeping stone-cold sober under our pusher from now on. One man awake all night."

Bell put his mind to the unsettling thought that of three acts of sabotage, only one could be connected to Harry Frost. Three acts of sabotage since the racers gathered at Belmont Park. Sir Eddison-Sydney-Martin twice a victim, Platov and poor Judd the mechanician the third.

Sir Eddison-Sydney-Martin's first smash had been so clearly a distraction engineered by Harry Frost to kill Josephine.

But how could he blame the second attack on Eddison-Sydney-Martin on Harry Frost? What would Frost get out of Eddison-Sydney-Martin smashing? Just as he had wondered back at Belmont, what would Harry Frost get out of Dmitri Platov's engine jumping the track and killing a mechanician? Was Frost attacking the entire race instead of concentrating on killing his wife? That didn't make sense at this stage. Frost was too single-minded to spread himself thin. He would concentrate on killing his wife first, a crime which, if successful, would have the collateral effect of besmirching Preston Whiteway's race as well.

But to what purpose had Platov's engine been destroyed by a saboteur not employed by Frost? And to what purpose had the headless pusher been made to smash?

To eliminate a potentially strong competitor, seemed the likeliest answer.

Who would gain? Three possibilities hovered in Bell's mind,

two likely, one odd but not entirely unlikely. The saboteur could be a competitor—one of the birdmen—eliminating his strongest rivals. Or the saboteur could be a gambler trying to throw the race by getting rid of front-runners. Or, oddly, it could be the race sponsor himself trying to generate publicity.

The likeliest was a competitor trying to gain an edge by eliminating his strongest rivals. Fifty thousand dollars was a huge prize, more money than a workingman would earn in a lifetime.

But the money wagered as the race progressed across the country would be even more than could be made by fixing a horse race. High rollers like Johnny Musto could rake it in.

Preston Whiteway presented a third, strange possibility. Bell could not forget that the publisher had stated unabashedly that the best thing that could happen to keep people excited about the race would be half the male contestants smashing to the ground before Chicago. "A natural winnowing of the field," as he had put it coldly, "will turn it into a contest that pits only the best airmen against plucky tomboy Josephine."

Too far-fetched? But was Preston Whiteway above engineering aeroplane smashes to sell newspapers? Truth, facts, and moral decency hadn't stopped him from trying to start a war with Japan over the Great White Fleet. Nor had they restrained him from using the sinking of the battleship *Maine* to incite the Spanish-American War.

JOSEPHINE JOSEPHS FELL farther behind on the one-hundred-forty-five-mile leg from Albany to Syracuse when the hastily re-paired *alettone* seized up, and its entire mounting had to be replaced.

Then she lost half a day between Syracuse and Buffalo when the Antoinette blew a cylinder.

Isaac Bell reminded her that she was not the only competitor running into difficulty. Three aeroplanes were already out of the race. A big Voisin tangled terminally with a pasture fence, a fast Ambroise Goupy biplane broke apart when a down current dropped it into a stand of trees short of the field where it was attempting to alight, and the formidable Renee Chevalier splashed into the Erie Canal, reducing his Blériot to matchwood, and nearly drowned in the shallow water, unable to stand or swim having broken both legs.

Josephine, whom Bell had noticed had become rather standoff-ish ever since they left Belmont, surprised him with one of her exuberant grins that made her look much more herself. "Thanks for the thought, Isaac. I guess I should be grateful I haven't broken any bones yet."

Bell hired a third mechanician—a skillful Chicago boy named Eustace Weed, who had lost his job on the ruined Voisin—to keep his *Eagle* running. That gave Andy spare time to investigate the mechanical cause of each of the smashes, with an eye to pinning down evidence of sabotage. The meticulous policeman's son gathered evidence carefully, and reported that since Eddison-Sydney-Martin's smash into New York Harbor most accidents had a legitimate mechanical explanation for what went wrong. The possible exception was Chevalier's, but key parts of his machine were on the bottom of the Erie Canal.

Bell followed up by questioning the mechanicians. Who was near the machine? Who was in your hangar car? Any strangers? None they remembered. Sometimes the mechanicians found evidence to show the Van Dorns—a broken strut, a crushed fuel line, a kinked stay wire—sometimes there was none.

Preston Whiteway kept railing at Bell that there was "a murderer among us." Bell kept his counsel, knowing that Whiteway could be him—not a murderer in the strictest sense but a cold-blooded saboteur with little regard for the fate of the drivers when they smashed.

As the racers struggled west, smashes grew increasingly common. Machines faltered, winds sprang up with no warning, and birdmen made mistakes. Others suffered breakdowns that added hours to their time. Joe Mudd's sturdy red Liberator was leaking so much oil that the entire front of the machine turned black. Then it nearly killed him when the oil caught fire over Buffalo. Mudd was luckier than Chet Bass. Bass's Army Signal Corps Wright Flyer skidded sideways on landing at Erie, Pennsylvania, throwing him thirty feet across the grass.

Bell listened closely to the heated discussions that followed. The fact Bass would lose two days in the hospital with a brain concussion prompted the birdmen and mechanicians to debate the value of installing belts to keep the drivers from falling off their machines. An Austrian aristocrat flying a Pischof monoplane ridiculed the "cowardly" idea of strapping in with a belt. Many agreed that belting on would be unmanly. But Billy Thomas, the race-car driver who had proven his bravery repeatedly on the raceways before learning how to fly the Vanderbilt syndicate's big Curtiss Twin Pusher, announced that the Austrian could go to hell, he would wear a belt.

The day he did, a Great Lakes gale blew his Curtiss against a railroad semaphore mast atop a signal tower on a depot building. The Curtiss ricocheted into twenty strands of telegraph wire and bounced back through the second-floor windows of the signal tower.

Billy Thomas's belt kept him in the wreckage, but he was nearly cut in half by the force of the sudden stop against the rigid leather. Internal organs ruptured, he was out of the race.

Discussion that night at the Cleveland Fairgrounds shifted toward the concept of elastic belts. Mechanicians got busy tinkering with the thick rubber bands already on hand to spring the aeroplanes' wheels.

The Austrian aristocrat still scoffed. The next day, a gust heeled his Pischof sharply, and he fell off the monoplane a thousand feet over Toledo, Ohio.

At the funeral, Eddison-Sydney-Martin announced that his wife insisted "vehemently" that he be strapped onto his aeroplane, wearing a broad belt fashioned from a horse sling.

Josephine's and Isaac Bell's similar craft had them seated deeper within the fuselage, making falling off slightly less likely. Josephine ignored Preston Whiteway's pleas that she wear a belt. Having survived a smash in a burning biplane, she explained, she was afraid of being trapped.

Isaac Bell, at Marion Morgan's suggestion, instructed Andy to anchor a wide motorcyclist's belt to the *Eagle* with rubber bands. Sheathed next to one of the bands was a razor-sharp hunting knife.

NOTHING WAS HEARD NOR SEEN of Harry Frost since he escaped from Isaac Bell under the Weehawken piers. Bell suspected that Frost was waiting for the race to reach Chicago. Chicago was where he had begun his meteoric rise to the criminal pinnacle from which he had launched his legitimate fortune. In no other city on the continent was Frost better established with gang associates and corrupt politicians. In no other city had he so deeply infiltrated the police.

Try it, Bell thought grimly. The Van Dorn Detective Agency had started in Chicago, too. They, too, knew the city cold. When the race was stopped in Gary, Indiana, by lakeshore storms that the Weather Bureau predicted would last for days, he went ahead by train to scout the city.

"We'll beat him if he tries it here," Bell vowed to Joseph Van Dorn while conferring by long-distance telephone from the agency's Palmer House Chicago headquarters.

Van Dorn, who was in Washington, reminded Bell that he had promised to keep a clear head.

Bell changed the subject to sabotage. Van Dorn listened closely, then observed, "The weakness of that line of inquiry is that flying machines are perfectly capable of smashing without help from miscreants."

"Except," Bell retorted, "in the cases of Eddison-Sydney-Martin and Renee Chevalier, and even Chet Bass, it's the front-runners who are smashing. Soon as a fellow pulls ahead of the pack, something goes wrong."

"Steve Stevens hasn't smashed yet. I read here in the *Washington Post* that Stevens holds the lead."

"Josephine is catching up."

"How much have you bet on her?"

"Enough to buy my own detective agency if I win," Bell answered darkly.

In fact, the newspapers were starting to take notice that a bird-man heavier than the rotund President Taft was flying faster than five men who tipped the scales at half his weight and a woman who barely weighed a third.

"According to the *Post*," Van Dorn chuckled, "the *dark horse* is the heaviest horse."

Bell had seen similar headlines in Cleveland.

SEVEN DAYS FROM NEW YORK TO CHICAGO?

the *Plain Dealer* speculated breathlessly, before the weather gods put the brakes on overoptimism.

MIRACLE FLIGHT. HEAVYWEIGHT COTTON FARMER
STILL IN LEAD.

"You've got to hand it to Whiteway," Van Dorn said. "He's pulling a regular P. T. Barnum. The whole country's talking about the race. Now that the other papers have no choice but to cover it, they're backing favorites and smearing rivals. And everyone's got an opinion. The sportswriters say that Josephine couldn't possibly win because women have no endurance."

"The bookmakers agree with them."

"Republican papers say that labor should not rise above its station, much less fly. Socialist papers demand aristocrats stay on the ground, as the air belongs to all. They're all calling your friend Eddison-Sydney-Martin the 'lucky British cat' for his nine-lives habit of surviving smashes."

"As Whiteway told us, they love the underdog."

"I'll grab a train," said Van Dorn. "I'll catch up in Chicago. Meantime, Isaac, keep in mind, sabotage or no, our first job is protecting Josephine."

"I'm going back to Gary. The weather ought to break soon."

Bell rang off with much to ponder. While keeping the clear head he promised, he could not ignore the evidence that more was afoot than Harry Frost's murderous attacks on Josephine. Something else was going on, something perhaps bigger, more complicated, than one angry man trying to kill his wife. There was a second job to do, another crime to solve, before it wrecked the race. Not only did he have to stop Harry Frost, he had to solve a crime that he did not yet know what it was, or would be.

24

ISAAC BELL WIRED DASHWOOD IN SAN FRANCISCO, repeating his earlier order to investigate Di Vecchio's suicide. In addition, he wanted to know what Marco Celere had done when he first arrived from Italy.

His telegraph caught Dashwood at a rare moment when the dogged young investigator was not out in the field. Dashwood wired back immediately.

APOLOGIZE DELAY. DI VECCHIO SUICIDE COMPLICATED.

MARCO CELERE ARRIVED SAN FRANCISCO. TRANSLATOR FOR

ROMAN NEWSPAPER CORRESPONDENT TOURING CALIFORNIA.

Isaac Bell read the telegram twice.

"Translator?"

Josephine told him it had been difficult to communicate with Marco Celere. She couldn't understand his accent.

Miss Josephine? Bell smiled to himself. What are you up to? Were you trying to throw off suspicion about cheating on Harry Frost? Were you assuring your new benefactor Preston Whiteway and his censorious mother that your heart was pure? Or were you covering for Marco Celere?

WHEN DETECTIVE JAMES DASHWOOD heard the opening notes of the opera aria "Celeste Aida" pierce the fog on San Francisco Bay, he told the nuns he had brought with him, "They're coming."

"Why are the fishermen singing Verdi?" asked Mother Superior, gripping tightly the arm of a beautiful young novitiate who spoke Italian.

Dashwood had led them onto the new Fisherman's Wharf, where they were surrounded by water they could not see. The cold murk coiled around them, chilling their lungs and wetting their cheeks.

"The fishermen sing to identify their boats in the fog," the slim, boyish Dashwood answered. "So I am told, though I personally have a theory that they navigate by listening to their voices echo from the shore."

Finding an Italian translator in San Francisco had not been difficult. The city was filled with Italian immigrants fleeing their poor and crowded homeland. But finding one that clannish, frightened old-world fishermen would talk to had thus far been impossible. Schoolteachers, olive oil and cheese importers, even a fellow from the chocolate factory next to the wharf, had encountered a wall of silence. This time would be different, Dashwood hoped. It had taken a warm introduction from the abbot of a wealthy monastery down the coast with whom he had dealings in the course of the Wrecker investigation, plus his own promise of an extortionate contribution to the convent's poor box, to persuade Mother Superior to bring the girl to Fisherman's Wharf to translate his questions and the fishermen's answers.

The singing grew louder. Ship horns resonated deep bass counterpoint, and tug whistles piped, as unseen vessels made their cautious way about the invisible harbor. The fog thinned and thickened in shifting patches. The long black hull of a four-masted ship materialized suddenly and just as suddenly disappeared. A tall steamer passed, transparent as a ghost, and vanished. A tiny green boat under a lateen sail took form.

"Here they come," said Dashwood. "Pietro and Giuseppe."

"Which has one arm?" asked Mother Superior.

"Giuseppe. He lost it to a shark, I was told. Or a devilfish."

The beautiful Maria made the sign of the cross. Dashwood said soothingly, "That's what they call the octopus."

Giuseppe scowled when he saw the detective who had visited Fisherman's Wharf so often, some thought he was buying fish for a wholesaler. But when his sea-crinkled eyes fell on the nuns' black habits, he crossed himself and nudged Pietro, who was preparing to throw a line around a cleat, and Pietro crossed himself, too.

Better, thought Dashwood. At least they weren't throwing fish heads at him, which was how his previous visit had ended.

"What do you want Maria to inquire of them?" Mother Superior asked.

"First, is it true they overheard an argument in the street outside their rooming house between two inventors of flying machines?"

"And if they did?"

"Oh, they did, for sure. The trick will be to convince them that I mean no harm and am merely trying to right a wrong, and that it has nothing to do with them nor will it cause them any trouble."

Mother Superior—a straight-talking Irishwoman who had led her convent through the recent earthquake and fires and taken in refugees like Maria from displaced orders whose motherhouses had tumbled down—said, "Maria will have her hands full convincing them of half that, Detective Dashwood."

AFTER WAITING OUT THREE DAYS of wind and rain in a muddy Gary, Indiana, fairground, the Whiteway Atlantic-to-Pacific Cross-Country Air Race took to the air in hopes of reaching Chicago's Illinois National Guard Armory ahead of another storm. In the bleachers erected along the broad avenue that served as the armory's parade ground, the impatient spectators were read a telegraph message that said thunder and lightning had driven the aviators back to the ground at Hammond.

The National Guard's fifty-piece brass marching band played to soothe the crowd. Then local aviators took to the air in early-model Wright Fliers to entertain them by attempting to drop plaster "bombs" on a "battleship" drawn in chalk in the middle of the avenue. The cobblestones were splotched with broken plaster when, finally, another message echoed from the megaphone.

The sky over Hammond had cleared. The racers were off the ground again.

An hour later, a shout went up.

"They're here!"

All eyes fixed on the sky.

One by one, the flying machines straggled in. Steve Stevens's white biplane was in the lead. It circled the parapet of the fortress-like armory, descended to the broad avenue, and bounced along the cobbles, its twin propellers blowing clouds of plaster dust. A company of soldiers in dress uniforms saluted, and an honor guard presented arms.

———

TWO VAN DORN PROTECTIVE SERVICES operators guarding the roof of the armory were leaning in the notches of the parapet, gazing at the sky. Behind them, a broad-shouldered, heavyset figure emerged silently from the penthouse that covered the stairs, circled a skylight and another penthouse that enclosed the elevator machinery, and crept close.

"If I were Harry Frost coming up the stairs I just climbed," his voice grated like a coal chute, "you boyos would be dead men."

The PS operators whirled around to see "Himself," the grim-visaged Mr. Joseph Van Dorn.

"And the murdering swine would be free to kill the lady bird-man the agency is being paid good money to protect."

"Sorry, Mr. Van Dorn." Milago ducked his head contritely.

Lewis had an excuse. "We thought the National Guard soldiers guarded their own stairs."

"The Sunday soldiers of the National Guard," the livid Van Dorn growled sarcastically, "emerge from their mamas' homes to defend the city of Chicago against rioting labor strikers and foreign invaders from Canada. They wouldn't recognize Harry Frost if they met him in an alley. Nor would they know how to conduct their business in an alley. *That's why you're here.*"

"Yes, sir, Mr. Van Dorn," they chorused.

"Do you have your posters?"

They whipped out Harry Frost wanted posters, with and without a beard.

"Do you have your pistols?"

They opened their coats to show holstered revolvers.

"Stay sharp. Watch the stairs."

———

DOWN ON THE PARADE GROUND, Marco Celere—disguised as Dmitri Platov—stood shoulder to shoulder with the mechanicians who had come ahead on their support trains. The mechanicians were anxiously scanning the sky for signs of more bad weather.

Celere clapped enthusiastically when Steve Stevens landed first—the least Platov would be expected to do. But all the while that he was smiling and clapping, he imagined fleets of flying machines mowing down the soldiers with machine guns and demolishing their red brick armory by raining dynamite from the sky.

25

THE SLAUGHTER FROM THE HEAVENS that Marco Celere dreamed of would demand flying machines not yet built. Such warships of the sky would have two or three, even four, motors on enormous wings and carry many bombs for long distances. Smaller, nimble escort machines would protect them from counterattack.

Celere was fully aware that his was not a new idea. Visionary artists and cold-blooded soldiers had long imagined speedy airships capable of carrying many passengers, or many bombs. But other men's ideas were his lifeblood. He was a sponge, as Danielle Di Vecchio had screamed at him. A thief and a sponge.

So what if Dmitri Platov, the fictional Russian aeroplane mechanician, machinist, and thermo engine designer, was his only original invention? An Italian proverb said it all: Necessity is the mother of invention. Marco Celere *needed* to destroy his competitors' flying machines to guarantee that Josephine won the race with his machine. Who better to sabotage them than helpful, kindly "Platov"?

Celere was truly an expert toolmaker, with a peculiar talent for picturing the finished product at the outset. The gift had set him above common machinists and mechanicians when he apprenticed at age twelve in a Birmingham machine shop—a position that his father, an immigrant restaurant waiter, had procured by seducing the owner's wife. When metal stock was put on a lathe to be turned into parts, the other boys saw a solid block of metal. But Marco could visualize the finished part even before the stock started spinning. It was as if he could see what waited inside. Releasing the part waiting inside was a simple matter of chiseling away the excess.

It worked in life, too. He had seen inside Di Vecchio's first monoplane a vision of Marco Celere himself winning contracts to build warplanes to defeat Italy's archenemy, Turkey, and seize the Turkish Ottoman Empire's colonies in North Africa.

Soon after the machine he copied had smashed, he saw vindication "waiting inside" a luxurious special train that rolled into San Francisco's First California Aerial Meet. Off stepped Harry Frost and his child bride. The fabulously wealthy couple—the heavy bomber and the nimble escort—richer by far than the King of Italy—had given him a second chance to sell futuritial war machines.

Josephine, desperate to fly aeroplanes and starved for affection, was seduced without difficulty. Remarkably observant, decisive, and brave in the air, she was easily led down on earth, where decisiveness turned impulsive, and where she seemed curiously unable to predict the consequences of her actions.

Along had come the Whiteway Cup Cross-Country Air Race to prove his aeroplanes were the best. They had to be. He had copied only the best. He had no doubt that Josephine would win with her flying skill and with him sabotaging the competition. Winning would vindicate him in the eyes of the Italian Army. Past smashes would be forgotten when his warplanes vanquished Turkey, and Italy took Turkey's colonies in North Africa.

Two yellow specks appeared in the distance: Josephine, with Isaac Bell right behind and above, following like a shepherd. The crowd began cheering "Josephine! Josephine!" Whiteway was a genius, Celere thought. They truly loved their Sweetheart of the Air. When she won the cup, everyone in the world would know her name. And every general in the world would know whose flying machine had carried her to victory.

If Steve Stevens managed to finish, all the better—Celere would sell the Army heavy bombers as well as nimble escorts. But that was a very big if. Uncontrollable vibration, due to a failure to synchronize the twin engines, was shaking it to pieces. If Stevens smashed before he finished, Celere could blame it on the farmer's weight and poor flying. He had to admit that, by now, young Igor Sikorsky would have solved the vibration problem, but it was beyond Celere's talents. And it was too late in the game to steal those ideas even if Sikorsky were here instead of in Russia. If only the thermo engine he had bought in Paris had worked out, but that, too, had been beyond his talents.

THE VAN DORN PROTECTIVE SERVICES operators guarding the roof of the armory had kept a sharp eye on the door from the stairs, as instructed by Joseph Van Dorn, though every cheer that went up had drawn their attention to the parade ground and bleachers below and the next machine descending from the sky.

Now they lay unconscious at Harry Frost's feet, surprised by hammer blows of his fists after he sprang not from the stairs' penthouse but from the elevator's, where he had hidden since dawn.

Frost steadied a Marlin rifle on a square stone between two notches in the parapet and waited patiently for Josephine's head to completely fill the circle of his telescopic sight. She was coming straight at him, preparing to circle the armory as required by the rules, and he could see her through the blur of her propeller. This might not be as satisfying a kill as strangling her, but the Van Dorns had left him no opportunity to get close. And there were times a man did best to take what he could get. Besides, the telescope made it seem as if they were facing each other across the dinner table.

THE INSTANT ISAAC BELL saw the stone notches in the armory's crenellated parapet, he rammed his control wheel forward as hard as he could and made the *Eagle* dive. That roof was precisely where *he* would lay an ambush. The rules of the race guaranteed that Frost's victim would have to fly so close, he could hit her with a rock.

Driving with his right hand, he swiveled his Remington autoload rifle with his left. He saw a startled expression on Josephine's face as he hurtled past her. Ahead, among the stone notches, he saw the sun glint on steel. Behind the flash, half hidden in shadow, the bulky silhouette of Harry Frost was drawing a bead on Josephine's yellow machine.

Then Frost saw the *American Eagle* plummeting toward him.

He swung his barrel in Bell's direction and opened fire. Braced on the solid roof of the armory, he was even more accurate than he had been from the oyster boat. Two slugs stitched through the fuselage directly behind the controls, and Bell knew that only the extraordinary speed of his dive had saved him when Frost underestimated how swiftly he would pass.

Now it was his turn. Waiting until his spinning propeller was clear of the field of fire, the tall detective triggered his Remington. Stone chips flew in Frost's face, and he dropped his rifle and fell backwards.

Isaac Bell turned the *Eagle* sharply—too sharply—felt it start to spin, corrected before he lost control, and swept back at the armory. Frost was scrambling across the roof, leaping over the bodies of two fallen detectives. He had left his rifle where he had dropped it and was holding a hand to his eye. Bell fired twice. One shot shattered glass in the structure that housed the elevator machinery. The other nicked the heel of Frost's boot. The impact of the powerful centerfire .35 caliber slug knocked the big man off his feet.

Bell wrenched the *Eagle* around again, ignoring the protesting shriek of wind in the stays and an ominous grinding sound that vibrated through the controls, and raced back at the red brick building to finish him off. Across the roof, the door of the stair house flew open. Soldiers with long, clumsy rifles tumbled through it and fanned out, forcing Bell to hold his fire to avoid hitting them. Frost ducked behind the elevator house. As Bell roared past, he saw the killer open a door and slip inside.

He looked down at the avenue in front of the building, saw that Josephine had alighted and that there was space for him. Down he went, blipping his motor. He hit the cobblestones hard, spun half around, recovered, and, when the tail skid had slowed him nearly to a stop, jumped down and ran up the front steps of the armory, drawing his pistol.

An honor guard of soldiers in dress uniforms holding rifles at port arms blocked his way.

"Van Dorn!" Bell addressed their sergeant, a decorated man of action whose chestful of battle ribbons included the blue-and-yellow Spanish-American War Marine Corps Spanish Campaign Service Medal. "There's a murderer in the elevator house. Follow me!"

The old veteran sprang into action, running after the tall detective and calling upon his men. The inside of the armory was an enormous cathedral-like drill space as wide as the building and half as deep. The coffered ceiling rose as high as the roof. Bell raced to the elevator and stair shafts. The elevator doors were closed, and the brass arrow that indicated its location showed that the car was at the top of the shaft.

"Two men here!" he ordered. "Don't let him out if the car descends. The rest, follow me."

He bounded up four flights of stairs, with the soldiers clattering behind, reached the roof, and stepped outside just as Joe Mudd's red Liberator roared around the building, yards ahead of Sir Eddison-Sydney-Martin's blue Curtiss Pusher.

Bell ran to the elevator house. The door was locked.

"Shoot it open."

The soldiers looked to their sergeant.

"Do it!" he ordered. Six men pumped three rounds of rifle fire into the door, bursting it open. Bell bounded in first, pistol in hand. The machine room was empty. He looked through the steel grate floor. He could see into the open, unroofed car, which was still at the top of the shaft immediately under him. It, too, was empty. Harry Frost had disappeared.

"Where is he?" shouted the sergeant. "I don't see anyone. Are you sure you saw him in here?"

Isaac Bell pointed at an open trapdoor in the floor of the car.

"He lowered himself down the traction rope."

"Impossible. There's no way a man could hold on to that greasy cable."

Bell dropped into the elevator car and looked down through the trap. His sharp eyes spotted twin grooves in the grease that thickly coated the braided steel wire that formed the traction rope. He showed the sergeant.

"Where the heck did he get a cable brake?"

"He came prepared," said Bell, climbing up the side of the car to run for the stairs.

"Any idea who he was?"

"Harry Frost."

Fear flickered across the old soldier's face. "We were chasing Harry Frost?"

"Don't worry. He won't get far."

"Chicago's his town, mister."

"It's our town, too, and Van Dorns never give up."

THAT EVENING, Isaac Bell parked a big Packard Model 30 within pistol shot of the three-story mansion on Dearborn Street that housed the Everleigh Club, the most luxurious bordello in Chicago. He kept the bill of a chauffeur's cap low over his eyes and watched two heavyset Van Dorns climb the front steps. Out-of-town men who would not be recognized by the doorman and floor managers, they were dressed in evening clothes to appear to be customers wealthy enough to patronize the establishment. They rang the bell. The massive oak door swung open, the detectives were ushered in, and it swung shut behind them.

Bell watched the sidewalks for cops and gangsters.

Stealthy movement beside a pool of streetlamp light caught his attention. A slight figure, a young man in a wrinkled sack suit and bowler hat, eased past the light, then veered across the sidewalk on a route that took him close enough to the Packard for Bell to recognize him.

"Dash!"

"Hello, Mr. Bell."

"Where the devil did you come from?"

"Mr. Bronson gave me permission to report in person. Got me a free ride guarding the Overland Limited's express car."

"You're just in time. Do you have your revolver?"

James Dashwood drew from a shoulder holster a long-barreled Colt that had been smithed to a fare-thee-well. "Right here, Mr. Bell."

"Do you see those French doors on the third-floor balcony?"

"Third floor."

"Those stairs lead up from the balcony to the roof. I'd prefer not to engage in a public gun battle with anyone trying to escape from that room through those doors. Do you see the knob?"

Dashwood's keen eyes penetrated the shadows to focus on the barely visible two-inch bronze knob. "Got it."

"If it moves, shoot it."

Bell tugged his gold watch from its pocket and traced the second hand. "In twenty seconds, our boys will knock on the hall door."

Twenty-three seconds later, the knob turned. Dashwood, who had been trained by his mother—a former shootist with Buffalo Bill's Wild West Show—fired once. The knob flew from the door.

"Hop in," said Bell. "Let's hear what this fellow has to tell us."

Moments later, the heavyset Van Dorns exited the front of the bordello, balancing a man between them like friends helping a drunk. Bell eased the Packard along the curb, and they bundled the man into the backseat.

"Do you realize who I am?" he blustered.

"You are Alderman William T. Foley, formerly known as 'Brothel Bill,' less for your handsome mug than for your management prowess in the vice trade."

"I'll have you arrested."

"You're running for reelection on the reform ticket."

"The alderman was carrying these," said one of the detectives, presenting Bell with two pocket pistols, a dagger, and a sap.

"Where is Harry Frost?"

"Who?" Bill Foley asked innocently. Like any successful Chicago criminal who had graduated to public office, Foley could recognize Van Dorn detectives when seated between them in the back of a Packard. He was emboldened by the knowledge that they were less likely to shoot him in an alley or drown him in Lake Michigan than certain other parties in town. "Harry Frost? Never heard of him."

"You were spending his money tonight in the most expensive sporting house in Chicago. Money he paid you this afternoon to cash a five-thousand-dollar check at the First Trust and Savings Bank. *Where is he?*"

"He didn't leave a forwarding address."

"Too bad for you."

"What are you going to do, turn me in to the sheriff? Who happens to be my wife's uncle."

"You're running for reelection on the reform ticket. Our client publishes a newspaper in this town that you would not want as your enemy."

"I'm not afraid of Whiteway's papers," Foley sneered. "Nobody in Chicago gives a hang for that California pup who—"

Bell cut him off. "The people of Chicago may continue to put up with your bribery and corruption a bit longer, but they will draw the line at even a hint that Alderman William T. Foley would endanger the life of Miss Josephine Josephs, America's Sweetheart of the Air."

Foley wet his lips.

"Where," Bell repeated, "is Harry Frost?"

"Left town."

"Alderman Foley, do not try my patience."

"No, I ain't kidding. He left. I saw him leave."

"On what train?"

"In an auto."

"What kind?"

"Thomas Flyer."

Bell exchanged a glance with James Dashwood. The Thomas was a rugged cross-country auto, which was why Bell had chosen them for his support train. Such a vehicle—capable of traversing bad roads and open prairie, and even straddling railroad tracks when washouts and broken ground made all else impassable—would make Frost dangerously mobile.

"Which way did he go?"

"West."

"Saint Louis?"

Alderman Foley shrugged. "I got the impression more like Kansas City—where your air race is going, if I can believe what I read in the newspapers."

"Is he alone?"

"He had a mechanician and a driver."

Bell exchanged another look with Dash. There was five hundred miles of increasingly open country between Chicago and Kansas City, and Frost was prepared for the long haul.

"Both are gunmen," Foley added.

"Names?"

"Mike Stotts and Dave Mayhew. Stotts's the driver. Mayhew's the mechanician. Used to be a telegrapher 'til they caught him selling horse-race results to the bookies. Telegraphers are sworn to secrecy, you know."

"What I don't know," said Bell, frowning curiously at Foley, "is why you've turned unusually talkative all of a sudden, Alderman. Are you making this up as we go along?"

"Nope. I just know Harry ain't coming back. I done him his last favor."

"How do you know Frost isn't coming back?"

"Never thought I'd see the day, but you damned Van Dorns ran him out of town."

ISAAC BELL LED JAMES DASHWOOD into a chophouse to feed him supper while the kid reported what he had discovered in San Francisco.

"Last you wired me, Dash, you found that Celere and Di Vecchio were both in San Francisco last summer. Celere had arrived earlier, working as a translator, then built a biplane he subsequently sold to Harry Frost, who shipped it back to the Adirondacks and hired Celere to work on Josephine's flying machines at their camp. Both Celere and Di Vecchio had fled Italy one step ahead of their creditors. Di Vecchio killed himself. What new do we know?"

"They got in a fight."

Two immigrant Italian fishermen, Dashwood explained, had overheard a long and angry shouting match in the street outside their boardinghouse. Di Vecchio accused Marco Celere of stealing his wing-strengthening design.

"I already know that," said Bell. "Celere would claim it was the other way around. What else?"

"Di Vecchio started it, shouting that Celere copied his entire machine. Celere shouted back that if that was true, why had the Italian Army bought his machines and not Di Vecchio's?"

"What did Di Vecchio answer?"

"He said that Celere had poisoned the market."

Bell nodded impatiently. This, too, he had already heard from Danielle. "Then what?"

"Then he started yelling that Celere better keep his hands off his daughter. Her name is—"

"Danielle!" said Bell. "What did keeping his hands off his daughter have to do with the Italian Army buying his aeroplane design?"

"Di Vecchio shouted, 'Find another woman to do your dirty work.'"

"What dirty work?"

"He used a word that my translators found very hard to repeat."

"A technical word. *Alettone?*"

"Not technical. The girl knew what it meant, but she was afraid to say it in front of Mother Superior."

"Mother Superior?" Bell echoed, fixing his protégé with a wintery eye. "Dash, what have you been up to?"

"They were nuns."

"Nuns?"

"You always told me people want to talk. But you have to make them comfortable. The girl was the only Italian translator I could get the fishermen to talk to. Once they started telling the story, they wouldn't shut up. I think because the nun was so beautiful."

Isaac Bell reached across the tablecloth to slap Dashwood on the shoulder. "Well done!"

"But finding her was what took me so long. Anyway, she was translating great guns until that word stopped her dead. I pleaded with them. I even offered to pray with them, and she finally whispered, 'Gigolo.'"

"Di Vecchio accused Marco Celere of being a gigolo?"

Bell was hardly surprised, recalling that soon after Josephine and Harry Frost appeared in San Francisco the young bride had persuaded her husband to buy Celere's biplane. "Did he mention any specifics?"

"Di Vecchio said that Celere persuaded an Italian Army general's daughter to get him to buy his machine. From what they heard, the fisherman thought it wasn't the first time he'd gotten women to make deals for him."

"Did he accuse Celere of taking money from women?"

"There was some sort of engine he bought at a Paris air meet. It sounded like a woman put up the money. But in San Francisco, he was broke again. I think the Army deal fell through."

"The machine smashed with the general on it."

"*That's* why Di Vecchio kept yelling that Celere sold them a lousy flying machine and ruined it for other inventors."

"Did Di Vecchio accuse Celere of trying a gigolo stunt with Danielle?"

"That's what Di Vecchio was warning him off about. 'Don't touch my daughter.'"

"Sounds like your fishermen stumbled onto a heck of a shout fest."

"They didn't exactly stumble. They lived there, too."

Bell watched the young detective's face closely. "You've turned up a lot of information, Dash, maybe enough to make it worth the wait. Did you get a lucky break or did you know what you were looking for?"

"Well, that's the thing, Mr. Bell. Don't you see? They were arguing outside the hotel where Di Vecchio died. The night he died."

27

ISAAC BELL FIXED HIS PROTÉGÉ with an intense gaze, his mind leaping to the possibility that an angry argument had ended in murder. "The *same* night?"

"The same night," answered James Dashwood. "In the same house where Di Vecchio asphyxiated himself by blowing out a gaslight and leaving the gas on."

"Are you certain he killed himself?"

"I looked into the possibility. That's why I thought I should report face-to-face, to explain why I'm thinking what I'm thinking."

"Go on," Bell urged.

"I was already investigating the suicide, like you ordered, when I heard about the shouting match. You told me about Marco Celere's original name being Prestogiacomo. I discovered he was staying there under that name. You always say you hate coincidences, so I reckoned there had to be a connection. I spoke with the San Francisco coroner. He admitted that they don't do much investigating into how an Italian immigrant happens to die in San Francisco. There's a lot of them in the city, but they keep to themselves. So I wondered, what if I pretended that the dead man wasn't Italian but American? And pretended he wasn't poor but earning three thousand dollars a year, and had a house and maids and a cook? What questions would I ask when *that* fellow got gassed in a hotel room?"

Bell concealed a proud smile, and asked sternly, "What do you conclude?"

"Gas is a heck of a way to get away with killing someone."

"Did you turn up any clues that would support such speculation?"

"Di Vecchio had a big bump on his head, the night clerk told me, like he fell out of bed when he passed out. Could have woke up groggy, tried to get up, and fell. Or he could have been conked on the head by the same fellow who turned on the gas. Trouble is, we'll never know."

"Probably not," Bell agreed.

"Could I ask you something, Mr. Bell?"

"Shoot."

"Why did you ask me to investigate his suicide?"

"I'm driving the last flying machine Di Vecchio built. It does not operate like a machine made by a man who would kill himself. It is unusually sturdy, and it flies like a machine made by a man who loved making machines and was looking forward to making many more. But that is merely an odd feeling, not evidence."

"But if you add your odd feeling to the odd bump on Di Vecchio's head, together they're sort of like a coincidence, aren't they?"

"In an odd way," Bell smiled.

"But like you say, Mr. Bell, we'll never know. Di Vecchio's dead, and so's the fellow who might have conked him."

"Maybe . . ." said Isaac Bell, thinking hard. "Dash? This engine in the Paris air meet that Di Vecchio said Celere bought with a woman's money. You said some sort of engine. What did you mean by 'some sort of engine'?"

Dashwood grinned. "That confused the heck out of the poor nuns. Threw them for a loop."

"Why?"

"The fishermen called it *polpo*. *Polpo* means 'octopus.'"

"What kind of engine is like an octopus?" asked Bell. "Eight-cylinder Antoinette, maybe."

"Well, they also call the octopus a devilfish. Only that doesn't make sense when it comes to engines."

Bell asked, "What happened when the nuns got confused?"

"The fishermen tried another word. *Calamaro*."

"What is that? Squid?"

"That's what Maria said it meant. Maria was the pretty nun."

"An engine like a squid or an octopus? They're quite different, actually: squid long and narrow with tentacles in back, octopus round and squat with eight arms. Dash, I want you to go to the library. Find out what Mr. Squid and Mr. Octopus have in common."

EUSTACE WEED, Andy Moser's Chicago-born helper who Isaac Bell had hired so Andy could spend time investigating the mechanical causes of the racers' smashes, asked for the evening off to say good-bye to his girl, who lived on the South Side.

"Just get back before sunrise," Andy told him. "If the weather holds, they'll be starting out for Peoria."

Eustace promised he'd be back in plenty of time—a promise

he knew he would keep if only because Daisy's mother would be sitting on the other side of the parlor door. His worst fears proved true. At nine p.m., Mrs. Ramsey called from the other room, "Daisy? Say good night to Mr. Weed. It's time for bed."

Eustace and the beautiful red-haired Daisy locked eyes, each certain it would be a better time for bed if Mother weren't there. But Mother was, so Eustace called, politely, "Good night, Mrs. Ramsey," and received a firm "Good night" through the closed door. In an unexpected flash of insight, Eustace realized that Mrs. Ramsey was not as coldheartedly unromantic as he had assumed. He took Daisy in his arms for a proper good-bye kiss.

"How long before you're back?" she whispered when they came up for air.

"We'll be racing three more weeks, if all goes well, maybe four. I hope I'll be home in a month."

"That's so long," Daisy groaned. Then out of nowhere she asked, "Is Josephine pretty?"

In his second wise flash of insight that evening, Eustace answered, "I didn't notice."

Daisy kissed him hard on the mouth and pressed her body against his until her mother called through the door, *"Good night!"*

Eustace Weed stumbled down the stairs, his head reeling and his heart full.

Two toughs were blocking the sidewalk, West Side boys.

It looked to Eustace like he had a fight on his hands, and one he wasn't likely to win. Running for it seemed the better idea. He was tall and thin and could probably leave them in the dust. But before he could move, they spread out and, to his astonishment and sudden fear, flashed open flick-knives.

"The boss wants to see you," one said. "You gonna come quiet?"

Eustace looked at the knives and nodded his head. "What's this about?"

"You'll find out."

They fell in on either side and walked him a couple of blocks to a street of saloons, where they entered a dimly lighted establishment and led him through the smoky barroom to a backroom office. The saloonkeeper, a barrel-bellied man in a bowler hat, vest, and necktie, sat behind a desk. On it, heated by a candle, bubbled a little cast-iron pot of boiling paraffin. It gave off a smell similar to the burnt castor scent of Gnome engine exhaust. Beside the pot was a short length of copper pipe, a water pitcher with a narrow spout, a leather sack a little longer than the pipe, and a vicious-looking blackjack with a flexible handle and a thick head.

"Shut the door."

The toughs did and stood by it. The saloonkeeper beckoned Eustace to approach his desk. "Your name is Eustace Weed. Your girl is Daisy Ramsey. She's a looker. Do you want to keep her that way?"

"What do you—"

The saloonkeeper picked up the blackjack and dangled the heavy end so that it swung side to side like a pendulum. "Or do you want to come home from the air race to find her face beaten to a pulp?"

In his first flush of panic, Eustace figured it was mistaken identity. They were thinking he owed gambling debts, which of course he didn't because he never gambled except when shooting pool, and he was too good at it to call it gambling. Then

he realized it wasn't mistaken identity. They knew he was working on the air race. Which meant they also knew that he was
working on the flying machine owned by the chief investigator of the Van Dorn Detective Agency. And they knew about
Daisy.

Eustace started to ask, "Why—" He was thinking this had to
do with Harry Frost, the madman trying to kill Josephine.

Before he could finish his question, the saloonkeeper interrupted in a silky voice. He had eyes that reflected the light as if
they were as hard and polished as ball bearings. "Why are we
threatening you? Because you're going to do something for us. If
you do it, you will come home to Chicago and find your girl
Daisy just like you left her. You got my promise, the word goes
out tonight: anybody so much as whistles at her, he's dragged in
here to answer to me. If you *don't* do what we ask, well . . . I'll let
you guess. Actually, you don't have to guess. I've already told you.
Understand?"

"What do you want?"

"I want you to tell me that you *understand* before we go on to
what we *want*."

Eustace saw no way out of this mess other than to say, "I
understand."

"Do you understand that if you go to the cops, you'll never
know which cops are our cops."

Eustace had grown up in Chicago. He knew about cops and
gangsters, and he'd heard the old stories about Harry Frost. He
nodded that he understood. The saloonkeeper raised an inquiring eyebrow and waited until Eustace repeated out loud, "I
understand."

"Good. Then you and Daisy will live happily ever after."

"When will you tell me what you want?"

"Right now. Do you see this here pot?"

"Yes."

"Do you see what's in there boiling?"

"It smells like paraffin."

"That's what it is. It's paraffin wax. Do you see this?" he held up the three-inch length of three-quarter-inch copper tubing.

"Yes."

"Do you know what it is?"

"It's a length of copper pipe."

"Blow out the candle."

Eustace looked puzzled.

The saloonkeeper said, "Lean down here and blow out the candle so the paraffin wax stops boiling."

Eustace leaned down, wondering if it was a trick, and they were going hit him or throw the boiling wax in his face. The back of his neck tingled as he blew out the candle. No one hit him. No one threw hot wax in his face.

"Good. Now we'll wait a moment for it to cool."

The saloonkeeper sat in complete silence. The toughs at the door shifted on their feet. Eustace heard a murmur of conversation from the saloon and a bark of laughter.

"Pick up the copper tube."

Eustace picked it up, more curious now than afraid.

"Dip one end in the paraffin. Careful, don't burn your fingers on the pot. Still hot."

Eustace dipped the tube in the paraffin, which was congealing and growing solid as it cooled.

"Hold it there . . ." After sixty seconds the saloonkeeper said, "Take it out. Good. Dip it in that water pitcher to cool it . . . Hold it there. All right, now you gotta move quick. Turn it over so the wax plug is down . . . That's a plug you made, you see, the wax plugs that end of the tube. Do you see?"

"The bottom is plugged."

"Now take the pitcher and pour the water into the tube. Careful, it doesn't take much. What would you say that is, two tablespoons?"

"Just about," Eustace agreed.

"Now, holding it upright, not spilling it, take your finger of your other hand and dip it in the wax . . . Don't worry, it won't burn you . . . Still warm, might sting a little, is all."

Eustace dipped his index finger into the warm, pliable wax.

"Almost done," said the saloonkeeper. "Scoop up some wax on your finger and use it to plug the other end of the tube."

Eustace did as he was told, working the wax into the opening and smoothing the edges.

"Do it again, work it in a little more, make sure it is sealed watertight—*absolutely watertight*. Do you understand?"

"I understand."

"O.K., turn it over. Let's see if no water drips out."

Eustace turned it over tentatively and held it out the way he used to present A+ projects in shop class.

The saloonkeeper took it from his hand and shook it hard. The plugs held. No water escaped. He dropped it in the leather sack, tugged the drawstrings tight, and returned it to Eustace Weed. "Don't let it get so warm it melts the wax."

"What am I supposed to do with it?"

"Keep it out of sight 'til somebody tells you where to put it. Then put it where he tells you."

Utterly mystified, Eustace Weed weighed the sack in his hand and asked, "Is that all?"

"All? Your girl's name is Daisy Ramsey." The short, round saloonkeeper picked up the sap and slammed it on his desk so hard the pot jumped. "That is *all*."

"I understand." Eustace blurted quickly, though he understood very little, starting with why the saloonkeeper went through the whole rigmarole with the wax pot. Why didn't he just hand him the wax-sealed tube in the sack?

The man looked hard at him, then he smiled. "You wonder why all this?" He indicated the pot.

"Yes, sir."

"So if you lose that which I gave you, you got no excuse. You know how to make another. You're a flying-machine mechanician, top of the trade. You can make anything. So when someone tells you where to put it, you'll be ready to put it where he tells you when he tells you. Understand?"

"I understand."

"O.K., get outta here!"

He signaled the toughs.

"They'll see you safe out of the neighborhood. You're a valuable man now, we don't want folks wondering why you got bruises. But don't forget, don't let nobody see that there tube of water. Anybody starts asking questions, and the city of Chicago loses a pretty face."

They started him out the door. The saloonkeeper called, "By the way, if you're wondering what it is and how it'll work, don't. And if you happen to figure it out and you don't like it, remember Daisy's pretty little nose. And her eyes."

ISAAC BELL DROPPED DASHWOOD around the corner from the
Palmer House at a small hotel that gave out-of-town Van Dorns
a discount. Then he drove to the Levee District and parked on a
street that hadn't changed much in a decade. Motortrucks lined up
at the newspaper depot instead of wagons, but the gutter was still
paved with greasy cobbles, and the ramshackle buildings still
housed saloons, brothels, lodging houses, and pawnshops.

By the dim light of widely scattered streetlamps, he could make
out the intersection of old and new brick where Harry Frost's
dynamite had demolished the depot walls. A man was sleeping in
the doorway the frightened newsboys had huddled in. A street-
walker emerged from the narrow alley. She spotted the Packard
and approached with a hopeful smile.

Bell smiled back, looked her in the eye, and pressed a ten-dollar
gold piece into her hand. "Go home. Take the night off."

He did not believe for one minute that the Van Dorn Detective
Agency had run Harry Frost out of Chicago. The criminal mastermind had left town under his own steam for his own reasons.
For it was chillingly clear to Bell that Harry Frost was as adaptable
as he was unpredictable. Roving in that Thomas Flyer, the city
gangster would take deadly, free-ranging command of the Mid-
west's prairies and the vast plain beyond the Mississippi while the
politicians and bankers and crooks in his Chicago organization
covered his back, wired money, and executed his orders.

Bringing a telegrapher in the Thomas was a stroke of warped
genius. Harry Frost could send Dave Mayhew climbing up railroad
telegraph poles to tap into the wires, eavesdrop on the Morse alphabet, and tell him what the stationmasters were reporting about

the progress of the race. Diabolical, thought Bell. Frost had drafted hundreds of dedicated assistants to track Josephine for him.

A drunk rounded the corner, smashed his bottle in the gutter, and burst into song.

"Come Josephine, in my flying machine . . .
"Up, up, a little bit higher
"Oh! My! The moon is on fire . . ."

JAMES DASHWOOD CAUGHT UP with Isaac Bell one hundred and seventy miles west of Chicago in a rail yard near the Peoria Fairgrounds on the bank of the Illinois River. It was a sweltering, humid evening—typical of the Midwestern states, Bell informed the young Californian—and the smell of coal smoke and steam, creosote ties, and the mechanicians' suppers frying, hung heavy in the air.

The support trains were parked cheek by jowl on parallel sidings reserved for the race. Bell's was nearest the main line but for one other, a four-car special, varnished green and trimmed with gold, owned by a timber magnate who had invested in the Vanderbilt syndicate and had announced that he saw no reason not to ride along with the rolling party just because his entry smashed into a signal tower. After all, Billy Thomas was recuperating nicely, and was a true sportsman who would insist the show go on without him.

Whiteway's yellow six-car *Josephine Special* was on the other side of the *Eagle Special*, and Bell had had his engineer stop his train so that the two flying-machine support cars stood next to each other. Both had their auto ramps down for their roadsters, which were off foraging for parts in Peoria hardware stores or scouting the route ahead. Laughter and the ring of crystal could be heard from a dinner party that Preston Whiteway was hosting.

Dashwood found Bell poring over large-scale topographic maps of the terrain across Illinois and Missouri to Kansas City, which he had rolled down from his hangar-car ceiling.

"What have you got, Dash?"

"I found a marine zoology book called *Report on the Cephalopods.* Squid and octopuses are cephalopods."

"So I recall," said Bell. "What do they have in common?"

"Propulsion."

Bell whirled from the map. "Of course. They both move by spurting water in the opposite direction."

"Squid more than octopus, who tend more toward walking and oozing."

"They *jet* along."

"But what sort of motor would my fishermen be comparing them to?"

"Platov's thermo engine. He used the word 'jet.'" Bell thought on that. "So your fishermen overheard Di Vecchio accuse Celere of a being a gigolo because he took money from a woman to buy some sort of engine at a Paris air meet. A jet motor. Sounds like Platov's thermo engine."

A heavy hand knocked on the side of the hangar car, and a man stood perspiring copiously at the top of the ramp. "Chief Investigator Bell? I'm Asbury, Central Illinois contract man."

"Yes, of course. Come on in, Asbury." The contractor was a retired peace officer who covered the Peoria region on a part-time basis, usually for bank robbery cases. Bell offered his hand, introduced "Detective Dashwood from San Francisco," then asked Asbury, "What have you got?"

"Well . . ." Asbury mopped his dripping face with a red hand-kerchief as he composed his answer. "The race has brought a slew of strangers into town. But I've seen none the size of Harry Frost."

"Did any pique your interest?" Bell asked patiently. As he moved west with the race, he expected to encounter private de-tectives and law officers so laconic that they would judge the closemouthed Constable Hodge of North River to be recklessly loquacious.

"There's a big-shot gambler from New York. Has a couple of toughs with him. Made me out to be the Law right off."

"Broad-in-the-beam middle-aged fellow in a checkerboard suit? Smells like a barbershop?"

"I'll say. Flies were swarming his perfume like bats at sunset."

"Johnny Musto, out of Brooklyn."

"What's he doing all the way to Peoria?"

"I doubt he came for the waters. Thank you, Asbury. If you go to the galley car on Mr. Whiteway's train, tell them I said to rustle up some supper for you . . . Dash, go size up Musto. Any luck, he won't make you for a Van Dorn. You not being from New York," Bell added, although in fact Dashwood's best disguise was his altar boy innocence. "Give me your revolver. He'll spot the bulge in your coat."

Bell shoved the long-barreled Colt in his desk drawer. His hand flickered to his hat and descended holding his two-shot derringer. "Stick this in your pocket."

"That's O.K., Mr. Bell," Dashwood grinned. He flexed his wrist in a jerky motion that caused a shiny new derringer to spit from his sleeve into his fingers.

Isaac Bell was impressed. "Pretty slick, Dash. Nice little gun, too."

"Birthday present."

"From your mother, I presume?"

"No, I met a girl who plays cards. Picked up the habit from her father. He plays cards, too."

Bell nodded, glad the altar boy was stepping out. "Meet me back here when you're done with Musto," he said, and went looking for Dmitri Platov.

He found the Russian strolling down the ramp from Joe Mudd's hangar car, wiping grease from his fingers with a gasoline-soaked rag.

"Good evening, Mr. Platov."

"Good evening, Mr. Bell. Is hot in Peoria."

"May I ask, sir, did you sell a thermo engine in Paris?"

Platov smiled. "May *I* asking why *you* asking?"

"I understand that an Italian flying-machine inventor named Prestogiacomo may have bought some sort of a 'jet' engine at the Paris air meet."

"Not from me."

"He might have been using a different name. He might have called himself Celere."

"Again, not buying from me."

"Did you ever meet Prestogiacomo?"

"No. In fact, I am never hearing of Prestogiacomo."

"He must have made something of a splash. He sold a monoplane to the Italian Army."

"I am not knowing Italians. Except one."

"Marco Celere?"

"I am not knowing Celere."

"But you know who I mean?"

"Of course, the Italian making Josephine's machine and the big one I am working for Steve Stevens."

Bell shifted gears deliberately. "What do you think of the Stevens machine?"

"It would not be fair for me discussing it."

"Why not?"

"As you working for Josephine."

"I protect Josephine. I don't work for her. I only ask if you can tell me anything that might help me protect her."

"I am not seeing what Stevens's machine is doing with that."

Bell changed tactics again, asking, "Did you ever encounter a Russian in Paris named Sikorsky?"

A huge smile separated Platov's mutton-chop whiskers. "Countryman genius."

"I understand vibration is a serious problem with more than one motor. Might Sikorsky want your thermo engine for his machines?"

"Maybe one day. Are excusing me, please? Duty calling."

"Of course. Sorry to take so much of your time . . . Oh, Mr. Platov? May I ask one other question?"

"Yes?"

"Who was the one Italian you *did* know in Paris?"

"The professor. Di Vecchio. Great man. Not practical man, but great ideas. Couldn't make real, but great ideas."

"My Di Vecchio monoplane is a highflier," said Bell, wondering why Danielle said she didn't know of Platov. "I would call it an idea made real."

Platov shrugged enigmatically.

"Did you know Di Vecchio well?"

"Not at all. Only listening to lecture." Suddenly he looked around, as if confirming they were alone, and lowered his voice to a conspiratorial mutter. "About Stevens's two-motor biplane? You are correct. Two-motor vibrations very rattling. Shaking to pieces. Excusing now, please."

Isaac Bell watched the Russian parade across the infield, bowing to the ladies and kissing their hands. Platov, the tall detective thought, you are smoother than your thermo engine.

And he found it impossible to believe that the ladies' man never introduced himself to Professor Di Vecchio's beautiful daughter.

BELL CONTINUED STUDYING his topographic maps to pinpoint where Frost might attack. Dash returned, reporting he had spotted Johnny Musto, buying drinks for newspaper reporters.

"No law against that," Bell observed. "Bookies live on information. Like detectives."

"Yes, Mr. Bell. But I followed him back to the rail yard and saw him slipping the same reporters rolls of cash."

"What do you make of it?"

"If he's bribing them, what I can't figure out is what they would do for him in return for the money."

"I doubt he wants his name in the papers," said Bell.

"Then what does he want?"

"Show me where he is."

Dash pointed the way, saying, "There's a boxcar over by the river where the fellows are shooting dice. Musto's taking bets."

"Stick close enough to hear, but don't let him see you with me."

Bell smelled the Brooklyn gambler before he heard him when a powerful scent of gardenia penetrated the thicker odors of railroad ties and locomotive smoke. Then he heard his hoarsely whispered "Bets, gentlemen. Place your bets."

Bell rounded the solitary boxcar in a dark corner of the yard.

A marble-eyed thug nudged Musto.

"Why, if it ain't one of my best customers. Never too late to increase your investment, sir. How much shall we add to yer three thousand on Miss Josephine? Gotta warn youse, though, de odds is shifting. The goil commands fifteen-to-one, since some bettors are notin' that she's pullin' up on Stevens."

Bell's smile was more affable than his voice. "I'm a bettor who's wondering if gamblers are conspiring to throw the race."

"Me?"

"We're a long way from Brooklyn, Johnny. What are you doing here?"

Musto objected mightily. "I don't have to throw no race. Win, lose, draw, all de same to me. Youse a bettin' man, Mr. Bell. And a man of the woild, if I don't mistake youse. Youse know the bookie never loses."

"Not so," said Bell. "Sometimes bookies do lose."

Musto exchanged astonished glances with his bodyguards. "Yeah? When?"

"When they get greedy."

"What do youse mean by dat? Who's greedy?"

"You're bribing newspaper reporters."

"Dat's ridiculous. What could dos poor hack writers do for me?"

"Tout one flying machine over another to millions of readers placing bets," said Isaac Bell. "In other words, skew the odds."

"Oh yeah? And what machine would I happen to be toutin'?"

"Same one you've been touting all along: Eddison-Sydney-Martin's headless pusher."

"The Coitus is a flying machine of real class," Musto protested. "It don't need no help from Johnny Musto."

"But it's getting a lot of help from Johnny Musto regardless."

"Hey, it's not like I'm fixin' the race. I'm passin' out information. A public service, youse might call it."

"I would call that a confession."

"You can't prove nothin'."

Isaac Bell's smile had vanished. He fixed the gambler with a cold eye. "I believe you know Harry Warren?"

"Harry Warren?" Johnny Musto stroked his double chin. "Harry Warren? Harry Warren? Lemme think. Oh yeah! Ain't he de New York Van Dorn who spies on the gangs?"

"Harry Warren is going to wire me in two days that you reported to him at Van Dorn headquarters at the Knickerbocker Hotel at Forty-second Street and Broadway in New York City. If he doesn't, I'm coming after you—personally—with all four feet."

Musto's bodyguards glowered.

Bell ignored them. "Johnny, I want you to pass the word: betting fair and square on the race is fine with me, throwing it is not."

"Not my fault what other gamblers do."

"Pass the word."

"What good'll that do youse?"

"They can't say they weren't warned. Have a pleasant journey home."

Musto looked sad. "How'm I goin' ta get back ta New York in two days?"

Isaac tugged his heavy gold watch chain from his vest pocket, opened the lid, and showed Musto the time. "Run quick and you can catch the milk train to Chicago."

"Johnny Musto don't ride no milk train."

"When you get to Chicago, treat yourself to the Twentieth Century Limited."

"What about da race?"

"Two days. New York."

The gambler and his bodyguards hurried off, muttering indignantly.

James Dashwood climbed down from his listening post on the roof of the boxcar.

Bell winked. "There's one out of the way. But he's not the only high-rolling tinhorn following the race, so I want you to keep an eye on the others. You're authorized to place just enough bets to make your presence welcome."

"Do you think Musto will show up again?" Dash asked.

"He's not stupid. Unfortunately, the damage is done."

"How do you mean, Mr. Bell?"

"The reporters he bribed have already wired their stories. If, as I suspect, there's a saboteur trying to derail the front-runners, then bookie Musto has put Eddison-Sydney-Martin in his crosshairs."

29

ILLINOIS THUNDERSTORMS STRUCK AGAIN, cutting the race in half. The trailing fliers, those who had gotten a late start from Peoria due to mechanic failures and mistakes made by tiring birdmen, put down in Springfield. But the leaders, Steve Stevens and Sir Eddison-Sydney-Martin, defied the black clouds towering in the west and forged on, hoping to reach the racetrack at Columbia before the storms blew them out of the sky.

Josephine, midway between the leaders and the trailers, pushed ahead. Isaac Bell stuck with her, eyes raking the ground for Harry Frost.

The leaders' support trains steamed along with them, then shoveled on the coal to race ahead to greet them at the track with canvas shrouds to protect the aeroplanes from the rain and tent stakes and ropes to anchor them against the wind.

Marco Celere played his kind and helpful Dmitri Platov role to the hilt, directing Steve Stevens's huge retinue of mechanicians, assistants, and servants in the securing of the big white biplane. Then he scooped up three oilskin slickers and ran to help tie down Josephine's and Bell's machines as they dropped from a sky suddenly seared by bolts of lightning.

The twin yellow monoplanes bounced to a stop seconds ahead of a downpour.

Celere tossed a slicker to Josephine and another to Bell, who said, "Thanks, Platov," then shouted, "Come on, Josephine. The boys'll tie it down." He threw a long arm over her shoulder and dragged her away, saying to Platov, "Imagine reporting to Mr. Van Dorn that America's Sweetheart of the Air got struck by lightning."

"Here helping, not worrying." Platov pulled on his own slicker. Enormous raindrops started kicking up dust. For a moment they sizzled in the blazing heat. Then the sky turned black as night, and an icy wind blasted rain across the infield. The last of the spectators ran to the hotel attached to the grandstand.

Bell's men—Andy Moser and his helpers—dragged canvas over the *Eagle*.

Eustace Weed, the new mechanician Bell had hired in Buffalo, said, "That's O.K., Mr. Platov. We've got it."

Celere ran to help Josephine's ham-handed detective-mechanicians tie down hers and he was reminded how frustrating it was not to be able to work on Josephine's aeroplane—his aeroplane—to keep it flying at its best. Josephine was good, but not that good. He may be a *truffatore* confidence man, but if there was one skill he truly possessed, he was a fine mechanician.

Celere waited until the machines were covered and tied down and he was sure that Isaac Bell was not coming back from escorting Josephine to her private car. Then he ran through the pouring rain to where Eddison-Sydney-Martin's headless pusher was tied down. He made a show of checking the ropes, though it was not likely anyone could see him through the dark and watery haze. The baronet and his mechanicians had fled to their train. It was an opportunity to do mischief. But he had to work fast and do something unexpected.

Thunder pealed. Lightning struck the grandstand roof, and green Saint Elmo's fire trickled along the gutters and down the leaders. The next bolt struck in the center of the infield, and Marco Celere began to see the wisdom of Bell's retreat from Mother Nature. He ran for the nearest cover, a temporary wooden shed erected to supply the flying machines with gasoline, oil, and water.

Someone was sheltering in it ahead of him. Too late to turn away, he saw that it was the Englishman Lionel Ruggs, the baronet's chief mechanician and the chief reason why he had steered clear of the headless pusher, other than surreptitiously drilling a hole in its wing strut back at Belmont Park.

"Whatcha doin' to the guv's machine?"

"Just checking its ropes."

"Spent a long time checkin' ropes."

Celere ducked his head as if he were embarrassed. "O.K., you are catching me. I was looking at competition."

"Lookin' or doin'?" Ruggs asked coldly.

"Doing? What would I be doing?"

Lionel Ruggs stepped very close to him. He was taller than Celere, and bigger in the chest. He stared inquiringly into Celere's eyes. Then he cracked a mirthless smile.

"Jimmy Quick. I thought that was you hidin' in those curls."

Marco Celere knew there was no denying it. Ruggs had him dead to rights. It had been fifteen years, but they'd worked side by side in the same machine shop from ages fourteen to eighteen and shared a room under the eaves of the owner's house. Celere had always feared that he would bump into his past sooner or later. How many flying-machine mechanicians were there in the small, tight-knit new world of flying machines?

Jimmy Quick had been his English nickname, a good-natured play on Prestogiacomo that the English found so hard to pronounce. He had recognized Ruggs from a distance and stayed out of his way. Now he had stumbled, face-to-face, into him in a thunderstorm.

"What's this Russian getup?" Ruggs demanded. "I bet you been caught stealin' somethin', like you was in Birmingham. Doin' the old man's daughter was one thing—more power to you—but stealin' his machine tool design he worked on his whole life, that was low. That old man treated us good."

Celere looked around. They were alone. No one was near the shed. He said, "The old man's dream didn't quite work. It was a bust."

Ruggs turned red. "A bust because you stole it before he perfected it . . . It was you, wasn't it, drilled our wing strut?"

"Not me."

"I don't believe you, Jimmy."

"I don't care if you believe me or not."

Lionel Ruggs pounded his chest. "*I* care. The guv's a good man. He may be an aristocrat, but he's a good man, and he deserves to win, fair and square. He don't deserve to die in a smash caused by a schemin' little bludger like you."

Marco Celere looked around again and confirmed they were still alone. The rain was coming down harder, pounding the tin roof. He couldn't see six feet from the shed. He said, "You're forgetting I make machine tools."

"How could I forget that? That's what the old man taught us to do. Gave us a roof over our heads. Gave us breakfast, lunch, and tea. Gave us a good-paying trade. You paid him back by stealin' his dream. And you ruined it 'cause you were too damned lazy and impatient to make it right."

Celere reached under his slicker and took a slide rule from his coat. "Do you know what this is?"

"It's the slide rule you wave around with your disguise."

"Do you believe that my slide rule is only a slide rule?"

"I seen you wavin' it around. What of it?"

"Let me show you."

Celere raised the instrument to the thin light in the open door. Ruggs followed it with his eyes, and Celere whipped it back toward him like a violin bow. Ruggs gasped and clutched his throat, trying to hold in the blood.

"This one's a razor, not the one 'Dmitri Platov' waves around. A razor—just in case—and you are the case."

Ruggs went bug-eyed. He let go his throat and grabbed Celere. But there was no strength left in his hand, and he collapsed, spraying blood on the Italian.

Celere watched him dying at his feet. It was only the second time he had killed a man and it did not get easier, even if the effect was worthwhile. His hands were shaking, and he felt panic flood his body and threaten to squeeze his brain into a lump that could not think or act. He had to run. There was no place to get rid of the body, no place to hide it. The rain would stop, and he would be caught. He tried to form a picture of running. The rain would wash the blood that sprayed all over his slicker. But they would still chase him. He looked at the razor, and he suddenly pictured it cutting cloth.

Swiftly, he knelt and slashed at Ruggs's pockets, taking from them coin and a roll of paper money and a leather wallet with more paper money in it. He stuffed them in his pockets, slashed Ruggs's vest, and took his cheap nickel pocket watch. He looked over the body, saw gold, and took Ruggs's wedding ring. Then he ran into the rain.

There was no time for sabotage. If by a miracle he got away with murder, he would come back and try again.

ONE HUNDRED AND TWENTY MILES from Columbia, Illinois, but still short of the Mississippi River, the westbound passenger train slowed down and pulled onto a siding. Marco Celere prayed they were only stopping for water. In his panicked run, he had clung to a groundless hope that if he could somehow get across the Mississippi, they couldn't catch him. Praying it was only a water siding, he pressed his face to the window and craned his neck for a view of the jerkwater tank. But why would they stop so close to the next town?

Two businessmen seated across the aisle of the luxurious extra-fare chair car that Celere had reckoned would be safer to flee in rather than an ordinary day coach seemed to be staring at him. There was a commotion at the vestibule. Celere fully expected to see a burly sheriff with a tin star on his coat and a pistol in his hand.

Instead, a newsboy sprang aboard and ran up the aisle, crying, "Great air race coming our way!"

Marco Celere bought a copy of the *Hannibal Courier-Post* and scanned it fearfully for a murder story that included his description.

The race occupied half the front page. Preston Whiteway, described as "a shrewd, wide-awake businessman," was quoted in boldface print, saying, "Sad as the recent death of Mark Twain—

Hannibal's own bard—sadder still that Mr. Twain did not live to
see the flying machines in the Great Whiteway Atlantic-to-Pacific
Cross-Country Air Race for the Whiteway Cup alight in his beloved hometown of Hannibal, Missouri."

Celere looked for the short out-of-town stories that these local
newspapers plucked from the telegraph. The first he saw was an
interview with a "prominent aviation specialist" who said that
Eddison-Sydney-Martin's headless Curtiss Pusher was the aeroplane to beat. "Far and away the sturdiest and fastest, its motor is
being improved every day."

It would improve less rapidly with Ruggs out of the picture,
Celere thought. But the famous high-flying baronet would have
no trouble attracting top mechanicians eager to join up with a
winner. The headless pusher was still the machine that posed the
worst threat to Josephine.

Celere thumbed deeper into the paper, looking for his description. The state militia was being called out. His heart skipped a
beat until he read that it was to quell a labor strike at Hannibal's
cement plant. The strike was blamed on "foreigners," egged on by
"Italians," who were seeking protection from the Italian consulate
in St. Louis. Thank God he was disguised as a Russian, Celere
thought, only to look up at the grim-faced businessmen lowering
their newspapers to stare at him from across the aisle. He did not
look Italian in his Platov getup, but there was no denying it made
him look like the most foreign passenger in the chair car. Or had
they already seen a story about the murder and a description of
his curly hair and mutton chops, his ever-present slide rule, and
his snappy straw boater with its stylish red hatband?

The nearest leaned across the aisle. "Hey, there!" he addressed
him bluntly. "You . . . mister?"

"Are you speaking to me, sir?"

"You a labor striker?"

Celere weighed the risk of being a foreign agitator versus a murderer on the run and chose to deal with the more immediate threat. "I am being aviation mechanician in Whiteway Cup Cross-Country Air Race."

Their suspicious expressions brightened like sunshine.

"You in the *race*? Put 'er there, feller!"

Soft pink palms thrust across the aisle, and they shook his hand vigorously.

"When are all you getting to Hannibal?"

"After thunderstorming over."

"Let's hope we don't get tornadoes."

"Say, if you was a bettin' man, who would you put your money on to win?"

Celere held up the newspaper. "Is saying here that Englishman pusher is best."

"Yeah, I read that in Chicago, too. But you're right there in the thick of it. What about Josephine? That little gal still behind?"

Celere froze. His eye had fallen on a telegraphed story down the page.

MURDER AND THEFT IN SHADOW OF STORM

"Josephine still behind?"

"Is catching up," Celere mumbled, reading as fast as he could:

An air race mechanician was found diabolically murdered at the Columbia fairground with his throat slashed, the victim of a robbery. According to Sheriff Lydem, the murderer could well be a labor agitator on the run from the cement strike in Missouri, and willing to stop at nothing to facilitate his escape. The victim's body was not discovered for many hours due to the violence of last night's storm.

Marco Celere looked up with a broad smile for the businessmen.

"Josephine is catching up," he repeated.

The train trundled loudly onto an iron-girder bridge, and the sky suddenly spread wide over a broad river.

"Here's the Mississippi. I read birdmen wear cork vests when they fly over bodies of water. Is that so?"

"Is good for floating," said Celere, gazing through the girders at the famed waterway. Brown and rain-swollen, flecked with dirty whitecaps, it rolled sullenly past the town of Hannibal, whose frame houses perched on the far side.

"I thought was wider," he said.

"Wide enough, you try crossing it without this here bridge. But you want to see real wide, you get down below Saint Louis where it meets up with the Missouri."

"And if you want to see really, really wide, wide as the ocean, you take a look where the Ohio comes in. Say, mister, what are you doing on the train when the race is back in Illinois?"

Suddenly they were staring again, suspecting they'd been hoodwinked.

"Scouting route," Celere answered smoothly. "Am getting off train in Hannibal and going back to race."

"Well, I sure do envy you, sir. Judging by the smile on your face, you are one lucky man to be part of that air race."

"Happy being," Celere replied. "Very happy being."

A good plan always made him happy. And he had just come up

with a beauty. Kindly, bighearted, crazy Russian Platov would volunteer to help the baronet's mechanicians by filling in for poor murdered Chief Mechanician Ruggs.

Steve Stevens would complain, but the hell with the fat fool. Dmitri Platov would help and help and help until he had finished the job on Eddison-Sydney-Martin's infernal headless pusher once and for all.

30

ISAAC BELL SAID, "Eustace, I've been watching you and you don't look happy. Are you homesick?"

They were getting the machine ready to take off from Topeka, Kansas. The Chicago kid he had hired to help Andy Moser was pouring gasoline through layers of cheesecloth to strain out any water that may have contaminated the supply. It was a daily ritual performed before mixing in the castor oil that lubricated the Gnome engine.

"No, sir, Mr. Bell," Weed answered hastily. But judging by the expression knitting his brow and pursing his lips, Bell thought something was very much wrong.

"Miss your girl?"

"Yes, sir," he blurted. "I sure do. But . . . You know."

"I do know," Bell said sincerely. "I'm often away from my fiancée. I'm lucky on this case, as she's around filming the race for Mr. Whiteway, so I get to see her now and then. What's your girl's name?"

"Daisy."

"Pretty name. What's her last name?"

"Ramsey."

"Daisy Ramsey. There's a mouthful . . . But wait. If you marry, she'll be Daisy Weed." Bell said it with a grin that coaxed a wan smile out of the boy.

"Oh, yes. We kid about that." The smile faded.

Bell said, "If something is troubling you, son, is there anything I can do to help?"

"No, thank you, sir, I'm O.K."

Eddie Edwards, the white-haired head of the Kansas City office, approached Bell, muttering, "We got trouble."

Bell hurried to the hangar car with him.

Andy Moser, who had been working nearby, tightening the *Eagle*'s wing-stay turnbuckles, said, "You sure you're O.K., Eustace? Mr. Bell seems concerned about you."

"His eyes go through you like iced lightning."

"He's just looking out for you."

Eustace Weed prayed that Andy was right. Because what Isaac Bell had spotted on his face was his sudden horrified realization of what they would force him to do with the copper tube of water sealed with paraffin wax.

He had been hoping that the criminals threatening Daisy had changed their minds. No one approached him in Peoria or Columbia, or Hannibal, Missouri, to tell him what to do with it. After Hannibal, where the race crossed the Mississippi River, he assumed it would happen in Kansas City. It was the only real city on the map since Chicago, and he had developed a picture in his mind of big-city saloonkeepers knowing one another but disdaining their counterparts in small towns. So he had dreaded Kansas City.

But no one had approached him there, either, nor when the race pulled up on the far side of the Missouri River. There had even been a letter from Daisy waiting for him, and she sounded fine. This very morning, camped by the Kansas River outside

Topeka, preparing Mr. Bell's machine to head south and west over
the empty plains toward Wichita, the terrified mechanician had
begun to wonder, would the whole nightmare simply go away?
Trouble was, he couldn't stop thinking about it. And just now,
while Mr. Bell watched him strain the gas before mixing the fuel,
Eustace Weed suddenly knew that Harry Frost's man would order
him to drop the tube in Isaac Bell's flying-machine fuel tank.

He had figured out how that little copper tube would make
Bell's flying machine smash. It was as ingenious as it was horrific.
The *Eagle*'s Gnome rotary engine was fuel lubricated. It had no
oil reservoir, no crankcase, no pump to maintain oil pressure—
in fact, no oil at all. The castor oil suspended in the gasoline did
the job of oil, greasing the passage of the piston through each of
the cylinders. It mixed in readily because castor oil dissolved in
gasoline.

Like paraffin. The paraffin wax that plugged the copper tube
would also dissolve in gasoline. When the gas melted the plugs, in
an hour or so, the water would leak out and contaminate the fuel.
Two tablespoons of water in a flying-machine gas tank was more
than enough to stop Isaac Bell's engine dead. Were he flying high
at the time, he might manage to volplane down safely. But if he
was taking off, or attempting to alight, or making a tight turn low
to the ground, he would smash.

ISAAC BELL LISTENED WITH DEEP CONCERN, but not much surprise,
as Eddie Edwards reported grim news he had just learned from a
contact in the United States Army. Someone had executed a daring raid on the arsenal at Fort Riley, Kansas.

"The Army's hushed it up," Eddie explained, "criminals busting into their arsenal not being the sort of event they want to read in the newspaper."

"What did they get?"

"Two air-cooled, belt-fed Colt-Browning M1895 machine guns."

"Had to be Frost," said Bell, picturing in his mind the four-hundred-and-fifty-rounds-per-minute weapons enveloping Josephine's monoplane in blizzards of flying lead.

"You gotta hand it to him, that man's got nerve. Right under the nose of the U.S. Army."

"How'd he break in?" Bell asked.

"The usual way. Bribed a quartermaster."

"I find it hard to imagine that even a quartermaster more larcenous than most his ilk would risk the Army not noticing missing *machine guns*."

"Frost tricked him into thinking he was stealing surplus uniforms. Said he was selling them in Mexico, or some cock-and-bull story the quartermaster believed. Or wanted to believe. A drinking man, needless to say. Anyhow, he got the surprise of his life when he woke up in the stockade. But by then the guns were long gone."

"When did this happen?"

"Three days ago."

Bell pulled the topographic map of Kansas down from the hangar-car ceiling. "Plenty of time for Frost to get between us and Wichita."

"That's why I said we have trouble. Though I do wonder how he'll fit two machine guns in a Thomas Flyer. Much less hide them. Takes three men to mount one of those guns. They weigh nearly four hundred pounds with their landing carriage."

"He's strong enough to pick one up himself. Besides, he has two helpers in that Thomas."

Bell traced on the map the rail line they would follow to Wichita. Then he traced those converging at Junction City, the nearest town to Fort Riley. "He'll move the guns by train, then freight wagon or motortruck."

"So he can attack anywhere between Kansas and California."

Bell had already concluded that. "We know by now that he doesn't think small. He'll hire more men for the second gun and spread them apart on either side of the railroad track we're flying along. They'll rake her coming and going from both sides."

Bell did some quick calculations in his head, and added darkly, "They'll open up at a mile. If she somehow makes it past them, they'll whirl the guns around and keep firing. As she's coming down the line at sixty miles per hour, they will be able to fire accurately for two full minutes."

STEVE STEVENS SHOOK a copy of the *Wichita Eagle* under Preston Whiteway's nose and roared indignantly, "They're quoting your *San Francisco Inquirer* quoting *me* saying I'm glad that crazy Russian is helping that English feller because everyone's in the race together, like we're all one big family."

"Yes, I read that," Whiteway said mildly. "It didn't sound like you."

"Darned right, it don't sound like me. Why'd you print it?"

"If you read it carefully, you will see that my reporters quoted Mr. Platov, who quoted you saying that the Great Whiteway Atlantic-to-Pacific Cross-Country Air Race for the Whiteway Cup and fifty thousand dollars is for everyone, and we're all one big family."

"I didn't say that."

"You might as well have. Everyone believes it now."

Stevens hopped angrily from foot to foot. His belly bounced, his jowls shook and turned red. "That crazy Russian put those words in my mouth. I didn't say—"

"What's the trouble? Everyone thinks you're a good man."

"I don't give a hoot about being a good man. I want to win the race. And there's Platov sashaying off to help Eddison-Highfalutin-Sydney-Whatever when my own machine is rattling to smithereens."

"You have my sympathy," said Preston Whiteway, smiling at Stevens's confirmation of happy rumors his spies had reported: the fast-flying farmer might not go the distance. "Now, if you'll excuse me, sir, I want to see my own entry—which is not rattling to smithereens, thank you very much—take to the air in the capable hands of Josephine, America's Sweetheart of the Air, who will win the race."

"Is that so? Well, let me tell you, Mr. Fancy-Pants Newspaperman, I hear tell folks is losing interest in your race now that we're so far west there's no one to watch it but jackrabbits, Indians, and coyotes."

Preston Whiteway arched a disdainful eyebrow at the rotund cotton farmer who was very rich but not as rich as he was. "Keep reading, Mr. Stevens. Events reported soon will surprise even you and keep ordinary folk on the edge of their seats."

ISAAC BELL FLICKED the blip switch on his control post to slow the Gnome. Andy Moser had tuned the motor so finely that he was unintentionally overtaking Josephine's Celere monoplane while riding herd above and behind her. Ironically, as her Celere began to suffer the wear and tear of the long race, his *American Eagle* seemed to get stronger. Andy kept repeating that Danielle's father "built 'em to last."

They were navigating by the railroad tracks.

Two thousand feet below, Kansas's winter wheat crop spread dark yellow to the horizons on either side of the rails. The flat, empty country was broken now and then by a lonely farmhouse, in a cluster of barns and silos, and the occasional ribbon of trees lining a creek or river. It was from one of those ribbons that Bell expected Frost would rake Josephine's aeroplane with machine-gun fire, and he had persuaded her to fly a quarter mile to the right of the tracks, to increase the range, and to steer clear of clumps of trees. If Frost did attack, Bell instructed her to veer away while he would descend in steep spiral dips, firing his mounted rifle.

They had just crossed a railroad junction helpfully marked with canvas arrows when Bell sensed motion behind him. He was not surprised to see Sir Eddison-Sydney-Martin's blue headless pusher overtaking them. The baronet's new Curtiss motor just kept on getting faster. Andy Moser credited "the crazy Russian" with its performance. Bell was not so sure about that. A conversation with Eddison-Sydney-Martin's regular mechanicians led him to believe that the six-cylinder engine was the real hero, being not only more powerful but smoother than the other flyers' fours. They certainly were not inclined to credit the Russian volunteer with more than helping out.

"The six might not be so smooth as your rotary Gnome, Mr. Bell," they said, "but it's considerably easier to keep tuned. Lucky for you you've got Andy Moser to keep it running."

The blue pusher sailed past Bell, and then Josephine, with a jaunty wave to each from the baronet. Bell saw Josephine reach up to fiddle with her gravity-feed gas tank. Her speed increased, but at the expense of gray smoke pouring from her motor. Eddison-Sydney-Martin continued to pull ahead, and was several hundred yards past her, when Bell saw something dark suddenly fly back in the Englishman's wake.

It looked like he had hit a bird.

But when the Curtiss staggered in the air, Bell realized that the dark object falling behind Eddison-Sydney-Martin was not a bird but his propeller.

Suddenly without power, forced to volplane, Eddison-Sydney-Martin tried to dip his elevator. But before the pusher could descend in a controlled glide, a piece flew from the tail. It was followed by another, and another, and Bell saw that the departing propeller had chopped parts of the tail as it flew away, still spinning like a buzz saw.

The biplane's elevator broke loose and trailed in blue shreds. The vertical tail with its rudder went next. A thousand feet above the ground, the baronet's swift headless pusher fell like a stone.

31

"CAT RAN OUT OF LIVES."

"Don't say that!" Josephine rounded on the mechanician who had muttered what they all feared. She ran to Abby, who was weeping. But when she tried to hold her, the baronet's wife pulled back and held herself stiff as a marble statue.

All Josephine could think of was Marco promising her, "You will win. I will see that you win. Don't you worry. No one will stay ahead of you."

What had he done?

They were gathered on the banks of a wide creek twenty miles southwest of Topeka, she and Isaac Bell, who had both alighted on a dirt road beside the tracks, and Abby and all the mechanicians, who had seen the smash from their support train. The blue pusher—what was left of it—was floating in the creek, caught on a snag halfway across.

Had Marco sabotaged Abby's husband's machine so that she could win? There he was, in his crazy Russian disguise. She was the only one who knew who he really was and the only one who suspected he had done something terrible. But she was afraid to ask.

I must, she thought. I have to ask him. And if it is true, then I have to admit everything, all the lies. She walked up to Marco. He was waving his Dmitri slide rule, and he looked as distraught as the others, but she realized with a terrible sense of lost trust that she could not be sure he wasn't pretending. She said, in a low voice, "I have to talk to you."

"Oh, poor Josephine!" he cried in full Platov mode. "You are seeing all happening in front of eyes."

"I have to ask you."

"What?"

Before she could speak, she heard a scream. Abby was screaming. Then, miraculously, a cheer from every throat. She whirled toward the creek. Everyone was looking downstream. Baronet Eddison-Sydney-Martin was limping unsteadily along the bank, soaking wet, covered in mud and fumbling with a cigarette he could not light.

BELL TOLD ANDY MOSER that he was certain that he had seen Eddison-Sydney-Martin's propeller fall off. "Is it common?"

"It happens," said Andy.

"What would cause it?"

"Lots of things. A crack in the hub."

"But he inspected the machine every time he flew. He walked around it and checked mounts and stays and everything. Just like all of us do. So did his mechanicians, just like you do for me."

"Could have hit a rock bouncing on the field."

"He would have noticed, felt it, heard it."

"He'd notice if it shattered the propeller," said Andy. "But if a rock hit right on the hub at the same moment he had his hands full just getting her into the air and his motor was straining loudly, maybe he didn't. Couple of months ago I heard about a propeller getting unstable because it was stored standing up. Moisture sunk into the bottom blade."

"His was brand-new and used nearly every day since he got it."

"Yeah, but you get these cracks."

"That's why it was painted silver," countered Bell, "so little cracks would show." That was standard procedure on pushers. His own propeller was not because a silver propeller spinning in front of the driver would dazzle him.

"I know, Mr. Bell. And obviously it wasn't around long enough to rot, either." Moser looked up at the tall detective. "If you're asking me was it sabotage, I'd say it sure as heck could have been."

"How? If you wanted a fellow's propeller to fly off, what would you do?"

"Anything I could to throw it out of kilter. When the propeller is off balance, it vibrates. Vibrations will break it or rattle the hub loose, or even shake the motor right off its mounts."

"But you wouldn't want it shaking that much because the fellow you're trying kill would notice and stop his motor and vol-plane down as fast as he could."

"You're right about that," Andy said gravely. "The saboteur would have to really know his business."

But that, Isaac Bell had to admit, was true of every mechanician in the race, with the possible exceptions of Josephine's disguised detectives. Another truth he could not ignore was that Preston Whiteway had gotten the wish he had so unabashedly hoped for back in San Francisco. He had had to wait long past Chicago and halfway across Kansas, but a "winnowing of the field" had indeed turned the race into a contest that pitted the best airmen against plucky tomboy Josephine.

Eddison-Sydney-Martin had probably been the best—and his

winnowing by sabotage had hardly been natural. But steady Joe Mudd was proving himself to be no slouch, while the thoroughly unpleasant but undeniably courageous Steve Stevens was a fast flier who pushed ahead unintimidated by the vibrations endangering his machine.

Bell had no way of knowing who the saboteur would try to attack next. In fact, the only thing that the tall detective knew absolutely for sure was that his first job was still what it had always been: keep Harry Frost from killing Josephine.

BELL WONDERED WHETHER the machine-gun raid at Fort Riley could have been an elaborate feint by Harry Frost, a distraction to lull Josephine's protectors into loosening the cordon they kept around her each night at the fairgrounds and rail yards. With that possibility in mind, Bell laid an ambush. He waited for dark—after sad good-byes with the Eddison-Sydney-Martins, whose support train steamed out of the tiny Morris County Fairgrounds rail yard back to Chicago—and climbed onto the roof of Josephine's private car. For hours, he lay in wait, scanning the trains parked on the other side of Whiteway's special and listening for the crunch of boots on gravel ballast.

It was a hot night. Windows, skylights, and roof hatches were open. Murmured conversations and occasional bursts of laughter mingled with a quiet sighing of locomotives bedded down with banked fires producing just enough steam to power lights and warm water.

Around midnight, he heard someone knock at Josephine's rear vestibule. Whoever it was, he must have come through the train, as Bell had seen or heard no one on the ballast. Nonetheless, Bell drew his Browning and aimed it through an open roof hatch at the door. He heard Josephine call sleepily from her stateroom, "Who is it?"

"Preston."

"Mr. Whiteway, it's kind of late."

"I must speak with you, Josephine."

Josephine padded into the front parlor, wearing a simple dressing gown over cotton pajamas, and opened the door.

Whiteway was dressed in a suit with a silk necktie, and his hair was combed in grand golden waves. "I want you to know that I've put a lot of thought in what I am about to say to you," he said, and began pacing about the narrow parlor. "Odd. I feel a little tongue-tied."

Josephine curled up in an overstuffed chair, tucked her bare feet under her, and watched him warily. "I hope you are not changing your mind," she said. "I'm doing much better. My times are improving. I've been catching up. And now that the poor baronet is out of the race, I have a very good chance."

"Of course you have!"

"Joe Mudd isn't as fast. And Steve Stevens can't keep going much longer."

"You're going to win. I'm sure of it."

Josephine grinned. "That's a relief. You looked so nervous, I thought you were dropping me . . . But what are you trying to say?"

Whiteway stood to his full height, thrust out his chest and belly, and blurted, "Marry me!"

"*What?*"

"I'll make a wonderful husband, and you'll be rich, and you can fly aeroplanes every day until we have children . . . What do you say?"

After a long silence, Josephine said, "I don't know what to say. I mean, it's very nice of you to offer, but—"

"But what? What could be better?"

Josephine took a deep breath and climbed to her feet. Whiteway opened his arms to embrace her.

"THEN WHAT HAPPENED?" whispered Marion when Bell reported to her at breakfast in the *Josephine Special*'s lavish dining car. Her enormous coral-sea green eyes were wide and so beautiful that for a long moment Bell lost his train of thought.

"Did she say yes?" Marion prompted.

"No."

"Good. Preston is too in love with himself to be a loving husband. If she's as sweet a girl as I read in the newspapers, she deserves better."

"You've seen more of her than the newspaper readers."

"We've only said hello in passing. But I would have thought she would have answered 'Maybe.'"

"Why?" Bell asked.

Marion thought on that. "She strikes me as someone who gets what she wants."

"It was a sort-of maybe. She said she had to think about it."

"I suspect she has no one to talk to. I'll give her an ear. And an opinion, if she wants one."

"I was hoping you would say that," said Bell. "In fact, I was hoping you would put your mind to what Harry Frost meant when he said that she and Celere were up to something."

Marion glanced out the window. A stiff wind was spinning

miniature tornadoes of coal smoke, wheat chaff, and cinders around the trains. "No flying today. I will do it right now."

"I WANT TO BE LIKE YOU WHEN I GROW UP," Josephine grinned at Marion. They were alone in the front parlor of Josephine's private car, curled up in facing armchairs. Coffee cups sat between them untouched.

"I hope I don't seem that old. Besides, you *are* grown up. You're driving a flying machine across the continent."

"That's not the same. I want to be a straight shooter like you."

"What do you mean?"

"You told me straight off that Isaac overheard Preston asking me to marry him."

Marion said, "I also told you that I'm very curious what you think of his proposal."

"I don't know. I mean, what does he want to marry me for?" She gave Marion one of her big open grins. "I'm just a silly girl two seconds off the farm."

"Men are strange creatures," Marion smiled back. "Most of them. Maybe he loves you."

"He didn't say he loved me."

"Well, Preston is not very bright in many ways. On the other hand, he is handsome."

"I suppose."

"And very, very wealthy."

"So was Harry."

"Unlike Harry, Preston, for all his many, many faults, is no brute."

"Yes, but he's big like Harry."

"And getting bigger," laughed Marion. "If he isn't careful, he'll end up like President Taft."

"Or Steve Stevens."

They both laughed. Marion watched her closely, and asked, "Are you considering it at all?"

"Not at all. I don't love him. I mean, I know he'd buy me aeroplanes. He said he'd buy me aeroplanes at least until we have children. Then wants me to stop flying."

"Good Lord," said Marion, "Preston is even a bigger fool than I thought."

"You don't think I should marry him . . . do you?"

Marion said, "I can't tell you that. You have to know what you want to do."

"You see, if I win the fifty thousand dollars, I'll have my own money. I'll buy my own aeroplanes."

Marion said, "Dear, if you win the cross-country race, they'll be lining up to *give* you aeroplanes."

"Really?"

"I am sure of it. They know that customers will buy aeroplanes you fly. So marrying Preston really has nothing to do with aeroplanes, does it?"

"If I win."

"Isaac says you have no doubt you'll win. And," she added with another laugh, "*he* has no doubt you'll win. He's bet three thousand dollars on you."

Josephine nodded distractedly and looked out her railcar window. The wind was still rattling the glass. She closed her eyes and started to form words with her lips, then pressed her lips tightly together. She was aching to talk, Marion thought. It seemed as if

Preston's proposal was forcing to her think about things she would prefer not to.

"What is it?" she asked. "What's really troubling you?"

Josephine pursed her lips and exhaled sharply. "Can you keep a secret?" Her hazel eyes bored pleadingly into Marion's.

"No," Marion answered, "I can't. Not from Isaac."

Josephine rolled her eyes. "Why are you so honest, Marion?"

"I prefer to be," said Marion. "What do you want to tell me?"

"Nothing . . . When I saw Marco shot, I was so surprised."

"I would think so."

"It was the last thing I expected."

"AND THEN," Marion Morgan confessed to Isaac Bell, "I blundered. Instead of keeping my silly mouth shut while she completed her thought, I said something imbecilic like 'Who would expect to see one's husband shoot one's friend?' and Josephine shut up tight as a clam."

"The last thing she expected," Bell mused, "implying she expected something else to happen. As if she was 'up to something,' just like Harry Frost said . . . Is she going to marry Preston?"

"She finally said, no, absolutely not."

"Will she change her mind?"

"Only if she were to fear that she would definitely not win the race."

"Because she wouldn't win the fifty thousand dollars, and Preston is rich?"

"You should have seen her eyes light up when I told her that if she wins inventors will give her aeroplanes. I don't think she ever thought of that before. It's like she doesn't think very far ahead.

She'll do anything she has to to keep herself in flying machines. Including marrying Preston. But only for the machines. She's not the kind of girl who wants a bunch of kids, jewels, and houses."

"Which reminds me," asked Isaac Bell, taking Marion in his arms, "when are *you* going to marry *me*?"

Marion looked at the emerald on her finger. Then she smiled into his eyes. She traced his golden mustache with the tip of her finger and kissed him firmly on his lips. "The moment you absolutely insist. You know I would do anything for you. But until then, I am very, very happy and totally content to be your fiancée."

THE KANSAN WIND howled all that day and through the night and into the next morning.

With no one flying anywhere, Andy Moser took the opportunity to completely disassemble Bell's Gnome and put it back together, cleaned, polished, tuned, and tweaked.

Joe Mudd's bricklayers, masons, plasterers, and locomotive firemen tore the Liberator's engine down into small pieces and finally isolated the cracked copper tube that was the source of the oil leak which kept turning the red machine black.

Russian Dmitri Platov directed Steve Stevens's mechanicians in another futile effort to permanently synchronize the biplane's twin motors. When Stevens complained rudely and threatened to dock everyone's salary, the usually easygoing thermo engine inventor stalked away to help Josephine take the head off her Antoinette to replace a leaky gasket.

Isaac Bell watched them. Platov kept talking to her in an urgent, low voice. Bell wondered whether she was discussing Whiteway's proposal with the Russian—an odd thought, but their conversation seemed so intense. Whenever he drifted close to overhear, they stopped talking.

"WHY IS DETECTIVE BELL LURKING?" asked Marco Celere, giving Bell a friendly wave with his Dmitri Platov slide rule.

"He's looking out for me."

"Surely he is not afraid for your safety in the presence of kindly Platov?"

"I doubt he's afraid of anything," said Josephine.

Celere began chiseling the old head gasket off Josephine's engine block. "You are somewhat prickly today, my dear."

"I'm sorry. I've got a lot on my mind."

"Starting with Mr. Whiteway's proposal?"

"What do you think?" she retorted sullenly.

"I think you should marry him."

"Marco!"

"I'm serious."

"Marco, that's disgusting. How could you want me to marry another man?"

"He's more than 'another man.' He's the richest newspaper publisher in America. He, and his money, could be very helpful to you. And me."

"What good will it do us if I'm married to him?"

"You would leave him for me, when the time is right."

"Marco, it makes me sick to think you would want me to be with him."

"Well, I'd expect you to postpone the honeymoon until after the race. Surely you could plead the necessity to concentrate on winning."

"What about the wedding night?"

"Don't worry, I'll think of something."

THE WINDS DROPPED. The Weather Bureau published reports that it might be calm for a few hours. Late in the afternoon, the racers swarmed off the Morris County Fairgrounds. Before dark, all alighted safely in Wichita, where Preston Whiteway strode dramatically into the glare of Marion Morgan's Picture World Cooper-Hewitt mercury-arc lamps.

Marion's operators were cranking two movie cameras, the second being an expense Whiteway had refused to bear until now despite Marion's insistence that two cameras would create exciting shifts of view that would draw bigger audiences. She had one camera aimed at the publisher, the other trained to capture the reactions of the newspaper reporters.

Tomorrow, Whiteway announced, would be an official off day. It would not count against the fifty-day limit because, "Tomorrow I am going to throw the biggest party the state of Kansas has ever seen to celebrate my engagement to Miss Josephine Josephs— America's Sweetheart of the Air."

Marion Morgan looked up from her station between the cameras to lock astonished gazes with Isaac Bell. Bell shook his head in disbelief.

A *San Francisco Inquirer* correspondent had been primed to call out, "When's the wedding, Mr. Whiteway, sir?" Other Whiteway employees chorused, as they had been instructed to, "Do we have to wait until the race is over?"

"Josephine wouldn't hear of it," Whiteway boomed back heartily. "At my beautiful bride's special request we're having a Texas-

sized wedding in the great city of Fort Worth's North Side
Coliseum, which is known far and wide as 'the most opulent and
dynamic pavilion in the entire Western Hemisphere.' We'll be married the moment the Great Whiteway Atlantic-to-Pacific Cross-
Country Air Race for the Whiteway Cup and fifty thousand dollars
flies into Fort Worth, Texas."

Marion flashed Bell a private grin and mouthed the word
"Shameless."

Bell grinned back, "Unabashedly."

But there was no denying that when "booming" his air race,
Preston Whiteway could lather up the public hotter than P. T.
Barnum, Florenz Ziegfeld, and Mark Twain combined.

The only question was, why had Josephine changed her mind?
Her times were improving, often surpassing the others. And her
flying machine was running beautifully. She had no reason to fear
she couldn't win the race.

32

INVESTIGATE DMITRI PLATOV,

Isaac Bell wired Van Dorn researchers in Chicago and New York. He was sure that the Russian inventor had somehow influenced Josephine to marry Preston Whiteway. *Why* Platov would want her to marry Whiteway was an enigma. But what intrigued the tall detective as much was how Platov had the power to change Josephine's mind about a decision as deeply important and intensely personal as marriage.

Bell could not ignore such mystery about a man who had the run of the air race infields and was welcomed in every hangar car. Particularly since Dmitri Platov had volunteered to fill in for Eddison-Sydney-Martin's murdered mechanician days before the Englishman's propeller broke loose and smashed him into a Kansas creek. And if there was any one mechanician in the race who knew his business, it was Platov.

The researchers' preliminary report, wired back in half a day, was baffling.

The only information on Dmitri Platov was found in Van Dorn files that contained newspaper clippings about the Whiteway Cup preparations at Belmont Park, and Isaac Bell's own reports from the infield. Similarly, newspaper reporters had described, with varying degrees of accuracy, Platov's revolutionary thermo engine, but only in articles about its destruction in the accident that had killed Steve Stevens's chief mechanician.

Bell pondered the meaning of such a lack of information. It jibed with Danielle Di Vecchio's assertion that she had never met Platov at the International Aeronautical Salon in Paris nor even heard his name there.

Was it possible that Platov had never been at the Paris air meet?

But if he had not been in Paris, then from whom had Marco Celere bought his so-called jet engine?

Bell wired Research:

CONCENTRATE ON THERMO ENGINE.

ON THE JUMP!

Then he called Dashwood into his headquarters car. "I'm taking you off the gamblers. Watch Dmitri Platov. Don't let him know, but stick to him like his shadow."

"What am I looking for?"

"He's making me uncomfortable," said Bell. "He could be as innocent as he looks. But he had the opportunity to sabotage the Englishman's pusher."

"Could he be Harry Frost's inside man?" asked Dashwood.

"He could be anything."

ISAAC BELL HALED the few Van Dorns in the Southwest he could get his hands on to defend Josephine's wedding from Harry Frost's Colt machine guns. As the private detectives hurried into Fort

Worth and reported aboard the *Eagle Special*, he drummed in his strategy: "Make it impossible for Harry Frost to sneak close enough to do damage. Ransack your contacts. There are darned few of us, but if we pool our links to lawmen, railroad police, informers, gamblers, and criminals beholden to us, we can try to establish a perimeter equal to the Colts' range and keep him outside it."

The stolen Colts' long range was the threat. The machine guns were deadly up to a mile. But Frost could nearly treble the threat by elevating the barrels to loft indirect "plunging fire," where bullets would rain down on the party indiscriminately from a distance as great as four thousand five hundred yards—the better part of three miles.

"Not as tough as it sounds," Bell assured the Van Dorns. "Fort Worth's sheriff is kindly lending a hand with a whole passel of temporary deputies, including ranch hands in the immediate area. They'll recognize strangers. And we're getting railroad dicks. The Texas & Pacific line and the Fort Worth & Denver are cooperating."

"What if Harry Frost gets the same idea and hires his own locals?" asked a Los Angeles detective who had just stepped off the train, wearing a cream-colored bowler hat and a pink necktie.

Bell said, "What do you say to that, Walt?" nodding to his old friend "Texas" Walt Hatfield, who had arrived on horseback.

Lean as a steel rail and considerably tougher, the former Texas Ranger turned Van Dorn detective squinted under the brim of his J. B. Stetson at the California dandy. "Nothin' to stop Frost from roundin' up a salty bunch," he drawled. "But he can't drive them into town, as they would be types well known by peace officers. However, Isaac," he said to Bell, "spottin' Harry Frost ain't stoppin' him. I reckon from readin' reports of your adventures thus far, Frost ain't scairt of nothin'. He'd charge Hell with a bucket of water."

Bell shook his head. "Don't count on Frost acting rashly. We'll see no reckless attack, no hopeless charge. He told me straight, he's not afraid of dying. But only after he kills Josephine."

HAVING SET UP HER CAMERAS and Cooper-Hewitt lamps in the North Side Coliseum, Marion Morgan joined Isaac Bell in his Van Dorn headquarters car. Bell complimented her new split riding skirt, which she had discovered in a Fort Worth department store that catered to wealthy ranchers' wives, then asked, "How does the wedding venue look?" Preoccupied with establishing the perimeter, he had yet to inspect the inside of the coliseum.

Marion laughed. "Do you recall how Preston described it?"

"'The most opulent and dynamic pavilion in the entire Western Hemisphere'?"

"He left out one word: 'livestock.' The opulent and dynamic livestock pavilion is where they hold their National Feeders and Breeders cattle show. Josephine laughed so hard, she started crying."

"She's a dairy farmer's daughter."

"She said, 'I'm getting married in a cow barn.' In actual fact, it's a grand building. Plenty of light for my cameras. Skylights in the roof, and electricity for my lamps. I'll do fine. How about you?"

"Indoors makes it easier to guard," said Bell.

When he did inspect it, he discovered it was indeed a wise choice, with enormous rail yards for the support trains and wedding guests' specials, and easily dismantled corrals to make airfield space for the flying machines.

———

AFTER A THOUSAND-MILE RUN from Chicago on awful roads, Harry Frost's sixty-horsepower, four-cylinder Model 35 Thomas Flyer touring car was caked in mud, gray with dust, and festooned with towropes and chains, extra gas and oil cans, and repeatedly patched spare tires. But it was running like a top, and Frost felt a kind of freedom he never experienced on a railroad, even steaming on his own special. Like Josephine used to prattle on about flying in the air—*on* the air, she called it, insisting that air was almost solid—in or on, a man could auto anywhere he pleased.

Thirty miles from Fort Worth, a meatpacking city that was smudging the sky with smoke, Frost ordered a halt on a low rise. He scanned the scrub-strewn prairie with powerful German field glasses he had bought for African safaris. A mile off was the railroad. A freight car sat all by itself on a remote siding that had once served a town since wiped from the map by a tornado.

"Go!"

Mike Stotts, Frost's mechanician, cranked the Thomas's motor. Three hours later, twenty-five miles on, they stopped again. Frost sent Stotts ahead on a bicycle, which they had stolen in Wichita Falls, to scout the territory and establish contact with Frost's men in Fort Worth.

"You want I should go with him?" asked Dave Mayhew, Frost's telegrapher.

"You stay here." He could always get another mechanician, but a telegrapher who was also handy with firearms was a rare animal. Stotts was back sooner than Frost had expected. "What's going on?"

"Picket line. They've got men on horses patrolling."

"You sure they weren't ranch hands?"

"I didn't see any cows."

"What about in the city?"

"Police everywhere. Half the men I saw were wearing deputy stars. And a fair portion of those who weren't looked like detectives."

"Did you see any rail dicks?"

"About a hundred."

Frost ruminated in silence. Clearly, Isaac Bell was operating under the assumption that the Colt machine guns stolen from Fort Riley were in his possession.

There were other ways to skin a cat. Frost sent Mayhew up a pole to wire a Texas & Pacific Railway dispatcher in his employ, then headed west, skirting Fort Worth.

After dark, the Thomas Flyer climbed the embankment onto the railroad, straddled the tracks, and continued west. Frost ordered the mechanician to watch behind them for locomotive headlamps. He and the telegrapher watched ahead. Five times in the night, they pulled off the tracks to let a train pass.

HALFWAY TO ABILENE late the next day, Harry Frost watched through his field glasses as a large chuck wagon, drawn by six powerful mules, stopped next to a freight car parked on a remote Texas & Pacific Railway siding. The siding served an enormous ranch ten miles away that was owned by a Wall Street investment combine in which Frost held a controlling interest. Six gunmen dressed like cowboys were riding with the wagon. They dismounted, unlocked a padlock, slid open the boxcar door, and wrestled heavy crates stenciled HOLIAN PLOW WORKS SANDY HOOK CONN into the wagon.

Frost raked the endless empty miles of brush and grass with

the field glasses, checking as he had repeatedly that there was no one in sight to interfere. Prairie speckled with brown clumps of mesquite grass rolled to the horizon. Clouds, or perhaps low hills, rose in the west. He spied, eight or ten miles north, a single spindly structure that could be either a windmill to pump water or a derrick to drill for oil. The tracks gleamed in a straight line east and west, edged by a ragged ribbon of telegraph wire strung along weathered poles.

They finished loading the chuck wagon. It trundled west on the rutted dirt track that paralleled the railroad, guarded by the men on horses. The Thomas caught up two miles from the siding. Up close, the appearance of the horsemen would cause any peace officer worth his salt to draw his guns for they looked less like cowboys than bank robbers. Their hands lacked the calluses and scars of range work. They wore six-guns in double holsters low on the hips and packed Winchester rifles in saddle scabbards. Surveying the three men in the Thomas, the hard-bitten gang turned expectantly to a tall man in their midst. Harry Frost had already spotted him as the leader with whom he had communicated through an intermediary he trusted from the old days.

Frost asked, "Which of you was in the Spanish War?"

Four men in campaign hats nodded.

"Did you fire the Colt?"

They nodded again, eyes still shifting toward their leader.

"Follow me. There's a creek bed where we can mount the guns."

No one moved.

"Herbert?" Frost said amiably. "My fellows in Chicago tell me you're one tough outlaw. Can't help but notice that everyone's looking at you like you're about to impart some wisdom. What's on your mind?"

Herbert answered by drawling, "We was debatin' why instead of shootin' at flyin' machines we oughtn't to take your money now, and your auto, and your machine guns, and if you don't give us no trouble, allow you all to hop a freight back to Chicago—you bein' only three, us bein' six."

Gripping the stock in one powerful hand, Harry Frost raised a sawed-off double-barreled ten-gauge from between his boots.

The outlaw looked fearlessly down the twin muzzles. "Ah don't cotton to a man drawin' a bead on me. Particularly with a coach gun."

"I'm not drawing a bead on you, Mr. Herbert," Harry Frost replied. "I'm blowing your head off." He jerked both triggers. The shotgun thundered like a cannon, and a swath of double-ought buckshot threw Herbert out of his saddle.

There was no echo on the open range, just a single blast of thunder and the neighing of frightened horses. When the dead man's gang got their mounts under control, Stotts and Mayhew were pointing revolvers in both hands, and Harry Frost himself had reloaded. His face was red with righteous anger.

"Who else?"

They uncrated the guns, mounts, ammunition boxes, and landing carriages in the meager shade of the scrub brush and low trees that grew beside the creek. They disassembled and cleaned the guns and mounted them on the two-wheeled landing carriages. The weapons weighed nearly four hundred pounds, including the ammunition boxes. Cursing the weight, they rolled them up and down the dry creek bed, which was deep and narrow as a military slit trench. Positioned two hundred yards apart and elevated on their carriages, the Colts commanded the railroad tracks that the aeroplanes would follow to Abilene.

To ensure the guns were in working order, they fed the canvas cartridge belts into the breeches and fired fifty rounds from each, killing some cows grazing half a mile away.

Harry Frost handed Stotts his hunting knife. "Go slice off some supper. Better cut enough for breakfast. We'll be here awhile."

He ordered Mayhew to climb a pole and tap into the wires.

The telegrapher strung wire down to the ground, connected it to a key, sat propped against the pole with the key in his lap, and translated the messages that railroad dispatchers were transmitting between their distant stations. Several times, he warned that a train was coming. They hid under the trestle that spanned the creek bed until the train had thundered overhead. Most of the telegraph traffic was about shunting extra trains—rich men's specials and newspapers' charters—into Fort Worth for the big wedding.

33

ISAAC BELL WAS SURPRISED when Preston Whiteway asked him to be his best man until he realized that the only people the newspaper magnate ever spent time with were people who worked for him, and the high-handed manner in which he treated employees guaranteed they would never be friends.

"I would be honored," Bell said, glad to stand near Josephine to protect her personally if Harry Frost somehow pulled a fast one and breached the outer defense lines. He was not as pleased when Josephine asked Marion to be her maid of honor. It put his fiancée directly in the line of fire, but Marion made it clear there was no saying no to such a request from Josephine, who was thousands of miles from her family and the only woman in the race.

In answer to Joseph Van Dorn's queries from Washington about "wedding hoopla," Isaac Bell wired back:

PRESTON PREEMINENT PROMOTER.

Hundreds of invited guests and hordes of spectators converged on Fort Worth in automobiles, buckboard wagons, carriages, and on horseback. Packed trains steamed in from Chicago, New York, Los Angeles, and San Francisco. The Northern Texas Traction

Company ran extra trolleys from Dallas. A company of state militia was called up to control the crowds and protect the flying machines. Additional companies were under orders at Tyler and Texarkana. Marion Morgan's camera operators were trampled by legions of newspaper sketch artists and photographers until Whiteway himself stepped in to remind them that, as owner of Picture World, he would not take kindly to his cameras being jostled.

The ceremony itself was delayed by every hitch imaginable.

The North Side Coliseum, which Whiteway had furnished with church pews and an altar shipped in from St. Louis, had been designed more for the movement of cattle than people, so it took a very long time to get everyone seated. Then summer thunderheads blackened the western sky, and every mechanician and birdman in the race, including the bride, ran out to the field to tie down their machines and shroud wings and fuselages with canvas.

Thunder shook the coliseum. Fierce winds swept in from the prairie. Steve Stevens's biplane tore its anchors. The bride, though widely known to despise the obese cotton farmer, led another charge outdoors to save his machine. They got it nailed down, but not before torrential rain struck.

Josephine was dried off by her ladies-in-waiting—a rough-and-tumble crowd of Fort Worth society matrons who had volunteered to fill in for the famous aviatrix's faraway family. The Bishop of San Francisco's stand-in—the Right Reverend himself pleaded prior responsibilities raising funds to erect a cathedral on earthquake-ravished Nob Hill—had just reassembled the flock in front of the temporarily consecrated altar when the floor was set to shaking by a colossal jet-black 2-8-2 Mikado locomotive rumbling into the yard. With deep fireboxes, superheated boilers, and eight drive wheels, the powerful Mikados usually sped immense strings of boxcars at sixty miles per hour. This one towed a single long black private car, which it parked beside a cattle chute that led directly into the building.

"Good God," whispered Preston Whiteway, "it's Mother."

From the private car, swathed head to toe in black silk and crowned with raven feathers, stalked the Widow Whiteway.

The newspaper publisher turned beseechingly to the Van Dorn Agency's chief investigator. "I thought she was in France," he whispered. "Bell, you're best man. It's your job to do something. *Please.*"

The tall, golden-haired detective squared his shoulders and strode to the cattle chute. Scion of an ancient Boston banking family, polished at boarding school and educated at Yale, Isaac Bell was steeped in the tradition of best men saving the day, whether by locating lost rings or defusing inebriated former fiancées, but this was as far beyond his ken, as if he were a Texas cowhand asked to rope a rhinoceros.

He offered his hand and a princely bow.

"At last," he greeted the groom's uninvited mother, "the ceremony can begin."

"Who are you?"

"I am Isaac Bell, Preston's best man and a devoted reader of your columns in the Sunday supplements."

"If you've read them, you know I cannot abide divorce."

"Neither can Josephine. Were her unfortunate marriage not properly annulled, she would never marry again. Here she is now." Josephine was hurrying from the altar with an open smile.

Mrs. Whiteway muttered, "She's braver than my son. Look at him, afraid of his own mother."

"He's mortified, madam. He thought you were in France."

"He *hoped* I was in France. What do think of this girl, Mr. Bell?"

"I admire her pluck."

Josephine approached, eyes warm, extending both hands. "I'm so glad you made it, Mrs. Whiteway. My own mother couldn't, and I felt all alone until now."

Mrs. Whiteway looked Josephine up and down. "Aren't you the plain Jane?" she announced. "Pretty enough, but no beauty, thank goodness. Beauty spoils a woman, turns her head . . . Who is that woman in maid-of-honor costume directing those men to point moving-picture cameras at me?"

"My fiancée," said Bell, who had already stepped out of the line of focus, "Miss Marion Morgan."

"Well, there may be exceptions to what I said about beautiful women," Mrs. Whiteway harrumphed. "Young lady, do you love my son?"

The aviatrix looked her in the eye. "I *like* him."

"Why?"

"He gets things done."

"That is the one good trait he inherited from my husband." She took Josephine's hand and said, "Let's get on with this," and walked her back to the altar.

Mrs. Whiteway was settled in the front pew, and the bishop's stand-in was repeating for the third time "We are gathered here today . . ." when through the skylight above Josephine and Preston the heavens suddenly glowed a steely green.

"Twisters!" cried the Texas plains dwellers who knew that weirdly tinted sky could only mean tornadoes.

Fort Worthians fled to storm cellars, inviting as many guests as they could squeeze in. Visitors who had steamed in on special trains retired to their dubious shelters. Those without cellars or trains found saloons.

The tornados roamed the rangeland until long after dark, roaring like runaway freights, hurling cattle and bunkhouses to the skies. They spared the city, but it was past midnight before a grateful congregation finally smelled the wedding feast cooking and at last heard the words "I now pronounce you man and wife."

Preston Whiteway, flushed from reciprocating multiple toasts to the bridegroom, planted a kiss on Josephine's lips. Maid of Honor Marion Morgan assured all who asked that, from her close vantage, she had observed that Josephine returned it gamely.

A roar of "Let's eat" drove hundreds to the tables.

Whiteway raised his glass high. "A toast to my beautiful bride, America's Sweetheart of the Air. May she fly ever higher and faster in my arms and—"

However Whiteway intended to continue his toast was drowned out by the distinctive grinding clatter of two pump-driven, eight-cylinder Antoinette motors clawing Steve Stevens's overburdened biplane into the night air.

JOSEPHINE JUMPED from the bridal party's table and ran full tilt through a canvas flap that covered a cattle chute leading to the flying field. Spitting fire from both motors, Stevens's machine cleared a fence and Mrs. Whiteway's locomotive, headed straight at a line of telegraph wires, cleared them by inches, lurched over a barn, and disappeared into the night.

Marco Celere was standing with the chocks he had pulled from its wheels at his feet, waving good-bye with his Platov's slide rule and his red-banded straw boater.

"I told you I'd think of something for your wedding night."

"Where's he going?"

"Abilene."

"That sneaky, fat . . ."

"I convinced him to go ahead so we'd have time to work on the motors."

"How can he see where he's flying?"

"Stars and moon on shiny tracks."

Josephine yelled for her mechanicians to pour gas and oil into her flying machine and spin it over. Marco raced after her as she ran to it, dragging her wedding dress like a cloud of white smoke. He pulled the canvas off the monoplane's wings while she knelt by tent pegs to release the tie-downs.

"I have to warn you . . ." he whispered urgently.

"What?" She loosened a taut-line hitch, tugged the rope off the strut, and knelt to loosen another.

"If something were to happen to 'Dmitri Platov,' don't worry."

"What do you mean? . . . *Hurry it up!*" she shouted to her detective-mechanicians, who were tipping cans of gas and oil into the tanks. "What are you talking about? *You're* Dmitri Platov."

"'Dmitri Platov' is being watched by Bell's detectives. He may have to suddenly disappear."

Josephine untied the last tie-down, jumped up on the soapbox, and scrambled onto her machine, desperate to get up in the air. The train of her wedding dress tangled in a stay. "Knife!" she yelled to a detective-mechanician, who flicked open a sharpened blade and slashed the train off her dress.

"Keep it out of the propeller!" she ordered, and the mechanician dragged it away. Marco was still standing on the soapbox, his whiskered face inches from hers. "What about you?" she asked.

"I'll be back. Don't worry."

She plunged her control post forward and pulled it back and tilted it sideways, checking that her elevator, rudder, and *alettoni* moved properly. "O.K., I won't. Get out of my way . . . *Contact!*"

She raced off the ground ten minutes behind Stevens.

Isaac Bell was already circling the field, having instructed Andy Moser to keep the motor warm and gas and castor oil topped off. From high in the air, he saw the North Side Coliseum, and all of Fort Worth, as a dull glow lost in the infinite sea of darkness that was the night-blackened Texas rangeland.

Josephine raced west, following the railroad tracks by the light of the moon.

The tall detective was right behind her, tracking the aviatrix by the pinprick of fire that marked her Antoinette's exhaust. For the first ten miles, he kept slowing his engine so as not to overtake her. But when the glow of Fort Worth had completely disappeared, and the ground was as dark behind as it was ahead, he fixed his eyes on the double line of moonlit steel, took his finger off the blip switch, and let the *Eagle* fly.

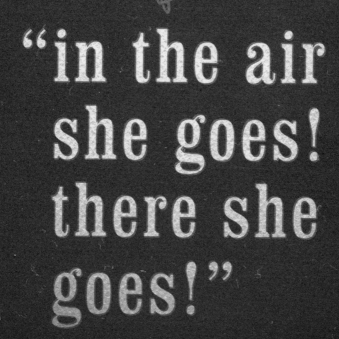

BOOK FOUR

"in the air
she goes!
there she
goes!"

Rifle vs. Machine Gun

34

HARRY FROST THOUGHT he heard something coming from the east. He saw no glow of a locomotive headlamp. But he knelt anyway and pressed his good ear to the cold steel rail to confirm that it was not a train. The track transmitted no tuning-fork vibration.

Dave Mayhew hunched over his telegraph key. It was he, eavesdropping on the railroad dispatchers, who had suddenly reported the startling news that several flying machines had ascended from Fort Worth in the dark. The blushing bride Josephine's was among them.

"This time," Harry Frost vowed in grave tones that chilled the hard-bitten Mayhew to the bone, "I'll give her a wedding night she will never forget."

He had been watching the eastern sky for nearly an hour, hoping to see her machine silhouetted against first light. So far, nothing. Still dark as a coal mine. Now he was sure he heard a motor.

He turned left and called into the dark, "Hear me?"

"Yes, sir, Mr. Frost."

He turned right and shouted again.

"Yes, sir, Mr. Frost."

"Get ready!"

He waited for a return shout, "Ready!" turned to his right, shouted again, "Get ready!" and heard, "Ready!" back.

Sound carried in the cold night air. He heard the distinctive metallic *snick* when, to either side of him, the machine gunners levered open their Colts' action to chamber their first rounds.

There were three men on each gun, knee-deep in rainwater left by the evening storms: a gunner, a feeder to the gunner's left guiding the canvas belt of cartridges, and a spotter with field glasses. Frost kept Mike Stotts standing by to run with orders if they couldn't hear him.

The noise grew louder, the sound of a straining machine. Then Frost distinguished the clatter of not one but two motors. They must be flying very close to each other, he thought. Too close. Something was wrong. Suddenly he realized that he was hearing two poorly synchronized engines driving Steve Stevens's biplane. Stevens was in the lead.

"Hold your fire! It's not her. Hold your fire!"

The biplane passed over, motors loud and ragged, flying low so the driver could see the rails. Josephine would have to fly low, too, making her an easy target.

Ten minutes elapsed before Frost heard another machine. Once again, he saw no locomotive light. Definitely an aeroplane. Was it Josephine? Or was it Isaac Bell? It was coming fast. He had seconds to make up his mind. Bell usually flew behind her.

"Ready!"

"Ready, Mr. Frost."

"Ready, Mr. Frost."

The gunner to his left yelled excitedly, "Here she comes!"

"Wait! . . . Wait!"

"Here she comes, boys!" cried the men on his right.

"Wait!"

Suddenly Frost heard the distinctive hollow-sounding blatting exhaust of a rotary motor.

"It's a Gnome! It's not her. It's a Gnome! He's ahead of her. Hold your fire! *Hold your fire!*"

He was too late. The excited gunners drowned him out with long bursts of automatic fire, feeding the ammunition belts as fast as the guns could fire. Spitting brass cartridges and empty cloth, the weapons spewed four hundred rounds a minute at the approaching machine.

ISAAC BELL LOCATED both machine guns by their muzzle flashes, two hundred yards apart to the north and south of the tracks. There was no way the gunners could see him, blinded by those flashes. But they were shooting accurately anyway, aiming at the sound of his motor, firing thunderously, stopping to listen, firing again.

Flying lead crackled as it passed close to the *Eagle*'s king posts.

Bell blipped the motor off, glided silently, then blipped it on again. The guns caught up and resumed firing. Heavy slugs shook struts behind him. The rudder took several hits, and he felt them kick his wheel post.

Bell turned the *Eagle* around and flew back up the tracks in the direction from which he had come. Facing east, back toward Fort Worth, he saw the gray glow of first light. His keen eyes detected a dot several miles distant. Josephine was coming at sixty miles at hour. He had two minutes to disable the machine guns before she ran into the clouds of lead they were shooting into the sky. But armed with a single Remington rifle, he was badly outgunned. His only hope was to sow confusion.

He blipped his motor off again, banked, and glided silently to the right. He blipped on. The south gun chattered, tracing the noise of his motor but revealing its position. Bell steered for the flashes, swooped low, and fired his rifle. He blipped off the motor and glided over the machine gun. Well past it, he blipped the Gnome again, roared around, and headed back, flying in line with the guns on a course perpendicular to the tracks.

Both guns, the closer south gun and the north gun on the far side of the tracks, opened a deadly sheet of fire. Bell swooped low over the nearer. By its muzzle flashes, he could see three men had the gun mounted on a light landing carriage, which they wheeled skillfully as he passed to rake him from behind.

Bell dropped under the stream of bullets, so low he could see flashes on the tracks. Harry Frost was firing a shotgun at the Gnome's brightly flaming exhaust. Bell dropped almost to the ground, practically parted Frost's hair with his skids, and fired his rifle at the north machine gunners, drawing their attention and causing them to wheel their gun and fire at him continuously. Had they held the trigger any longer, the air-cooled Colt would have burned up. As it was he could see the barrel glowing red-hot. But they stopped firing abruptly and scattered for their lives as their emplacement was hit by a burst from the south gunners, whom Bell had tricked into strafing their opposite position while trying to rake him from behind.

A second later, the south gun exploded when the last bullets from the northern emplacement they put out of action ignited their ammunition boxes.

Bell slammed the *Eagle* in another tight turn and fired his last shots from the Remington at the shotgun flashes. He stood little chance of hitting Frost in the dim light from his racing machine but hoped that Remington .35 slugs shrieking near Frost's head would make the murderer dive for cover.

Frost didn't budge.

He stood erect, firing repeatedly, until his shotgun was empty.

Then he jumped from the tracks into the creek bed and ran with astonishing agility the hundred yards to the machine gun whose gunners had fled. As Josephine flashed by low overhead, Frost spun the heavy weapon's carriage and fired a long burst after her. Bell drove his machine straight at him. The Remington was empty. He drew his pistol and fired as fast as he could pull the trigger. Bracketed by flying lead, Harry Frost fired back until the ammunition belt, with no one to guide it into the breech, jammed.

Bell saw Josephine's machine dip a wing. It dropped toward the ground, skimming the tracks, and Bell feared that she was wounded or her controls so badly damaged that she would slam a wing into the ground and cartwheel to oblivion. Heart in his throat, he watched with terrible anticipation that turned to astonished relief as the Celere monoplane lifted its wing, straightened up, and wobbled into the sky.

ISAAC BELL STUCK CLOSE to Josephine all the way to Abilene, where the tracks of the Abilene & Northern Railway, the Abilene & Southern, and the Santa Fe crossed the Texas & Pacific. She landed clumsily, skidding half around in front of the freight station. Bell alighted nearby.

He found her slumped over her controls, clutching her arm. A machine-gun slug had grazed her, tearing the skin and furrowing flesh. Her wedding dress was streaked with blood and engine grease. Her lips were trembling. "I nearly lost control."

"I am so sorry. I should have stopped him."

"I told you he's animal sly. Nobody can stop him."

Bell tied a handkerchief around the wound, which was still oozing blood. Small boys had come running, trailed by old men with long Civil War beards. Men and boys gaped at the yellow machines side by side in the dust.

"Run, you boys," Bell shouted, "bring a doctor!"

Josephine straightened up but did not try to climb down from her machine. Her entire body seemed rigid with the sustained effort to keep flying. She was pale and looked utterly exhausted. Bell threw an arm around her shoulders.

"It's all right to cry," he said gently. "I won't tell anybody."

"My machine's O.K.," she answered, her voice small and distant. "But he ruined my wedding dress. Why am I crying? I don't even care about this silly dress. Wait a minute!" She looked around, suddenly frantic. "Where's Steve Stevens?"

The doctor came running with his medical bag.

"Did you see a white biplane with a big fat driver?" Josephine demanded.

"Just left, ma'am, headed for Odessa. Said he's hoping to make El Paso in a couple of days. Now, let's help you off this machine."

"I need oil and gasoline."

"You need a proper bandage, carbolic acid, and a week in bed, little lady."

"Watch me," said Josephine. She raised her bloody arm and opened her fingers. "I can move my hand, do you see?"

"I see that the bone is not broken," said the doctor. "But you have had terrible shock to your system."

Isaac Bell observed the determined set to her jaw and the sudden fierce gleam in her eye. He beckoned the boys and tossed each a five-dollar gold piece. "Rustle up oil and gasoline for Josephine's flying machine. Gasoline and castor oil for mine. On the jump!"

"She can't operate a flying machine in her condition," the doctor protested.

"Patch her up!" Bell told the doctor.

"Do you seriously believe that she's flying to El Paso in her condition?"

"No," said Isaac Bell. "She's flying to San Francisco."

35

TWO DAYS LATER, Josephine circled El Paso's business district while Isaac Bell swept field glasses across the rooftops in search of Harry Frost with a rifle. Her Celere monoplane had taken the lead on the run today from Pecos, as it had the day before from Midland to Pecos.

The ground below was seething with ten thousand El Paso Texans who had turned out to greet the aviatrix, primed for her arrival by newspaper headlines blaring:

HERE COMES THE BRIDE!

They crammed the business district to watch from streets, city squares, windows, and sixth-story roofs. Mindful of the mobs they encountered in Fort Worth, Bell had demanded that Whiteway move the actual alighting spot to a more easily guarded rail yard beside the Rio Grande. Looking at the mad scene below, he was glad he had.

Josephine was still giving them a show when Steve Stevens's big white biplane appeared in the east with Joe Mudd's red Liberator laboring after it. She circled once more for the crowd, embellished the maneuver with a string of steep spiral dips that set them ooohhhing and aaahhhing, and descended to the rail yard.

Bell landed beside her.

The air racers had battled strong headwinds all day, and their support trains had already arrived. The crews were celebrating. With the state of Texas behind them now, the finish line seemed almost in sight. South, across the river, exotic Mexico shimmered in the hot sun. But it was the west that gripped their interest—the New Mexico Territory, the Arizona Territory, and finally California at the edge of the Pacific Ocean.

They weren't there yet, Bell knew, his eye captured by a series of blue mountain ranges that pointed toward the Continental Divide. To clear even the low end of the Rockies, the machines would have to climb higher than four thousand feet.

He found telegrams waiting. One lifted his spirits mightily. Archie was recovered enough to risk traveling west with Lillian on Osgood Hennessy's special train to see the end of the race. Bell wired back that they should light a fire under the lawyers angling to free Danielle Di Vecchio from the asylum and bring her with them so she could see her father's machine had flown across the continent while guarding the race—provided, of course, Bell thought, knocking ruefully on wood, that he didn't smash it to pieces or get shot out of the sky by Harry Frost.

Less happy news was contained in a long telegram from Research:

PLATOV UNMET UNSEEN UNKNOWN,

Grady Forrer had begun, confessing his failure to turn up anything about the Russian inventor Dmitri Platov beyond the reports from Belmont Park. The head of the Van Dorn Research Department added an intriguing slant that deepened the mystery:

THERMO ENGINE DEMONSTRATED AT PARIS INTERNATIONAL

AERONAUTICAL SALON BY AUSTRALIAN INVENTOR/SHEEP

DROVER ROB CONNOLLY.

NOT PLATOV.

AUSTRALIAN SOLD ENGINE AND WENT HOME.

CURRENTLY INCOMMUNICADO OUTBACK.

THERMO ENGINE BUYER UNKNOWN.

???POSSIBLY PLATOV???

Isaac Bell went looking for Dmitri Platov.

He found James Dashwood, whom he had assigned to watch the Russian, staring at the back of Steve Stevens's support train. A perplexed expression clouded his face, and he ducked his head in embarrassment when he saw the chief investigator striding purposefully straight at him.

"I surmise," Isaac Bell said sternly, "that you lost Platov."

"Not only Platov. His entire shop car disappeared."

It had been the last car on Stevens's special. Now it was gone.

"It didn't steam off on its own."

"No, sir. The boys told me when they woke up this morning, it was uncoupled and gone."

Bell surveyed the siding on which the Stevens special sat. The rails pitched slightly downhill. Uncoupled, Platov's car would have rolled away. "Can't have gotten far."

But a switch was open at the back end of the yard, connecting the support train siding to a feeder line that disappeared among a cluster of factories and warehouses along the river.

"Go get a handcar, James."

Dashwood returned, pumping a lightweight track inspector's

handcar. Bell jumped on, and they started down the factory siding. Bell lent this strength to the slim Dashwood's effort, and they were soon rolling at nearly twenty miles per hour. Rounding a bend, they saw smoke ahead, the source hidden by clapboard-sided ware-houses. Around the next twist in the rail, they saw oily smoke rising into the clear blue sky.

"Faster!"

They raced between a leatherworks and an odoriferous slaugh-terhouse, and saw that the smoke was billowing from Platov's shop car, which had stopped against the bumper that blocked the end of the rails. Flames were spouting from its windows, doors, and roof hatch. In the seconds it took Bell and Dashwood to reach it, the entire car was completely engulfed.

"Poor Mr. Platov," Dashwood cried. "All his tools . . . God, I hope he's not inside."

"Poor Mr. Platov," Bell repeated grimly. A shop car filled with tanks of oil and gasoline burned hot and fast.

"Lucky the car wasn't coupled to Mr. Stevens's special," said Dashwood.

"Very lucky," Bell agreed.

"What is that smell?"

"Some poor devil roasting, I'm afraid."

"Mr. Platov?"

"Who else?" asked Bell.

Horse-drawn fire engines came bouncing over the tracks. The firemen unrolled hoses to the river and engaged their steam pump. Powerful streams of water bored into the flames but to little ef-fect. The fire quickly consumed the wooden sides and roof and floor of the rail car until there was nothing left but a mound of ash heaped between the steel trucks and iron wheels. When it was out, the fireman found the shriveled remains of a human body, its boots and clothes burned to a crisp.

Bell poked among the wet ashes.

Something gleaming caught his eye. He picked up a one-inch square of glass framed with brass. It was still warm. He turned it over his fingers. The brass had grooves on two edges. He showed it to Dashwood. "Faber-Castell engineering slide rule . . . or what's left of it."

"Here comes Steve Stevens."

The fast-flying cotton farmer waddled up, planted his hands on his hips, and glowered at the ashes.

"If this don't beat all! Ah got a socialist red unionist creepin' up on me. Every sentimental fool in the country is rootin' for Josephine just 'cause she's a gal. And now my high-paid mechanician goes and barbecues hisself. Who the heck is goin' to keep my poor machine runnin'?"

Bell suggested, "Why don't you ask the mechanicians Dmitri helped?"

"That's the dumbest idea Ah ever heard. Even if that damn-fool Russian couldn't synchronize my motors, nobody else knows how to fix my flying machine like him. Poor old machine might as well have burned up with him. He knew it inside and out. Without him, Ah'll be lucky to make it across the New Mexico Territory."

"It's not a dumb idea," said Josephine. Bell had noticed her glide up silently behind them on a bicycle she had borrowed somewhere. Stevens had not.

The startled fat man whirled around. "Where the heck did you come from? How long have you been listenin'?"

"Since you said they're rooting for me because I'm a girl."

"Well, darn it, it's true, and you know it's true."

Josephine stared into the smoldering ruins of Platov's shop car. "But Isaac is right. With Dmitri . . . gone . . . you need help."

"Ah'll get on fine. Don't count me out 'cause I lost one mechanician."

Josephine shook her head. "Mr. Stevens, I have ears. I hear those motors chewing your machine to bits every time you take to the air. Do you want me to have a look at them?"

"Well, Ah'm not sure—"

Bell interrupted. "I'll ask Andy Moser if he would look them over with Josephine."

"In case you think I'm going to sabotage your machine when you're not looking," Josephine grinned at Stevens.

"Ah didn't say that."

"You were thinking it. Let me and Andy lend you a hand." Her grin got wider, and she teased, "Isaac will tell Andy to watch me like a hawk, so I don't 'accidentally' bust anything."

"All right, all right. Can't hurt to have a look."

Josephine pedaled back toward the rail yard.

"Hop on," Bell told Stevens, and pumped the handcar after her. Stevens was silent until after they passed the slaughterhouse and the factories. Then he said, "'Preciate yer tryin' to help, Bell."

"Appreciate Josephine."

"She took me by surprise."

"I think it's dawning on both of you that you're all in this together."

"Now you sound like that fool Red."

"Mudd is in with you, too," said Bell.

"Damned unionist."

But the best intentions could not overcome the stress of running rough for three thousand miles. Josephine and Andy tried their wizardry on Stevens's two motors all afternoon before they admitted defeat.

Josephine took Bell aside and spoke urgently: "I doubt Stevens will listen to me, but maybe if he hears it from Andy he might listen."

"Listen to what?"

"That machine will never make it to San Francisco. If he tries to force it, it'll kill him."

Bell beckoned Andy. Andy said, "Best I could do was synchronize 'em for a few minutes before they started running haywire again. But even if we could *keep* 'em synchronized, the motors are shot. He won't make it over the mountains."

"Tell him."

"Would you come with me, Mr. Bell? In case he gets mad."

Bell stood by as Andy explained the situation to Steve Stevens.

Stevens planted his hands on his hips and turned red in the face.

Andy said, "I'm real sorry, Mr. Stevens. But I'm just telling you what's true. Those motors will kill you."

Stevens said, "Boy, there is no way Ah'm goin' home to Mississippi with my tail between my legs. Ah'm goin' home with the Whiteway Cup or Ah ain't goin'." He looked at Bell. "Go ahead, speak your piece. You think Ah'm crazy."

"I think," said Bell, "there's a difference between bravery and foolishness."

"And now you're goin' to tell me what that difference is?"

"I won't do that for another man," said Bell.

Stevens stared at his big white biplane.

"Was you ever fat, Bell, when you was a little boy?"

"Not that I recall."

"You would," Stevens chuckled bleakly. "It's not somethin' you'd ever forget . . . Ah been a fat man my whole life. And a fat boy before that."

He walked in front of the biplane, trailed a plump hand over the taut fabric and stroked one of the big propellers.

"My daddy used to tell me no one will ever love a fat man. Turned out, he was right as rain . . ." Stevens swallowed hard. "Ah know damned well when Ah go home, they still won't love me. But they're sure as hell goin' to respect me."

36

JOSEPHINE WAS SPOOKED BY THE MOUNTAIN AIR. It felt thin, particularly in the hottest part of the day, and not as strong as she was used to even at speed. She watched her barometer, hardly believing her eyes, as she circled in the bluest sky she had ever seen, trying to work on altitude above the railroad city of Deming, New Mexico Territory. The makeshift altimeter seemed stuck. She tapped it hard with her finger, but the needle didn't move. When she looked down, the Union Depot and its Harvey's Restaurant, which sat between the parallel Atchison, Topeka & Santa Fe and Southern Pacific tracks, appeared no smaller, and she realized that her machine was climbing as slowly as the instrument indicated.

Steve Stevens and Joe Mudd were far below her, and she could only wonder how they were faring. She at least had mountain experience, flying in the Adirondacks. Though, to tell the truth, it wasn't much help when Wild West crosscurrents grabbed her wings, updrafts kicked like a mule, and the same air that knocked her down seemed unwilling to pick her up again. She looked over her shoulder. Isaac's *Eagle*, on faithful station above and behind her, was bouncing up and down like it was on an elastic string.

At last she worked up to three thousand feet, gave up on any more, and headed for Lordsburg, hoping to keep climbing high enough to clear the mountains. She followed the Southern Pacific Railroad tracks and soon overtook an express train that had left Deming thirty minutes ahead of her. The locomotive was spewing smoke straight up, slowly climbing a heavy grade, clear warning that the land was still rising, and she had to climb with it.

Grim thoughts of Marco suddenly wrenched at her concentration.

She did not fear that he had actually died in Platov guise. He had warned her in Fort Worth that he would "disappear." But when he reappeared in whatever form he conjured next time, the first question she had to ask was, who had died in the fire in his place? It was a terrible question. She could not think of an answer she could accept. Thank goodness, she had her hands full for now, trying to get over the Continental Divide, and she had to shove all of that out of her mind.

Ahead she saw the rails enter a pass between two mountain peaks. Despite the pure blue sky everywhere else, a thick cloud bank hung over the pass. It looked like someone had stuffed cotton between the mountains and railroad-tunneled through it. She had to climb even higher to stay above the clouds. If she got inside them, she would get lost and have no clue where the peaks were until she ran into one.

But hard as she tried manipulating her elevator and *alettoni*, and coaxing effort out of her straining Antoinette, she found herself enveloped by cold mist. Sometimes it was so thick that she couldn't see the propeller. Then, for a moment, it thinned. She spotted the peaks, corrected her course, and braced for the next blinding. All the way, she had to coax the monoplane to climb. Again the mist thinned. She saw that she had steered to the right, not even realizing it. She corrected hastily. The cloud closed around her. She was blind again. But, at the same time, she felt something in the cloud that made the air stronger.

Suddenly she was above it all, higher than the pass, higher than the cloud, even higher than the peaks, and the sky was as blue as she had ever seen in her whole life in every direction.

"Good girl, Elsie!"

For a crazy moment, she thought she could see the Pacific Ocean. But that was still seven hundred miles ahead. She looked back. Isaac Bell was *above* her, and she swore that when she won the race the first dollar she would spend of the prize money would be to buy a Gnome rotary.

Farther back, Joe Mudd's sturdy red tractor biplane was flying in circles as he patiently fought for altitude before tackling the pass. Steve Stevens soared under Mudd, passed him, and shot for the pass, using the power of his two engines to force his machine higher. It dove into the cloud bank straight in line with the railroad tracks. Josephine looked back repeatedly to see him emerge.

But instead of the white biplane suddenly boring out of the cloud, a bright red flower of fire suddenly erupted from the bank. She heard no explosion over the roar of her engine, and it took her a moment to realize what had happened. Josephine's breath caught in her throat. Steve Stevens had smashed into the mountain. His biplane was burning, and he was dead.

Two terrible thoughts pierced her heart.

Stevens's twin-motor speedster—Marco's amazing big and fast heavy-lifting machine—was out of the race, leaving Joe Mudd's slow Liberator her only competition. She hated herself for thinking that way; not only was it uncharitable and unworthy but she realized that even though she disliked Stevens, he had been part of her tiny band of cross-country aviators.

Her second terrible thought was harder to bear. Sir Eddison-Sydney-Martin would probably have won if Marco hadn't caused damage to his Curtiss Pusher.

That night in Willcox, Arizona Territory, having stopped in Lordsburg only long enough for gas and oil, Josephine overheard Marion tell Isaac Bell, "Whiteway is pleased as punch."

"He's gotten what he wanted," Isaac replied. "A neck and neck flying race between America's plucky Sweetheart of the Air and a union man on a slow machine."

EUSTACE WEED'S WORST NIGHTMARE came true in Tucson. The race was held up by a ferocious sandstorm that half buried the machines. After they got them dug out and cleaned up, Andy Moser gave him the afternoon off to shoot pool downtown. There, Eustace encountered a Yaqui Indian, who tried to take his money shooting eight-ball. The Indian was good, very good indeed, and it took Eustace Weed most of the afternoon to take the Yaqui's money and that of his friends, who were laying side bets that the Tucson Indian would beat the kid from Chicago. When Eustace left the pool hall at suppertime, the Yaqui named him "the Chicago Kid," and he felt like he was on top of the world until a fellow waiting on the sidewalk said, "You're on, kid."

"What do you mean?"

"Still got what we gave you in Chicago?"

"What?"

"Did you lose it?"

"No."

"Let me see it."

Reluctantly, Eustace Weed produced the little leather sack. The guy shook out the copper tube, inspected that the seals were intact, and handed it back. "We'll be touch . . . soon."

Eustace Weed said, "Do you understand what this will do to a flying machine?"

"You tell me."

"It's not like your motor quitting in your auto. He's up in the sky."

"That makes sense, it being a flying machine."

"Water in the gas will stop a motor dead. If that happens when he's way high up, the driver might be able to volplane down safely. *Might.* But if his motor stops dead when he's lower down, his machine will smash, and he will die."

"Do you understand what will happen to Daisy Ramsey if you don't do what you're told?"

Eustace Weed could not meet the guy's eye. He looked down. "Yes."

"Enough said."

Eustace Weed said nothing.

"Understand?"

"I understand."

37

"TEXAS" WALT HATFIELD showed up suddenly on a thundery morning in Yuma, Arizona Territory. The town sat on the banks of the recently dammed Colorado River. Across the wide water lay California. The racers were itching to make Palm Springs by nightfall. But it was thunderstorm season in California, and the locals advised waiting a few hours for the risk of lightning strikes and torrential rains to diminish. The machines were tied down under canvas, and the support trains were still in the rail yard.

"Does Mr. Van Dorn know you're here?" Bell asked, knowing the Texan's penchant for bulling off on his own.

"The range boss ordered me to hightail it here and report in person."

"You have something on Frost?"

Texas Walt shoved his J.B. back on this head. "Ran down his Thomas Flyer outside of Tuscon. How the heck he drove it that far, I don't know. But neither hide nor hair of him or his boys. I had a strong inkling they caught a train. Found out yesterday they rode out in style, having reserved a stateroom on the Limited."

"Which way?"

"California."

"So why did Mr. Van Dorn send you here?"

Texas Walt grinned, a blaze of startling white teeth in a stern countenance as sun-browned as a saddle. "'Cause he had every reason to. Isaac, old son, wait 'til you clap eyes on who I brung with me."

"There's only two men I want to clap eyes on: Harry Frost. Or Marco Celere, back from the dead."

"Damn! You are always one step ahead. How in heck did you know?"

"Know what?"

"I brung Marco Celere."

"Alive?"

"Darned tootin', alive. Got him from some Southern Pacific rail dicks I'm acquainted with. They caught a hobo hopping off a freight who swore up, down, and sideways that he's part of the air race. Claimed to know Josephine personally and demanded to see the Van Dorn detectives guarding her. As that information is not printed in the newspapers, the boys believed him enough to wire me."

"Where is he?"

"Got him right in the cookhouse. The man's starving."

Isaac Bell charged into the galley car and saw a ragged stranger, forking eggs and bacon off a plate with one hand and stuffing bread in his mouth with the other. He had greasy black hair, parted by a red scar that traveled from his brow across the crown of his skull, another red scar on his forearm, and intensely bright eyes.

"Are you Marco Celere?"

"That is my name, sir," he replied, speaking with an Italian accent somewhat heavier than Danielle Di Vecchio's though not as difficult to understand as Josephine had led Bell to believe. "Where is Josephine?"

"Where have you been?"

Celere smiled. "I wish I could answer that."

"You're going to have to answer that before I let you within a mile of Josephine. Who are you?"

"I am Marco Celere. I came awake two weeks ago in Canada. I had no idea who I was or how I got there. Then, gradually, my memory returned. In tiny bits. A trickle to start, then a flood. I remember my aeroplanes first. Then I saw a newspaper account about the Whiteway Cup Air Race. In it, I read, I have not only one but two machines, my heavy biplane and my swift *monoplano*, and suddenly it all came back."

"Where in Canada?"

"A farm. To the south of Montreal."

"Any idea how you got there?"

"I do not honestly know. The people who saved me found me by the train tracks. They assumed that I rode on a freight train."

"What people?"

"A kindly farm family. They nursed me through winter into spring before I began to remember."

Challenging the man who Danielle had called a thief and a confidence man, who had changed his name from Prestogiacomo to Celere while fleeing his past, and who James Dashwood suspected might have murdered Danielle's father in San Francisco and disguised the crime as a suicide, Bell kept peppering him with questions.

"Any idea how you happened to get amnesia?"

"I know precisely how." Celere ran his fingers along the scar on his scalp. "I was hunting with Harry Frost. He shot me."

"What brings you to the Arizona Territory?"

"I have come to help Josephine win the race in my flying machine. May I see her, please?"

Bell asked, "When did you last read a newspaper?"

"I saw a scrap of one last week in the Kansas City yards."

"Are you aware that your heavy biplane smashed?"

"No! Can it be fixed?"

"It ran into a mountain."

"That is most disturbing. What of the driver?"

"What you would expect."

Celere put down his fork. "That is terrible. I am so sorry. I hope it was not the fault of the machine."

"The machine was as worn out as the rest of them. It's a long race."

"But a magnificent challenge," said Celere.

"I should also warn you," said Bell, watching his eyes closely, "that Josephine has remarried."

Celere surprised him. He would have thought Celere would be troubled to learn that his girlfriend had married. Instead, he said, "Wonderful! I am so happy for her! But what of her marriage to Frost?"

"Annulled."

"Good. That is only right. He was a terrible husband to her. To whom has she been married?"

"Preston Whiteway."

Celere clapped his hands in delight. "Ah! Perfect!"

"Why is that perfect?"

"She is a racer. He is a race promoter. A marriage made in Heaven. I can't wait to congratulate him and wish her happiness."

Bell glanced at Texas Walt, who was listening at the door, then asked the Italian inventor, "Would you care to get cleaned up first? I'll find you a razor and some fresh clothes. There's a washroom in the back of the hangar car."

"*Grazie!* Thank you. I really must look a sight."

Bell exchanged glances with Texas Walt again and answered with a smile that didn't light his eyes. "You look pretty much like a fellow who crossed the continent in a freight car."

Bell and Hatfield led him to the washroom and gave him a towel and razor.

"Thank you, thank you. Could I ask one more favor?"

"What would you like?"

"Would there be some brilliantine?" He ran his fingers through his dirty hair. "That I might smooth my hair?"

"I'll rustle some up," said Texas Walt.

"Thank you, sir. And some mustache wax? It will be wonderful to be myself again."

"LIKE A FELLOW WHO CROSSED the continent in a freight car?" Texas Walt echoed Isaac Bell's assessment with a dubious grin.

Bell grinned back. "What do you think?"

"Looked more to me like the man rode the cushions," said Hatfield, using the hobo expression for buying a ticket for a parlor car. "Doubt he hit the rails 'til the last hundred miles."

"Exactly," said Bell, who had ridden many a freight train while investigating in disguise. "He's not dirty enough."

"Ah suppose some lonely ranch wife might have sluiced him off in her horse trough."

"Might have."

Texas Walt rolled a cigarette, exhaled blue smoke, and remarked, "Can't help wonderin' what Miss Josephine is gonna think. Suppose she'd have agreed to marry Whiteway if she had known Celere was alive?"

"I guess that depends on what they meant to each other," answered Bell.

"What do we do with him, boss?"

"Let's see what he's up to," answered Bell, wondering whether in Marco Celere's miraculous return lay the explanation for Harry Frost's angry *You don't know what* they *were up to.*

MARCO CELERE EMERGED from Bell's hangar car bathed, shaved, and brilliantined. His black hair gleamed, his cheeks were smooth, his mustache curled at the tips. Bell's own mustache twitched in the thinnest of smiles when Texas Walt glanced his way. The sharp-eyed Texan had noticed, as had he, that Celere's clean-shaven cheeks were slightly paler in color than his nose and chin. The difference was almost imperceptible, but they were looking for false notes, and there it was, an indication that he had until recently worn a beard.

Josephine expressed astonishment that Celere was alive. She said she had never given up hope that he had somehow survived. She took his hand and said, "Oh, you poor thing," when he told his story. She seemed happy to see him, Bell thought, but she turned quickly to the business of the race.

"You couldn't have come at a better time, Marco. I need help keeping the aeroplane running. It's getting pretty worn down. I'll have my husband put you on the payroll."

"There is no need for that," Celere replied gallantly, "I will work gratis. After all, it is in my interest, too, that my machine win the race."

"Then you better get to work," said Bell. "Weather's clearing.

Weiner of Accounting just announced we're taking off for Palm Springs."

MINDFUL THAT ISAAC BELL was watching him like a hawk, Marco Celere waited patiently to have a private conversation with Josephine. He made sure he was never alone with her until after she arrived at Palm Springs. Only the next morning, while they fueled the machine for the short flight to Los Angeles, did he dare to chance speaking. They were alone, pouring gasoline into the overhead gravity tank, while the mechanicians joined the police in clearing spectators from the field.

Josephine spoke first. "Who died in the fire?"

"I found a body in the hobo jungle. Now Platov doesn't exist."

"Dead already?"

"Of course. A poor old man. They die all the time. What did you think?"

"I don't know what to think."

"Maybe married life confuses you."

"What do you mean?"

"What is it like?" Marco teased. "Being Mrs. Preston Whiteway?"

"I postponed my 'honeymoon' until after the race. You know that. I told you I would."

Marco shrugged. "This is like opera buffa."

"I don't know anything about opera."

"Opera buffa is the funny kind. Like vaudeville comics."

"This is not funny to me, Marco."

"To me, it's worth getting shot."

"How? Why?"

"It's just that if something were to happen to Preston White-way, you would inherit his newspaper empire."

"I don't want his empire. I just want to fly aeroplanes and win this race." She searched his face, and added, "And be with you."

"I suppose that I should feel grateful you still feel that way."

"What would happen to Preston?"

"Oh, now Mr. Whiteway is 'Preston'?"

"I can't call my husband Mr. Whiteway."

"No, I suppose you can't."

"Marco, what is it? What are you getting at?"

"I just wonder, will you keep helping me?"

"Of course . . . What did you mean, if something happens to Preston?"

"Such as Harry Frost, your insanely jealous former husband, murdering your new husband."

"What are you saying?"

Marco reached over and turned back the sleeve of her blouse, uncovering the bandaged bullet wound on her forearm. "Nothing you don't already know about the man."

A LOUD, BRIGHT CARNIVAL pitched its tents near Dominguez Field, just south of Los Angeles, and was doing a roaring business from the spillover of the quarter-million spectators who thronged to cheer the arrival of the last two contestants for the Whiteway Cup and send them off to Fresno in the morning.

Eustace Weed was sick with fear over the impending order to contaminate Isaac Bell's aeroplane fuel and had no desire to go to a carnival. But Mr. Bell insisted that "all work and no play made Jack a dull boy." He backed up this observation with five dollars' spending money and strict orders not to bring any change back from the midway. A friend of Mr. Bell's, a guy Eustace's age named Dash who'd been hanging around, placing a lot of bets on the race, ever since Illinois, walked over with Eustace from the rail yard and promised they'd meet up later to walk back to the support train.

Eustace won a teddy bear by knocking over wooden milk bottles with a baseball. He was debating mailing it to Daisy or delivering it in person—as if somehow everything would turn out fine—when the toothless old barker who handed him his prize whispered hoarsely, "You're on, Eustace."

"What?"

"Tomorrow morning. Drop it in Bell's gasoline tank right before he takes off."

"What if he sees me?"

"Palm it when you fill the tank so he don't."

"But he's sharp as all heck. He might see me."

The toothless old guy patted Eustace's shoulder in a friendly way and said, "Listen, Eustace, I don't know what this is about and I don't want to. All I know is, the fellows who told me to pass you the message are as bad as they get. So I'm advising you, whoever this sharp Bell is, he better not see you."

The carnival had a Ferris wheel in the middle. It looked eighty feet tall, and Eustace wondered would they leave Daisy alone if he rode to the top and killed himself by jumping off. Just then, Dash showed up.

"What happened? Lose all your money? You look miserable."

"I'm O.K."

"Hey, you won a teddy bear."

"For my girl."

"What's her name?"

"Daisy."

"Say, if you married her, she'd be Daisy Weed," Dash joked like it was a new idea. Then he asked if Eustace was hungry and insisted on buying him a sausage and a beer that went down like sawdust and vinegar.

TWO HARD-FACED MEN with hooded eyes were waiting for Isaac Bell outside the *Eagle Special*'s hangar car. They were dressed in slouch hats, shirts with dirty collars, four-in-hand ties loose at the neck, and dark sack suits bulging with sidearms. One man had his arm in a sling that was noticeably fresher and whiter than his shirt, as was the bandage on his companion's forehead. Josephine's detective-mechanicians were eyeing them closely, scrutiny the two men returned with sullen bravado.

"Remember us, Mr. Bell?"

"Griggs and Bottomley. You look like you tangled with a locomotive."

"Feel that way, too," Griggs admitted.

Bell shook their hands, taking Bottomley's left in deference to his sling, and told the detective-mechanicians, "They're O.K., boys, Tom Griggs and Ed Bottomley, Southern Pacific rail dicks."

The Van Dorns looked down their noses at the railroad police, who commonly represented the bottom of the private detective heap, until Bell added, "If you remember the Glendale wreck, Griggs and Bottomley were instrumental in getting to the bottom of it. What's up, boys?"

"We had a hunch you'd be the Van Dorn ramrodding the Josephine case."

Bell nodded. "Not something I want to read in the newspaper, but I am. And I have a funny feeling, based on the evidence of recent ministrations by the medicos, that you're going to tell me you ran into Harry Frost."

"Ed plugged him dead center," said Griggs. "Gut-shot him. Didn't even slow him down."

"He wears a 'bulletproof' vest."

"Heard of them," said Griggs. "I didn't know they worked."

"We do now," observed Bottomley.

"Where did this happen?"

"Burbank. Dispatcher wired us someone was busting into a maintenance shop. Thieving louse was just piling into a motortruck when we got there. Louse opened fire. We shot back. He walked straight at us, walloped me in the head, and shot Tom in the arm."

"By the time we could see straight," said Bottomley, "he was gone. Found the motortruck in the morning. Empty."

"What did he steal?"

"Five fifty-pound crates of dynamite, some blasting caps, and a coil of fuse," answered Griggs.

"I can't say I'm surprised," said Bell. "He loves his dynamite."

"Sure, Mr. Bell. But what has Tom and me racking our brains is how's he's fixing to blow up a flying machine."

"The race is headed to Fresno in the morning," answered Bell. "I'll telephone Superintendent Watt, tell him what you boys turned up, and ask him to set the entire California division of the Southern Pacific Railroad Police to inspecting main-line bridges and trestles for sabotage."

"But flying machines don't use bridges."

"Their support trains do," Bell explained. "And just between us, at this point in the race, after four thousand miles, the mechanicians and spare parts in their hangar cars are all that's keeping them in the air. By any chance did you wound him at all?"

"I think I creased his leg when I went down. Wouldn't be surprised if he limps a mite."

"Well done," said Isaac Bell.

EUSTACE WEED DECIDED that since he had no other choice than to do this terrible thing to Isaac Bell, he would at least do it right so nothing bad happened to Daisy by mistake. That would be the worst, to get caught doing the terrible thing but also have Daisy hurt.

To steady his nerves, he pretended that he was back in Tucson, hustling hick-town pool players in their hick-town parlor. One thing he knew for sure: if you wanted to win at pool, you had to trust yourself. At the end of the game, the dough was won by the guy who didn't lose his nerve.

He snugged the copper tube inside his left hand and kept it hidden while he poured the strained gasoline–and–castor oil mix into the *American Eagle*'s tank right under Isaac Bell's nose. That way, he wouldn't look suspicious pulling it from a pocket. Andy came over to report that the machine was ready. Bell turned away to speak to Andy. Eustace reached for the gas cap to screw it on with his right hand.

Bell said, "Andy, let's check the control post again."

Eustace passed his left hand over the open mouth of the tank.

Isaac Bell's thumb and forefinger closed around his wrist, hard as a steel shackle.

"Eustace. You've got some explaining to do."

EUSTACE WEED OPENED HIS MOUTH. He could not speak. Tears welled in his eyes.

Bell watched him sternly. When he spoke, the chief investigator's voice was glacial: "I'll tell you what happened. You nod. Understand?"

Eustace was trembling.

"Understand?" Bell repeated.

Eustace nodded.

Bell let go his wrist, palming the copper tube as he did, shook it speculatively, then tossed it to Andy Moser, who took one look and glowered, "When the gas melts the wax, what's inside leaks out. What is it? Water?"

Eustace Weed bit his lip and nodded.

Bell pulled a notepad from his coat. "Do you recognize this fellow?"

Eustace Weed blinked at a drawing like you'd see in the newspaper.

"A saloonkeeper in Chicago. I don't know his name."

"How about this one?"

"He worked for the saloonkeeper. He took me to him."

"And this one?"

"He's the other one who took me to see him."

"How about this man?"

Bell showed him a sketch of a grim-faced man, more frightening than the others, who looked like a prizefighter who had never lost a bout. "No. I never saw him."

"This fellow is a Van Dorn detective who has lived for the past two weeks across the hall from Miss Daisy Ramsey and her mother. He shares his rooms with another fellow, a bigger fellow. When one has to go out, the other is there, across the hall. When Daisy goes to work at the telephone exchange, a Van Dorn man watches the sidewalk and another watches the telephone exchange. Do you understand what I'm saying to you, Eustace?"

"Daisy is safe?"

"Daisy is safe. Now, tell me everything. Quickly."

"How do you know her name?"

"I asked you her name back in Topeka, Kansas. You told me, confirming what we were already turning up in Chicago. It's our town."

"But you can't watch over her forever."

"We don't have to." Bell held up the pictures again. "These two will be locked back in Joliet prison to resume serving well-deserved twenty-year sentences. This saloonkeeper is about to go out of business and open a small dry-goods store in Seattle, a city to which he is moving for his health."

ON A REMOTE STRETCH of dun-colored ranchland between Los Angeles and Fresno, the Southern Pacific West Side Line that the air racers were supposed to follow crossed the tracks of the Atchison, Topeka & Santa Fe. Intersecting at that same point were local short-line railroads that served the raisin growers and cattlemen of the San Joaquin Valley. The resultant junction of rails, switches, and underpasses was so confusing that dispatchers and train conductors called it the Snake Dance. The Whiteway Cup Air Race stewards had marked the correct route with a conspicuous canvas arrow.

Dave Mayhew, Harry Frost's telegrapher, climbed down from a pole and read aloud his Morse alphabet transcriptions.

"Josephine's way in the lead. Joe Mudd had trouble getting off the ground. Now he's stuck in a cotton field in Tipton."

"Where's her support train?" asked Frost.

"Keeping pace. Right under her."

"Where's Isaac Bell?"

"The Tulare dispatcher heard his motor sputtering when he saw Bell and Josephine fly over. No one's spotted him since. The last dispatcher who spotted her said Josephine was flying alone."

"Where is Bell's support train?"

"Sidelined north of Tulare—probably where he went down."

Harry Frost pulled his watch from his vest and confirmed the time. By this hour, the water in his gas should have made Isaac Bell smash.

"Get the auto," he told Mayhew.

With decent luck, Bell was dead. But, at the very least, the Van Dorn posed no threat to Frost's plan to shoot Josephine out of the sky and wreck Whiteway's support train.

To Stotts, Frost said, "Move the pointer."

Mike Stotts ran onto the Southern Pacific main line, rolled up the canvas arrow pointing north and unrolled it pointing north-west up the short line that angled toward the dry hills that rimmed the valley to the west. Then he threw the switch to divert Jose-phine's train in the same direction.

Dave Mayhew drove a brand-new Thomas Flyer onto the short line. Frost and Stotts climbed in, and the three raced northwest.

39

THE ONLY NOISE ISAAC BELL HEARD was the wind humming in the wing stays as he volplaned his yellow machine in gently descending circles. Beef cattle grazed peacefully under him, and a flock of white pelicans stayed on course, proof that he was passing over the ground as silently as a condor.

A storm from the distant Pacific was surmounting the coastal mountains, and the shadow cast by his machine flickered and faded as the sun was covered and uncovered by cloud fragments racing ahead of the heavy thunderheads. As his shadow crept across the rolling hills in lazy curves, Bell maneuvered carefully so as not to let it fall on the Thomas Flyer racing ahead of a dust trail on the short-line tracks.

There were three men in the Thomas. Bell was too high in the air to identify them, even with his field glasses. But the massive bulk of the figure hunched in the backseat of the open auto, and the canvas arrow that had been shifted away from the main line, coupled with poor Eustace's attempt to sabotage his engine, told him it had to be Harry Frost.

He had spotted the dust trail ten miles after he followed the canvas arrow at the Snake Dance junction and immediately shut off the noisy Gnome. Josephine was safe on the ground thirty miles back, fuming at the delay despite an official time-out sanctioned by Preston Whiteway to give Bell the opportunity to capture Frost.

Bell turned back toward the junction and restarted the Gnome. When he saw the long yellow line that was the *Josephine Special*, he swooped down to the train, skimmed the roof of the hangar car, which bristled with rifle-toting detectives, turned around again, and led the train after the Thomas, rising to only five hundred feet above the locomotive.

After ten minutes he thought that they would have caught up, but the tracks were empty and the dust trail gone. A broad dry creek appeared ahead, a dip in the rolling land, as the tracks began veering alongside the foothills of the Coast Range mountains. It was bridged by a long wooden trestle.

The tall detective held his control wheel in one hand and scrutinized the trestle with his field glasses. The maze of timbers would offer excellent cover for men with rifles. And they could have hidden the Thomas in its shadows. But he saw neither the men nor their auto. Suddenly he heard two sharp explosions— louder than the roar of the Gnome. He knew they weren't gunshots. Nor had they come from the trestle but from directly beneath him, as if from the locomotive.

The big black Atlantic slowed abruptly. Its high drive wheels ground sparks from the rails as the engineer fought to stop his long train as fast as he could. The loud reports, Bell realized, had been caused by torpedoes—detonating caps of fulminate of mercury attached to the rails with lead straps to signal trouble ahead. When a locomotive passed over them, they exploded loudly enough for the engineer and fireman to hear over the roar of the firebox and the thunder of the steam.

Bell saw white smoke spewing from the brake shoes under

every car, and the train clashed and banged to a halt halfway across the trestle. Instantly, the locomotive emitted five puffs of steam from its whistle. Five whistles signaled a brakeman to jump from the rear car—Preston Whiteway's private carriage—and run back along the tracks waving a red flag to warn trains steaming behind it that the special had stopped suddenly for an emergency and was blocking the tracks. By then Bell had overflown the train and the trestle.

He saw the glitter of sunlight on glass.

In the same instant, he spotted the Thomas parked in the shadow of a rail-maintenance shack. The sun flashed again on a telescope sight. He counted two rifles braced on the roof of the shack, spitting red fire.

It was a brilliantly laid trap—the train stopped as a distraction, the rock-steady shooting position, the shock of total surprise. And Bell knew that if he were the young aviatrix whose name was painted on the side of his yellow monoplane, Frost would have killed her in the second hail of fire when she veered away instinctively, thus presenting a bigger target broadside.

Isaac Bell dove straight at the shack, sheered away at the last moment to aim clear of his propeller, and emptied his Remington's five-shot magazine so fast that the sound of the shots blended together in a roar like a cannon. Circling up and back, he saw that he had hit the gunmen to either side of Frost. He extracted the empty magazine, slipped a full one in its place, and dove again.

Frost did not shoot at him. Bell wondered if he had hit Frost, too, and wounded him too badly to fight. But, no, Frost was running to the Thomas. He cranked the motor, jumped in, and drove onto the tracks. Then, to Bell's puzzlement, he jumped from the auto and knelt briefly beside the rails.

Frost jumped back on the Thomas and drove toward the hills.

Less than ten seconds had expired since the shooting started. Detectives were still leaping from the hangar car. Bell banked hard to chase after the Thomas. But as the *Eagle* tipped on its side, Bell's experience with Harry Frost's relentless cruelty made him look carefully where Frost had knelt.

He saw smoke, a thin white trail of smoke.

Without hesitation, Isaac Bell rammed his blip switch, shoved his wheel forward, and dropped the *Eagle* toward the tracks. In the midst of the smoke, traveling along the rail, was a moving stud of red fire. Harry Frost had knelt on the rails and coolly lit a fuse— the fuse he had stolen from the Burbank maintenance shop along with detonators and dynamite.

He had packed the trestle with explosives, Bell realized. The attack he had planned had been twofold: shoot Josephine out of the sky, and blow Preston Whiteway's train to Kingdom Come— along with every Van Dorn riding on it.

Bell forced the *Eagle* down and straddled the rails with the skids. He hit so hard, the machine bounced and tried to rise again. It would have been safer to pour on the power and take her up again, but there wasn't a moment to lose. He drove the machine down hard and felt the skids shatter on the crossties. Splintering wood, shrieking metallic protest, the *Eagle* slid along the railroad tracks. Bell leaped and hit the ground running.

The smoke was racing ahead of him, picking up speed as it closed with the trestle. Bell ran faster, gaining on it, and was within yards of stomping it out when it slipped over the lip of the gorge and under the trestle where he couldn't reach.

"Back your engine!" he shouted, running onto the trestle. "Back off the bridge."

There was no time for that. He saw the engineer gaping from his cab and his detectives running to help him, not realizing the danger. He saw Dashwood among them.

"Dash!" he shouted. "There's a detonator fuse under the tracks. Shoot it."

Bell climbed over the edge and down through the wooden timbers beneath the track. He saw the fuse strung timber to timber, burning brightly. Dash was quick—he, too, went over the side, scrambled among the timbers, and spotted the dot of fire fifty feet away. Clinging to a timber with one arm, the young detective drew his long-barreled Colt, took aim, and fired. The bullet threw splinters. The fuse kept burning. Dash fired again. The fuse leaped and jumped, and kept burning.

Bell pulled himself along under the tracks, jumping from timber to timber. Ahead, in the shadow of the locomotive, he saw bundled dynamite—dozens and dozens of sticks, enough to destroy the trestle, the train, and everyone on it. Dash fired again. The fuse fire danced on.

Isaac Bell leaped onto a horizontal cross timber, drew his Browning smoothly from his coat, and fired once.

The dancing flame vanished. A wisp of smoke stood in its place, wavered in a puff of wind, then drifted away as if the fuse had been a candle snuffed out to end a pleasant evening.

Bell scrambled back up on the tracks and ran to the train to issue orders.

Josephine's Van Dorn mechanicians were good men but city men, next to useless out of doors. "Crank Whiteway's roadster," he told them, "and run it down the ramp. Defuse the dynamite under the bridge. Then fix the skids so my machine can fly.

"Dash! You cover the boys working on my machine. Shoot

Frost in the head if the sidewinder doubles back." He gestured
Dash closer, and added under his breath, "Don't let Celere near
my machine. Oh, by the way, I know your mother gave you that
Colt. But I would take it kindly if you would allow my gunsmith
to fix you up with a proper Browning.

"Texas Walt! You come with me!"

Bell jumped behind the steering wheel of Preston Whiteway's
yellow Rolls-Royce. Walt Hatfield piled in next to him with a couple of lever-action Winchesters, and they drove off the trestle and
raced up the railroad tracks toward the foothills of the Coast Range.

After three miles of the grade steepening and scrub growth
and clumps of low trees intruding on the grassland, they found the
Thomas Flyer stopped in the middle of the tracks with two tires
punctured by loose railroad spikes. Texas Walt spotted Frost's trail,
first from loose ballast where he had run down the railroad embankment, then from his trampling through the knee-high grass.

Bell covered the thickets and rock outcroppings ahead with a
Winchester while Hatfield loped from a scuff in the sand to a bent
blade of grass to a broken twig. Bell himself was an experienced
tracker, but Texas Walt could read the ground like the Comanches
who had raised him.

Above the hills, thunder muttered and lightning flickered inside
the swelling storm clouds. The wind puffed cold in their faces,
then hot.

A blue jay bounced up from a thicket of evergreen oaks a half
mile ahead.

It was mighty long range for a rifle, but Bell snapped, "Down!"

A shot echoed off the hills. Walt crumpled beside him.

40

BELL CUT TO THE RIGHT, seeking the shelter of a boulder. A .45-70 slug parted the air six inches from his cheek. Instead of diving for cover, he bounded past the boulder and into a narrow arroyo.

He raced silently up the dry creek bed, one eye ahead, the other guiding his boots around anything that would make noise. The arroyo veered more to the right—farther from Frost—even as it climbed the steepening slope. Bell put on speed. He ran flat out for a full mile, climbing all the distance. When he finally stopped to catch his breath, it was where a ledge would allow him to survey the ground he had put behind him. Slithering flat on his belly, he edged forward until he could see the back of the thicket from which Frost had fired.

Now half a mile below him, it covered nearly an acre of the hillside. Frost could be hidden anywhere inside it or he might have retreated up the slope and could now be more at Bell's level. If he were smart, he would have withdrawn. But Bell was betting that Frost was making a big-game hunter's mistake by staying still or moving only a short distance to lay another ambush for his quarry. Most animals ran when hunted. Some, like panther and elephant, might occasionally charge. Very few slipped past to attack from behind.

Bell chose the route for his attack down a shallow arroyo and past a thicket. He eased back from the ledge to stay out of sight and started down. He was silent and he was quick, loath to give Frost time to reconsider his position. When the arroyo grew too shallow to hide him, he crawled to the nearest thicket and kept going.

The leaden arch of sky was pierced suddenly by jagged lightning.

Drops of rain scattered the dust.

Again the wind rattled the hard-leafed chaparral, first hot, then cold.

Suddenly he skidded off balance. He kicked a rock, which rolled noisily downhill.

A shot cracked, the bullet kicking dust fifteen feet below him. Bell instantly grabbed another rock and threw it far to his right. It landed with a clatter that drew more fire. Let Frost wonder which rock had been accidentally dislodged and which thrown. Bell started down again. The location from where Frost had fired his rifle was almost exactly where Bell had guessed. He was staying put in the thicket, which was now less than three hundred yards below him. But now Frost knew to look behind him.

Without warning, he exploded into action, shoving out of the dense undergrowth running for the cover of a depression in the land that looked to Bell like the mouth of a small canyon. Frost was limping, as Tom Griggs had speculated, but still covering ground at a startling speed for a man his size. Bell snapped a shot at him that missed. He levered a fresh round into the Winchester and stood erect to deliberately line up a second shot, leading the running man and calculating the effect of the rising wind over the two hundred yards that separated them. His rifle spoke.

Frost flung his arms high. His Marlin went flying. The distance was too long to hear him yell, but Bell thought he had hurt him badly until he saw Frost scoop his fallen rifle off the ground and disappear into the canyon.

Isaac Bell ran down the slope, bounding from hummock to hummock, leaping brush and boulders. He lost his footing, pitched to the ground, rolled on his shoulder, and sprang to his feet again, still running and clutching his Winchester.

He sensed more than saw a flicker of movement at the mouth of the canyon and dove headlong to the ground. A pistol slug whistled through the air he had just vacated. He tucked the Winchester tight to his chest, rolled, and this time when he sprang to his feet he came up firing, levering slug after slug into the breech, spraying a deadly fusillade that sent Frost in retreat.

For some reason, Frost wasn't using his Marlin. Bell guessed that his Winchester shot that had set it flying had damaged it, in which case Frost was down to sidearms. He burst into the canyon, which was no wider than a town house but appeared to bore deeply into the hillside. Thick brush clogged the mouth. Bell pushed through thorny chaparral. Pistol shots booming close at hand revealed Frost, crouching and firing his snub-nosed Webley-Fosbery automatic revolver with which he had almost killed Archie Abbott. The range was too long for the sawed-off barrel. The manstoppers flew wildly, scattering splinters of wood.

Bell tried to fire back. His Winchester was empty.

Frost charged, plowing through the brush like a buffalo, triggering his heavy pistol as he halved the range and burst from the thicket. It was Bell's first close look at him. One eye was cloudy, the socket scarred where Bell's Remington rifle shots had hurled stone chips in his face at the Chicago armory. The ear Bell had winged was a ragged appendage. The jaw Archie had broken was misshapen. But his good eye burned hot as a gasoline fire, and he ran with the unstoppable gait of a locomotive.

Bell dropped to one knee, pulled his throwing knife from his boot, and flung it hard. It slid between the bones of Frost's forearm, and the deadly Webley-Fosbery fell from his convulsing fingers. Before it hit the ground, Frost pulled out a pocket pistol with his left hand.

Bell drew his Browning and triggered it twice. Their weapons echoed in unison. Frost's vest deflected both of Bell's bullets. One of Frost's shots fanned Bell's cheek, the other plucked his sleeve. Frost's pocket pistol jammed, and he drew his own Browning, a far deadlier threat than the pistol. Bell ran straight at him and shot the Browning out of Frost's hand. Frost threw a roundhouse left, spraying Bell with blood from his skewered forearm.

Bell deflected some of the impact with his shoulder. But the giant's punch rocked him to the core, knocked him halfway to his knees. White flashes stormed before his eyes. His hands felt heavy as lead. He sensed a second pile-driver punch coming at him, rolled with it, and hurled his own punch, aiming for the jawbone that Archie had broken.

His tightly clenched fist connected, staggering the giant and drawing a grunt of pain. But Frost whirled around and back-handed him with a blow that knocked the detective to the ground. Frost picked up his ruined rifle and raised it to the sky like a long steel club. Isaac Bell whipped his derringer from his hat.

"Drop it!" he said. "You're a dead man."

Frost swung the rifle.

Bell squeezed the trigger.

A blaze of light and an explosion fifty times louder than a pistol shot sent the rifle pinwheeling forty feet. Frost was smashed flat on the ground. Six feet away, Isaac Bell remained on his feet, ears ringing, staring down at his fallen adversary in astonishment. The smell of burning flesh hung in the air. Frost's face was black, his beard burned, his shirt and trousers smoldering, the soles blown off his boots.

Life was leaking from Frost's eyes. He sucked air through his charred lips. But his voice was still strong, harsh and thick with scorn. "You didn't get me. Lightning bolt hit my rifle."

"I had you dead to rights," answered Bell. "The lightning just happened to get you first."

Frost croaked bitter laughter.

"Is that why Van Dorns never give up? You got weather gods on your side?"

Isaac Bell gazed down triumphantly at the dying criminal. "I didn't need weather gods," he said quietly. "I had Wally Laughlin on my side."

"Who the hell is Wally Laughlin?"

"He was a newsboy. You murdered him and two of his friends when you dynamited the Dearborn Street news depot."

"Newsboy? . . . Oh yeah, I remember." He shuddered with pain and forced out another jibe. "I'll hear about it in Hell. How old was he?"

"Twelve."

"Twelve?" Frost lay back. His voice grew weak. "Twelve was my grand year. I'd been a little runt getting used by every Tom, Dick, and Harry. Then all of a sudden I started growing and growing, and everything went my way. Won my first fight. Got my first gang. Killed my first man—twenty years old, he was, full grown."

A hideous parody of a smile twisted Frost's burnt lips.

"Poor little Wally," he muttered sarcastically. "Who knows what the little bastard could have made of himself."

"He made a memory of himself," said Isaac Bell.

"How'd he do that?"

"He had a kind soul."

BELL STOOD UP and gathered his weapons.

Harry Frost called after him. Suddenly there was fear in his voice. "Are you leaving me here to die alone?"

"You've left crowds to die alone."

"What if I told you something you don't know about Marco Celere?"

Bell said, "Marco Celere showed up in Yuma three days ago, fit as a fiddle. You ran from the only murder you didn't commit."

Frost levered himself up on one elbow and shot back, "I *know* that."

Intrigued, Bell knelt beside the dying man, watching his hands for a hidden knife or another pocket pistol stashed in his smoldering garments. "How?"

"Marco Celere showed up at Belmont Park *six weeks ago*."

"Celere gave me the impression he was in Canada six weeks ago."

"He was right in the middle of the race," Frost crowed. "Prancing around the infield like he owned it. You damned Van Dorns never knew."

"*Platov!*" said Bell. "Of course!" Marco Celere was the saboteur, though proving it in a court of law would be next to impossible.

"A little late on that one, Mr. Detective," Frost sneered.

"How did you happen to see him?"

"He spotted me one night I was trying to get near Josephine's machine. Walked up to me, big as life, and offered a deal."

"I'd have thought you'd kill him on sight," said Bell.

"You know that sawed-off coach gun the Italians call a *lupa*? He had it pointed at my head. Both hammers on full cock."

"What deal?"

"Should I give you a gift for little Wally?" Frost asked mockingly. "Information you can use to get Celere? You think if I do you a favor, they'll be nice to me in Hell?"

"I don't see you getting a better chance than this one. What was the deal?"

"If I held off killing Josephine until after she won the race, then Marco would take me to a place where I could hide out in luxury for the rest of my life."

"Where would this paradise be?" Bell asked skeptically.

"North Africa. Libya. The Turkish colonies that Italy is going to win in North Africa. He said we'd be safe as houses and live like kings."

"Sounds like con-man palaver."

"No. Celere knows his business. I've been over there, I seen it with my own eyes. The Ottomans—the Turks—they're on their last leg and Italy's so poor and crowded, they're itching to grab their colonies. So Celere's setting himself up to be the Italian Army's gold-haired boy by supplying aerial war machines. He'll be the national hero when Italy beats Turkey with his machine-gun aeroplanes and bomb carriers. But he knows he's got to prove himself. They'll only buy his machines if Josephine wins the race."

"Why didn't you take him up on it?"

Rage stiffened Frost's ravaged face. "I *told you*, I'm not a chump. If he was so fixed there in North Africa that he could protect me, then he'd hold the key to my cell. I might as well be back in the orphanage."

"Why didn't he blow your head off with his *lupa*?"

"Celere's like a juggler, always tossing a bunch of balls in the air. He bet on you protecting her and hoped I would change my mind—*and* that I would kill Whiteway when the time came."

"What time came?"

"The wedding. He knew Whiteway was angling for Josephine. Marco figured I'd be so mad, I'd kill Whiteway, and Josephine would inherit the money and marry him. And if later I killed her, too, he'd get it all."

Frost's one good eye sought Bell's two. "Marco started this. He's the one who turned her head. So I reckoned the juggler seeing all his balls come crashing down was my sweetest revenge."

"Another reason to kill her?" asked Bell.

"Marco knew the Stevens biplane would never make it. He needed Josephine to prove that his flying machines can be fighting machines."

Bell shook his head. "All she wants is to fly."

"I gave her the chance, she turned it against me. She deserves to be killed," Frost whispered.

"You're dying with hatred on your lips."

ISAAC BELL WAS DEEPLY RELIEVED to find Texas Walt, sitting in the rain, holding his head.

"Feels like John Philip Sousa's playing a steam calliope where my brain used to be."

Bell walked him to the Rolls-Royce and drove it to the trestle, Walt cussing a blue streak at every bump. The mechanicians had repaired the *Eagle*'s undercarriage. Bell made Walt comfortable on the train. Then he took to the air and headed for Fresno, the last overnight stop before San Francisco. Josephine's yellow machine and Joe Mudd's red tractor biplane were tied down fifty yards apart on a muddy fairground. Joe Mudd leaned on crutches, joking with the mechanicians working on his undercarriage.

"Hard landing?" Bell asked.

Mudd shrugged. "Just a busted leg. Machine's O.K. Mostly."

"Where's Josephine?"

"She and Whiteway are at the fairground hotel. I'd steer clear, if I were you."

"What's wrong?"

"Stormy weather."

Bell beckoned Josephine's detective-mechanicians, who were ferrying tools and parts for Marco Celere, who was shaking his head over her motor. "Keep a sharp eye on Celere. Do not let him near Joe Mudd's machine."

"What if he makes a run for it?" asked Dashwood.

"He won't. Celere's not going anywhere as long as there's any chance Josephine will win the race."

He went to the fairground hotel. Preston Whiteway had rented the top floor of the two-story structure. Bell quickened his pace up the stairs when he heard the publisher shouting at the top of his lungs. He knocked loudly and entered. Whiteway was standing over Josephine, who was curled in a tight ball in a parlor chair, staring at the carpet.

Whiteway saw Bell, and instead of asking what had happened with Harry Frost he shouted, "You talk sense to her! Maybe she'll listen to you!"

"What's the matter?"

"My wife refuses to finish the race."

"Why?"

"She won't tell me. Maybe she'll tell you. Where the hell's my train?"

"Just pulled in."

"I'll be in San Francisco for the end of the race."

"Where is Marion?"

"Gone ahead with her cameras," Whiteway answered. He lowered his voice to a hoarse stage whisper that Josephine could have heard in the next county and pleaded, "See if you can talk sense into her—she's throwing away the chance of a lifetime."

Bell replied with a silent nod.

As Whiteway backed out of the room, he appeared to see Bell for the first time. "You look like you've been wrestling grizzly bears."

"You should have seen the other guy."

"Help yourself to the whiskey."

"I intend to," said Isaac Bell.

41

"WANT SOME?" Bell asked Josephine.

"No."

Bell filled a short glass, tossed it back neat, filled it again, and sipped. "Josephine, what did you say when Marco asked you to come with him to North Africa?"

She looked up from the carpet, eyes wide. "How did you know that?"

"He made Harry Frost the same offer."

"*Harry?* Why?"

"Marco wanted Frost to kill your new husband."

Josephine's eyes went dead. "Marco's worse than Harry," she whispered.

"I'd say they were neck and neck. What was your answer, Josephine?"

"I told him no."

Bell watched her closely as he said, "I'll bet Marco thinks you'll change your mind when you're a rich widow."

"Never . . . Is Preston in danger?"

"Harry Frost is dead."

"Thank God . . . Do you think Marco has the guts to kill Preston without Harry's help?"

Instead of answering that question, Isaac Bell said, "I know why you're quitting the race."

"No you don't."

"You're quitting because Marco Celere, disguised as Dmitri Platov, sabotaged the best of the other machines."

She looked away. "I wondered," she whispered. "I didn't just wonder, I suspected. But I didn't stop him. Losing the race will be my punishment. I have been terrible."

"Because you didn't stop him or because you went along with Marco's plan to frame Harry for murder?"

"Did Harry tell you that, too?"

Bell smiled. "No, I stumbled on that on my own."

"Looking back, I know it was an evil plan. I knew it then but Harry deserved to be locked up again."

"Why did you let Marco talk you into marrying Whiteway?"

"I was too tired to argue. I just wanted to win the race—"

"Perhaps you thought that if one marriage could be annulled, so could another?"

"Sure, if we had no honeymoon. And I swear, Isaac, I had no idea Marco planned to kill Preston. Poor Preston, he's just so . . . Poor Preston, he is such a fool, Isaac, he really loves me."

Bell gave her a gently teasing smile. "Maybe Preston thinks that when you fall in with the wrong men and don't see what they're doing, that you're not so terrible—just single-mindedly myopic in your determination to fly? Maybe that's why he can't believe you won't finish the race."

"I do not deserve to win . . . Are you going to arrest Marco?"

"I can't, yet. I don't have enough proof to make a case in court. Besides, I want him free to work on your machine in case you change your mind."

"I won't. The winner should win fair and square."

"You and Joe Mudd are neck and neck. It would be good for the winner, and good for aviation, if you raced right down to the wire. Whatever you've done wrong, it doesn't change the fact that you've driven a flying machine across the continent. Why don't you sleep on it? Meantime, I'll let Marco work on the machine overnight."

EPILOGUE

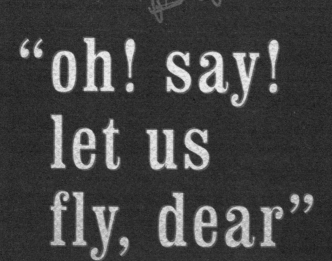

"oh! say! let us fly, dear"

Let Us Fly, Dear

MARCO CELERE SAW a way out of his predicament. Rather than wait helplessly for Josephine to change her mind, and fearing she would not, he placed a long-distance call from the hotel telephone. Preston Whiteway snatched up his telephone like a man who had been waiting all night for news from Fresno. "Will she fly?"

"This is Marco Celere, inventor of your aeroplane and chief mechanician."

"Oh . . . Well? Will she fly?"

"I understand," Celere answered suavely, "that Mr. Bell is discussing it with her over breakfast. There's time still—there's a low fog on the field the sun hasn't burned off yet. But I have a suggestion. If Josephine cannot win the Whiteway Cup, surely her flying machine can."

"What are you talking about?"

"If she doesn't agree to finish the race, I will fly the last leg from Fresno and win the race for her."

"Against the rules. One driver, one machine, all the way."

"We are men of the world, Mr. Whiteway. They are your rules. The Whiteway Cup is your race. Surely you can change your own rules."

"Mr. Celere you may know something about building flying machines, but you don't know the first thing about newspaper readers. They'll buy any lie you print—unless it's a lie about some-thing you've already convinced them to love. They love Josephine. They want her to win. They don't give a hang about your flying machine."

"But it would be so good for aviation—" Celere pleaded.

"And even better for you. I wasn't born yesterday."

The telephone banged dead in Celere's ear.

Celere listened outside the hotel dining room. He heard Bell speaking urgently. Then he heard Josephine say loudly and clearly, "No."

Celere hurried out on the field to his monoplane. The fog was still heavy, and he could barely see Joe Mudd's and Isaac Bell's machines. Josephine's Van Dorn mechanicians were watching him suspiciously even though he had been guiding their efforts since Yuma, Arizona.

"We should start the motor," he said.

"Why? She's not going anywhere."

"Mr. Bell is very persuasive. He still may convince Josephine to change her mind. Let us fill her tanks, spin her motor, and make it warm for her." They exchanged glances. Celere said, "I don't see Joe's Mudd's mechanicians hanging about this morning. They'll be ready to go when the fog lifts. Shouldn't we be? Just in case?"

That got them going. It was after all a race, and though they were better detectives than mechanicians, they had been compet-ing daily for forty-eight days and four thousand miles.

"Start fueling. I will be right back."

He went to the tiny stateroom they had given him on the train and returned carrying a yard-long, six-inch-wide corrugated paper tube sealed at either end and shoved it into the driving nacelle.

"What's that?" asked a detective.

"*San Francisco Inquirer* flag, which Josephine is supposed to wave when she lands at the Presidio. What is wrong with motor?"

"What do you mean?"

"I do not like the sound."

"Sounds fine to me."

Celere looked the detective-mechanician in the eye. Then he flashed his most winning smile. "Let us make a deal, you and me, sir. I will not arrest criminals. You will not tell me that a flying-machine motor sounds like it will not suddenly stop in the sky."

"Sorry, Celere. You're right. What do you hear?"

"Bring me soapbox." He climbed on the box and into the nacelle and played with the throttle, revving and slowing the Antoinette. He cocked his ear, shaking his head in puzzlement. "Pull chocks. Let's taxi her around a little."

"Careful you don't run into anything. Can't see fifty feet."

The mechanicians pulled the wooden blocks that were holding the wheels in place.

Celere revved the motor. "You hear? You hear?"

"I'm not sure."

"Listen . . . Here, I make go faster."

He opened the throttle all the way. The Antoinette's crisp burble increased to a roar. He turned the rudder, shaped the wings, raced fifty yards along the grass, and soared into the fog.

BELL ORDERED his *Eagle* made ready to fly, but there was no following Celere in the fog because no one knew which way he had gone. He had to wait until some railroad dispatcher wired a report that he had been spotted. Nearly an hour later, Isaac Bell received a telephone call from the railroad detectives Tom Griggs and Ed Bottomley.

"Are you sure you got Harry Frost?"

"I laid him personally on a slab of ice in the Fresno police station."

"Yeah, well, we just had our second dynamite robbery in two days. Fellow walked into our Merced shop with a coach gun, terrorized the poor old clerk into loading two hundred pounds of dynamite, detonators, and ice tongs on a track inspector's handcar, and pumped off. We found the handcar three miles down the line next to an empty hayfield. Not a trace of the fellow or the dynamite or the ice tongs."

"Ice tongs?" Bell echoed, mystified. "What else did he take?"

"Isn't two hundred pounds of dynamite enough?"

"What else?"

"Hold on! . . . Hey, Tom, Mr. Bell wants to know did he take anything else . . . Oh yeah. Tom says he took a flashlight and some electric cable."

"What kind of detonators? Fulminate of mercury?"

"Electric."

"Did you find any truck or wagon tracks?"

"That's the funny thing. The only wheel tracks were out in the middle of the field. Nothing by the road except footprints. Strange, don't you think?"

"*Not if he came and left on a flying machine!*"

"Oh. Never thought of that . . . You still there, Mr. Bell?"

Isaac Bell was running to his *American Eagle*. "Spin her over!"

The Gnome's urgent *Blat! Blat! Blat!* caused Joe Mudd to turn aside and let Bell take off ahead of the Liberator. Bell picked up the Southern Pacific tracks and headed north toward San Francisco. He had less than two hundred miles in which to catch up with Marco Celere.

The stolen electric detonators, the flashlight, and the electric cable were the clues that told Bell exactly what Marco Celere intended to do. He had stolen the ingredients to make an aerial bomb with an electric detonator. Fulminate of mercury detonators that exploded on contact would be deadly on a flying machine that bounced as it took off from the ground and was battered sharply by air currents in the sky. Any sudden motion would make them detonate the dynamite and the flying machine with it.

But an *electric* detonator could be controlled by a simple switch between the flashlight batteries and the detonators. As long as the switch was off, the dynamite was safe. Switch it on, and the dynamite would explode.

Celere would have fashioned it to be moved into the on position after it was dropped—then only when it fell on its target. He would have installed two switches, one to make the bomb ready at the moment he was ready to drop, the second that would cause the explosion on impact.

Bell could not imagine why Celere had taken ice tongs.

But the rest was clear. Whiteway had refused to let him demonstrate that his machine could win the race, even without Josephine, leaving Celere with no way to prove to the Italian Army that his aeroplane could be a war machine.

Dropping two hundred pounds of dynamite would prove its military value with a bang heard around the world. As to what he would drop his bomb on, the answer was obvious. A con man like Celere was essentially the same as a boomer like Preston Whiteway. Both had an instinct for how to get the most publicity. Few buildings in San Francisco were as tall, and none more famous, than the San Francisco Inquirer Building. A flying machine destroying it would be a shot heard by every army general in the world.

And if Whiteway were to die in his penthouse office atop the San Francisco Inquirer Building, so much the better: the wealthy Widow Josephine would be available, Celere would think. Bell knew she would never fall for him again, but Celere didn't. By the Italian's reckoning, he would kill two birds with one bomb, Bell thought grimly: demonstrate the power of his warplane and marry a wealthy widow.

It was good flying weather. The wind had dropped. The sky was clear, the air cool enough to cool the motor and rich enough to make it run at top power. The Gnome rotary would give him the speed to overtake Celere. But when he finally saw the break in the hills that the rail line followed toward Oakland and then the blue bays of Oakland and San Francisco, he still had not caught up. Celere might have smashed along the way, in water or woods, where Bell hadn't seen him. It was possible. The machines were tired.

Then, abruptly and with a sinking heart, Isaac Bell saw the yellow speck that told him Celere was crossing the bay and closing in on the city. He was flying lower than Bell, perhaps dragged down by the weight of the explosives or perhaps descending to make it easier to hit his target. But it gave Bell a slim advantage, and he took it, pushing his control post forward and diving to increase speed.

Ahead, the Oakland Mole jutted far into San Francisco Bay. It was the pier that carried trains to the ocean freighters and city ferries, and, as he flew the length, he saw parked on it the famous dark green Southern Pacific special owned by the president of the line, Osgood Hennessy. Archie and Lillian had arrived with Danielle Di Vecchio.

He was catching up.

He was well over the water while Celere hadn't yet crossed to the shore.

Bell pulled his rifle up from the nacelle and clipped it into the swivel. High-power Remington slugs crackling past Celere's head ought to concentrate his mind more on escaping than dropping a bomb, which would be a cumbersome exercise with lead howling by.

But when Bell located the monoplane in his powerful field glasses, he got a shock.

Now he knew why Celere had stolen the ice tongs. He had forgotten that whatever his failings, Celere was a darned clever machinist. There would be nothing cumbersome about dropping the dynamite, no clumsy hoisting it over the side of the machine.

All four boxes of dynamite were dangling below the monoplane, directly under Celere, where the two hundred pounds would be well balanced, and they were hanging from the ice tongs. Bell saw a rope running from the ice-tong handle up the side of the aeroplane into the steering nacelle where Celere sat.

To drop the dynamite, all he had to do was arm the electric detonator switch and tug the rope.

Bell dropped his glasses and took aim with the Remington auto rifle. The range was still too great. But now Celere was crossing the forest of sailing masts that marked the waterfront. He was mere minutes from Whiteway's Market Street headquarters. Bell steepened his dive and picked up a little more speed. It made the difference: now he, too, was crossing the waterfront, and Celere was in rifle range. But he was flying above Bell now because the dive had taken him so low, he was nearly scraping building tops.

Ahead was the Inquirer Building, taller than all around it, with the yellow race banner on top. Bell tweaked his elevator, rose slightly, and found Celere's machine in his rifle sight. Just as Bell was about to pull the trigger, he saw something glitter on the out-door terrace of Whiteway's penthouse office. Bell whipped his field glasses to his eyes.

Immediately ahead of Celere's dynamite-laden monoplane, smack in his line of fire, operators where cranking moving-picture cameras. Directing them was a tall blond woman in a white shirt-waist with her hair swept up so she could inspect what they saw through their lenses. Marion had chosen to shoot the finish from the dramatic setting of the roof where the aviators would circle before landing at the Presidio.

Bell banked hard right to change his field of fire. Celere was flying straight at the building. He was less than one hundred feet higher, and closing fast, when Bell saw him reach for the rope.

Bell had no clear shot at Celere without endangering Marion.

But if he didn't shoot, Celere would drop his bomb.

Bell whipped his machine hard left. The wings rattled, and the stays groaned. The motor screamed as the propeller hacked the shifting air. He soared away from Celere's course to shift the angle so he could fire. The range increased radically. He had one second to fire. The gun kicked. Marco Celere ducked his head and looked around wildly, eyes locking in astonishment on Bell's *Eagle* racing back at him.

He grabbed the bomb-release rope. But he was too late. His

flying machine had flown past the Inquirer Building. He banked to swing back and make another run.

"Not on my watch," said Isaac Bell.

With the people on the penthouse terrace safely behind them, Bell pegged another shot at Celere. This one came closer, he guessed by the violent motion of Celere's head, followed by a steep climbing turn away from Bell. Bell followed. The trick, he realized, was to stay behind and stay inside Celere's turn so that he could keep firing to drive Celere farther and farther from his target.

Celere went up, Bell followed. Celere went down, Bell followed again, drawing so close that he could see Celere's face as if they were about to commence a boxing match. Celere ducked down, reaching for something inside the nacelle, and brought up a stubby weapon that Bell recognized as his sawed-off *lupa* shotgun. Buckshot screeched and pinged through his wing stays.

"You have teeth? So do I."

Bell fired his swivel gun.

Celere's hand flew from his control post as if it were red-hot. Bell fired again.

Celere jerked *alettoni* and rudder, and the machine soared toward San Francisco Bay. Bell followed, thinking to force him down over the water. But Celere turned around and raced back at the Inquirer Building. Bell turned more sharply. The *Eagle* went exactly where he pointed it, and he was suddenly aware that after four thousand miles across the continent he was getting the hang of flying.

He pulled alongside, leveled his swivel gun at Celere, and let go the wheel to motion that Celere should descend and land before he shot him. Celere whipped up the *lupa* and blasted back point-blank. Buckshot shrieked again, most of it missing, except for a single slug that struck the breech of the Remington, jamming it.

Isaac Bell drew his Browning and raked Celere's machine with pistol fire.

The answering bellow of the *lupa* told him that Celere was not impressed. And now the Italian pressed his advantage of heavier firepower, skillfully reloading and firing repeatedly. Only the short range of the shotgun saved Bell from being hit as Celere lined up again to drop the bomb.

Bell saw him reach for the arming wire that would close the first electric switch.

He wrenched the *Eagle* onto a collision course. He saw sudden panic on Celere's face. About to ram into the side of the yellow monoplane, Bell turned at the last second to cross directly in front. Celere whirled the double-barreled *lupa*, tracking Bell until Bell was so close he could see deep inside its gaping muzzles.

When he could not miss, Marco Celere triggered both barrels. Isaac Bell saw flame jet from them.

A torrent of buckshot roared at him, and the tall detective knew that his tactic had worked. He had won the battle. Celere's whirling propeller blocked the buckshot. The speeding lead shattered the eight-foot wooden airscrew into splinters. The yellow monoplane staggered in the air. Celere tried to volplane by gaining speed with a diving turn. The weight of the dynamite was too much for the suddenly powerless flying machine. Instead of turning, it began to spin. One wing brushed the parapet of the Inquirer Building and snapped off.

Momentum lost, the wrecked monoplane tumbled toward Market Street.

Isaac Bell held his breath. He could only pray that he had distracted Celere sufficiently to keep him from arming the dynamite. If he hadn't—if Celere did close the electrical circuit—the falling aeroplane would explode on impact. In two seconds, which stretched like eternity, it hit but did not explode, harming only its murderous inventor and Preston Whiteway's yellow Rolls-Royce on which it landed.

ISAAC BELL CIRCLED the Inquirer Building and exchanged joyous waves with Marion Morgan.

Then he skirted Nob Hill and steered across the city toward the Golden Gate.

Far behind him, he saw a red speck in the sky. Joe Mudd's Liberator was approaching Oakland. Bell grinned with genuine pleasure. Mudd and his sturdy little tractor biplane had only ten miles to go to win the Whiteway Cup. The expression on Whiteway's face would be priceless.

Ahead, a splash of green on the tip of the peninsula that sheltered San Francisco Bay from the Pacific Ocean marked the Presidio. The grounds of the Army post appeared to be in motion, rippling like a wind-stirred field of grain. It was an illusion, Bell realized as he drew nearer, created by a horde of spectators who filled parade grounds, streets, and barracks roofs in the tens of thousands. Closer still, he even saw them clinging to the tops of trees.

The only place with room to alight was the sloping parade ground in front of Infantry Row, the red brick barracks on Montgomery Street, which was guarded by a company of soldiers holding back the crowd.

Bell steered into a salty Pacific wind, blipped his Gnome to slow it down, and landed his machine on the narrow stretch of ground that the Army had secured. The roar of the crowd drowned out his motor. He scanned their faces and felt his heart lift. There was Archie Abbott, standing on his own two feet, pale but smiling, with Lillian bracing one arm. It took Bell a moment to recognize the tall, stylishly dressed brunette with them as Danielle Di Vecchio, who was smiling proudly at her father's machine. Next to her, considerably less stylish looking but grinning as proudly, was Andy Moser, and Bell surmised that the railroad had cleared the tracks for the Van Dorn Agency's *Eagle Special* to speed to San Francisco.

As Bell jumped down from the *Eagle*, Weiner of Accounting bustled up, trailed by the many assistants he had acquired in the course of the race.

"Congratulations, Mr. Bell."

"For what?"

"You won."

"Won what?"

"The Atlantic-to-Pacific Cross-Country Air Race. The Whiteway Cup is yours."

"What the devil are you talking about, Mr. Weiner?"

The accountant explained that in the course of protecting Josephine, Isaac Bell had flown his *American Eagle* monoplane all the way across America and landed first, with the best overall time.

"I wasn't in the race. How could I win?"

"I am a certified accountant, sir. I and my staff kept track of every minute flown by every contestant. You won. Fair and square."

"But I didn't register. I never even got my flying license."

Weiner, Bell soon discovered, had put his race time to good use by mastering the art of booming in addition to accounting.

"I am sure," he answered with a knowing wink, "that Mr.

Whiteway will overlook certain minor technicalities when he considers how many newspapers we will sell touting a winner who is not only a dashing detective but is engaged to a beautiful blond moving-picture director. Your public awaits."

Weiner indicated the mob of photographers and correspondents poised to pounce on the winner. "Don't worry about the details, Mr. Bell, we'll make you the most famous man in America."

Off to the side, out of the hoopla, Bell saw a bandaged "Texas" Walt Hatfield quietly celebrating with James Dashwood. They were passing a flask and puffing on cigars. Dash coughed on the smoke. The Texan slapped him on the back. Dash responded by flicking his new derringer from his wrist, and, when both men laughed, it struck Isaac Bell that if he accepted the Whiteway Cup, the most famous man in America would be far too well known to ever again operate as a Van Dorn detective.

Marion Morgan raced up in a taxi, urging her camera operators to plant their tripods. She threw a glorious smile to Bell and pointed him out to her operators, with the usual stern warning to keep him out of the picture.

Preston Whiteway arrived right behind her, careening onto the field in a newspaper-delivery van driven by his demolished Rolls-Royce's chauffeur.

"Who won?" he bellowed.

Weiner of Accounting turned expectantly to Isaac Bell.

"You're looking at him," said the tall, golden-haired detective.

"Who?"

Isaac Bell took one long last look at the cheering crowds. Then he turned slowly on his heel and pointed at the sky. Joe Mudd's Revolution Red Liberator wobbled over the hill, lined up into the ocean wind, and floated to the grass.

"Labor?" gasped Whiteway.

"Bricklayers, masons, plasterers, and locomotive firemen."

"*Unionists* won my race?"

"Tell your readers they worked for it."

MARION AND ARCHIE AND LILLIAN crowded around while Andy and Danielle helped Isaac Bell refuel his flying machine. Andy assured him it was still sound despite a few bullet holes, repeating, "Danielle's old man built a heck of a strong machine, didn't he, Danny?"

"*Elastico!*" said Danielle, bathing Andy and Bell with her dazzling smile. "You did him proud, both of you."

"Your father made it easy for us," answered Isaac Bell.

Then he turned to Marion Morgan and took her hand.

"I promised you a ride."

Marion squeezed into the nacelle behind him and wrapped her arms around his waist. Andy spun the propeller, and Bell raced up from the grass. The *Eagle* climbed quickly in the heavy sea air.

High above the blue waters of San Francisco Bay, Isaac Bell blipped off the motor.

When the only sound was the wind sighing in the stays, he turned around and kissed her.

"My darling, we are not going back down until we set a wedding date."

Marion kissed him back. Her eyes roamed the blue bays, the green peninsulas, and the sun descending from scarlet clouds into the immensity of the Pacific Ocean. She kissed him again and leaned forward to lay her head on his shoulder.

"This is so beautiful," she said. "Let's stay up forever."